A DEATH IN SHEFFIELD

ANNE CLEELAND

ARTEMIS
PRESS

OTHER REGENCY ADVENTURES BY
ANNE CLEELAND:

For Aspen's mom, who loves a good horse; and for all others like her.

CHAPTER 1

I *believe this wretched ball is worse than the Siege of Burgos,* thought Artemis; *at least there was no mystery as to who was the enemy, at Burgos.*

She was stationed at her aunt's side, doing her best not to appear self-conscious whilst the woman engaged in a very civil argument with the Portuguese Ambassador, who'd asked permission to dance with her. Artemis observed that the stout little man had beads of perspiration lining his upper lip, which was no surprise; he was no doubt uneasy in his unaccustomed role as abductor of young maidens. *He'd never make a reconnaissance officer,* she thought with some scorn; *he'd start at his own shadow.*

Artemis's Aunt Stanhope replied with finality, "I'm afraid Miss Merryfield is promised to her cousin for this dance, Excellency, and he should be along at any moment."

"Matters are pressing," the man insisted in an urgent undertone, glancing over his shoulder. "Droughm has lately arrived."

Artemis's aunt regarded the man from beneath hooded lids. "Has he indeed?"

The Portuguese Ambassador lowered his voice. "He cannot

be allowed to interfere with her." With some firmness, the diplomat tugged on Artemis' elbow. "Come, Miss Merryfield—we will dance, yes?"

"You will wait for your cousin," countered her aunt, her gaze never leaving the Ambassador's.

"I am not one for dancing," Artemis explained to the combatants in an apologetic tone, "having never learned." On the other hand, she was adept in the loading of musketry, but this particular skill seemed irrelevant—or at least not relevant as yet, depending on whether she would be called upon to shoot some or all of the other persons present. It was beginning to seem as though this was not entirely beyond the realm of possibility.

"Then I shall walk with her on the terrace—he will not look for her to be with me," the Ambassador insisted, meeting her aunt's gaze with a hint of exasperation. "Come, madam; we both wish that she should avoid Droughm."

Aunt Stanhope made no response, but allowed her calculating gaze to sweep the room in a rare display of wariness.

Oh-ho, thought Artemis with great interest. *She is indeed contemplating a strategic retreat; that the unknown Droughm has the ability to shake my formidable aunt can only be regarded as an excellent omen.*

Pressing his advantage, the man offered his arm to Artemis. "I will take your niece out to take some air—she is a bit faint from the heat and the crowd, I think."

Artemis, who had never been faint in her life, slid her gaze back to her aunt to await the next counter-parry.

But instead the woman bowed her head in reluctant acquiescence. "Very well; but Torville will join you when he arrives—he must be seen to dance with her."

"You presume," the other said in a clipped tone. "Matters are not yet settled."

"We shall see," replied the lady, her gaze unflinching.

It is so very provoking—to be treated as though one does not exist, thought Artemis as she curtseyed prettily. *"Obrigado,"* she said to the Ambassador, and took his arm.

The man stared at her in abject horror, as well he should. Earlier in the evening she'd stood near the windows, listening in as the honorable Ambassador covertly identified her to his young and handsome attaché. Whilst her Portuguese was not good—having mostly been gleaned from curse words and military terms—Artemis had managed to follow the alarming gist of their urgent conversation. *I probably should not have let him know I understood what he said,* she thought, observing his reaction; *I'd not make much of a reconnaissance officer, myself.*

As he steered her toward the terrace doors, the Ambassador drew his mouth into what he obviously hoped was a reassuring smile. "I was not aware, Miss Merryfield, that you spoke my language."

"You live and you learn," Artemis noted piously.

"I was upset earlier, you must understand—your aunt—"

Artemis soothed, "Pray do not concern yourself; I understand that tempers are short, the circumstances being what they are."

"Exactly." He bent his head to hers, adding in an urgent undertone, "I wished to ask—you have heard nothing from your uncle, Miss Merryfield—nothing?"

"No—I've had no word from Sheffield." Artemis firmly quashed the memory of the last time she'd seen Uncle Thaddeus, watching solemnly as the flames ignited around her feet. *I very much fear I am running short on time and strategy,* she thought; *an ally is needful, and with any luck he has indeed lately arrived in the form of the dreaded Droughm.*

With barely-suppressed urgency, the Ambassador led her from the overheated ballroom and onto the terrace, which overlooked a beautiful formal garden—a rarity in crowded London. Hanging paper lanterns were strung between the trees and the effect was magical; Artemis would have liked to stand

and admire pretty gardens, but she was too preoccupied with plotting out a potential retreat route.

"Your aunt; she is a very hard woman," her companion continued, his tone bordering on the peevish. "She does not listen to reason."

"I have been saddled with a very strange assortment of relatives," Artemis agreed. "Small wonder the Colonel never mentioned them—he was probably too busy, what with fighting the French at *Torres Vedras*, and *Corunna*." The reference to the besieged Portuguese towns was deliberate; the Ambassador did not seem to appreciate the sacrifices made by others in the defense of his country, particularly if he was truly planning to abduct the daughter of a fallen war hero.

The man had the grace to look a bit ashamed, and patted the hand on his arm in a conciliatory gesture. "Believe me, Miss Merryfield, if there was any other option I would gladly leave you and your aunt alone. I have no other choice in the matter." Nervously, he glanced over his shoulder.

"Why are you all so afraid of Droughm?" She glanced up at him, genuinely curious. "He appears to feature as the bogeyman, in this tale."

"It is nothing to concern you," the man replied in a curt tone, his temporary contrition gone in an instant. "Now, come along and we shall meet up with Marco—he is very taken with you, he tells me."

They navigated across the terrace, the Ambassador practically tugging on Artemis' arm as he urged her down the far steps and into the dimly-lit garden. Almost immediately, they encountered the young attaché who'd listened to his superior's musings about potential abductions, earlier in the evening.

As he bowed, the dark-eyed young man rendered a charming smile, his teeth flashing white against his swarthy skin. "Good evening, Miss Merryfield."

"*Ela pode falar Portugues,*" the Ambassador warned his cohort.

Without missing a beat, the attaché offered his arm and invited her to walk with him in his own language, his head bent to hers and his attitude deferential. Artemis acquiesced with her own shy smile, after deciding that her best strategy was to behave as though her head had been turned by her handsome escort. Taking his arm, she pretended not to notice the significant glance the two men exchanged. *I was indeed safer at the Siege of Burgos,* she concluded, as she contemplated the ground in a show of maidenly shyness; *and certainly better informed.*

"You are very beautiful tonight," the attaché murmured, his head bent close to hers. "Your eyes, they are the most extraordinary color—"

"My father," Artemis responded abruptly, her mouth pressed into a thin line. "I have my father's eyes."

Thrown off by her tone, her companion glanced at her for a moment, then recovered and continued with his flirtation. "Shall we admire the lilacs? Come—no one will miss you."

Foolish man, she thought; *every man jack has been watching my every move since I first set foot in this miserable city.* "With pleasure." She smiled up into his admiring eyes and concluded that he was probably trying to maneuver her toward the back gate—it was dark and deserted over there, so it was well-suited for an abduction. *I've half a mind to let him take me away from my horrible aunt,* she thought, as she allowed him to lead her toward the corner gate; *he is a handsome fellow, and I imagine he receives a fine stipend from the Portuguese government.*

Hard on this thought, she paused and bent as though to retrieve something she'd dropped on the ground. When her escort immediately stooped to assist, she grasped his head with both hands and brought her knee to his forehead with as much force as she could muster. With a grunt, the handsome Ambassador's attaché slumped to the ground.

Walking briskly, Artemis retreated down the graveled path back toward the terrace, smoothing out her gloves and breathing in the heavy scent of lilacs. Suddenly, the figure of a man rose before her, and she came to an abrupt halt, as the strains of the orchestra could be heard floating out from the terrace. Although they'd never met, she could guess the gentleman's identity, and awaited events.

"Miss Merryfield." He bowed.

"Mr. Droughm." He was tall, and—although it was difficult to see his features with his back to the torches—his hair was very dark. *We would have dark-haired children, between us,* she thought dispassionately, and belatedly realized that she should have curtseyed.

He tilted his head. "I'm afraid it is just 'Droughm'."

"Ah." *He was a peer, then—it wanted only this.* "I beg your pardon."

They regarded each other for a silent moment. "I thought perhaps you might require some assistance."

"No," she responded, and offered nothing more.

"How old are you, Miss Merryfield?" She noted that he spoke in an abrupt manner—he was not one for roundaboutation, it seemed.

She let out a breath and admitted, "I am turned seventeen."

He put his chin to his chest, thinking over this unfortunate fact. She gauged him to have perhaps thirty-five years in his dish, perhaps more. "Do they know you are not yet eighteen?"

"I am afraid I confessed to my age before I knew what was afoot."

This remark made him raise a dark brow. "Do you know what is afoot, then?"

"I've a good guess," she countered. "Perhaps you will be kind enough to fill in the particulars."

"We may have to marry," he announced in his blunt manner.

"Yes—or at least pretend to marry," she temporized. It made her uneasy that he held a title; he was probably overly-proud of his exalted ancestors, and such. "And speaking of which, what have you done with my cousin Torville—have you killed him?" This last asked in a hopeful tone.

She had the brief impression he was amused. "Torville has been unavoidably detained, I'm afraid. Has he offered you insult?"

She could be equally blunt. "Daily, since I've arrived. I keep the 'tweenie in my room at night."

In a grim tone, he assured her, "Such measures will no longer be necessary; I will see to it."

Lifting her chin, she regarded him steadily. "I've no doubt of it—you terrify them. They are all rolling their eyes like green recruits under fire."

If she'd hoped to hear of the nature of his involvement in the mysteries that abounded here in London, she was to be disappointed. Contemplating her thoughtfully, he said only, "They have engaged with very dangerous people, and are becoming desperate."

This was of interest, and spoke of unseen forces at work. She probed, "The Ambassador is no danger, surely—you could fell him with one blow."

"Indeed." It was evident from his ironic tone that he had witnessed her own blow to the attaché.

Crossly, she defended herself, "It is no easy thing to be an heiress, I assure you—I'd rather face the French."

With mock-humility he bowed his head. "You misunderstand—I would not be so impertinent as to question your actions."

Ignoring the mockery, she pointed out with exasperation, "That is the problem *exactly*—I am at an extreme disadvantage because I must not ask impertinent questions of my betters."

But he was unmoved, and pointed out reasonably, "Unfortunately, there is no other kind of question; not to one's betters."

"You are of no help." She made a wry mouth, because he

was going to make her laugh, despite her best efforts to resist. "There are such goings on—am I supposed to say nothing, and be as mild as milk?"

"Unimaginable."

She flashed him a look, aware that he was enjoying himself at her expense. "Why do they fear you?" He had avoided an answer, before.

"That," he noted, "is an impertinent question."

"You are provoking," she chided, cross again. "I am tempted to reject your suit out-of-hand."

"Do not, I beg of you—I think we will have much to say to one another."

Artemis met his level gaze for a long moment, there, with the scent of lilacs hanging heavy in the air, and the lamplight flickering off his profile, and found that she could make no reply, impertinent or otherwise.

"You had best return. I will ask you to dance."

"I do not dance," she admitted, rather wishing that she did.

In his brusque manner he declared, "You will dance with me, regardless."

She blinked, and decided he was rather appealing, in his autocratic way. "You will put the cat among the pigeons," she cautiously advised. "Mayhem is the certain result."

"You terrify me," he replied, unperturbed. "Go."

Thoughtfully, Artemis sidled back through the crowded room as she returned to her aunt's side. It did seem—at long last—that matters were looking up. *But I must watch myself*, she thought; *he sees far more than he ought, this one, and I must discover why he wields such power.*

"Why, Artemis," said her aunt, her thin brows raised in surprise. "Where is your escort?"

"He was unavoidably detained," she replied, deciding that she approved of Droughm's phrase. She then looked about her with feigned surprise. "Heavens—has my cousin Torville not yet made an appearance?"

"Not yet arrived." Her aunt's eyes narrowed as she canvassed the crowded room again. "I am rather vexed with him—he spoke with such enthusiasm of partnering you tonight."

"A very dutiful nephew," Artemis agreed, and earned a sharp glance from her aunt. Aunt and Uncle Stanhope were childless, and Torville was her Uncle Stanhope's eldest nephew. The extant scheme was to marry Artemis to Torville, thus keeping her Uncle Thaddeus' mining operations in the family. Artemis could scarcely blame them for this scheme; she was an unexpected heiress without protectors, and their only other alternative was to be hanged for treason.

CHAPTER 2

*H*aving decided that the ball was not going to be as unpleasant as she'd first feared, Artemis scanned the crowded room, waiting to spy a certain tall figure. The orchestra was preparing for the next set, and the candlelit room was filled with fashionable members of the *ton*, the men dressed in understated black in contrast to the sumptuous silks and satins worn by the women. Because she was not yet "out," Artemis was unfortunately dressed in white, and—even though she paid little attention to such things—she knew she did not look well in white, considering the fairness of her skin. She hoped that it had not been quite so obvious, in the torch-lit garden.

"Whatever has happened to the Ambassador, Artemis; what did he say to you?" It seemed that Artemis' aunt trusted her partner-in-crime as little as the man trusted her in turn, and small blame to either of them, since they were both facing the wrath of England's Minister of the Treasury. And it had come as no surprise when Droughm had hinted that her relatives had engaged with unspecified "dangerous people"; after all, *someone* had set up an elaborate counterfeiting operation, and Artemis would bet her teeth that the Portuguese Ambassador wasn't up to the task—the man was incapable of seeing to a simple abduction, for heaven's sake.

"He asked if I had heard from mine uncle," Artemis answered. "And I explained that I had not."

Making an impatient sound, her aunt allowed a rare display of frustrated emotion. "It is very like Thaddeus—to disappear and leave us with no clue as to whether he yet lives."

In the event his fond sister was unaware, Artemis offered, "He was mad, you know."

"Fie, Artemis," her aunt reproached her. "We do not yet know that he is dead."

"As you say." Artemis made an equivocal response, as she had first-hand knowledge that her great-uncle Thaddeus no longer walked the earth. She duly noted that her aunt had made no attempt to refute her brother's madness, and decided that the Colonel had done her no favors when he'd sent her off to his wretched relatives. *I have been ill-used*, she thought, and then felt a stab of guilt for thinking badly of the Colonel—*he could not possibly have known*, she assured herself; *not possibly*.

Artemis could feel her aunt's reaction even before Droughm approached; the woman stiffened and turned to grasp hold of Artemis's elbow. "Come with me, Artemis—"

But before they could make a strategic retreat, the enemy had blocked their path. "Lady Stanhope; I am Droughm." He bowed.

"Lord Droughm." With palpable reluctance, her aunt bowed.

"I understand Lord Stanhope is from home."

If it was possible, her aunt's expression grew more guarded. "Indeed; he will be sorry to have missed making your acquaintance, my lord."

"He is already acquainted with my nephew Wentworth, I understand."

Artemis watched the byplay with some admiration, having never had the opportunity to hold the whip-hand over her aunt.

12

She wondered who Wentworth was, and why his name had been thrown down like a challenge.

Lady Stanhope paused, wary, and debating what to say. "I believe there is an acquaintanceship, yes."

He has her back on her heels, thought Artemis with satisfaction. *I indeed have an ally—and a formidable one, at that; I have no doubt he will hold his position under fire.*

"May I beg an introduction to your charming companion, Lady Stanhope?" Droughm turned to Artemis and rendered a small bow as she belatedly remembered to sink into a curtesy.

Green, she thought with surprise; his eyes were a pale green —which was unexpected, as he'd seemed so dark, outside in the garden. His hair was very brown, with a slight sprinkling of grey at the temples.

"May I present Miss Merryfield?" offered her aunt in a reluctant tone. "Lately visiting from Sheffield."

Droughm lifted his quizzing glass and regarded Artemis through it. "Miss Merryfield, would you care to dance?"

"Lay on," said Artemis easily.

But her aunt disclaimed in alarm, "I am afraid she is not yet 'out', my lord."

Ignoring her, Droughm offered his arm, and Artemis took it, thinking he had been forewarned, and thus any potential disgrace was wholly his own.

"But—but my lord, I must protest," Lady Stanhope continued in an undertone, as it was apparent the interaction was inviting unwelcome attention from those who stood nearby. "Miss Merryfield awaits her cousin."

"My abject apologies to him," said Droughm, his tone bordering on rudeness, and he led Artemis away as her aunt stood, speechless.

Rolled up; foot and guns, thought Artemis with extreme satisfaction—*I can only admire his technique.* She could not dwell on the skirmish for long, however, because their movement toward the dance floor was attracting a great deal of attention, with women whispering behind their fans and a buzzing undercurrent erupting in their wake as they passed by. Artemis knew she was not such a curiosity in her own right, and so she surmised that her escort must be an object of great interest.

And while it was one thing to attempt one's first public dance in a quiet corner of the ballroom, it was quite another to be the cynosure of attention, and Artemis felt a small qualm that was very uncharacteristic for her. *If this is one of those complicated dances where there is a great deal of crossing about and bowing,* she thought, *I am dead.*

As though reading her mind, her companion leaned in and said in an undertone, "It is a waltz—very simple."

"Then that is to the good." She tried to maintain an attitude of calm as they took up their position on the dance floor, and hoped for the best. Fortunately, the 'tweenie at Stanhope House was enthralled with the new dance, and—as Artemis had stood in as her practice partner on several occasions—at least she knew the basic steps.

This is as nothing, she assured herself stoutly, whilst the speculative whispering rose in volume. *Facing down Massola when the Prussians were delayed—now, that was something.* To change the direction of her thoughts, she turned her gaze to her partner, and decided that he was rather handsome in a rugged sort of way—capable, and no-nonsense.

For his part, he'd negligently lifted his quizzing-glass so as to study her, and she bore this scrutiny without a flinch. "You'll not discomfit me by wielding your quizzing-glass, you know. I am made of sterner stuff."

"I beg your pardon." He dropped it so that it fell on its ribbon to his chest. "The truth is I do not see up close as well as I was used."

"The wages of age," she commiserated. "Next, you will require an ear-trumpet."

A half smile tugged at his mouth. "Minx—small wonder you are pronounced impertinent."

"Hush," she begged, hearing the music start up. "I must concentrate."

He moved to her, lifting her right hand in his left, and placing his other hand at her waist. Artemis suddenly found that she was close enough to see the pulse beating in his throat, and then she caught the scent of sandalwood, very subtle, as he began the dance, keeping his movements simple, and his steps short.

After a few moments, Artemis felt she was responding passably well to the rhythm of the music and the guiding pressure at her waist, and thus could relax a bit. He said near her ear, "May I speak, or will you enjoin me to 'hush' again?"

Resisting the urge to count aloud—as she had done with the 'tweenie—Artemis said in a distracted fashion, "You may do as you wish; I don't have the ordering of you."

He was amused again—she could tell by the way he squeezed her hand slightly. "We must have a private conversation, you and I. Do you ride?"

This welcome question inspired her to take her gaze off her feet for a moment and meet his with a flare of hope. "Yes. But I have no mount, and no riding habit."

"Ah. How well do you ride?"

"Well." Her gaze returned to her feet, although she was gaining confidence—it was not so difficult, truly; once one got past the proximity of the gentleman, and the warm hand at one's waist.

"You were well-named, then; Artemis, the goddess of the hunt."

Feeling that she was comfortable enough to focus again on his face, she confessed, "It is a wretched thing to be saddled with—one can never quite live up to it."

He met her eyes with a small smile. "I completely understand; my own surname is St. John."

"That is nearly as wretched," she agreed. "But not quite."

She made a misstep, but then managed to make a recovery

whilst he waited a few beats to allow her to regain the rhythm. Smiling, she looked up to him. "This is rather enjoyable, isn't it?"

"I have never enjoyed myself more."

"I doubt that," she said dryly. "I think you very much enjoyed setting mine aunt back on her heels."

"Where is your chamber at Stanhope House?"

This was unexpected, and she shot him a look. "You are too old to be climbing vines, I think."

His eyes gleaming, he squeezed her hand again. "I've half a mind to prove you wrong, but I am asking because I will post a man to watch the house."

"Oh—oh, I am on the third floor over the mews; the next thing to a miserable garret, I'm afraid."

He offered quite seriously, "If you are in distress, you have only to signal."

She frowned. "I do keep my pistol with me."

Carefully, he executed a quarter-turn. "It would be best to hold your powder until the situation is resolved."

"And what is the situation, exactly? Where is Lord Stanhope, and who is Wentworth?" She felt she may as well ask him; she very much doubted he would tell her, and he didn't.

"We will discuss it at some other time," he replied as the strains of the music concluded. "Prepare yourself; I am going to court you."

"Lay on," she said agreeably, finding his abruptness rather endearing, in an odd way. The warm hand was removed from her waist, and she had to resist an impulse to take it in her own.

"*And damn'd be him who first cries, hold, enough.*"

Smiling with delight, she recited, "*So great a day as this is cheaply bought.*"

Pleased, he took her arm to escort her back to her aunt, the buzzing undertone slightly louder as they passed through the crowd. "You are well-versed in Shakespeare."

Disclaiming, she shook her head. "No—not truly. But my mad uncle was well-versed in *Macbeth*."

He cast her a keen glance. "He was mad?"

"Oh yes; quite mad."

Again, she could see that assorted spectators were openly watching them in their progress across the room, and so she strove mightily to appear unconcerned with her role as a freakish curiosity.

The green eyes sharp upon her, her escort asked, "Does your uncle yet live?"

"We will discuss it at some other time," she parroted his own words back at him. *The Four Terrible Things*, she thought; *I will have to confess them to him and hope for the best; I have little other choice.*

"Fair enough." With a bow, he delivered her back to her aunt.

CHAPTER 3

*A*rtemis was young but she was no fool; upon her arrival, she'd shrewdly assessed the inhabitants at Stanhope House and almost immediately decided that the better part of valor was to listen at doors. The snatches of conversation she'd overheard whilst walking about soft-footed had featured Droughm's name more than once; usually pronounced by her aunt in tones of loathing when the older woman was closeted with Torville, trying to deal with the dire emergency that had arisen when Artemis' great-uncle Thaddeus had mysteriously disappeared.

Artemis had made the acquaintance of her Stanhope relatives when they came to fetch her from Thaddeus' manor house in Sheffield, and at the time she'd been willing to flee the area with all speed, unaware that she'd leapt from the boiling pot into the fire. *Well*, she thought fairly; *not exactly—it was mine uncle who tried to set me on fire, after all, so it was more like I leapt from one blaze to the next.*

That some terrible crisis had arisen due to Uncle Thaddeus' disappearance seemed evident, and that the particulars could not bear the light of day also seemed evident; behind her cold manner, Artemis' aunt behaved like an enemy general under siege—all frustration and barely-concealed rage. Almost immediately after Artemis arrived in London, Lord Stanhope had departed for parts unknown, and the tension at Stanhope House was so thick that one could cut it with a bayonet.

Listening at the keyhole, Artemis had pieced together the nature of the crisis: "I am at my wit's end, Torville; we cannot allow any type of disruption—if the Treasury Inspector catches wind—"

"Wentworth will do as he is told, madam; be easy. And Droughm is half-way around the world in Algiers."

"You must marry the chit, and as soon as possible."

"—don't know if she holds title until we know for certain that he is dead—"

"Nevertheless—"

"Be reasonable, madam—who can give consent? She is underage—"

Yes, thought Artemis, assessing the situation thoughtfully as she crept back into her own little room; *I am underage, and there is literally no one to give the needed consent for my marriage, even if they assume mine uncle is dead, which they cannot—or at least not yet. And as they have need of my cooperation, it does not appear that they can seize the fortune against my will—which perhaps they could have done in the Middle Ages, but surely is frowned upon nowadays.*

In sum, it appeared that everyone was stymied and she was safe, so long as no one knew what had happened to Uncle Thaddeus. Or at least she'd thought she was safe, until recent days when—with the silence from Sheffield becoming more and more ominous—Torville had begun pursuing her aggressively, with the apparent aim of taking all choices away from her; if she was ruined, even the authorities would reluctantly hand her over to him.

Matters had not yet progressed to where Artemis felt compelled to either flee or shoot him, but she was in a rare tangle because there seemed to be no way out of this mess—or at least no simple retreat route. She had her own reasons to keep the authorities away from the strange circumstance of her missing uncle, so she couldn't approach them. She couldn't disappear into the night because she had—quite literally—no one to flee to, not to mention there would be an immediate hue and cry because she was the sole heiress to her uncle's silver mining fortune.

Therefore, it was with no little relief that she welcomed Droughm's appearance on the scene, and for more reasons than one. Her aunt's greatest fear, as far as Artemis could determine, was that Droughm—for reasons which were as yet unclear— would come and seize Artemis for himself. Now that she'd met the gentleman, Artemis thought this an excellent strategy, and was more than willing to encourage him in this aim.

To this end, she volunteered to sit for Katy so as to allow the young maid to practice arranging her hair. Katy was not fazed by the fact she'd been relegated to the lowly task of waiting on Artemis, and was instead unswerving in her ambition to become a real lady's maid. Artemis had little doubt the girl would succeed—she was as determined as Wellington, when he'd sworn to re-take Badajoz.

"Try to make me appear older," Artemis suggested thoughtfully, watching the 'tweenie's ministrations in the mirror. Artemis' hair was long, black and thick, falling nearly to her waist. She had invariably worn it in a long plait down her back, but now decided it would appear too school-girlish to continue with this habit.

"For the gentleman who danced with you," Katy remarked matter-of-factly. "They're all abuzz about it, downstairs."

Apparently, there was little of which the servants were unaware. "I waltzed," Artemis confessed with a smile, watching the girl in the mirror. "You would have been proud of me, Katy."

"Did you remember not to watch your feet, miss?" Katy frowned in concentration as she experimented with a twisted style.

"No, but he didn't seem to mind—he was very kind." Artemis winced when Katy tugged too hard. "Although everyone was staring."

"Cook says he's twice your age, and only did it to pull on her ladyship's tail."

Smiling at herself in the mirror, Artemis admitted, "I cannot disagree—which only made the experience that much more enjoyable."

Katy laughed. "Will he call upon you today, miss?" According to the complicated protocols of the *ton* with which Artemis was not very familiar, a lady's dance partners were obligated to make a visit the following day.

"I honestly don't know—it may come to blows, if he does." Thinking she'd do a little probing, Artemis asked, "Do you know why mine aunt dislikes him so?"

Katy met her eyes in the mirror and shrugged, speaking around the pins she held in her mouth. "I only know it has something to do with the mines in Sheffield—it is grand-dad's opinion that they fear being ruined, and that Lord Droughm is the one to do it."

Katy's grand-dad was Hooks, the butler of the establishment, and so it could be assumed he knew of what he spoke, being best situated to listen at doors.

"Yes," Artemis agreed thoughtfully. "They are very much afraid of something—but mainly, they are afraid of Droughm."

Her hands pausing for a moment, Katy met her eyes in the mirror and offered, "My grand-dad said to tell you that if you need him to take a whip to Torville, he'll do it even if he gets the sack."

Touched, Artemis replied, "Tell your grand-dad I will keep it to mind, and thank him for me."

Katy resumed her work, arranging ringlets and then stepping back to consider the result with a critical eye. "He says you're well-able to take care of yourself, but he's worried you might be taken by surprise."

I have such champions, thought Artemis with a small pang; *I wonder if I deserve them.*

Katy continued, "We'll have to make up some blacks for you, if it turns out your uncle is dead—I think you would look very nice in blacks, with your complexion, and your eyes."

"Perhaps we'll never know what happened to him," suggested Artemis hopefully.

Misinterpreting her response, Katy lowered her hands and apologized. "Oh—I'm that sorry, miss; I shouldn't have spoken so. He'll turn up, don't you worry."

But Artemis only shrugged a shoulder. "I was only with him for two months, Katy—and I can't say I was very fond of him. He was a mean old miser."

Surprised, Katy paused to stare. "Is that so? And him leaving all his money to you—it's a wonder, it is."

"It was not so much he left it to me as there is no one else to claim it," Artemis explained. "The Colonel was his only nephew, but he was killed on the Continent."

The girl nodded in sympathy. "I'm that sorry, miss; it's like one of those fairy tales—all the terrible things that have happened to you."

A Grimm's tale, thought Artemis; *and I am afraid the worst part of this tale is yet to be told.*

"What'll you wear for the visiting hour, miss?" Katy ruthlessly pushed the last pin in place, and then walked over to survey Artemis' scant wardrobe with a critical eye. "A shame that you aren't allowed to wear colors yet."

Artemis could only agree—Droughm seemed the sort of man who would take notice of such things, and pale colors only reinforced the fact that she was of tender years. "The ivory, perhaps? The yellow looks hideous on me."

"There is nothing to prevent me from threading a cherry ribbon through your hair," the maid suggested with a touch of defiance. "That will turn his head."

"He doesn't seem the sort to have his head turned," Artemis remarked. "But I would like to wear a ribbon, if you have one."

After this artifice was complete, the two girls gazed in satisfaction at Artemis' reflected glory. "Just the thing," said Katy. "Best get ye downstairs—I mean, best get *you* downstairs." Katy was keenly aware that a lady's maid needed to speak like a lady, and was carefully cultivating her vocabulary. "Visiting hour is upon us, and your gentleman may be first in line."

Privately, Artemis thought her gentleman was more likely to seize her on the street and sling her over his shoulder rather than comply with polite protocols. With this agreeable scenario in mind, she thanked Katy and descended the stairs.

CHAPTER 4

*A*rtemis arrived at the house's main floor, dressed in her ivory gown and wishing she'd slept better the night before—she was not used to such late nights, and there had been much to think about.

Hooks met her at the foot of the stairs with a small bow. "Flowers have arrived for you, miss; I took the liberty of placing them on the entry table." As always, his manner was dry and correct, and Artemis was hard-pressed to imagine him wielding a whip.

"I thank you, Hooks." Artemis wandered into the foyer to observe an impressive bouquet of lilacs on display, with a card propped up against the vase that containing a single-word signature in a heavy scrawl—there was no mistaking the sender. Leaning in to breathe the scent, Artemis could not suppress a smile; perhaps it was only a shot across the bow aimed at her aunt, but it was also a deft compliment, and much appreciated.

The sound of murmured voices told her that her aunt was already entertaining visitors in the drawing room, and so—with an inward sigh—she dutifully went in to take up her post; Artemis was not well-versed in the making of polite conversation, having spent little of her life thus far in polite company.

She was soon to discover the reason for the prompt assemblage in her aunt's drawing room, and her aunt addressed her from the settee with a brittle smile that was not reflected in her eyes. "Artemis," she said. "You are much sought after—come sit beside me, if you please."

As Artemis settled into the silk-lined seat, the three other ladies present scrutinized her with unveiled curiosity. One of them leaned forward to ask without preamble, "Had you a previous acquaintanceship with Lord Droughm, Miss Merryfield? Was he a friend to your father, perhaps?"

Folding her hands in her lap, Artemis decided this pointed questioning may actually be enjoyable, since her aunt's rigid posture made it clear she found no joy in it whatsoever. "No ma'am—I hadn't met him, before." Artemis was not about to mention the lilac-scented meeting in the garden, preferring to keep the memory to herself.

The three visitors assimilated this surprising information, alert and motionless as though they were hounds at the point. A second woman asked, "And yet he asked you to waltz on your first encounter?"

"Yes," Artemis confirmed. "I believe he thought it would be simpler than something more complicated—I do not dance well." There seemed to be no harm to making the confession; the fact being self-evident to anyone who had witnessed the event.

There was a stunned silence, and the first woman gently informed her, "But, my dear—you are not allowed to waltz, if you are not yet 'out'."

"Oh." Artemis reviewed the slightly scandalized faces focused upon hers. "I did not know this." And little mind my lord Droughm would pay to such strictures—Artemis had the distinct impression that he was a force unto himself.

Daringly, the third visitor cut to the nub of the matter. "Did

Lord Droughm say anything that would indicate his intentions, Miss Merryfield?"

If I told them the truth, they would all fall off their chairs, thought Artemis, *and mine aunt would probably suffer an apoplexy.* Therefore, it was with sincere regret that she temporized, "He did say he admired my name."

"Your *Christian* name?" ventured the second lady in disbelief. "Are you saying he asked for permission to use your Christian name?"

I am in a minefield, thought Artemis, *and I have no idea of my bearings.* "I suppose so," she equivocated.

This revelation appeared to be the clincher, as no one present could find her voice for a moment. "He is *courting* her," her interrogator breathed.

"Nonsense," interjected Artemis' aunt, who'd lost all patience. "He was kind to the daughter of a war-hero—nothing more."

"Lord Droughm is not renowned for his kindness," the second lady observed with a titter, and the others exchanged arch glances that promised a thorough dissection of these events as soon as they were away from the premises.

"I wonder who will inform Lady Tallyer?" The first woman asked the question with an edge of malice in her tone, but one of her companions gave her an admonishing look, and so she subsided.

Ah, thought Artemis—*so the gentleman has a mistress.* This was unsurprising to her, as a bachelor of his stamp had probably maintained more than a few, throughout his career. She had seen many such arrangements amongst the officers in the Peninsula, where the wives back home were beloved, but nevertheless not close enough to hand.

"You may not be aware," announced Lady Stanhope in icy tones, "that an understanding has been reached between Miss Merryfield and my nephew Torville."

This was news to Artemis, but she did not refute the

falsehood, certain that Droughm would not allow a paltry "understanding" to dissuade him from his goal—whatever that goal was. Hopefully, it was to include more dancing.

With varying degrees of open skepticism, those assembled digested the news that the House of Stanhope hoped to secure the heiress' fortune despite Lord Droughm's superior rank. Seeing this, Artemis's aunt added with some defiance, "And I cannot credit that the gentleman meant anything by his attentions last night. Why, Artemis is not yet out of the schoolroom."

More accurately, I've never been in a schoolroom, Artemis thought, but any correction of the record would have to wait because—as if on cue—Hooks bowed at the entrance to the drawing room and announced, "Lord Droughm, madam."

The effect of the announcement on those assembled in the drawing room was immediate; everyone froze in a room so silent that Artemis was worried they could hear her heightened pulse.

"Pray send him in, Hooks."

Droughm entered, and suddenly Artemis was aware that she'd been waiting for this moment, marking time, since they'd parted last night. He met her eyes for the merest instant, and then looked to her aunt and bowed.

"Lord Droughm; a very pleasant surprise. I believe you are acquainted with my niece, Miss Merryfield."

After greetings were exchanged all around, the other women in the room decided they could not very well sit and stare, and so a murmuring conversation resumed among them, even though Artemis was fully aware that all ears were on the stretch.

Droughm seated himself across from Artemis and negligently asked, "How does your Uncle Thaddeus, Miss Merryfield? I have not heard from him of late."

Wretched man, thought Artemis, struggling to control her countenance in the face of this direct attack on her aunt; *I do not know my lines.* She was saved from making a reply by Lady Stanhope, who observed with hooded eyes, "I did not know you were acquainted with Artemis' uncle, my lord."

"Great-uncle," he corrected her.

Oh-ho, thought Artemis; *someone has been doing some sleuthing.*

But her aunt was not to be deflected. "And the nature of your acquaintanceship?"

Matching her stare for stare, Droughm answered, "I am an investor in the mines, madam."

This disclosure did indeed seem to quell her aunt, who made no reply.

Artemis was not one to sit quietly by whilst silent warfare was going forward, and so she offered, "I believe mine uncle mentioned your visit, and spoke very fondly of you, sir."

"My lord," corrected her aunt, embarrassed by the lapse.

"My lord," Artemis repeated dutifully, and had the pleasure of seeing a gleam of amusement in the gentleman's eye.

Droughm replied, "Indeed, we toured the refining sites together; I was very interested in the details of the operation." This said with an edge to his tone.

"I do not believe there are refining sites at the mines," noted her aunt sharply.

"They are in Buxton, which is very near," Artemis corrected her aunt gently. "And I am afraid I have not heard from mine uncle since I arrived in London, sir."

She heard her aunt sigh with impatience at her repeated use of the wrong honorific, but Artemis cared only for smile that tugged at her visitor's mouth. "I imagine Uncle Thaddeus misses me sorely, but he is sadly disorganized, and unlikely to write."

"Has he sent your horse to town?"

"Not as yet, I am afraid." Artemis did not bat an eyelash at the mention of this phantom beast. "I do miss her."

"Then allow me to arrange for the use of a lady's mount until she arrives."

"We cannot stable an additional horse, my lord," Lady Stanhope interrupted with some impatience. "We have hardly room for the carriage horses."

"No matter—I shall provide a mount from my stables." Droughm stood, and added in a careless manner, "I will bring a mare by tomorrow, with your permission."

There was a slight pause, but Lady Stanhope had no choice, and bowed her head slightly. "Splendid."

Masterful, thought Artemis in all admiration; *another direct hit.*

Their exalted guest said his farewells, and as all the ladies rose, he met Artemis' eye with a message that compelled her to accompany him to the foyer. As he walked beside her, he asked in an undertone, "Are there indeed refining sites in Buxton?"

"I've no idea, but neither does mine aunt. You should warn me before you make things up out of whole cloth."

But the pale green eyes were sharp upon hers. "You are quite capable of telling a fish tale, yourself. How old are you—give me the unbarked truth."

Discomfited by this question, she answered steadily, "I'm afraid I am seventeen, barked or unbarked."

He scrutinized her face, and made no move to leave. "I thought perhaps you were undercounting, so as to keep them from forcing you into an unwanted alliance."

Hooks entered the foyer, and stood at a discreet distance.

"No," she said only.

He lowered his gaze and thought for a moment. "Torville will return, but you have nothing to fear from him."

"I am glad to hear it; thank you."

"You are welcome, Artemis—or whatever your true name is."

With an effort, she maintained her poise. "It is indeed

Artemis," she whispered. Of the Four Terrible Things, it appeared he was now aware of at least one.

Hooks took a reluctant step forward. "I am afraid I have been asked to fetch the young lady, my lord."

"I will call to take you riding tomorrow." With a final, unreadable glance, Droughm donned his hat, and left.

CHAPTER 5

*A*fter Droughm's departure, the morning visitors hastily made their farewells, no doubt in a fever to be the first to spread this extraordinary tale to others—which was probably Droughm's intention all along, in making such a public visit. After this, any hasty attempt to secure Artemis for Torville would be looked upon with grave suspicion, if my lord Droughm were indeed in the running as a potential suitor. It was very well done, and Artemis would have been all admiration if she weren't convinced the gentleman was just as ably cooking her own goose.

Artemis's aunt wasted no time in leaving Stanhope House for an undisclosed location, and Artemis was torn between a desire to discover who she went to meet, and an equally strong desire to retreat to her chamber and wring her hands for the first time in her life.

Droughm had unearthed at least one of her secrets in a twinkling, which was ominous and impressive at the same time. It seemed clear that he had access to information few others had, and this gave her pause; her inclination was to trust him, but there must be good reason that all the other players held him in dread, and she should proceed with caution.

On the other hand, the Stanhopes held some means to keep him in check; her eavesdropping had revealed their conviction that Droughm could not report their counterfeiting operations to the authorities for some undisclosed reason.

In light of this stalemate, the immediate and logical solution for either side was to be the first to marry Artemis, and thus lay a husband's claim to the silver mines. It was a race to see who would succeed in this aim, but matters were further complicated by the fact that Artemis was underage and without a legal guardian, and—as yet—it had not been proved that her great-uncle was, in fact, dead.

Taking a breath, Artemis mounted the steps to her room, somewhat consoled. That some horrific scandal was brewing seemed evident, but whatever-it-was, it tainted Droughm, also, so it was very unlikely that he would hand her over to the authorities as an imposter—not to mention he didn't wish the Stanhopes to discover that she was not what she seemed. Instead, she need only await her next encounter with him, and try to come up with an explanation—although this appeared to be a tall order, as he was not one who was easily fooled. *Hell and damnation,* she swore to herself; *but I am in a fix.*

There was a soft knock at the door, and Artemis squared her shoulders before opening it, but it was revealed to be only Hooks, who informed her with a correct bow of his head that she had a visitor, downstairs. "A Miss Valdez."

Artemis brought to mind the very short list of her acquaintances in London. "I haven't a clue, Hooks—friend or foe?"

Hicks considered. "I believe the young lady hails from Spain."

Brightening, Artemis declared, "Friend, then—it must be someone I knew from the war."

She descended into the drawing room to observe a pretty dark-haired woman, bent over the writing cabinet as she quickly rifled through the drawers. Artemis watched her for a moment, knowing they'd never met, and thinking this a very interesting development, indeed.

Approaching in a brisk manner, she bent to join in the search alongside the young woman. "What is it that are we looking for?"

Startled, the visitor turned and held out a hand, her smile bright and disarming. "Fah; it is my terrible curiosity—I do beg your pardon."

"No need to beg *my* pardon, it is not my house; but I'm afraid there isn't anything of interest hidden anywhere—I've already looked."

The woman regarded her with frank curiosity. "*Deus*, you are a strange one."

So; not Spanish but Portuguese, thought Artemis, who was suddenly wary. "You must forgive me; I've forgotten where we met."

Her visitor trilled a laugh, and reached to take Artemis' hands in her own, her manner vivacious and charming. "I am not surprised; it was at the Ballantine House ball—we met very briefly. I was in attendance with my father, Ambassador Valdez."

"Your father is the Portuguese Ambassador?" For whatever reason, Artemis knew this was not, in fact, the truth.

Drawing her mouth down, the young woman tilted her head in contrition. "My poor father sends me with his apologies —Marcos insulted you, he believes."

"Not at all," Artemis demurred, gently retrieving her hands from the other's grasp. "More like I insulted Marcos."

Artemis saw a flash of recalibration in the girl's eyes, quickly extinguished. "Then there is nothing to forgive, and we are friends, yes? My father tells me you do not know many people in town—I thought perhaps we could become good companions."

"That would be excellent—I am always on the lookout for good companions." Artemis did not invite her visitor to sit.

The other trilled a merry little laugh. "Wonderful! I am to be wed, soon, and I have need of someone to help me with my wedding arrangements—there is much shopping to be done, and a new trousseau to purchase."

"My best wishes," Artemis congratulated her with a small smile. "That sounds very exciting."

Pausing, the girl glanced at her sidelong, perhaps thinking that Artemis' reaction was not what was expected for such a proffered treat from her older, more dashing visitor.

"When do you wed?" asked Artemis, thinking she may as well show an interest so as to move this gambit along—whatever this gambit was.

"The end of summer—although my betrothed must discuss the settlements with his family." Her full, ripe mouth sobered, and she leaned in to say in a confiding manner, "They are unhappy because I am not English."

"If his affections are sincere, I am certain it will all work out." Privately, Artemis was not so optimistic—she had seen many a soldier marry a foreign bride, only to contend with the headaches that went along with such a match.

The other lifted her pretty chin in a determined fashion. "My darling has pledged to put his ring on my finger, even if his family does not approve—his family is very rich," she added candidly, "but it means nothing to him if he cannot marry me."

"He seems a worthy suitor, then."

Her visitor waited a beat, then hinted, "Indeed, he is; I will have an English title."

"Will you? Then everything will be worth it."

There was another small pause. *I am going to drive her mad,* thought Artemis, hiding a smile, *because I will not ask.*

With barely-concealed impatience, her visitor broached the subject herself. "My father tells me you are acquainted with the family—Lord Droughm."

"Ah," said Artemis with polite interest. "You are going to marry Lord Droughm?"

"No, no—" the girl trilled her pretty laugh again, but there was an edge of annoyance, this time. "I will marry his heir, Lord Wentworth."

"I wish you very happy," said Artemis, thinking this all very interesting. "Will you live in London, once you are wed?"

The girl tilted her head with regret. "That depends on his prospects—we may have to defy his family."

"I am certain it will all work out," Artemis offered.

The girl took Artemis's hands again, clearly hiding her frustration that the young Artemis had not leapt to be involved in any clandestine plan that might be put forward. "I am Lisabetta; may I call you Artemis?"

"Of course you may," agreed Artemis. "Whenever you wish."

"I cannot stay," the woman said, as though she had been invited to stay. "But I wanted to convey my father's apologies, and leave a letter for your aunt from my father—they have a common interest." This said with a sidelong glance that hinted of mysteries, and deep secrets.

Artemis took the letter only to leave it negligently on the tea table. "I will see that she reads it upon her return."

The girl flashed her pretty smile as Hooks saw her out the door, and Artemis had to admire her self-control—if their roles had been reversed, she would have been stamping her foot in frustration long before now.

But she wasn't allowed any time to dwell on the motivation behind this unlooked-for visitor, because as he closed the door, Hooks announced, "I hope you don't mind, miss; I took the liberty of having your riding habit pressed."

As Artemis did not own a riding habit, this was unexpected news. "I thank you."

The butler bowed, his expression wooden, and retreated into the kitchen.

Artemis quickened her pace up the stairs and once in her room, flung open the armoire doors. Hanging amongst the other offerings was an elegant riding habit, conservatively cut, in a midnight blue velvet that exactly matched her eyes. With a reverent hand, she reached up to stroke the sleeve, and found that she had a wild variety of emotions roiling within her breast. A wonder, that he had managed to have it made up on such short notice; it was a grand gesture, and much appreciated. Apparently, he was willing to forgive her for her deceptions—or at least those of which he knew. *I am longing to see him again*, she thought honestly—*and it is so unlike me that I scarce recognize myself.*

Slowly, she closed the armoire door and leaned her forehead against the smooth wood. *I have to sort out what I can tell him, and what I must not, and above all, I cannot be tempted to cast all my cares upon his capable shoulders—at least not until I find out how he fits into all this.*

Reluctantly acknowledging that she had no choice but to possess her soul in patience, she closed the curtains and lay down to sleep; she had a feeling the next few days would be eventful, and she was in sore need of rest.

CHAPTER 6

*T*hat afternoon, Artemis wandered down the servant's stairway with the intent of inveigling some bread and jam out of Cook; she was reluctant to join her aunt for tea in the drawing room but she was hungry, and a body needed to eat.

As she turned the corner at the foot of the narrow stairs, she came face-to-face with her cousin Torville, who was apparently edging his way out the back entry—no doubt he was avoiding their mutual aunt, also. Artemis was unsurprised to note that he looked the worse for wear—he'd a bruised area near his eye, and she could see several stitches on his forehead that had been obscured by the artful arrangement of his hair.

Upon sighting her, Torville bowed with mock-formality. "Cousin—I have missed you." There was always a snide edge of mockery whenever he spoke; it was very unattractive.

"Good afternoon, Torville," said Artemis. "How did you injure yourself?"

Smiling, he slapped the gloves he held in one hand against the other hand. "I'm afraid I had a nasty fall down a flight of stairs."

Hiding her extreme satisfaction, Artemis offered, "I hope it was not too painful."

"My only consolation is that I was drunk at the time."

"A happy coincidence," she agreed. "Now, if you do not mind, I am headed to the kitchen."

He stepped back, and then bowed with an overly-elaborate gesture as she brushed by him. There'd been a change in his usual manner, as ordinarily he'd bestow a lingering kiss on her cheek when he greeted her—in his odious, calculating manner. It seemed clear that he'd been threatened—and with good result —but he was not one to allow himself to be bested, and she'd do well to be wary when it came to Torville. Completely selfish and spoiled, he wouldn't have lasted ten days under the Colonel's command—that, or he'd have been shown the error of his ways in no uncertain terms. It was rather a shame; the army had been the saving of many a spoiled boy.

After deciding that Torville didn't deserve another thought, Artemis stepped into the happier, warmer climes of the house kitchen. The cook who presided there was a thin, unhappy woman who made wonderful pastries and complained constantly; at present, she was keeping a weather eye on her ovens but looked up to observe Artemis' entry with a dour eye. "There ye are; I thought ye'd sleep the day away."

"I'm very sharp-set, and hoping you will have the goodness to feed me, please." Artemis sat down on a stool at the work table, and wound her feet around the legs. "And I'm also hoping you have something other than cucumber sandwiches from the tea room, because no one will ever convince me that cucumber sandwiches are anything other than a sorry excuse."

With a show of being very much put-upon, the woman used the corner of her apron to serve up two scones that were already warming beside the hearth, and set them before Artemis. "Hot," she warned succinctly, and Artemis waited impatiently for the offerings to cool down, gauging with a quickly withdrawn fingertip.

Crossing her arms, Cook rested her thin frame against the edge of the table. "They say ye've got yerself a beau."

"It is the eighth wonder of the world," Artemis agreed, helping herself from the jug of milk that had been set out for her.

"His nibs'll be unhappy." This said with a derisive movement of the head which indicated the departed Torville. "He wants yer fortune."

"He'll not have it," Artemis assured her. "Unless I give it all to you, and you be the one to marry him."

Pursing her mouth, Cook expressed her extreme disapproval at this attempt at levity. "Best watch yerself, missy—a word to the wise." She pushed the jam pot a bit closer.

"For two pins, I'd sign the wretched mines over to you," Artemis declared as she spooned a dollop of jam onto a scone. "You could set-up a bakery for the poor miners, and thus brighten up their dreary days."

"Yer beau wouldn't like that," Cook reminded her. "If it's yer fortune he's after, better he have it than Torville."

"No question," Artemis agreed through a mouthful, remembering the feel of that gentleman's warm hand at her waist.

With a casual gesture, Cook wiped the corner of the table with her apron. "Heard he's a handsome fella."

"We're going riding, tomorrow," Artemis revealed. "Peek out the curtains, and see for yourself."

But Cook's brows had drawn together upon hearing this news. "Be wary," she warned. "There be strange doings afoot."

Yes, thought Artemis, as she spooned another dollop of jam onto the scone; *Droughm is trying to goad someone into doing something—aside from goading me into this courtship, of course. Unless—unless his goal is not truly a courtship, but some other goal altogether.*

With this unhappy thought, she picked apart the remains of the scone, trying not to think about how disappointed she would be if that wonderful awareness she could see in his eyes was all a sham. *I hope not,* she thought, and tried to console herself by reflecting that the new riding habit in her armoire seemed excessive, if indeed it was all a sham.

"Who was the furrin girl, come to visit?"

"I've no idea," answered Artemis in all honesty. "Perhaps she's after my mines, too."

Cook frowned mightily, and considered the opposite wall for a moment. "Strange doings afoot," she repeated. "And Old Crotchets is like a cat on hot bricks." This was Cook's derisive term for Hooks, even though Artemis was privately convinced that the spinster had a soft spot for the very correct butler.

"I'll not hear you disparage Hooks," Artemis protested, through another mouthful. "He has promised to give Torville a whipping, if needful."

The older woman paused in the act of checking her breads. "Has he? More than I would have expected of him." She sniffed.

Artemis eyed her covertly as she took a swallow from the milk jug. "I think the man has hidden depths; perhaps you should be kinder to him."

With a thunderous brow, Cook waved a bread-paddle at Artemis. "Ye'll do best to remember, missy, that the men-folk want one thing, and one thing only."

"Even Hooks?" Artemis teased.

"Some jest hide it better than most," Cook intoned darkly. "Mark me."

"I will respectfully disagree," Artemis decided, as she licked her fingers. "Mainly, they all seem to want my silver mines."

"Sauce," the cook muttered, and turned to address the waiting bread.

CHAPTER 7

*T*he following morning, Artemis was on pins and needles, worried that some unlooked-for calamity would prevent her promised ride with Droughm. A glance out the window showed the weather was cooperating, and the new riding habit fit her slim figure perfectly, being only a bit too long so that she would have to gather up her skirts in a hand whilst she managed the stairs.

"It's a lovely thing, miss—I didn't know you had it packed away." Katy was apparently innocent of her grandfather's machinations.

"Can you dress my hair again, Katy? Or do you think it best to wear a plait, so that it doesn't come down?"

After serious consideration, they compromised by securing Artemis' thick mane into a soft knot at the back of her head, and Artemis observed her reflection in the mirror with no small satisfaction, turning from side to side and admiring the finest piece of clothing she'd ever owned.

"You look a rare treat, miss—the color brings out your lovely eyes."

"Yes," said Artemis in a neutral tone. "I believe that was the intention."

Katy crossed over to the armoire, and rummaged at the foot. "Me grand-dad—I mean, *my* grand-dad—unpacked your riding boots for you."

The man is like a magician, thought Artemis; *conjuring up items out of thin air.*

With great reverence, Katy produced lady's riding boots, of butter-soft leather and polished to a glossy sheen. Artemis pulled them on and concluded that the fit had not been left to chance; Hooks must have measured another pair of shoes. She admired the boots, flexing and pointing her feet and thinking she'd never had boots so fine—the Colonel had such a pair, once, until he'd lost them at cards.

"Pray give your grand-dad a kiss for me, Katy—he is a trump."

"Yes, miss." Reminded, she warned, "Torville's back."

"That he is," agreed Artemis absently, wishing she had a decent pair of gloves—her gloves were in sorry shape.

"Cook thinks he's had a set-to, and did not come out the better."

"I think Cook is nobody's fool." Artemis regarded herself one last time in the mirror and then resolutely turned to descend to the drawing room. "*Come, put mine armor on; give me my staff.*"

"As you say, miss—don't fall off the horse." Katy was perhaps worried that Artemis could ride no better than she could dance. "And try not to shake your hair down."

Although Artemis felt she could handle her aunt, her cousin Torville, or any combination thereof, she'd waited until the last minute to come downstairs so as to avoid waiting for Droughm in their disapproving company. To her surprise, however, Droughm himself stood at the foot of the stairs, looking up at her as she descended with the tail of her skirt in her hand. The sight of him was as unexpected as it was welcome, and she could not suppress a smile. "Sir," she teased; "you are very prompt."

"Artemis," he returned, using her Christian name without compunction. "You look very fine."

"A new riding habit has turned up." She made a gesture, encompassing it. "It must have come from mine uncle."

Droughm produced his quizzing glass and reviewed her form, head to foot. "He has very good taste."

"I confess this would be the first evidence of it."

Hooks—who'd been attending the entry door—unbent enough to issue a dry smile at this exchange, and then opened the door for them; apparently, they were to bypass taking leave of her aunt, a bold strategy which Artemis could only admire.

As she passed before Droughm to head out the door, she was close enough to breathe in his now-familiar scent, and to observe the dark stubble on his chin—he must have a heavy beard. She felt almost intoxicated with the nearness of him, and had to firmly remind herself to stay sharp.

This resolution did not last long, however, because as Artemis emerged on the front steps she beheld a groom, holding a grey stallion and a bay Arab mare, the mare sidling with impatience.

"Oh," she breathed, and approached in awe to run a hand down the mare's glossy neck. "She is *perfect*, Droughm."

He was quiet, and she glanced up to see him watching her, the expression in his eyes very warm. Artemis had never been shy a moment in her life, but found that she had to look away for a moment, afraid that she would suffocate from this feeling in her breast. "Is she from your stable?"

He laid a hand on the mare's flank. "No—but I will stable her, and you have a fortnight to decide whether she suits you. If she does, she is yours."

She twisted her mouth whilst stroking the mare's soft nose. "I should *try* to bring myself to tell you that I cannot accept such a gift."

"Don't bother—it would be very tiresome."

There was no explanation offered of what would happen to

the mare when he returned to wherever-it-was that he came from, those events being the unspoken footnote to this exchange. *Apparently, I'm to be spoiled*, she thought; it was a very strange and unfamiliar sensation.

Although the groom stepped forward, Droughm himself helped her mount; his hands cupped for her boot. "I have a million things to tell you," she offered as she took up the reins. "I hope I don't gabble."

"Wait a bit, until you have her in hand," he suggested, mounting his grey but keeping his gaze upon her, assessing.

She settled into the side-saddle, and accepted a crop from the groom, arranging her skirts whilst the horse paced in a tight circle. Artemis was a good rider, and had to resist the urge to jump the wrought-iron border fence, so as to demonstrate this. "What is her name?"

"Her name is your choice."

She thought about it; there was little doubt such a creature would be swift of foot. "Callisto, I think."

"Another goddess, then. Are you ready, you and Callisto?"

"Lay on."

They stepped out in the direction of the park, and Artemis was quiet for a few moments, adjusting to the horse's movements and relishing the welcome sensation of riding again, mounted on this very agreeable horse and side-by-side with this very agreeable man.

Apparently, however, the very agreeable man had decided he'd controlled his blunt nature long enough. "I'll have some answers from you, Artemis."

Thinking of the ladies who'd visited her aunt's drawing room, she responded with mock-severity, "I don't believe I've given you permission to address me thus."

"Artemis," he repeated, unrepentant, and swinging his crop along his horse's side. "It is quite the best name I have ever heard."

"I am fond of it myself," she confessed with a smile. "Although I pretend otherwise, because it is expected of me."

He casually flicked his crop on the toe of his boot as the horses clip-clopped along the cobblestone street. "How did it come about?"

"I am informed there was a full moon, the night I was born."

He glanced at her. "Fortune's omen."

She felt compelled to look away. "No—not in truth. I was born on the second day of the Battle of Mantua."

But he had moved on to the next topic. "There is no record that Colonel William Merryfield ever married."

"No," she agreed in an even tone. "He never spoke of it to me, leastways."

He brought his grey up close beside her, and continued in a low voice, "Was he your father, nonetheless?"

"No." With a conscious effort, she tried to relax her hands on the reins. "I never knew my father."

There was a slight pause. "I see; you were Merryfield's convenient, then."

It took her a moment to understand what he meant, and then her reaction was swift and furious, as she stood in her stirrups and slashed her crop at him.

With a swift movement, he grasped the crop in his hand and thwarted her, his expression startled as they stared at each other for a long moment.

Horrified by her loss of composure in such a public place, she took hold of herself and said steadily, "You will recant that statement, sir."

His surprise still evident, he released her crop. "I do recant. I beg your pardon."

They walked forward, Artemis acutely dismayed and keeping her gaze fixed on her horse's ears. "I must beg your pardon, in turn. Is everyone staring?"

Droughm's voice held a trace of amusement. "Of course not

—why the devil would anyone take the slightest interest in the two of us?"

Turning to him, she smiled brightly, hoping any observers would think her actions had been in play, and not serious. "I am so very sorry."

"The fault is mine," he responded, and offered nothing further.

After a moment or two of silence, she took a steadying breath. "My mother was killed seven years ago—by the Spanish, not the French. It was during the Spanish retreat, and part of our regiment was cut off and captured near San Sebastian. The Spanish didn't know who to trust, and in their panic, they slaughtered everyone the next morning."

"But you survived?"

She pressed her lips together. "I was not there, actually—not there with my mother. I was traveling with the other women in the regiment. My father had already been killed at Salamanca."

"I am sorry for it," he offered quietly.

She continued, "Colonel Merryfield was our commanding officer, and had always been fond of me. When my mother died, he took me under his wing; I was ten at the time."

Unbidden, she had a clear memory of the Colonel on that terrible, terrible day; speaking kindly to her in his bluff manner, and handing her a rag doll—heaven only knew where he'd come across it. She'd decided, then and there, that the Colonel was the most wonderful human being who'd ever trod the earth.

Striving for a light tone, she concluded, "The Colonel may have had his faults, but he was not a debaucher of children."

"I should never have leapt to such a conclusion—forgive me." They walked together for a few moments, the horses hooves making their rhythmic sound on the pavement as the park came into view. "Did he adopt you?"

"I do not know," she answered, and then—because there was nothing for it—looked over at him. "I rather doubt it."

He frowned, considering for a moment. "I would ask that you say nothing of this to anyone."

This was of interest; she had revealed that she was not, in true fact, the heiress to the mines, but he was apparently not dissuaded from his plan to stymie all evildoers by marrying her out-of-hand. She couldn't decide if she was relieved or alarmed, and so instead asked, "Who is the rightful heir to the mines, if I am not?"

"That is unclear; I believe the Merryfield line would extinguish with your uncle's death. We will say nothing of this —and in any event, even if your claim were to be contested, you have no legal guardian to represent you. It is just as well—any delay is useful."

She corrected him, "I have no guardian as yet, although I believe Lord Stanhope has applied to the Court of Chancery to be my guardian." There was a great deal to be said for listening at doors.

"It will not come to that," he assured her, idly flicking his crop on his boot again.

So; he indeed planned to marry her out-of-hand, and it did seem the best potential solution; eighteen was a long ways off, she was caught up in some sort of treasonous plot, and—as she'd said to Cook—it was far better that Droughm lay claim to the mines than the odious Torville.

On the other hand, a hasty marriage to a near-stranger seemed a bit desperate, and Artemis had to remind herself that it was best to be cautious; she must not allow herself to be beguiled by him—however tempting the prospect. *Although I would like to see anyone try to take this fine mare away from me,* she thought with some defiance; *and I would very much enjoy being kissed—just once—by this fine man.*

"It is a damnable situation," he pronounced, and made no apology for his language, which she took in good part. "Tell me of your mad uncle."

She protested in a mild tone, "Why is it that I must tell you all my secrets, but you are as close as the sphinx?"

But he was unyielding, and shook his head slightly. "I must ask that you trust me, Artemis."

She made no immediate reply, but looked ahead, thoughtful. "Because I am unseasoned."

He flicked his crop on his boot for emphasis. "No; because you are too shrewd by half."

This was of interest; and she wondered what it was that he didn't want her to unearth. "And you cannot trust me to behave as I ought, once I know your secrets?"

He answered carefully, "You are not so seasoned as to be able to judge what is for the best, perhaps."

"Perhaps," she agreed. Artemis did not express her own opinion—that she was indeed a fair judge of such things, despite her youth. It came from having so few supporters that she could rely upon.

With this in mind, she waited until they had passed through the gates that led into the park before she said matter-of-factly, "I met Wentworth's betrothed—I believe she is a spy."

The green eyes were suddenly sharp upon hers, and she could sense his extreme surprise. Hiding a smile, she thought —*there; that will teach him to think me unseasoned.*

CHAPTER 8

*I*nto the silence, Artemis explained, "I met a spy once, in the hills of Spain—a woman who came to warn the Colonel of an ambush, up ahead. It was extraordinary—how she could change who she was, depending upon what she needed, and from whom she needed it. Miss Valdez—or whoever she is—reminds me of her."

The crop began hitting Droughm's boot again. "When was this?"

"Yesterday—I caught her rifling through the writing desk in the drawing room. What was she looking for?"

He had the grace to give her a glance of regret, after she'd just chastised him for being so secretive. "It is a sensitive matter, and cannot be bandied about, I'm afraid."

"You don't trust me," she concluded. "I understand." This said in a tone making it very clear she did not understand at all.

His gaze meeting hers, he said in his brusque way, "I confess I have to fight an inclination to trust you completely, and thank God that you have been thrown my way."

While this was a very welcome profession of tender feelings, it did not alter the fact that he was changing the subject. Making a sound of extreme impatience, she refused to look at him. "If I am at the center of this mystery, it is only fair that I know what is afoot."

"Plates," he relented. "She was looking for minting plates, the kind that are used for the pressing of coins. They are not very large." He indicated with his fingers.

Artemis frowned, thinking this over. "The Stanhopes are involved in counterfeiting coins?"

"I'm afraid it is much worse than that."

Counterfeiting was a form of treason, and punishable by hanging; it was hard to imagine how it could be much worse. Trying to decide what she should ask next, Artemis was forestalled by the approach of a gentleman, who doffed his hat to Droughm.

In his negligent manner, Droughm introduced Artemis, and offered no explanation for her presence beside him. As a result, Artemis could perceive a gleam of speculation in the gentleman's eye as he said all that was proper to her. *I am to be put on display, yet again*, she thought with resignation, and was somewhat comforted by the fact that she could ride much better than she could dance.

When they continued on their way, Artemis observed, "Your grey is voice-trained, I think."

"Trajan." Droughm laid a fond hand on his horse's neck. "We have been together a long time, now—he knows what I wish to do before I do."

"There is nothing so fine as a good horse." Artemis had been horse-mad from the day she was born.

He tilted his head slightly, as they walked along. "I may have to disagree."

Even though he did not look at her, Artemis felt herself grow a bit warm as they continued into the heart of the park, navigating through the press of visitors who were present at this fashionable hour. She did her best to appear unfazed by the covert scrutiny she attracted, whilst Droughm remained close-at-hand, pointing out an occasional landmark in his careless manner, and apparently oblivious to the attention they garnered.

The carriages along the pathways moved along at a snail's pace as occupants greeted each other, the ladies deftly wielding their decorated parasols and fans as the gentlemen drew up to engage in the fine art of flirtation.

"Where do we go to gallop?" asked Artemis, who was heartily bored.

Amused, her companion shook his head. "There is no galloping, I'm afraid; at least, not at this hour."

Perplexed, she looked about her. "You gave me this wonderful little mare for *this*?"

"Patience," he advised. "There are some strictures that we dare not flout—I cannot let it be thought that you are anything other than the gently-bred daughter of a war-hero, and as an added incentive, the heiress to a mining fortune."

She ventured candidly, "It hardly matters; it would still be a huge mismatch, no matter what tale was spun."

"Nonsense; it all depends on the size of the heiress' fortune."

Smiling at his cynicism, she could only agree. "I suppose that is true—how many thousand pounds' inheritance can be bartered for a barony?"

He tilted his head and confessed, "I am afraid that I am an Earl."

Staring at him in acute dismay, she faltered, "Oh; oh, Droughm—"

"Pen," he interrupted.

"Pen?" she asked, confused, and struggling with this latest revelation.

"Penderton," he explained. "My name—please use it, when it is just the two of us."

"Pen," Artemis addressed him, very seriously. "I *truly* cannot marry you—it would be *beyond* a mismatch." With a pang of regret, she wondered if she would indeed have to relinquish this fine mare, after all.

"Nonsense," he replied in his off-hand manner. "I think we are well-suited."

"You don't know the worst," she confessed. "I am afraid to even tell you."

Turning his head, he met her gaze with his own frank one. "There could be nothing worse than losing you, now that I have finally found you."

The thing was, she could swear he was completely sincere. Mesmerized, she could think of nothing to say whilst they regarded each other for a long moment. *Hell and damnation*, she thought yet again.

The spell was broken by a low, feminine voice that laughingly called out, "Droughm—do pay attention, I pray you."

The woman who addressed them was lovely; honey-blond with an admirable figure. Her riding habit was dashing without being showy, cut in the military style and highlighted with a mock shako, placed aslant on her curls. And—as if being a vision of loveliness weren't enough—she sat on a very fine-boned black gelding.

I cannot bring myself to be uneasy, Artemis decided; *if we were indeed competing, I would have no choice but to concede the field.*

"I'd no idea you were back in town; what a happy surprise." The other's twinkling gaze took in Artemis and her companion with all evidence of good will, but Artemis was not fooled, and awaited events.

For his part, Droughm greeted the woman in his easy manner. "Carena; it is a pleasure to see you again."

With no show of purpose, the woman nevertheless managed to fall in beside him and, as a result, Artemis was necessarily forced to follow, filled with admiration for the subtle piece of maneuvering. *She'd make a good tactical officer*, thought Artemis, and prepared to listen and learn.

The newcomer spoke to Droughm in a vivacious manner for a few minutes, but when they reached a broader pathway, the woman turned with a friendly gesture to Artemis. "Pray come up beside me—I am unpardonably rude to interrupt your outing."

Artemis smiled in return and did as she was bid, awaiting an introduction.

"Lady Tallyer, allow me to introduce Miss Merryfield," said Droughm. Again, he made no attempt to offer an explanation for Artemis' presence at his side.

"Is this your first visit to town, Miss Merryfield?" Lady Tallyer appeared genuinely interested, which was kind of her, particularly since Artemis was fully aware the lady was actually making a shrewd assessment of enemy terrain.

"It is indeed," Artemis admitted. "I am enjoying it very much." This for the benefit of the gentleman who knew that but for him, her circumstances were otherwise not at all enjoyable.

"Such an exciting time for you," the lady exclaimed in the manner of an indulgent adult to a small child. "Will you have a season?"

"No," confessed Artemis. "I am unseasoned."

Lady Tallyer turned to Droughm with delight. "Your young friend is a wit, Droughm."

"So it would seem," he agreed, and Artemis arched a brow at him behind the lady's back. *I am wicked*, she thought; *and I should not seek to discomfit him whilst he speaks with his admirer.*

The lady adjusted her reins in a manner that drew attention to her graceful hands. "Are you lately arrived from Somerhurst, Droughm?"

"Algiers, instead; I've not yet had an opportunity to visit Somerhurst."

Kindly including Artemis in the conversation, the lady disclosed, "The formal gardens at Somerhurst are breathtaking, this time of year."

A fusillade, thought Artemis with appreciation. *But sadly, it is only a pyrrhic victory; poor Lady Tallyer is not slated to be the person who will tend the gardens at Somerhurst, wherever they are.*

"I had the pleasure of visiting the formal gardens at the Ballantine House ball," Artemis reminisced for the gentleman's benefit. "It quite took my breath away."

"One should fondly remember one's first ball," the lady agreed indulgently. "No doubt once you are old enough to be out, you will attend many more." The glance she gave to the gentleman deftly conveyed a willingness to support and encourage a young girl on the cusp of adulthood.

Artemis decided it was past time to fire off a round, herself. "I confess I was coerced into waltzing when I had no business even making the attempt."

But the lady was not shaken, and responded with a smile. "Lord Droughm can be most persuasive."

She then slid the gentleman a knowing look from beneath her lashes that made Artemis feel all of ten years old. *Best retreat*, she cautioned herself, *and present no more openings for a double entendre.*

After a few more minutes of conversation, Lady Tallyer indicated she would return to her group. "Do you make an appearance at Montagu's card party tonight, Droughm? I believe we have need of a fourth."

But the gentleman was not one to be coerced by good manners. "I must first review my calendar, Carena."

The lady did not press, and instead smiled at Artemis. "I hope to meet you again soon, Miss Merryfield." With a cheerful little wave, she turned back, and even in retreat, her figure was impressive.

Her eyes alight, Artemis turned her gaze to Droughm, awaiting his reaction. He did not deign to give her one, although she could see that he was amused. She prompted, "A beauty, Pen—it is a shame she has no silver mines, lying about."

To his credit, he did not attempt to disclaim. "I will inform her that we will not resume our relationship."

"The Colonel always gave them a bracelet," Artemis suggested helpfully.

Although there was a small smile playing about his lips, he chided, "You should not be speaking of such things, Artemis."

But Artemis wanted him to know she was not missish about such subjects, and shook her head slightly. "I've grown up amongst soldiers, Pen. I am not shocked by much of anything."

"Nevertheless, you must try to be circumspect. We cannot allow anyone to entertain a suspicion about your antecedents."

This was a good point, and with a wry smile, she acknowledged, "Then I'm afraid you'll be more of a Dutch Aunt than a suitor, if you are going to try to steer me through London society. I am foundering in unfamiliar terrain."

He assured her, "Not much longer, Artemis—my promise on it. And speaking of which, can you tell me your dreaded confession? I may need to create a plausible tale."

Suddenly sober, she advised him, "There are actually four secrets—all of them equally horrifying. Perhaps you will want to reconsider giving Lady Tallyer her parting bracelet."

"In for a penny, in for a pound," he replied in a philosophical manner. "Tell me, if you please."

Looking ahead, she nodded, and tried to sort out her thoughts, finding that it was surprisingly difficult to know where to begin.

Suddenly, she felt his hand on her arm, and looked at him in surprise.

"No," he said softly, his expression concerned. "Not in such a public place—forgive me for being a clumsy fool."

"I need to gather my courage," she confessed.

"And I need to offer comfort—which I cannot do here."

"Soon," she pleaded. "I *must* tell you soon."

"You will," he assured her, and they turned for home.

CHAPTER 9

*A*rtemis sat with her hands folded in her lap as she underwent an uncomfortable debriefing at Stanhope House. She'd returned home only to find that Lady Stanhope requested a moment of her time, and was then led into the dining room with no further ado.

"I am informed he was quite particular in his attentions," her aunt said, as she regarded her niece from beneath hooded eyes.

"Lord Droughm was very kind." Artemis presented a guileless expression, and hoped to get over this rough ground as lightly as possible. Belatedly, she realized that she was ignorant of Droughm's strategy—whether she should openly admit his attentions to her aunt so as to trigger whatever reaction he was seeking, or whether she was supposed to pretend to be unaware of his pointed interest. *A pox on the man, for forgetting to strategize with me,* she thought; *I suppose it best to pretend to be unaware until I hear otherwise.* To this end, she recited as though she were ten years old, "He showed me the Serpentine Pond; there were all variety of ducks."

Her aunt made no reply, and Artemis had the uneasy

59

conviction that she'd overplayed her hand. Retrenching, she added, "And Lady Tallyer joined us for a time."

"Did she indeed?" Her aunt's thin brows rose in surprise.

That should confuse the issue, thought Artemis with satisfaction, and then heard the entry bell ring. She paused, hoping that the visitor meant an end to her debriefing; perhaps luncheon would be served soon—it had been hungry work this morning, sorting out the rest of her life.

But instead of a reprieve, Artemis could hear Hooks speaking with Torville in the foyer. *It wants only this*, she thought with resignation, and prepared herself for further interrogation.

"Aunt," her cousin greeted as he entered the room. "I am looking to be fed."

Artemis rose to curtsy, and he greeted her with a cynical smile. "Cousin."

Aunt Stanhope pulled the bell cord. "I am so happy you've joined us, Torville; Artemis is relating her experiences from this morning." This said with some meaning.

"Oh?" the gentleman asked as he moved over to the sideboard. "Which experiences are these?"

"Lord Droughm took her riding in the park." The older woman paused. "On a mare he brought especially for her."

As the servant brought in the cold-meat platters, Torville turned to regard Artemis with some surprise. "Did he? Am I to wish you happy, cousin?"

"Great heavens, Torville—he cannot think to marry her," her aunt interjected with a tinge of exasperation. "The man is a belted Earl." This being said, her aunt then turned to address Artemis in awful tones. "Did he indeed speak of marriage?"

Artemis did her best to appear bewildered. "We spoke of horses, ma'am—and gardens."

Her aunt subsided, and thoughtfully sank into her chair. "He plays a deep game, then."

But Torville had other concerns to raise. "I understand you

entertained a visitor here at the house, cousin—the Ambassador's daughter."

"I did," Artemis readily admitted, turning to her aunt. "I forgot to mention it, ma'am—she came by yesterday to leave a note for you."

If it were possible, Lady Stanhope's expression became even more basilisk-like. "Indeed?"

Since it seemed clear that this was very unwelcome news, Artemis decided to do a bit of probing. "We met at the ball, you see. Miss Valdez would like to stand as my friend, here in London."

"Artemis," her aunt scolded; "you must not entertain visitors when I am from home—you are no longer with the army, and must make an effort to behave with propriety."

"Yes, ma'am—I am truly sorry. I wasn't certain what I should do in such a situation."

"If neither I nor Torville is at home, you must not entertain visitors—I will inform Hooks. At your age you must be very circumspect."

"Yes, ma'am." Artemis decided that she probably shouldn't mention she'd been discussing the best way to dismiss a mistress with Droughm. "Miss Valdez did mention a potential shopping expedition—would such an outing be permissible?"

Her companions regarded her with mutual, silent consternation. "I would be remiss to allow such an expedition, Artemis," her aunt declared firmly. "I am afraid the young lady runs with a fast crowd, and I could not be easy."

"Do not leave the house with her," Torville advised bluntly. "Your reputation would suffer." He gave his aunt a covert glance of alarm, but she'd sunk her chin to her chest, and was lost in thought.

So—the Portuguese contingency still hopes to abduct me, Artemis thought. *It is strange, though; it takes little imagination to make the connection between counterfeiting coins and the silver mines in Sheffield, but I cannot see why Portugal would take such an interest. I will have to ask Droughm, next time I see him.*

"Perhaps you will escort your cousin to the lending library after luncheon," suggested Lady Stanhope, lifting her head to fix Torville with a silent message. "You have spent little time together, of late."

Artemis decided that this idea had merit; it was unlikely that Torville would continue to press his attentions on her—not after having the fear of Droughm beaten into him—and perhaps she could wheedle some information from him about how all this fit together

And so, Artemis stepped out onto the pavement with Torville, and immediately cast a casual glance behind them. She saw what she'd expected; Droughm's man, dressed in workman's clothes and following at a discreet distance—it was nice to know her flank was protected. She met the man's gaze for a long moment to make him aware she knew of his presence, and then brought her attention back to her companion. "Are you inclined to tell me what makes our mutual aunt so nervous?"

"Is she nervous?" Torville slid his mocking gaze sidelong to her. "I hadn't noticed."

"So—you are not inclined," she concluded. "It is all very puzzling. Where is our Uncle Stanhope?"

"I believe he is in Sheffield, trying to discover what happened to your great-uncle."

Artemis considered this. "Good luck to him."

His gaze speculative, it was Torville's turn to press. "What do you know of it?"

But she would not be drawn. "I am as little inclined to tell you anything as you are to tell me."

Twisting his mouth into a cynical smile, he returned his gaze to the street ahead. "We have a stalemate, then."

They walked a bit further in silence, coming upon the shops that served this fashionable area of town. "Are we truly going to the library?" Artemis asked. "I'm not much for reading."

"Your wish is my command," he replied in a tone that made her long to cuff him. "What you will."

"I'd like an ice," she decided, spying a confectioner's shop across the way. "I haven't had an ice since Barcelona."

"By all means, then." He escorted her into the establishment, and Artemis settled upon a table near the window, so that her guard would have an unobstructed view. They ordered dishes of the treat, neither one of them finding it necessary to maintain a conversation, even out of politeness. After scraping the last bit from the bottom of her dish, Artemis thought she'd take a cast, and asked, "What do you know about Ambassador Valdez's daughter?"

Torville eyed her in amusement. "You are a suspicious little package—why would I know anything about her?" This said in a manner that made it clear he indeed knew something, and was not going to tell her.

Although she realized he was trying to goad her, she continued to press, hoping he'd not miss a chance to feel superior. "Our aunt seem very reluctant to allow me to fraternize with her."

With his eyes holding hers, her companion licked the spoon in a deliberate and provoking manner whilst he considered his answer. *If Droughm were here*, thought Artemis, *he would punch him yet again, and I would be happy to hold his coat.*

"She is no doubt afraid that your reputation would suffer."

Artemis regarded him with a thoughtful gaze. "I think that you are all afraid of Miss Valdez, for some reason."

A cynical smile on his lips, Torville negligently leaned back. "Heavens no—where do you come by these fanciful notions, little cousin?"

She lifted a brow. "I suppose it comes of having all manner of secretive relations."

Cocking his head, Torville replied, "If you marry me, there

will be no more secrets. And I suppose I could do worse than have to look into those eyes of yours, across the breakfast table every morning."

"And think upon my silver mines," she added.

"That, too," he agreed without a qualm. "Quite the sweetener, they are."

"No, thank you," she said politely. She imagined he made the offer so as to be able to report to their aunt that he had done so—no doubt his aunt had commissioned him for this very purpose. If the Court of Chancery was told she wished to marry her cousin, presumably her guardianship issues would be resolved in short order.

"I am unsurprised that you scorn my suit—you have bigger fish to fry." This with another sly look.

But she would not be goaded into a response, and they returned to Stanhope House with little further discussion.

CHAPTER 10

*A*fter Artemis returned from her outing with Torville, she retreated into the kitchen but did not find the quiet sanctuary that she sought; Cook was banging the pots around and evidently in a foul mood. "Ye're lucky he brought ye back, ye young fool."

"He behaved himself," Artemis protested. "And anyway, I wanted an ice." *And I had reinforcements at the ready*, she added silently—*otherwise I wouldn't have gone; I may be young, but I am no fool.*

Grumbling, the woman produced a fresh lemon tart only with a show of reluctance. "I'm ready to wash me hands of ye."

"I still have my beau," Artemis pointed out, taking a bite. She truly wasn't very hungry— not after the ice—but she didn't want to hurt Cook's feelings.

But this reminder only instigated another bout of pots-banging. "You won't have 'im for long, if Old Crotchets has his way."

Amused, Artemis protested, "Surely, Hooks approves of Lord Droughm? Never say he thinks I can look higher?"

The older woman sniffed. "Lady Tallyer's housemaid was here, sweetenin' 'im up and askin' 'im questions—the old fool."

Oh-ho, thought Artemis, dropping her gaze to the table; *very enterprising—not that any information gained by my lady Tallyer will work to change the coming course of events.* Aloud, she proclaimed, "I'll not believe it; I cannot imagine that Hooks would betray me for a pretty face."

Cook had the grace to look a bit abashed. "I'll not say he would—only that it doesn't look right—'im bein' put to the touch by such a hussy." She snapped the lid on the tea kettle, for emphasis.

"Perhaps he is lonely, and craves feminine attention," Artemis suggested, watching her companion from beneath her lashes. "In the army, I saw many a man fall into female trouble out of sheer loneliness."

Frowning, the woman considered this, as she tested a cake with her finger. "I could play cribbage with 'im a' nights—I think he plays cribbage."

"It would be an act of kindness." Whilst the woman was distracted, Artemis folded the uneaten tart into her napkin, unseen. "And it would help him resist the temptations offered by all the hussies underfoot, here in London."

"Men," Cook sniffed, but Artemis felt she'd successfully planted a small seed, and hoped it would bear fruit—although the thought of either Cook or Hooks being romantically inclined boggled the mind; perhaps it would be a good match for that reason alone.

After excusing herself, Artemis retreated to her chamber to lie on her bed and contemplate the extraordinary events of the day, cautiously allowing full rein to the effervescing happiness within her breast. She thought about the morning's ride, and reenacted as much as she could remember in her mind—dwelling in particular on her escort's brusque and spontaneous confession of tender feelings. He was smitten, she was smitten, and now it only wanted a path to happiness—although the fact that the path was fraught with peril, spies and treason did make things a bit more complicated.

I need more information, she reminded herself, *before I can completely trust him.* Absently groping for her tattered rag doll, she tucked it into the crook of her arm.

"Are you awake, miss? We'll have to ready you for tea, soon." Katy came through the door, balancing a chipped ewer of hot water. "Small wonder you're weary—the men folk are all plying you with favors, today."

"It is a wondrous thing, to be an heiress," Artemis observed. "I highly recommend it."

"I think his lordship wouldn't care if you were barefoot and in your shift," the 'tweenie opined with no little satisfaction. "He's a grand one."

"He is indeed." Artemis smiled at the ceiling as she contemplated Droughm's imagined reaction if she were to appear before him, barefoot and in her shift.

With a fond gesture, Katy reached to touch one of the doll's thread-worn braids. "A good friend, miss."

Artemis lifted her doll between her hands, and could feel the edges of the minting plates, hidden within the rag-filled body. "A very good friend," she agreed.

CHAPTER 11

*V*ery early the following morning, Artemis opened sleepy eyes to behold Katy, illuminated by a single candle that she shielded with her hand. "Miss," she whispered, "My grand-dad would like to speak with you."

Startled, Artemis propped up on an elbow and attempted to draw together her scattered wits. "What's amiss, Hooks?" Artemis noted that the staid retainer stood behind Katy, his hands folded before him.

"There is no emergency, Miss Merryfield," he assured her with a small bow. "Lord Droughm is out front, and explains he requested your presence for an early ride this morning, but apparently the invitation went astray."

Artemis sat up, fully awake. "Did it indeed?"

"Apparently," the retainer repeated smoothly. "And as the other inhabitants are abed, I am at a loss."

"Hooks," Artemis declared, as she swung her legs over the side of the bed. "You are worth your weight in gold. I'll be down in five minutes."

"His lordship is accompanied by a groom." Hooks did not want her to think he was completely lost to all propriety as he bowed, and left her to Katy's ministrations.

A few minutes later, Artemis gathered her gloves and crept downstairs, dressed in her blue velvet habit. Awaiting her approach, Hooks quietly opened the door and then Artemis was outside in the weak morning light, Droughm and his groom waiting at the curb with the horses. Droughm helped her to mount Callisto, and then they were away, not speaking until they were a goodly distance from the house.

Artemis grinned at him, the cold air making her cheeks tingle. "You are the most complete hand."

"Sleepy-sides," he teased. "Don't fall off your horse."

She laughed with sheer pleasure. "Oh, I have taken many a tumble, I assure you—it comes of being a neck-or-nothing rider."

"Not to be confused with your good-for–nothing cousin, whom I ask that you avoid in the future."

So; he was unhappy with her, and she quickly looked over to him in apology. "I am sorry; I thought now that Torville's been defanged, I would ply him with some questions."

"No more," he said only. "And you are to equally avoid those who ruined your evening at Ballantine House, including Miss Valdez."

With a teasing smile, she offered, "I don't know, Pen; I regard the Ballantine House ball as the best night of my short life, thus far."

Apparently, she'd succeeded in putting herself back in his good graces, because he gave her a very meaningful look. "There will be better nights, I promise you."

Feeling a bit warm despite the chill, she contemplated her horse's ears for a moment. "Where do we go?"

He flicked his crop on the toe of his boot. "Rotten Row. It is a good place for a run, this early—there should be no one about."

"That is excellent, Pen—I would love a good run." She hoped he hadn't noticed that it was starting to drizzle.

The park was indeed deserted, as they came to the long,

sandy track. "Can we truly let them go?" She did not want to have him unhappy with her again.

"Careful—it is a bit wet," he cautioned.

With a serious expression, Artemis contemplated the stretch ahead. "Perhaps I should get off, then, and lead her."

With a half-smile, he bent his head in acknowledgment. "Your pardon—I cannot seem to help myself."

Artemis smiled to show she took it in good heart—it was rather nice, after all, to have someone worried about her. "I should take a tumble, my Dutch Aunt, just to set your mind at rest."

He gathered up his reins. "Pray resist the impulse. Let's see how she goes, then."

They moved into a gallop that went on for an exhilarating half-mile, until he finally signaled they should come to a stop. Artemis pulled in her mare, laughing in delight, and wheeled around to see that Droughm had already dismounted. With several long strides, he pulled her from her horse and into his arms, so as to kiss her rather roughly.

The reality was so much better than the imagining, as he lowered her to the ground, his arm unyielding across her back. *I shall never forget this as long as I live,* she thought, and tried to match his urgency.

After kissing her very thoroughly for a blissful space of time, he gentled his actions and kissed the edge of her lower lip, her cheek, and then her mouth again. When he finally ceased, he kept his face close to hers, stroking the hair back from her temples with light fingertips.

Closing her eyes, she leaned into him, overcome with the sensation of his nearness, and unable to speak.

"If it starts to rain in earnest, we will have to go back, I'm afraid."

She managed to find her voice. "Must we?"

"Let's take cover, and wait a bit." He indicated a pathway sheltered by leafy trees, and they retreated to stand beneath the broad-spread branches. Thankfully, the rain was only sporadic, and the gray morning mists were beginning to dissipate in the strengthening sunlight.

They stood together, Droughm's hand around her waist whilst Artemis leaned into him, noting that the groom was nowhere to be seen. *Good man*, she thought; *although no doubt he is operating under strict instructions—that kiss had the feel of pent-up anticipation.*

It was very quiet, the only sound being the horses, as they cropped the long grass. Whilst she fingered the sleeve of his coat, Artemis pressed her lips together for a moment, and then began: "My mother was married to an infantryman; her husband's regiment was called up to hold the Po Valley during the First Coalition. They had to move quickly, and so the camp followers—like my mother—were often left to join up as best they could. It was the way of it."

He bent his head to her, listening, as she gazed out over the sun-dappled landscape.

"An enemy brigade came in from the flank, and our camp was raided. My mother was raped, as were many of the women."

With a hand, he drew her head to rest against his cheek.

"The others tried to convince my mother that her husband could just as easily be the father, and that she shouldn't dwell on it, but my eyes—" She paused. "My mother found it difficult to look upon me, and so the other women helped to raise me."

"Artemis," he said quietly, so that it resonated against the bones of her face.

Heartened, she drew breath, and continued, "I told you about what happened at San Sebastian but I didn't tell you everything. At San Sebastian she was raped again, and became pregnant again. She was unable to face it, and killed herself." *There*, she thought, *I have done it—I have told him.*

"A sorry excuse for a mother," she could hear the

suppressed anger in his voice, "to even allow you to know of your heritage."

Leaning back in surprise, she gazed up at him. "Why—why that is what I've always thought, privately; but then I felt guilty for thinking it. The truth is the truth, after all."

But he disagreed, and pulled her firmly against his side. "Some things are more important than the truth; and if you think I am going to shy away from discussing your beautiful eyes—and at length—you have misjudged your man."

"Yes, sir." She used the wrong honorific, so as to lighten her next remark. "But you mustn't marry me, given the circumstances."

His immediate response was to say, "I'll have no more of your nonsense," and kiss her again. As she was now becoming accustomed, she moved her hands to his shoulders and responded with enthusiasm when he pulled her closer for further intimacies; caressing her in a way that was a clear precursor to an anticipated coupling.

His mouth finally broke away, and she could feel his chest rise and fall as he held her against him for a moment. For her part, she clung to him, trying to catch her breath and unable to step away. Years ago, when she'd puzzled out the events that took place in the marriage bed, she was a bit skeptical—it all seemed so awkward, and almost absurdly intimate. Now—now she was a convert, and yearned to run her hands across his bare chest. *There will be hair on his chest*, she thought, a bit dazed; *he has quite a heavy beard.*

"Do not look at me in such a way, Artemis. Your task is to keep me in check."

"I don't know if that is the best plan, Pen," she admitted in a thick voice.

He kissed her quickly. "Enough, now."

"Yes," she agreed. "Enough." Neither moved. Then they both began to laugh, and the perilous moment had passed. *This is exactly why they go on and on nattering about chaperones*, she thought—*it would be hard to control this inclination, if we were someplace truly private*. She put a finger up to trace his mouth, and he kissed the tip and cupped her face in his hand.

"Pen—exactly how long am I to keep you in check?"

He smiled, and from this proximity, she could see the network of crinkles at the corners of his eyes. "Not long." He gently touched an earlobe. "Your ears are unpierced—I could not remember."

Bemused, she regarded him. "Is it important?"

"I purchased a set of sapphires for you." He placed two fingers at the hollow of her throat and traced where the necklace would be. "Nothing ostentatious; very simple." He met her gaze and added, "To match your beautiful eyes."

Blushing with pleasure, she nevertheless reminded him, "You know that I'll not be old enough to wear proper jewels for some years, Pen."

He leaned in to place his cheek against her temple so that he spoke into her ear. "I thought you could wear them for me, when we are in private." Unspoken was the understanding that she would be wearing nothing else.

With a smile, she rubbed her face in his coat. "I am amazed you can sleep at night, Pen, weaving such strategies."

He chuckled again near her ear, and then stepped back. "Give me your foot and let's put you up before I lose my resolve." Suiting deed to word, they were underway again, and began heading back.

CHAPTER 12

     *T*he sun was rising in earnest as they approached the park's gate, but Artemis was not concerned; Lady Stanhope would breakfast in her room, and the only staff who would be up and about would not betray her. And besides, Lady Stanhope was afraid of Droughm, for reasons as yet unexplored.

"Miss Merryfield?" a voice called from the pathway perpendicular to their own.

Artemis turned in surprise to see two soldiers, apparently out for the same reason they were—to take an early morning run.

"Well met," the fellow called out with enthusiasm. "I knew it—Colonel Merryfield's Artemis."

"Hallo," she returned with a smile, finding she was very happy to see their uniforms—it reminded her of everything that used to be familiar, and now was not.

After introductions were made, the second young man offered, "A fine horse—a Barbary, I believe."

"Indeed she is," agreed Artemis, and decided she probably shouldn't discuss the particulars, not with Droughm at her side, and no chaperone in sight. "Where are you stationed?"

"The barracks at Woolwich, for the time being," offered the first. "But the latest rumor speaks of more action on the Continent."

"No rest for the weary," Artemis commiserated. "Is Boney swimming to shore?"

But the young man shook his head. "Don't joke—things are in such a shambles at the Congress that there's a real fear he'll escape, and try to raise another army."

This was a surprise; Napoleon was exiled on the Island of Elba whilst the Congress of Vienna tried to sort out what was to be done with post-war Europe. She'd heard nothing to indicate the former French Emperor would make another attempt to conquer the world, but of course, she'd been preoccupied of late —what with counterfeiting, murder, and attempted abductions. "Well, he'll never raise another *Grande Armée*," she declared with the scorn of the victor. "That ship has sailed."

"Oh—he can muster up the troops; he's famous for it," the first man said with a touch of exasperation. "But I can't believe he has a ha'pence left—not after the Moscow debacle."

"And if he dares to try, the Iron Duke will give him what for," the second man declared. "I almost hope he does escape— just so we have a chance to lay into him again."

Thinking to include Droughm, Artemis asked, "Do you think Napoleon will try to inflict another round of misery, my lord?"

"I think it inevitable," he said in his blunt way.

A bit taken aback, Artemis stared at him for a moment, but the others seemed to take his comment as confirmation of what they believed, and a lively discussion ensued as to when such an attempt would be made.

"Before the end of Spring," said the first soldier. "It's now or never. Is that your guess, my lord?"

"I make no guess," Droughm replied, and Artemis cast him a sharp look at his choice of words.

While the others discussed the swiftness of the anticipated

defeat, Artemis confessed, "I'd no idea of the rumors—it comes from being a paltry civilian."

"Yes—didn't they pack you off to Yorkshire, or somewhere?"

"Sheffield," she confirmed. "Then, like a bad penny, I was packed off here."

"I am sorry about what happened to the Colonel," the second soldier sympathized. "To have survived so much action, only to die in such a way—"

"Yes," she interrupted. "Thank you."

"Perhaps I could call upon you, Miss Merryfield," the man suggested in a self-conscious manner, and then looked to Droughm for permission.

"By all means," said Droughm handsomely.

Struggling to hide a smile, Artemis informed him, "I am staying at Stanhope House, on Berkeley Square." Then, for Droughm's benefit, she added, "For the time being, leastways."

Farewells were exchanged, and each group resumed their ride. With a gleam, Artemis glanced over at Droughm to await his comment, but he merely looked amused, and would not be drawn. *He is certain of me*, she thought; *as well he should be.*

"Tell me of Merryfield's death," he said after a moment.

"He was robbed and killed in San Pablo," she replied in a level voice. "He was leaving a gaming ken in the wee hours, and was set-upon by thieves."

He glanced at her, his expression thoughtful. "And?"

She debated. "Could I perform only one dreaded confession per day?"

"You may; but I should like to hear it, and soon."

To divert the subject—and because she'd caught something in his manner—she asked, "What do you know of Napoleon's plans?"

"We keep up a correspondence," he responded mildly, and flicked his crop.

She looked ahead again, knowing he was not going to tell

her whatever-it-was he knew. *Interesting*, she thought—*that we have not known each other very long, but we seem to know each other very well, indeed.*

Aloud, she offered, "It is incredible to think that the war may start up again—how many Coalitions have there been? Four or five?"

"Too many. But your friend has the right of it; Napoleon cannot hope to succeed without funding—and a great deal of it."

Unable to comprehend such foolishness, Artemis shook her head in amazement. "Who would dare back him now? It would be throwing good money after bad."

"Indeed," agreed Droughm, who offered nothing more.

The horses walked for a few minutes in silence, and Artemis was already regretting that they would soon be parted. "Will you come call upon me again—perhaps later this morning? Cook makes an excellent tart, and I can ensure that mine aunt has her smelling salts at the ready."

But his response was unexpected. "I have a different excursion in mind, and I must beg a favor from you."

"Willingly." Hopefully, whatever it was, it would lead the gentleman to take another round of gross liberties with her person.

"I would ask that you make arrangements to visit the British Museum with Miss Valdez, two mornings hence."

Staring at him in surprise, she faltered, "The one who is a spy?"

"The very same. But I would ask that you not discuss that particular subject with her."

With a knit brow, Artemis cautioned, "I have been forbidden by mine aunt to keep company with the young lady—being as how they seem to be terrified of her."

If she thought he might enlighten her, she was to be disappointed yet again. Instead, he absently began to flick his crop. "I see. Try to contrive the meeting, nevertheless."

She ventured, "Are they more terrified of you, or of her?"

"We shall soon see," was all he would say, and she decided not to press him any further; she was trying very hard to avoid any behavior that could be considered childish, the encounter with Lady Tallyer serving as both an inspiration and a warning.

With this in mind, Artemis contemplated her orders. "Will you be there—at the Museum?"

"I will meet up with you, but you must not allow her to know this."

Nodding, she asked, "What is our battle strategy?"

He tilted his head in apology. "I cannot tell you, I'm afraid—and not because I think you unseasoned, but because I fear you will embark on some course destined to make my hair turn grey."

"More grey," she countered, teasing.

"More grey," he agreed with a small smile.

"Come, Pen—I am not so reckless," she insisted. "And I must know whether I should bring my pistol."

"Bring it, if you'd like; pray refrain from shooting her, though."

They turned onto her street, and she realized with a pang of regret that she'd be home in a matter of minutes. "Will I see you before the Museum, Pen? Perhaps you should climb a vine, later." The suggestion was rather bold; if she entertained him in her room there would be no hope for it—but she could not muster up a shred of regret for her anticipated ruination.

"Don't tempt me," was his only response.

Reminded, she told him, "I wasn't certain what to say to mine aunt when she quizzed me about your intentions. I pretended to be rather simple, and unaware of the enormity of it all."

A half-smile played around his mouth. "There is not a soul alive who could be fooled into thinking you are rather simple."

"Do I tell her that you have spoken of a mutual future?" Honestly, the man was not exactly forthcoming. Besides,

Artemis rather enjoyed it when he spoke of a mutual future—it brought on that breathless feeling.

"For my purposes, it does not matter—she'll not believe it, in any event."

A bit soberly, Artemis considered this, as they halted before Stanhope House. "No; she didn't seem inclined to believe it— that someone like you would marry someone like me. And she is not even aware that I am the bastard daughter of an anonymous French soldier." Her eyes slid over to him, thinking she'd best emphasize this point, in the event he hadn't grasped its significance earlier.

But her companion was unaffected, and replied, "Just imagine your father's consternation, if he could but discover that he'd sired an English Countess."

"Oh; I suppose it serves him right." She was much struck, not having looked at it in quite this way.

"Just so," said Droughm, and left it at that.

CHAPTER 13

$\mathcal{H}$ ooks was on the watch for Artemis's return, and quietly let her back into the house. She'd already decided she'd say nothing of the outing unless she was asked, as she was certain Hooks would not betray her. She tried not to dwell on what sort of explanation she could possibly offer, and decided she'd face that test only if the need arose.

After undressing with the aid of a conspiratorial Katy—who was brimful of suppressed excitement—Artemis crept back into her bed to warm herself, and to dwell with delight upon the details of the morning's adventure. Despite her intention to mentally reenact the moment when Droughm pulled her from her horse to kiss her, she was almost immediately asleep.

She was gently shaken awake two hours later by the apologetic 'tweenie. "Wake up, miss; Lady Stanhope is asking for you."

Rubbing her eyes, Artemis concluded that her unauthorized outing must have been unearthed. "Tell her I'll be down straightaway, Katy. Is she very angry?"

The girl assured her, "Oh—oh no, miss; I don't think she knows about your ride this morning. Instead, she wants to speak with you before visiting hour starts because Lord Stanhope returned home this morning."

This did not bode well—that Lord Stanhope had returned and her presence was immediately requested, since it indicated she'd be subject to yet another round of interrogation about Droughm and Uncle Thaddeus, and not necessarily in that order. *I am not good at subterfuge,* Artemis thought in annoyance; *and I am having trouble keeping track of all the various deceptions I must practice.*

In fact, after the promising events of the morning's ride she was positively longing to confess the remaining Three Terrible Things to Droughm; judging by the look in his eyes he'd not abandon ship, and may even arrange matters so that she was not immediately thrown into prison.

Artemis rose and stepped quickly to the wash basin, the floor cold against her bare feet. On some level, she was aware that her inclination to trust Droughm was not necessarily wise; it was clear that his courtship was serving his own ends— indeed, he'd been very candid about it—and what those ends were was as yet unexplained. A notorious bachelor was now publicly making up to a much younger girl who had unexpectedly inherited silver mines in Sheffield—or at least she was the presumed heiress—and as Artemis allowed the water to run through her hands she admitted that anyone else would be forgiven for thinking the whole situation too smoky by half. *But not me,* she thought a bit fiercely—*I am not so young, nor so unseasoned that I do not recognize love when it stares me in the face.*

With Katy's assistance, she donned her yellow day dress and went below to face the enemy—there wasn't time to dress her hair, but as Droughm did not intend to call, this did not seem a calamity. Mentally girding her loins for the coming interview, Artemis consoled herself with the sure knowledge that Cook will have cooked-up something delicious and fortifying.

When she entered the drawing room, she saw that her aunt was speaking in an intense undertone to Lord Stanhope, who had poured himself a brandy even though it was yet mid-morning. Her aunt's husband had the red-veined nose of a man who drank over-much, but as he was married to her aunt there was small blame to him.

Upon sighting Artemis in the doorway, they broke off their discussion in a manner that made it very clear she had been its object, and settled into an ominous silence as she approached.

"Welcome back, Uncle." Artemis curtseyed, and decided to confront matters with direct action. "My cousin Torville tells me you sought word of Uncle Thaddeus—were you able to discover his fate?"

"Unfortunately not," her uncle replied, eying her sourly. "I have no news—other than the unhappy tidings that on top of everything else, there's been a major cave-in at the mines, and so all operations have necessarily halted."

Artemis carefully let out a breath she didn't realize she'd been holding. "That is a shame—it all seems such a mystery."

Her Uncle Stanhope viewed the contents of his glass, unable to contain his bitterness. "A pox on the old fool for thinking he would live forever—no one has any knowledge of a will, and I searched the place top to bottom looking for a safe where he might hide his valuables—but nothing." He looked to Artemis with little hope. "Are you aware of any hidey-hole he would have used to secret valuables, Artemis?"

"No, Uncle." Fortunately, he did not ask where Artemis would choose to secret any valuables—not that she would have told him, of course.

He looked with some significance at his wife, and added, "Apparently, I was not the only one to have conducted such a search."

Lady Stanhope looked away without comment, and Artemis decided that Lord Stanhope was somewhat cowed, despite his show of bravado. After all, this was not a surprise; Lady Stanhope was very much like the Lady Macbeth character from Uncle Thaddeus' favorite play—strong and unswerving in her ambitions—and therefore her husband necessarily had to be someone who was easily cowed, or they would have killed each other by now.

Not to mention, of course, that Lady Stanhope did not seem at all moved by the fact her only brother was missing and presumed dead; instead she was up to her elbows in schemes to maintain control of the silver mines. *Perhaps I did not miss out on much, never having had a family*, Artemis decided. *They all seem mightily inclined to dislike one another.*

Her thoughts were interrupted by her uncle's next comment. "Lady Stanhope tells me that Lord Droughm has been particular in his attentions, Artemis."

Tired of equivocating, Artemis simply replied, "Yes, Uncle." She did not add that his attentions this morning had been very particular, indeed.

Her uncle's brows drew together in consternation at this bald admission, whilst Lady Stanhope remarked in an exasperated tone, "I told you—it is the talk of the town."

But the gentleman turned aside with an impatient gesture. "He cannot think to marry her—he provokes us, nothing more." In contradiction of this expressed confidence, he took another healthy swallow of the brandy.

"He is provoking, indeed," Artemis's aunt agreed, a bitter edge to her voice. "He called here—bold as brass—and practically taunted me."

After thinking this over, her spouse mused aloud, "Perhaps we should go abroad, and take the chit with us until it is resolved." He spoke as though Artemis was not present, which she found rather disconcerting.

But the lady rallied him, "No—we cannot jeopardize the guardianship proceedings by making such a move. Everyone would think it very strange if we did not encourage Droughm's suit, and I imagine that is his intent; to goad us into doing something to alarm the Court. Instead, we must try to rush the guardianship proceedings, behind the scenes. Very shortly we will have the whip hand, and do not forget that he must protect Wentworth, at all costs. Droughm is stymied—we have only to hold firm."

She repeated this last with careful emphasis, as it seemed clear that her better half was in his cups.

Lowering her gaze, Artemis hid her alarm at the tenor of the discussion, but was spared having to participate further when Hooks came into the room to announce the arrival of visitors. "The Honorable Ambassador Valdez and Miss Valdez," he intoned.

Now, here's a surprise, thought Artemis into the sudden silence that ensued. After a quick glance was exchanged, Lord Stanhope straightened his cravat and advised Hooks to see them in, as Artemis dutifully took up her position next to her aunt.

The visitors were ushered in, and the other girl greeted Artemis with her vivacious smile, settling in beside her even though there wasn't really enough room on the settee. "Miss Merryfield," she complained in a teasing tone, "You have not sent me a note so that we may go shopping."

Before Artemis could respond, her aunt intervened. "My niece has had little free time, I'm afraid—Lord Droughm has been assiduous in his attentions."

There was a few moments ominous silence. *Ah—the answer to my question*, thought Artemis, watching her aunt stare down the Portuguese girl. *They are more afraid of Droughm, if mine aunt is willing to invoke him as a warning against the Portuguese contingent. I wonder why that is?*

The Ambassador drew his brows together and glanced uneasily at his daughter. "Droughm is courting the girl—you are certain?"

"Yes, Papa," said his daughter in a perfunctory manner that indicated to Artemis he was not her Papa at all. "Miss Merryfield is working to steal the title away from my poor Wentworth—she will undoubtedly have many fine sons."

Unwilling to be drawn, Artemis only smiled as though at a jest, whilst Lord Stanhope cautioned hastily, "Now, now; it is early days yet—let's not fill the girl's head with foolishness."

Hoping to forestall yet another round of questioning about what-Droughm-said-to-her, Artemis asked in a friendly manner, "How go your own wedding preparations, Miss Valdez? Or is it a sore subject?"

The other drew her mouth into a thin line. "Ah, we've had a terrible tragedy; a gift has been misplaced. It is a very valuable gift, and irreplaceable."

The others in the room sat frozen in dismayed silence. *Message received*, thought Artemis, who then asked artlessly, "Could you place an advertisement in the newspaper, perhaps? It may have been sent to the wrong recipient."

Her charming smile back in place, the young woman laid a hand on Artemis' arm. "That is a very good idea, and I thank you for it."

"Lady Tallyer," announced Hooks from the doorway.

CHAPTER 14

"*P*ray invite her in, Hooks," said Lady Stanhope, who rested a calculating eye on Artemis. "I quite look forward to making Lady Tallyer's acquaintance."

The lady entered the room, looking composed, well-dressed, and seemingly unaware that she was the source of any awkwardness. After the newcomer made her greetings to her hostess, she took Artemis' hand and reminded her with a warm smile, "We met yesterday, at the park."

"I do remember, my lady; you were mounted on a beautiful black, who looked to be a jumper."

"He is indeed—and steady as they come." Gracefully, the lady settled into a chair across from Artemis. "Although he is a bit head-shy."

"Ah; the two of you have much in common." Miss Valdez allowed an edge of malice to underlie this *double entendre*.

"Miss Merryfield is a fine rider," Lady Tallyer replied with equanimity.

"But without your experience—or at least, not as yet," added the other, with an arched brow.

Artemis lowered her gaze, and contemplated the very interesting fact that the Portuguese girl sounded a bit jealous, despite herself. Another of Droughm's former mistresses, perhaps; the man must go through them like handkerchiefs.

"How long do you stay in town, Lady Tallyer?" asked Artemis' aunt in an ingratiating manner. "Perhaps you will have an opportunity to reestablish old ties." This a thinly-veiled suggestion that she endeavor to take the problem that was my lord Droughm off their hands.

"*Very* old ties," added Miss Valdez, who had the felicity of being younger than Lady Tallyer.

But once again, Lady Tallyer gave no show of discomfiture, and replied in a friendly manner, "I intend to stay for the season, unless I am called away." She then turned to Artemis and asked kindly, "And you, Miss Merryfield? How long will you stay with your aunt and uncle?"

Artemis was spared the necessity of an answer by the entrance of Torville, who assessed the scene in his desultory manner, and then straightened up to make a beeline over to Lady Tallyer, pulling up a chair beside her. *Small blame to him,* thought Artemis—*I hear she is available.*

Lady Stanhope could not approve of Torville's oversetting her plans by making up to Lady Tallyer, and so she asked him in a pointed manner, "Lady Tallyer tells us that Artemis enjoys the park, Torville; perhaps you will take your cousin for an outing, later today. A good, long walk would be just the thing to allow the two of you to become better acquainted."

Torville bowed his head in mock-dutiful acquiescence. "Willingly—and I'll buy her another ice, if she'd like." He added in a smiling aside to Lady Tallyer, "It is a simple task, to entertain my young cousin."

But the lady did not come to engage in a flirtation with Torville, and instead turned her attention back to Artemis. "Will you ride today, Miss Merryfield? You have a very neat mare—I confess I've never seen a finer."

In an attempt to regain Lady Tallyer's wandering attention,

Torville interjected, "My little cousin does not have a horse, I'm afraid."

"No," Artemis agreed in a mild tone. "Instead, she is on loan from Lord Droughm."

"What?" Lord Stanhope bestirred himself to remonstrate with his wife. "You cannot allow Droughm to mount Artemis."

Torville stifled a chuckle behind a cough while Artemis did her best to appear oblivious to his unfortunate turn of phrase.

"I could not very well refuse, my dear," Lady Stanhope replied in an even tone, her cheeks a bit pink. "It was a generous offer."

"Very generous." Lady Tallyer leaned forward to touch Artemis' knee, which Artemis found she didn't like at all. "You are fortunate, in your friends."

"It is much appreciated," Artemis agreed; "Before I came to England, I rode quite a bit—nearly every day of my life—and I've missed it." She added fairly, "Although riding in London is not quite the same, of course."

"Will you return to Sheffield soon, Miss Merryfield?" Lady Tallyer tried a different tack to repeat her earlier, unanswered question. "The hills of Sheffield must offer excellent riding opportunities."

Artemis explained carefully, "I await news of mine Uncle Thaddeus, and once that is settled, I imagine I will find my way home." She did not specify the location of this happy place, as she was not yet certain where it was—although apparently the gardens were impressive. *I will finally have a home,* she thought, turning over this novel idea in her mind. *How strange—although I imagine we will travel; he seems a restless soul.*

Leaning to touch Artemis' knee again, Lady Tallyer offered with a full measure of sympathy, "How clumsy of me; please accept my apologies, Miss Merryfield. I understand that your great-uncle in Sheffield is missing; it must be very distressing, not to know what has happened to him."

"One can only presume the worst," acknowledged Artemis,

remembering how surprised that gentleman had looked, when she'd drawn and fired on him.

"Yes; we will shortly assume Artemis' guardianship," announced Lord Stanhope, a little too loudly and with a touch of defiance. "We are her only remaining relatives, after all."

Miss Valdez's eyes narrowed. "You are counting the chickens, perhaps."

But Artemis's uncle rose up in defiance, and Artemis decided that he must be a bit well-to-go, to be challenging the Portuguese contingent so openly. "There are no other chickens to count," he retorted a bit belligerently. "We will control the mines, and if anyone wishes for our cooperation, they must apply to us, and to us alone."

"My dear—" Lady Stanhope soothed, her smile stiff; "Won't you sit down for a moment? I believe you are distressing our dear Artemis."

Without a blink, Artemis sneaked an apricot tart and awaited Miss Valdez's rejoinder with interest.

The Portuguese girl, however, did not deign to argue with her inebriated host, and instead looked to Torville, her face alight and her dark eyes flashing with amusement. "So then —*you* must cut out Lord Droughm, and marry Miss Merryfield, yes? My Wentworth would very much appreciate it."

But Torville was intent upon his pursuit of Lady Tallyer, and so replied in a negligent manner, "Heaven forfend; Droughm is welcome to her."

Artemis could not help but note that the other three other ladies in the room betrayed varying degrees of chagrin at his response. *I hope they don't all come to cuffs*, she thought; *although I'd wager good money on Miss Valdez—she has the look of a gutter fighter.*

Lord Stanhope swayed slightly, and wagged a reprimanding finger at Torville. "You will do as you are told, nephew."

But before he could continue, his wife took him firmly by the arm and steered him into the kitchen, claiming a need to instruct the cook.

The Portuguese girl watched them leave with a thoughtful eye, and—since Torville had once again claimed Lady Tallyer's attention—Artemis seized on her chance to put Droughm's plan into play. Leaning toward the other girl, she offered in a conspiratorial aside, "My aunt will not allow me to go shopping with you—she thinks me too young." With an annoyed nod of her head, she indicated the kitchen. "You can see how unkind they are to me—*so* unreasonable, and they are not even my parents." This last said with a touch of defiance.

With a calculating expression in the depths of her dark eyes, the other girl tilted her head in sympathy. "I am so very disappointed—we would have such a happy time together."

"They only forbade shopping—it is not as though they forbade me to meet with you, altogether." Artemis did her best to appear guiltily self-conscious. *I am not good at play-acting,* she thought; *a pox on Droughm, for putting me up to this.*

"Indeed," agreed the other, quick to leap upon this opening. "I am certain they cannot object if we meet at, say, the Royal Art Exhibition."

"Could it be the Museum, instead?" Artemis asked artlessly. "I hear there is a famous Egyptian exhibition, there."

"Even better," pronounced the other. "Tomorrow?"

"The day after," countered Artemis. "Shall we meet at ten o'clock?"

"I quite look forward to it." The other girl's bright smile did not quite reach her eyes.

"What do you two whisper about?" asked Lady Tallyer, cutting off Torville mid-sentence. "Beaux?"

"I have no beaux; I am to marry my Wentworth." Miss Valdez shook her finger playfully at the other woman. "And Artemis must not have any beaux—not until she finds her uncle. Otherwise they do not know the size of the dowry she brings."

"Droughm wouldn't care—he is rich," intoned the Ambassador in a sour tone, and both ladies looked annoyed at this observation.

I probably should not mention the sapphires, although it would be so very enjoyable to do so, thought Artemis, and found a great deal of satisfaction in having the upper hand, for once. It felt rather like that day when the regiment had patiently waited on the hilltop at San Christoval— just before springing the trap on the unsuspecting French.

Lady Stanhope returned to the room, looking a bit grim, and absent her better half. "May I offer you more tea, Lady Tallyer? Our cook makes an exceptional pastry. "

But the lady declined, and rose to take her leave. "I do hope you hear good news, Miss Merryfield, and I hope to visit with you again very soon."

"Thank you, my lady," Artemis responded politely, thinking it very unlikely. The lady was clearly pressing for information, but there nothing else to tell—not anything that Artemis was willing to relate, leastways. Or that the lady would be anxious to hear.

"I'll walk you out." Torville offered his arm to Lady Tallyer, and Artemis hid a smile as Lady Stanhope viewed this development with a baleful eye.

Torville did not return, and the Portuguese visitors also rose to take their leave, Miss Valdez sending Artemis a conspiratorial glance as she expressed her desire to meet again soon.

In departing the drawing room, Artemis let out a breath, relieved to have got over that rough ground as lightly as possible. Seeing her bouquet of lilacs on the table, she paused to touch the signature on the card, breathing in the scent and wishing their sender would magically appear at the front door.

"Hooks," she asked diffidently, "would you mind saving the card for me?" She felt young and a bit silly, but the retainer assured her it had always been his intention. Unable to resist, she asked, "Have you mislaid another invitation to ride?"

"I am afraid not," the butler replied with regret. "But if you have any private letters to be delivered, miss, I shall see to it personally."

Fingering a petal, she frowned slightly. "No—I have only to be patient, I suppose."

"Indeed, miss," agreed the servant, and they parted in perfect understanding

*A*rtemis stood inside the entry doors of the British Museum, and looked around her with a great deal of interest. The marbled floors echoed with the footsteps of many visitors, but the atmosphere was nevertheless hushed, and serious with the weight of history. She had to suppress an inclination to step out into the crowd and wander about—it felt so liberating, not to be constrained by watchful chaperones. She was alone, as Katy had left her at the door on the understanding that Artemis was to have an unauthorized meeting with Droughm, and that the girl was to be tortured rather than confess to Artemis' misdeeds.

It was still a bit early for her rendezvous with Miss Valdez, and so whilst she waited, Artemis considered what she knew—and didn't yet know—about the present situation. That Droughm was setting up some sort of trap seemed evident; presumably, he sought to extricate his heir from whatever leverage the others had over him. *I wonder whether Wentworth's scandal trumps mine,* she thought. *I doubt it—and it only means that I must make my confession soon, and hope that Droughm can resolve all problems.*

Idly, she ran a finger along the handrail and tried to avoid thinking of a notion that had crossed her mind; that his involvement in these matters was not just personal—because of Wentworth—but in some sort of official capacity. Her hand paused. After all, he seemed to be privy to information which—one would think—would be closely guarded; Napoleon's plans, for instance, and the Colonel's marital status. And he'd come from Algiers without mentioning what it was he did there; with the situation being what it was in that area of the world, it seemed unlikely that it had been a pleasure trip. And he knew that Miss Valdez was a spy—although how she was involved in the Stanhopes' counterfeiting plot remained unclear. If Droughm was engaged in diplomacy on behalf of the Home Office, why wouldn't he openly admit it?

With a troubled brow, she stared unseeing toward the Great Exhibition Hall, shying away from her uneasy conclusion. He couldn't be a *spy*, for heaven's sake; he was an Earl—a belted Earl, whatever that meant. Artemis had a soldier's natural aversion to spies—not to mention such a role would create a major conflict of interest with respect to her own troubles. She'd been hoping that he'd be willing to help her outfox the authorities, but if he *was* the authorities, then it might be foolish to trust him, no matter the depth of his affection for her.

"Miss Merryfield—here I am."

Breaking away from her unhappy reverie, Artemis turned to greet Miss Valdez, who was dressed in a dashing bronze gown that was slashed at the sleeves and trimmed with gold braiding. *I should attempt a bit more dash, myself, if I'm to be a Countess,* she realized. Up until now, her clothing had always been practical linsey-woolsey, and usually smelt of cannon smoke. Smiling, she said, "*Bom-dia.*"

Miss Valdez laughed her pretty, trilling laugh. "You speak Portuguese," she exclaimed in that language.

"Only a little," Artemis demurred. "Mainly curse words."

With another chuckle, the other girl wound her arm around Artemis'. "I am so happy to see you again; you are very amusing, and it is a good thing for me to be amused, in my troubles. Come—let us go."

Artemis willingly fell into step beside her. "Have you found your missing gift?"

"I have not," the girl admitted. "It is of all things annoying. What shall we see?"

Artemis allowed the other girl to take the initiative, mainly because she was not certain what it was that Droughm had planned. "It truly doesn't matter to me; I am happy just to be out of the house. You must choose."

"This way, then." Their arms firmly linked, Miss Valdez led Artemis in the direction of the Parthenon display, with its massive marble ruins rising nearly to the ceiling. With a sly glance, Miss Valdez offered, "Lady Tallyer is jealous of you, I think."

"Surely not," Artemis protested. "She has no need to be jealous of anyone."

But the other girl shook her head, making her dusky curls dance. "No—I think it is true. Should she be? Tell me of Lord Droughm—what does he say to you?"

Artemis teased, "I am afraid to speak of him to you; he features as the ogre in your own romance, after all."

The girl frowned in confusion. "*Quel est 'ogre'*?"

"A monster," Artemis explained. "Like the ones in the fairy tales."

Nodding in agreement, her companion exclaimed, "Yes; Droughm is the ogre. I must convince you to flee from this ogre —he is not at all what he seems."

"Is he not?" Artemis asked in a mild tone. "Then again, it seems that no one is." She'd noted with interest that when the Portuguese girl had asked about the unfamiliar English word, she'd accidentally lapsed—only for a moment—into French. "How does your father feel about your engagement? Is he another ogre, or does he approve of Wentworth?"

"He approves—very much so," the girl confirmed happily.

"Although I think he wishes I would marry a *Portgueso*." With a knowing look, she added, "But the fathers, they do not object if the family is rich."

With a small smile, Artemis acknowledged this universal truth. "He hopes his son-in-law will pay for his horses, I imagine. Your father is famous for his Lipizzaners, and they are expensive to maintain."

The girl tossed her head, laughing. "Yes, indeed—they are his pride. Why, I believe he loves them more than he loves me."

Artemis added, "Even the enemy knew of them; they spared the town of Guarda, so as to avoid injuring his horses."

"Yes, yes—even when they are at war, the men can always agree about the horses."

So—not the daughter of the Ambassador, and not Portuguese, deduced Artemis; *there are no such Lipizzaners, and the people of Guarda were all massacred. Evidently, she is a French spy—and presumably Droughm already knows this, if we are setting up a trap, between us.*

The other girl announced, "You like ices, yes? There is a place for them in the street behind—we must go there." Playfully pulling on Artemis' arm, she steered her toward the rear entrance to the Museum.

"I believe they also sell ices at the café, here," Artemis stalled, uncertain what she was supposed to do—trust Droughm not to have briefed her ahead of time.

Miss Valdez drew her mouth into a pretty *moue*. "But if we go there, then you can come with me to the milliner's that is just around the corner—I must decide on my wedding hat, and I would hear your opinion." The vivacious Miss Valdez swept forward, firmly clasping Artemis' arm. "Come, it will be very much enjoyable."

Artemis took a quick survey of the area, and then decided that she should fall in with the other girl's plans until events indicated otherwise—at least she'd not be caught unaware, if there was indeed to be another abduction attempt.

As they approached the back entrance, suddenly a man's voice could be heard, hailing them from a small distance. "Lisabetta—my darling."

Although Miss Valdez paused to smile with delight, Artemis could sense the girl's chagrin, and looked with interest at the young man who approached them.

"Wentworth." Miss Valdez held out her hands to him. "*Querido*—what a pleasant surprise."

No discernable resemblance to Droughm, Artemis decided. Wentworth was slim and rather reedy, in his early twenties and not at all what one would consider a match for this vivacious and exotic young woman.

"This is Miss Merryfield; you must shake her hand, but then we have an appointment to keep, and we cannot be late. Will you come to visit me later, *querido*?"

"Instead, allow me to escort you, my dear; and Miss Merryfield too." Wentworth turned to address Artemis with a small bow. "I have heard a great deal about you, Miss Merryfield."

"Fah; you must not encourage her," the other girl cautioned with a brittle laugh. "She seeks to cut you out of your inheritance. Now, you must go away—we go to choose my wedding dress, and it is bad luck for you to see it before the wedding."

"Hat," corrected Artemis. "We go to choose your wedding hat."

"Either one," replied the other girl crossly. "You cannot see either one, Wentworth."

They'd come to a stand-still in the narrow hallway that led to the back entrance, and Artemis offered, "Perhaps we can postpone our visit to the milliner's, and instead Lord Wentworth can join us on a tour of the Museum."

But this was apparently not the correct tack to take, as Wentworth insisted, "No—no; if Lisabetta has such an important appointment, I must not divert her. Instead, I will provide an escort, and wait outside the shop—I won't peek, I promise." With a slightly nervous smile, he moved forward toward the door, so as to open it for them.

Ah—there is indeed a plan afoot, and I imagine I should move away from her, thought Artemis, as she casually began extricating her arm from the other's grip.

But with a swift movement, Lisabetta turned upon Artemis, her face inches away as she pressed a thin dagger against Artemis' breast. "You will come with me," whispered the woman in Portuguese. "I do not wish to hurt you, but I will."

"Understood," said Artemis with alacrity. "I am at your command."

The other girl then turned, her arm tight around Artemis as she pressed the tip of the dagger between Artemis' ribs. "No, no; I must insist that you stay behind, *querido*—I am losing the patience."

"Lisabetta—darling, please don't be angry." Wentworth spoke a bit too loudly, and he cast a quick, nervous glance over his shoulder.

Reinforcements were on the way, then. Whilst Miss Valdez propelled her out the door, Artemis chose her moment, and then quickly jerked her arm upward under Lisabetta's, forcing the dagger to lift. With her other arm, she smashed her elbow into the woman's throat, and then turned to quickly seize with both hands the wrist that held the dagger, bending it ruthlessly backwards. With a choking sound, her captor collapsed to her knees as the dagger clattered to the tiled floor.

Wentworth rushed in to help Lisabetta as though she'd merely fallen, and another man materialized to offer his assistance also, grasping the girl firmly from the other side.

Artemis was thus not surprised when Droughm strode forward, a worried frown on his brow. "You are unhurt?"

"I am." Artemis watched as the other two maneuvered Miss Valdez out the door whilst she continued to rasp and struggle for breath. In the event he was unaware, Artemis warned Droughm, "I believe she has reinforcements, waiting outside."

"No longer; it is I who have reinforcements, instead."

Artemis smiled, enjoying the irony. "The abductor is herself abducted."

"Not exactly," he demurred. "Instead, they are eloping, despite parental opposition. No one is quite certain where they went."

"*Pen*," she breathed, unable to contain her admiration. "That is *diabolical*."

He offered his arm to her. "If you are willing, I've a mind to take a tour of the Museum."

She took it without hesitation. "I am indeed willing. Is there to be any more hand-to-hand combat?"

"Nothing that you cannot handle," he assured her.

CHAPTER 16

*A*s though nothing untoward had occurred, Droughm steered Artemis back into the Main Exhibition Hall. "The boy's a fool—he was expressly instructed not to allow her to use you as a hostage."

"It truly wasn't his fault—she had a grip on me from the moment I entered the building."

Looking down at her, he was silent for a moment, and then said abruptly, "God, how I've missed you."

Gratified by this observation, she nevertheless noted, "It's only been two days, Pen."

"Too long. I've not the patience to be a suitor—no wonder I've never made the attempt before."

"Well, it would be hard to find a less-likely suitor than Wentworth," Artemis observed. "How did he get tangled up with someone like Miss Valdez? Is the betrothal a ploy, of some sort?"

"No—the betrothal is genuine. She told him she was pregnant."

This was plain-speaking—even for Droughm—and a bit taken aback, Artemis considered this news for a moment. "I doubt it."

"As do I; but the mere fact that it *could* be true is a problem in and of itself."

They stopped to admire the ancient Greek frescoes, but Artemis could cast only a cursory eye over the exhibit, thinking of the hapless Wentworth, who clearly did not have half the mettle Droughm did—Droughm would never allow himself to be caught in such a way. "She is so obviously a temptress; was he so foolish that he couldn't see it?"

"Unfortunately, yes. I was out of the country, and the boy is far too naïve. But in his defense, very little tempting is necessary for most men."

This was inarguably true, as Artemis had seen firsthand—time and again—amongst the troops. Perplexed, she observed, "It seems the height of foolishness, to be constantly subject to such a weakness."

"As my opinion would no doubt shock you, I shall withhold it."

She laughed, as he'd intended, and then belatedly realized that she probably shouldn't be discussing this particular topic with him—not when she was positively *longing* to go someplace private so that he could have his way with her. Firmly changing the topic, she offered, "Miss Valdez is not Portuguese; instead, I believe she is French."

"Yes. Or more correctly, she is from Martinique." He frowned slightly, as he bent to review a placard next to the carvings.

As it was a delicate subject, Artemis decided to plunge in. "There is a history between you, I think; was she another mistress?"

There was a pause, whilst she could see that he debated what to reveal. *I believe we are wandering into the subject of his mysterious work,* she thought, *and I am of two minds as to whether I truly wish to know the truth.* "Not a mistress," he finally said. "More along the lines of a brief *liaison*."

"Ah—then her seduction of Wentworth held a measure of revenge, too."

He made no response, and she squeezed his arm. "Should I not speak of it? I have lived my life amongst men, remember, so you must forgive me if I am too outspoken."

But his reaction was unexpected, as he turned to hold her gaze with his own, the expression in the green eyes intent. "I will confess that there have been more than a few women, Artemis—but no more, my promise on it. I would never dishonor you in such a way."

"I appreciate it," she replied with mock-gravity. "Being as I don't think I could temper my actions, and I am considered quite a good shot."

But instead of responding to her teasing, he ducked his head for a moment, gathering himself. "I love you," he offered in a gruff voice. "I should have said, before I mauled you about."

He was not well-suited for soft words, and she touched his arm gently. "I know it—I do not need constant reassurances, or poetry dedicated to my eyes."

"*Her eyes the brightest stars the heavens hold,*" he recited, looking a bit self-conscious at having been caught thinking of such things.

"Oh; oh—*Pen,*" she breathed, nearly undone. "Do you suppose we could go visit your residence?" She was in a fever to reward his poetry-reciting, so that he would be encouraged to persevere.

"No," he replied bluntly, and began moving her along the display again. "I am not going to dishonor you—remember?"

"I was right; you *are* a Dutch Aunt," she teased. "For two pins, I'd elope with Wentworth, myself—he's not one to operate under any such restrictions."

He lifted a corner of his mouth, amused. "You mustn't, though; if Wentworth ended up with control of the mines, we'd be right back where we started."

This was of interest, and as he seemed willing to speak of it, she asked, "Why did Miss Valdez entrap Wentworth—what was her aim?"

He gave her a glance. "It is complicated."

But Artemis decided to press—after all, she was now a player in this little drama, and there was a dagger-hole in the bodice of her ivory day dress, to prove it. "Give me a quick debriefing, then; I have it on good authority that I am too shrewd by half."

He thought about it for a moment. "I'd rather not; not just yet." With an apologetic gesture, he covered the hand tucked in his elbow, briefly.

The mysterious scandal, she thought. *The reason the Stanhopes feel emboldened to hold their course despite their fear of him— although now Droughm has arranged for Miss Valdez's abduction so as to spike their guns, in some undisclosed way. Why would any of it matter to the counterfeiting plot, though? It must indeed be complicated.*

They exited the Greek exhibit and he paused, looking over the murmuring crowds. "Where shall we go next?

"I know there is a famous Egyptian Exhibition, upstairs." Artemis nodded toward the staircase. "The Colonel was very interested in the Egyptian discoveries."

"Then by all means."

At a sedate pace, they proceeded up the stairs to the second floor, fielding covert glances from several curious women who passed them by. It seemed apparent that Droughm's aim was to openly court her in yet another public place, absent a chaperone and with her hand resting in the crook of his arm—therefore making it difficult for the Stanhopes to claim they had her best interests in mind when seeking to marry her off to Torville. *More guns spiked*, she thought; *a very clever man—hopefully he'll not spike my guns just as easily.*

They walked along the mezzanine level, Droughm deigning to nod to an occasional acquaintance, although no one dared halt his progress. Artemis decided it was very pleasant to spend this time with him—even though there was every chance she would suffer for it, later—and resolved not to dwell any more on those matters that he would rather not speak about. *In the end, I do trust him,* she decided, *although I need to make my confession, at some point. Only not just yet—not when we are having such a fine outing, and I am not yet certain whether he is truly some sort of spy.*

Searching for an innocuous topic, she asked, "How is Wentworth your heir, if I may ask—what is the relationship?"

He smiled slightly as he gazed though his quizzing glass to review a placard. "He is my great-nephew."

She laughed aloud. "As amusing as that is, Pen, even you are not that aged. How did this come about?"

He straightened up, and they moved along to the sarcophagus display. "My father had two families; with his first wife he had a daughter—my half-sister Maria. With his second wife he had me. Wentworth is Maria's grandson."

Artemis nodded, making a mental note that his father must have married a much younger woman, the second time—there was a precedent, then.

Pausing to admire a golden sarcophagus, Droughm studied the placard that described the artifact, lifting his quizzing glass and frowning slightly.

Artemis smiled. "I think that spectacles may be needful."

"No," he said shortly, as he straightened up. "They are not."

Laughing softly, she shook her head. "You are very vain, I think. Do you use spectacles when you are at home?"

"For the reading of very fine print," he admitted. "But nothing more—I can see perfectly well from a distance."

She readily confessed, "Then we are well-matched; I cannot see as well at a distance as I can up-close."

"Is that so?" Intrigued, he looked around the room and then indicated a placard that was suspended from the ceiling, across the room. "Can you read that sign?"

She pressed her lips together for a moment, but there was

nothing for it. "I've another dreaded confession, I'm afraid. I have never learned to read."

He turned to stare at her.

"I can write my initials," she assured him, coloring up with embarrassment under his scrutiny.

His expression very serious, he said slowly, "It is nothing short of extraordinary, that you have become who you are."

Her brow knit, she considered this observation for a moment. "I think I have always been who I am."

He turned abruptly and steered her to a less crowded alcove, between two glass display cases. "Thank God for it. I must marry you, Artemis, and take you to bed for at least a week. I will arrange for a private ceremony at St. George's."

While gratifying, this course seemed a bit rash, considering the dire but unknown situation whereby all participants seemed to be holding each other in check. "Despite having no guardian's consent?"

But he was adamant, and hardened his jaw. "The devil with a guardian's consent—I will present a special license, and no one would dare challenge it."

"As you wish," she agreed. "If I'd known my failings would make you so—so avid, I would have told you days and days ago."

With a bark of laughter, he took her hands in his. "It is not illiteracy that makes me avid, Artemis. And if you'd rather not learn to read, you needn't—it doesn't matter a whit to me."

After hesitating for a moment, she confessed, "I would rather like to learn, so as to read Shakespeare—if it is not so very difficult."

His expression softened. "Then I will teach you—in between those times when we are abed."

"Slow going, then."

But he was too busy making plans to respond to her jest. "We will go for an early morning wedding, tomorrow. Until then, you must give no indication to anyone that such is the plan—I will enlist Hooks."

For a moment, she toyed with the idea of pointing out that she hadn't actually agreed to marry him, but decided she shouldn't tease him—not so close upon his labored declaration of love; one step at a time, with this man.

As they paused before another display, he glanced around them, then removed the signet ring he wore on his little finger, to slide it onto her ring finger, and gauge the size. "A bit too large," he noted, and then replaced it on his own.

"Yes," she agreed, and could not suppress a smile. *I believe,* she thought cautiously, *that everything is actually going to work out—once I get the remaining Two Terrible Things out of the way, that is; I can't very well marry him before I tell him the truth.*

To this end, she waited until they were near the Roman antiquities display to broach the next subject. "Have you ever been to Sheffield, Pen?"

"No," he replied. "Are you hungry? I am rather hungry."

"Well," she persevered, "There were Vikings in Sheffield."

"Did you meet any?" He was in a light-hearted mood, she could see—having vanquished Miss Valdez and determined on marriage in one fell afternoon.

"No—it was a long time ago. There was a big battle near the hills where the mines are. They know that it happened because the Vikings left their weapons lying about."

He regarded the ancient Roman coins on display through his quizzing glass. "Did they? Seems rather careless of them."

"That is exactly what I thought," Artemis agreed, distracted from her theme. "And yet everyone seems to think they were so formidable."

"They lost to the English," pronounced Droughm, as though this disposed of the subject.

"Yes—yes, they lost at the big battle that I spoke of," Artemis persisted. "The Vikings were aligned with the Scots, and apparently Macbeth—from the play, you know—Macbeth was based on a real person, who took his title from a vanquished Viking."

With every indication that he wasn't much interested, Droughm straightened up to face her. "Is there any chance we could discuss the Vikings over luncheon, Artemis?"

Seizing on this excuse, she willingly abandoned the topic for a later time, and took his proffered arm. "Lay on."

CHAPTER 17

*a*rtemis had been called in for a dressing-down, and was fending off the questions as best she could, taking a penitent's pose with her head bent in shame. Her aunt was alarmingly agitated, her back rigid and her hands clasped before her as she paced back and forth. "You were instructed—directly!—not to consort with Miss Valdez."

"I am truly sorry, ma'am; she was going to show me her wedding ensemble, and I could not resist—I should not have disobeyed you."

"And then she left the Museum with Wentworth—not to return?" Lady Stanhope cast a significant glance at Lord Stanhope, who stood silently by, trying to control his own agitation by making heavy inroads into the brandy decanter.

"Yes, ma'am. As it turned out, he and Lord Droughm were also visiting the Museum." To her dismay, the Stanhopes appeared remarkably well-informed as to the events of the day—although to be fair, any number of persons had observed them, and could have made a report to her. Without the benefit of a briefing, Artemis decided she would hew as close to the truth as possible and accept her lumps; after all, in another day it would no longer matter—not to mention she would then outrank Lady Stanhope.

"Where did they go?" Her aunt paused before her, willing Artemis to give an acceptable answer.

"I do not know, ma'am." She decided to add, for flavor, "They seemed very fond."

Making a strangled sound, her aunt continued her pacing. "And I understand that Droughm was himself very fond—that there was no mistaking his intentions."

"Lord Droughm was very kind," Artemis agreed. To throw dust in her interrogator's eyes, she said it in the tone of a child who had been indulged, but her aunt's source of intelligence was too thorough.

"I am told there were clear indications that marriage was discussed."

Alarmed, Artemis could only surmise that someone had seen the exchange of Droughm's signet ring. "I received no proposal of marriage," she said in all honesty.

Pausing for a moment in her relentless pacing, the woman said over her shoulder to Lord Stanhope, "What is happening at the Court? Why *on earth* does it move so slowly?"

He shrugged, and swirled the brandy in his glass. "Our judge was attacked by brigands, and so the matter has been transferred to another judge, who I hope is more amenable. The matter should be concluded shortly."

Letting out a breath, the lady allowed her gaze to rest on her wayward niece. "I am most displeased, Artemis. You will remain in your room until further notice."

"Yes, ma'am; I am *truly* sorry, ma'am." Artemis ascended the stairs, very much looking forward to her escape from this wretched place on the morrow. Unfortunately, it appeared she was destined to be married in her hideous yellow dress, but there was nothing for it.

After Artemis retreated up to her room, Katy appeared almost immediately, her eyes wide as she softly shut the door behind her. "Are you all right, miss? Her ladyship is that unhappy with you."

"Small blame to her," Artemis observed fairly. "I disobeyed a direct order."

"Cook says she'll smuggle up some food; she says ye'll— *you'll* need your strength, in all your troubles."

"Much appreciated, Katy; I do feel as though I've gone over rough ground." She then paused as they heard the front door open and close. "Do you think you could you find out who went where, Katy?" With all this talk of judge-shifting, it would probably behoove her to keep a weather eye on the comings-and-goings.

"In a trice, miss." The 'tweenie slipped out the door.

Artemis had barely removed her shoes and stockings before the doorknob slowly turned and Cook entered on soft feet, carrying a napkin-covered tray. "Here's a ruckus," the woman pronounced sourly as she set it down on the bedside table. "Mayhap they'll pack ye off home."

"There's no place for them to send me," Artemis pointed out. "Although I suppose I could join Boney on Elba—I hear the weather is very fine, there."

After making a sound of disapproval at the tenor of such a jest, the woman removed the napkin, and Artemis settled on the bed's edge to address the generous portion of sliced lamb with carrots and pudding—Cook knew she was fond of lamb.

"Yer beau is persona non nobody," Cook pronounced, crossing her arms over her bony chest. "Ye'd think they'd be congratulatin' ye, and kissin' yer hand."

"They covet my silver mines," Artemis reminded her, her mouth full. "I imagine Droughm will not want to share."

"Will he have ye, then?" The other slid her a speculating glance.

Remembering Droughm's cautions, Artemis said only, "I shouldn't be surprised."

"Heh," said Cook with satisfaction. "It'll be a nine days' wonder."

"I shall steal you away," Artemis promised. "I imagine his own cook is a sorry excuse."

"G'wan wi' ye," the other said, very pleased, but pretending to be cross. "As though the likes o' me could manage fer an Earl."

"He will dote on his young bride—and I will insist on your apricot tarts."

But this was the wrong tack, and Cook shook a bony finger at her. "Ye'd do best to please yer man, and make no unreasonable demands."

"On the contrary," Artemis replied in a wicked tone, "I will comply with all his demands—that is exactly why he'll dote."

"Missy," the other breathed, thoroughly shocked. "I'll hear no more o' this kind o' talk."

But Artemis attacked her pudding, unrepentant. "I thought you told me it was the one thing the men-folk want."

Cook reconsidered. "That," she agreed, "and a nice brisket."

Struggling not to laugh, Artemis said solemnly, "I will keep it to mind, then."

"My lady is that angry at Torville—but he'll not come near ye."

"Torville is craven," Artemis pronounced in scorn, spearing a carrot with her fork. "A good riddance."

"I'd not trust any of 'em as far as I could throw 'em," the other warned.

"We are agreed, then."

Katy returned to close the door softly behind her and report, "His lordship left to go confer with someone about the mines."

Artemis thought this over. "Do we know who?"

"No, miss. But my lady said to him, 'You'd best let them know, and come up with some way to prod the Court along.'"

This information, Artemis surmised, was courtesy of Hooks, who had his finger on the pulse of the household.

Self-consciously, the girl added, "My grand-dad asked me to give you this, miss." Solemnly, Katy unfolded her handkerchief to expose a silver tuppence, nestled therein. "He said it was my grand-dam's."

"Thank you," said Artemis politely, taking it between her fingers.

Cook exclaimed impatiently, "Ye'll have to explain it to 'er, ye gowk—she doesn't know what it is, bein' as she's from heathen parts."

"Oh—right." Katy leaned in earnestly. "It's a lucky tuppence, miss. You put it in your shoe on your wedding day; it's a tradition."

Touched, Artemis closed her hand around the tuppence. "You must thank your grand-dad, Katy—and I will thank him myself, when I get the chance." That chance would come before dawn tomorrow, as she crept out of Stanhope House for the last time, wearing her second-best day dress and with a tuppence in her shoe. It was a shame she couldn't enlist Katy to dress her hair, but she imagined her bridegroom wouldn't care, being as how they were heading straight to bed for a week.

Katy couldn't suppress a smile. "It would be something like, miss—to have a grand wedding to such a grand lord."

The only thing Artemis cared about at this point was to be bound to Pen and start her new life; to this end, the quick, private ceremony already planned sounded perfectly adequate. "I wouldn't know what to do with a grand wedding, Katy; the only weddings I've ever been to were field weddings, where the Chaplain would marry the couple because the bridegroom was facing a battle the next day." She didn't add that most of the time the bride was pregnant, and the main concern was the soldier's pension.

"It's a shame your papa is no longer with us—he'd be that proud."

"Yes—it is a shame." Artemis had a sudden memory of the last conversation she'd had with the Colonel, as the rain poured

115

down on their bivouac in San Pablo. He was never one to be afraid, but there was no question he'd exhibited a heightened concern as he helped her ready for her trip, packing her few belongings in the kit.

"I'll send for you when matters have righted themselves, Artemis. I'm certain you'll rub along with my Uncle Thaddeus —he's a bit odd, don't let it throw you—and try to learn what you can about the mines; after all, they're slated to be mine, and I don't know the first thing about mining."

"A shame they're not yours now," Artemis had pointed out. The Colonel was at low water, due to the fact that—ever since Napoleon's surrender had been signed—he now had a great deal more idle time to spend in the new gambling kens that had sprung up in the area. "Perhaps he will give you an advance on your inheritance—shall I put it to the touch?"

The Colonel had laughed his deep laugh, but Artemis was not fooled, and knew he was troubled. "Not a chance; he's a miserable old miser. But feel free to try to sweeten him up—if anyone can do it, you can."

He had cautioned her about the importance of the minting plates. "Thaddeus is under contract with the Treasury to mint the new silver schilling, and production is already underway. The minting plates need to be replaced, every now and then, and these will be needed very soon, to make certain the production continues apace. Give them to Thaddeus and no one else, and don't let anyone know you have them—we can't let them fall into the wrong hands."

Artemis had examined the delicately engraved plates in the candlelight. "Shouldn't they be making the minting plates in England?"

"The engraver is here, on the Continent; not just anyone can do this kind of work."

Artemis may have been young, and she may have been eager to finally see the homeland that all the soldiers had fought so hard for, but she nevertheless knew the situation did not bear scrutiny. She could think of no legitimate reason why the Colonel would be smuggling printing plates to his odd uncle in Sheffield. Therefore, when she was informed that the Colonel had been killed, shortly thereafter, she was almost unsurprised.

Katy's voice interrupted her thoughts. "It's like a fairy story, it is—you an orphan, and his lordship coming to take you away from your cruel relations. "When did your mum die, miss?"

Bringing herself back to the present, Artemis replied, "I was ten."

Cook made a sympathetic sound with her tongue. "Sech a shame."

Artemis lifted her head to smile at them. "It truly didn't seem so—we managed, the Colonel and me; I wouldn't change it for anything."

Katy offered, "No, indeed—it brought you here to us, and to your beau."

"I've told Cook that I'll have Droughm steal her away," Artemis declared as she folded her napkin on the tray. "I'll need an ally."

Her eyes dancing, Katy cautioned, "But if you do, miss, who'll play cribbage with my grand-dad o' nights?"

"Never ye mind," advised the older woman in a gruff tone. "'Tis a means to pass the time, is all."

"I hear he likes a good brisket," Artemis offered slyly.

CHAPTER 18

*A*rtemis had learned, during the course of her brief life, that there were events over which one had no control, and therefore railing against fate was never a useful option. A good example was the miserable weather at the Siege of Burgos; just as Wellington was ready to spring the trap, they were forced to wait three days until the mud subsided—otherwise, the cannons would be mired—and with the additional time to prepare, the enemy had held, and lived to fight another day. A stoic acceptance of fate was needful in such a situation, even though one was inclined to swear and drum one's heels. She took a deep breath and with a conscious effort, unclenched her hands.

She was seated in the subdued atmosphere of the drawing room at Stanhope House, awaiting the Bow Street Investigator's questions. It was her wedding day, and after having been awakened by Hooks, she'd silently prepared for her trip to St. George's in the pre-dawn darkness. In the act of creeping down the stairs, however, she'd been surprised to hear visitors at the door, and Hook's voice, uncharacteristically alarmed. Lord Stanhope was dead—murdered; his body had been discovered in the Seven Dials District, notorious for brothels.

Lady Stanhope had held together well, rigidly insisting she had no idea why her husband would be visiting such a notorious neighborhood and disclaiming emphatically that he had any enemies.

"We are not certain it is a random crime, my lady," the Investigator had said. "After all, your brother in Sheffield has disappeared, and from what we have learned, your husband was an investor in his mining operations."

"I cannot imagine there is the slightest connection," the woman had insisted, her lips pale.

The rest of the household had been asked to wait in the drawing room to be questioned, with Artemis trying to decide how much she could withhold in good faith. Fortunately, she was not to be put to the test, because Droughm came in through the door, and at Hooks' gesture, strode toward her. He wore a formal morning coat for the wedding—very handsome and correct, and she felt an uncharacteristic prickling of tears behind her eyes, as he drew a chair close to hers. Taking her hand, he said, "I am sorry," and she knew he did not refer to her Uncle Stanhope. "Hooks sent word."

"What do you know of this?" It had occurred to her that her uncle's death had scotched the guardianship proceedings and all wedding plans with one ferocious blow—she could be forgiven for feeling very uneasy about this latest turn of events.

"Very little, as yet. You will stay indoors today—remember, my guard is stationed at the back—and we will reschedule our wedding for tomorrow morning."

Artemis stared at him, the inclination for tears gone as quickly as it had come. "We will?" She felt an inappropriate sense of relief, given the circumstances. "Oh, Pen; won't everyone think it very strange?"

"Everyone will assume you are pregnant," he answered in his abrupt way. "We won't care—we'll be in Sheffield."

"Oh—oh, I see," she stammered, hiding her alarm. "I didn't know we planned to go there for our wedding trip."

"It is important that we proceed to Sheffield with all speed. As your husband, I will have standing to assert control of the mines, pending your uncle's reappearance." He bent his head to look into her face, his expression softening. "Once the situation at the mines is resolved, then I promise we will take a proper wedding trip—anywhere you'd like."

"Anywhere other than Sheffield." She paused, and pressed her lips together. "And mine uncle will not make a reappearance."

"Did you kill him?" Based on the tenor of the matter-of-fact question, she was given to understand that he'd already guessed the answer.

"Yes—but it was justified, Pen."

"Filthy bastard," exclaimed Droughm with low heat. "I wish I'd killed him myself—"

"Oh," interrupted Artemis. "No; it was nothing like that—the man was over seventy, after all—but it was indeed self-defense, albeit for another reason; I tried to tell you at the Museum, but you were hungry—"

He drew his dark brows together, at sea. "Something about Vikings?"

"More *Macbeth* than Vikings. It's—it's rather a long story."

"Then save it for the trip to Sheffield. I'm afraid I must leave you, but you will be safe in the house—there are those who watch. Do not leave for any reason; I will have your promise."

"Yes, sir," she teased, feeling considerably better than she had ten minutes earlier.

"Miss Merryfield?" The Investigator approached; he was a tall, lean man, with shrewd grey eyes that gave away no reaction as he observed her huddling with an Earl of the realm.

"I am Miss Merryfield," acknowledged Artemis. And then, since Droughm offered no greeting, she added, "And this is Lord Droughm, come to pay his respects."

The grey-eyed man bowed. "My lord."

Something in the action—a barely discernable irony—told

Artemis that the two were already acquainted, and she eyed the newcomer in a speculative fashion, as she could think of no reason why a Bow Street Investigator would be on ironic terms with the aforesaid Earl.

The Investigator continued in a respectful manner, "I believe you were just leaving, my lord; pray do not allow me to detain you."

But Droughm was not to be ousted, and placed a hand on the back of Artemis' chair. "Miss Merryfield has been the recipient of upsetting news, and I would ask that she be treated very gently."

"I shall treat Miss Merryfield with the utmost respect, I assure you." This said with another ironic bow.

"See to it," said Droughm as he took his hat from Hooks. "Else I will speak to your superiors."

Artemis lowered her gaze, alive to the undercurrents in their conversation. If it was possible, the day became even worse than it already was. *Hell and damnation*, she swore to herself, *but I am in a fix.*

Taking Droughm's seat, the grey-eyed man began, "I confess I have prior knowledge of you, Miss Merryfield—although we have never met. I was at Bussaco, and remember that you rode the post when the Field Marshal's messenger was struck down."

Artemis recalled it well. "It was no hardship, sir; I stayed out of the range of fire, and the Colonel needed every soldier he had on the front. Were you stationed on the flank, with Captain Venables?"

"In a manner of speaking," was the oblique reply. "Tell me of your uncle."

Artemis was very much disinclined to cooperate, and wished Droughm had stayed behind to assist her through this minefield. In an even tone, she replied, "I have no uncles, but instead two great-uncles. To which one do you refer?"

The Inspector corrected, "You mean that you *had* two great-uncles."

"That is true," Artemis acknowledged. "Although it is not yet known if mine Uncle Thaddeus is dead."

The other regarded her for a long, silent moment, and Artemis had the impression he was hoping she would starting speaking out of sheer nervousness. He would be disappointed; she waited in silence.

"How did Lord Stanhope seem, when last you saw him?"

She thought about her interrogation in the drawing room, when the man had needed the aid of a strong dose of alcohol to hear of Artemis' visit to the Museum. "He was very unhappy with me; I was consorting with Lord Droughm, and there was a fear I would marry my silver mines away from the family."

"Do you intend to marry Lord Droughm?" the other asked abruptly.

"That is none of your business," she answered evenly.

"Do not trifle with me," he warned.

"No, sir."

In the ensuing silence, he bent his head, thinking, and took a different tack. "Are you aware your uncle's silver was being mined for the Treasury?"

"Yes," she answered readily. "The George the Third shilling —mine uncle was very proud of his contribution to his country."

The grey eyes watched her. "Sheffield is perhaps more famous for its tin mining, than its silver mining."

Artemis regarded him calmly. "I'm afraid I wouldn't know."

"Yes—I forgot," he agreed, leaning back. "You were only in Sheffield for a brief time."

Again, she had the feeling he was waiting for her to start speaking to fill the silence, but she declined, and sat quietly.

"Did Colonel Merryfield speak of Lord Stanhope?"

Artemis thought about it. "I don't recall—he spoke of Uncle

Thaddeus on rare occasions, but I don't remember hearing him ever speaking of the Stanhopes."

"Do you think there was a falling-out?"

She shook her head. "I honestly don't know."

The Investigator shrugged his shoulders. "Well—as you were adopted rather late, you may not be familiar with the Colonel's family history."

Artemis had already determined that she should not shield the truth about her parentage, because to do so might contribute to the theory that she was a murderess, hoping to inherit some silver mines. "I am not certain that I was ever adopted by the Colonel," she confessed in a steady voice.

The grey-eyed man lifted his brows in surprise. "On the contrary, the Colonel's military records indicate you were formally adopted in ought-nine. He never mentioned it?"

Artemis dropped her gaze to study her hands, clasped in her lap. "No—he was rather lackadaisical about such things." With stoic patience, she waited for whatever blow was to fall next; it could not be more evident that this man had been consulting with Droughm behind the scenes.

"Colonel Merryfield also met with an untimely end. If I were a suspicious man, I would wonder that you seem to leave a trail of dead men, in your wake."

"Yes, sir; it is alarming, indeed." There was another pause, and she met his gaze with her own steady one, bracing herself for the next, inevitable question.

"Tell me about the Colonel's death—had he any enemies? Any weaknesses that may have been exploited?" The grey eyes were sharp upon hers.

Lifting her gaze, she focused on the curtains, which had been drawn over the front window, so that only a small sliver of daylight filtered through. "He was a wonderful man; a bit reckless, but I think men in his position did not survive, absent a reckless streak—he had to trust his instincts without hesitation. He had a quick wit, and a generous heart—his men loved him, and would have died for him, as would I. There will never be another like him." To her horror, the prickling of tears returned, and she opened her eyes wide, so as not to cry.

He watched her for a moment, and even though she hadn't answered his question, he did not pursue it. Unexpectedly, he leaned forward, and briefly closed his hand over hers in her lap. "To better days," he offered.

"To better days," she agreed, nearly undone by the show of sympathy.

CHAPTER 19

*H*ooks put a black ribbon on the door in place of the knocker, and they were not at home to visitors. Artemis spent a desultory day with her own thoughts, which were as subdued as the atmosphere in this house of mourning. Lady Stanhope had retired to her chamber, not to emerge, and since Katy had been sent to deliver mourning announcements, Artemis did not even have the distraction of playing spillikins for imaginary stakes—not that such a pastime would have been at all appropriate.

Idly, she knelt on the settee and parted the curtains a few inches to watch the people pass by on the street. With forlorn hope, she watched for Droughm to come visit again, even though she knew he wouldn't—he wouldn't risk raising the alarm that his courtship of her hadn't, in fact, been thwarted by Lord Stanhope's sudden death. But—and here was a thought that lifted her spirits—by this time tomorrow—*this* time, without a doubt—they would be married, and she need never long to see him again. Except, perhaps, for those times when he traveled, to serve the Home Office as a spy.

With a long sigh, she idly admired a grey roan that passed by—a very fine horse, and with all the right points, as the

Colonel would say. She'd carefully thought it over, and decided there was nothing for it; she would marry Droughm, even though she was now certain he was allied in some secret way with the Inspector. The same instinct that had told her Miss Valdez was some sort of spy—a French one, apparently—told her the two men operated in the same sphere. The clincher had been the Inspector's casual confirmation of her mythical adoption, which only verified the suspicion she'd entertained when she'd watched the two men interact.

So—she was now knee-deep in some plot that appeared to involve French spies, the Treasury, the Portuguese and—of all things—*tin* mining, if she read the man aright, today. Meanwhile, she had secrets of her own which she'd planned to reveal to Droughm before they were married, but this course now appeared foolhardy, if indeed he worked in some capacity for the Crown.

Not to mention there was the added complication that Droughm had his own mysterious scandal brewing—a scandal that tied his hands in some way, or at least the Stanhopes seemed to think so. Of course, Lord Stanhope was now dead, and Wentworth and his French-spy betrothed had been spirited away, so perhaps all counter-checks had now been eliminated.

In any event, it seemed clear there were various forces ferociously working against each other with the object of controlling the mines in Sheffield, and this object was connected somehow to the last war, and the potential war to come. Her supposed adoption by the Colonel was only the latest foray in the behind-the-scenes war over the mines; each side was attempting to stymie the other, and she very much feared that things would look a bit bleak for her, once they discovered her own role in these events.

Leaning against the back of the settee, she rested her chin on her hands so as to watch the lucky passers-by, who went about their business without having to worry about murder, or abduction, or a healthy dose of treason. And—now that she'd no doubt of his role in this unfolding drama—Artemis also had to face the very real possibility that Droughm's appearance on the scene as her eager suitor was mere playacting, both to inveigle her secrets and to lay a husband's claim to the mines.

Indeed, to a dispassionate observer, this would make much more sense; men like him did not fall instantly in love with girls like her. Except he did love her—she would stake her life on it—and apparently, she would be called upon to do just that.

She watched another horse go by—a bit too short in the back—and reluctantly recalled Droughm's declaration that some things were more important than the truth. The present situation could easily be one of those things; he'd willingly lie to her if it meant exposing those who were plotting to betray England. Perhaps he'd been reluctant to give her any details about what was going forward because he was unsure of her allegiances.

With a mighty effort, she raised her head and righted her ship. It might be true that she was young in years, but she was not young in experience, or in gauging the character of others— whether it was her tormented mother, or the Colonel, who would stake anything on the next turn of a card, or those—the many, truly—who sought their own gain at the expense of the greater good. She was a fair judge of people, and her instincts had been proven sound, time and again. *If I know nothing else, I know he loves me,* she concluded; *and I love him.* For the first time, she examined this aspect, as—aside from the Colonel—she'd never transferred her allegiance to another person. *It is true,* she decided; *I do love him. And so I shall simply have to trust him.*

Hooks knocked discreetly on the doorjamb. "A message for you, miss." In his stately way, he approached and held out a silver salver that contained a plain envelope, unaddressed.

This was of interest, as Artemis was certain no messenger had come to the door. "Thank you, Hooks." She opened the note to reveal a card upon which was drawn a small bouquet— perhaps lilacs, although the artist was clearly not over-talented.

Smiling, Artemis held the card to her lips for a moment; she would not have been able to read a note of encouragement, and so Droughm had done the next best thing.

Tomorrow, she thought, holding the card between her hands and wondering where all those ridiculous doubts had come from; *tomorrow we shall be wed, and I will bare my soul, and he will come up with a plan—I have the feeling he is a prodigious planner, which is to the good, because I am currently at a standstill.*

Artemis looked up to observe that Hooks still hovered near the doorway, and surmised that he was minding her. "How does mine aunt, Hooks—is she lying down?"

"Her ladyship has found it necessary to visit her physician so as to seek a physic, miss."

With some surprise, Artemis observed, "She does not seem the sort to resort to physicking."

Bowing his head slightly, the butler replied in his diplomatic manner, "I cannot say."

Artemis turned to look out the window again, resting her chin on her fist. "All I know is that if I were her, I would flee this place with all speed." With a pang, Artemis remembered that this, in fact, had been Lord Stanhope's expressed preference —a pity that he hadn't followed his inclination. "Where is Torville?"

"I believe he accompanied her ladyship to her physician."

She turned to stare at him. "He is offering her his support? I wouldn't think he was capable of such a thing."

The butler, of course, would not betray any like-minded thinking, but instead offered, "I believe a funeral is planned for the day after next, miss."

"Oh." Artemis hadn't considered the funeral plans, and could only imagine the awkwardness of having to publicly mourn a husband who'd been found murdered in a low brothel. With a teasing light in her eye, she ventured, "I'll be very sorry to miss it, Hooks."

Hooks did not miss a beat, and bowed slightly. "Every happiness, miss."

She smiled warmly at him, now that he had spoken of it. "I thank you for the tuppence; I'll be certain to return it to Katy, pending her own need of it."

Further conversation was curtailed by the entrance of Katy herself, back from her errands. "I'm here, grand-dad."

With some relief, Artemis turned from her post at the window. "I suppose spillikins is out of the question, Katy, but do you think we could play a quiet game of lottery? I am bored to flinders."

With a measured pace, Hooks retreated to the kitchen, whilst Katy retrieved a deck of lottery cards from the secretary desk. "Have they found out who killed Lord Stanhope, miss?"

Artemis knit her brow. "The Investigator didn't say, but I believe he suspects Lady Stanhope."

Aghast, the girl turned to stare at her in shock, and Artemis laughed. "I am teasing—for heaven's sake, Katy."

The 'tweenie leaned forward to confide, "I shouldn't be surprised, miss."

"Nor would I," agreed Artemis. "Now, deal."

*a*s Lady Stanhope had not returned, Artemis visited the kitchen to beg a pot-luck dinner from Cook, who wore a black armband to emphasize her state of mourning, since her uniform was already black and she could not wear gloves.

"I saw a blackbird out o' my window, yesterday," that worthy revealed in the tones of the jeremiad. "A portent, it was."

"Can you predict the weather?" Artemis wound her legs around the stool. "The army would pay you handsomely."

"None o' your sauce," Cook warned. "'Twas a bad omen, and worse to come, I'm thinkin'."

"I'm not certain what could be worse," Artemis pointed out reasonably. "Murder is at the top, I think."

Cook shook her head sorrowfully. "And to be struck down in such a place—"

"I don't think he was looking for a nice brisket," opined Artemis.

"That lawman asked me questions." The woman sniffed, as she dished up a plate of cold ham and tomatoes. "Impertinent."

"Did he? What did you tell him?" Artemis began to eat, awaiting the answer with interest.

"Asked if I'd heard of his lordship's goin' to sech places before—" Cook ducked her chin "—I tole him I had not." She slid Artemis a glance. "Asked about ye."

"Ah," said Artemis, slicing a tomato. "Then I'm to be arrested for certain."

The older woman smiled her grim smile. "I stood bluff—ye needn't worry."

"Did you reveal that I like my beefsteak rare?"

"Impertinent, he was," she sniffed again. "Thinkin' I'd tell tales."

"He didn't strike me so much as impertinent as shrewd," Artemis admitted, helping herself to the milk jug. "He'd have made a good reconnaissance scout."

Before Cook could make a response, they were joined by Torville, who asked Cook to make up a plate as he drew up a stool beside Artemis. "A thoroughly wretched day; but one must eat, I suppose."

Artemis could see he was not his usual self—he seemed subdued, and his usual air of insolence was absent. *Spooked*, she thought; *and small blame to him—he's the one who does inhabit the brothels.* "Is our mutual aunt still from home?"

"Yes, but I've been discharged from accompanying her on her errands." He paused, cutting into the ham and chewing on a bite. "I will admit, though, that she was a bit easier to endure; this has been a humbling experience for her, and she's not one easily humbled."

Artemis said frankly, "I thought perhaps she'd fled."

He slid his thoughtful gaze toward her for a moment, but said only, "No reason to, surely. And no suspect has been identified as yet."

Apparently, then, he was going to pretend that this was a random crime, although Artemis was certain he knew as well as she did that this was not the case—perhaps he didn't wish to discuss the counterfeiting scheme in front of Cook. "Will you stay in town?" Artemis was a little vague about mourning protocol, but it seemed unlikely that Torville could wander off to engage in his usual pursuits, these next few days.

"For the near future. I should help out, I suppose."

This sentiment was unlooked-for, and engendered in Artemis a twinge of guilt, because she was going to leave this vale of tears first thing tomorrow morning, and never look back. "That's very kind of you, Torville; I can't imagine it will be an easy thing, these next few days."

Indicating with his knife, he observed, "Well, someone should look after you—aside from you-know-who."

She had to smile. "I can't imagine that you-know-who requires any assistance."

With a sigh, he dropped his hands and regarded her with a touch of exasperation. "Pray do not quash the first glimmerings of a conscience, I beg of you."

"I will not," she agreed. "Instead, I welcome all lookings-after."

"Good." Lifting his utensils again, he continued his meal.

"Where is mine aunt now?"

"I left her at the dressmaker's; she needs mourning-clothes, and she tells me she will have them make-up a dress for you, too."

With a pang, Artemis realized she'd have to leave her beautiful new riding habit behind—since she couldn't very well be married in it—but then consoled herself by thinking that Droughm would no doubt conjure up another one as easily as the first.

After taking another bite, Torville added, "I hope a black armband will suffice for me. I imagine I will be asked to say a eulogy, which is weighty assignment, and may be beyond my powers."

"You *cannot* speak ill of him," Artemis cautioned; with Torville, one never knew.

But he only twisted his mouth as he chewed his ham. "It

wouldn't matter what I said—everyone will be thinking of where he died, and what he was doing there."

"Poor you," Artemis sympathized.

"Poor both of us; I will rely upon your moral support."

"Of course," she lied without a qualm. "Anything to help."

He turned his speculative gaze to her. "What does your friend have to say—or is he unaware of the tragedy, as yet?"

Artemis did not pretend to misunderstand to whom he referred. "He came by this morning to offer his condolences—he was here when the Bow Street Investigator was here."

Torville paused, and then asked in an overly-casual manner. "Oh? What did the Investigator have to say?"

"I told him Cook did it," Artemis offered. "Being as how the deceased had dared to criticize her bread pudding."

"Sauce," muttered Cook, as she tended to the hearth.

"We are in for a very uncomfortable few days," Torville declared, as he pushed away from the table.

As she was in for a very blissful few days, Artemis made no reply.

He paused at the door. "We should have another ice, cousin, to fortify us for the trials ahead. And you aren't old enough to share a bottle of brandy—more's the pity."

Artemis eyed him in bemusement. "We can't go have an ice, Torville—only think of how it would look."

With heavy patience, he explained, "No, nodkin; I will bring it here. I'll return in a bit." He then sauntered out the door.

Cook watched him go, her hands folded beneath her apron. "All on end, 'e is."

Artemis lifted a bread-end from his plate. "It comes of having responsibility suddenly thrust upon him. He'll have to stay away from his gaming hells for the foreseeable future, and instead help arrange for mine aunt's mourning affairs—what could be worse?"

"It's not like 'im," Cook mused, her chin on her chest. "It's more like 'im to slip away to Newmarket or somewheres, and leave 'er ladyship to deal with 'er own troubles."

Artemis teased, "Maybe he'll redeem himself, and live the rest of his life doing good works, and such."

"Not 'im," said Cook succinctly, turning back to her hearth. "Ye'll see."

But Torville returned as promised with the proffered treat, and sat with Artemis in the drawing room whilst they partook. Since he'd gone to the trouble, Artemis felt obligated to ask about what he'd done the past week, and so was required to listen to tales of the racecourse, and the perfidy of favorites who threw a splint at the most inopportune time.

Slouching in his seat, her cousin complained, "It's ridiculous —I've had such a run of bad luck that the bookmakers won't allow me to punt my bets any longer."

Holding the empty dish in her lap, Artemis listened with half an ear, staring at the fire that burned in the grate. "You mustn't gamble, Torville," she said in disapproval, her mouth having trouble forming the words. "It causes no end of trouble."

He made some reply, but she wasn't listening to him, as he wasn't very interesting, and she was tired of listening. The officers would race, sometimes, when everyone was waiting for the next deployment, and the soldiers would bet on the races even though it was against regulations—the Colonel was not one to put protocol above morale. If the weather was hot, the men would race in their shirtsleeves, and everyone would shout, just to have the opportunity to do so; eager for a distraction from the unending hardship of war, and a chance to vie good-naturedly against each another. She'd always longed to participate, but the Colonel wouldn't hear of it—he was very protective of her, in his own way. Captain Venables had an inky-black mare that was unbeatable, even though she didn't have the stride of a champion; she simply would not allow any other horse to pass her. Tremendous heart, had that horse. Artemis stared into the fire, and wondered whatever had happened to Captain Venable's black mare.

With an effort, she lifted her gaze to see that Cook had come to gather-up the dishes, and to wish her good night in a pointed manner. *She doesn't want me to linger here with Torville,* thought Artemis, amused. Thus prompted, she thanked Torville and then mounted the stairs rather slowly, as her legs felt unaccountably heavy. *I must go to sleep,* she thought; *tomorrow — tomorrow is important, for some reason, but I can't remember why.*

CHAPTER 21

*A*rtemis gazed, mesmerized, at the single candle on her bedside table. She thought of the Battle of Vitoria, and of the young lieutenant for whom she'd carried such a *tendre*, until he was killed crossing the Zadorra River, along with so many others—so very many. The next morning, the blood-soaked battlefield had been shrouded in a heavy fog, making everything so silent, and she could remember watching the cranes as they flew—their wing-tips barely skimming—along the river; and how it had been hauntingly beautiful, despite the horror of it all.

She could hear a ruckus of some sort, downstairs, but she found she could not take her gaze from the candle, lost in the memory of the monochromatic tones of the battlefield, when it was covered by the morning fog. Dimly, she was aware of a violent pounding and muffled curse words, and then footsteps, hurrying up the stairs with some urgency. *I should see what is afoot*, she thought lazily, and closed her eyes.

"Missy, missy look at me—hold the lamp up, ye old fool!"

With an effort, Artemis managed to open her eyes to see Cook, her thin, anxious face a bit too close—

"Bring the basin, Katy—quick now; help me get this down 'er gullet."

"No." Artemis twisted away from the hands that grasped her. "Quick—sound the alarm!"

"Miss Merryfield," said Hooks in a firm tone, "You must drink Cook's potion."

"Put 'er on the floor," commanded Cook. "I'll kneel on 'er arms."

Pinned to the floor, Artemis gritted her teeth and turned her head from side to side whilst Hooks tried to force open her jaw. Opening her eyes, she could see Katy's frightened face, upside-down, and hovering over hers. "Please hold still and drink it, miss—*please*."

"Hold 'er head between yer knees—ready? On the count of three—"

And then Artemis was gasping and sputtering as she swallowed a vile-tasting liquid, and almost simultaneously began retching miserably. The many hands turned her over, and she vomited and heaved the contents of her stomach into the basin, Katy holding her hair back and Cook saying something unintelligible in a soothing voice.

Spent, Artemis knelt on her hands and knees, gasping for air. Muffled shouting and pounding could be heard from downstairs. "What is the enemy's position?" she rasped.

After a pause, Hooks answered her. "Torville is locked away in the hall closet, miss."

Cook said to him, "We've got to get 'er out of the house. Someone'll be comin' soon as a witness, and if she's here in the house alone with 'im it won't matter that 'e hasn't done the deed—she'll be ruined, just the same."

Raising her face, Artemis closed her eyes against the spinning room, and gasped, "There—there is a Lance Corporal, posted out the window—Droughm has him stationed to guard the flank. You—you have only to signal."

There was a small silence. "Do you think it true?" asked Katy of the others.

"Go see," commanded Cook, and Katy sprang to the window with the lamp, whilst Hooks and Cook helped Artemis sit up on the floor.

"I am going to be sick again," Artemis announced, and then suited action to word. Dimly, she could hear the casement window opening, and Katy communicating in an urgent whisper.

"Let him in the servant's entrance," directed Hooks. "Quietly, now."

"Make certain—make certain he knows the password," Artemis cautioned between retching, and then realized she'd forgot what it was—it changed every day, and she couldn't remember it—it was *so* important to remember the password—

But apparently he knew it, because the Lance Corporal was lifting her to her feet and bundling her in the coverlet from the bed. "I have a side-arm," she told him, struggling to keep her eyes open. "It is under my pillow."

"I have it, miss," said Hooks, securing her pistol.

"I'll take her to his lordship's," said the man, "and he'll decide what's to be done."

"Mind the perimeter," Artemis warned.

"She's goin' nowhere without me," said Cook in a grim tone. "She may need another dose."

"We'll all go," Hooks decided, "That way, there will be no witnesses, and no one will know where's she's gone."

"Secure him in the brig," suggested Artemis. "There is no time for a court-martial."

"Here you go, miss." The Lance Corporal lifted her up, bundled in the coverlet.

"My doll," remembered Artemis, struggling to stay conscious. "I—I must keep her with me."

"Here she is, miss," said Katy, who quickly tucked the doll inside the coverlet.

Artemis leaned her cheek against the Lance Corporal's shoulder, and closed her eyes, immediately falling into a dream about their camp near the Spanish vineyards, and Happy Jack, the Colonel's horse, who used to come to the Colonel's whistle.

"*A drum, a drum, Macbeth doth come,*" she recited to Droughm.

"We must be away, and quickly," he said over his shoulder. "Give her your clothes, if you please."

"Yes, my lord," said Katy.

With an effort, Artemis focused on Droughm as he searched her eyes, his hand cradling the back of her head. He was in a murderous rage. "Don't kill anyone," she cautioned.

"She'll just sleep, now," Cook's voice said. "Strong coffee, when she wakes."

"I must keep my doll," Artemis told him, the words careful and distinct.

"I will bring her with us. Go to sleep, Artemis."

"You can't send the others back into the ambush," she pleaded. "Not after they've risked their lives."

"No; they will go to Somerhurst. You must try to sleep, now."

"Yes, sir," she said, teasing him, and he pulled her head to his coat lapel and held her close, his breath on her hair.

CHAPTER 22

"*A*rtemis."

She'd been having disturbing and disjointed dreams, and heard his voice with an enormous sense of relief. On several previous occasions she'd tried to lift her eyelids, but they would not respond; this time she tried again and blinked, focusing on Droughm, who sat on the bed beside her, watching. He was worried, and so she smiled. "Hallo."

"Hallo." He ran his hand along her arm. "Are you all right?"

"Perfectly," she said, her tongue thick.

"You'll not thank me, Artemis, but I'm afraid we must leave soon."

"Right." She propped herself up on an elbow, and as the movement caused her head to ache abominably, she paused, willing the pain to subside. She noted they were in a small, low-ceilinged chamber, with a banked fire burning in the grate. Blinking, she tried to remember if she knew where they were.

"We're at an inn near Epping Forest," he informed her. "I'd like to leave out the window, if you are able."

"Right," she said again. "I'm sorry, Pen—my head hurts and I cannot think."

"You were drugged," he said in a grim tone. "I should

probably try to find you some hair of the dog, but it will have to wait."

But Artemis had made a much more interesting discovery. "Did we get married?" She wore a wedding band on her ring finger, and stared at it in bemusement.

"We are pretending to be married; I am not about to allow you out of my sight. Can you stand, do you think?"

"Yes," she replied, and hoped it was true. She swung her legs over the side of the bed, and he steadied her as she stood, trying to control her heaving stomach and her pounding head. Droughm was dressed in plain leather breeches and a corduroy jacket; he looked very un-Earl-like—except for the fact he wore an aura of suppressed rage that did not bode well for the peasantry.

"Steady—shall I carry you?"

"I'm much better," she assured him. "Truly, Pen."

"They will pay." He said it in a grim tone, as he lifted the curtain aside to watch out the window for a moment.

"I am glad to hear it." She tried not to sway, and pressed her palms to her temples to ease the aching. "A firing squad comes to mind."

Glancing at her, he instructed, "I'll drop down and then catch you, when you come after me."

Looking out, she saw it was early morning, and a light rain was falling on the fallow fields which were visible from the window. Being unfamiliar with English geography, she had no idea where Epping Forest was, but it seemed suitably obscure, if they were in retreat.

He raised the casement and swung a leg over, then hung onto the sill whilst he lowered himself down to leap the remainder of the way to the ground. Artemis determinedly followed suit, only to discover that the fall into Droughm's arms was too much for the tenuous state of her stomach. Retching miserably, she was sick alongside the wall whilst her companion patted her back in sympathy and muttered, "Quickly, if you please."

"Sorry," she gasped, and straightened up, embarrassed by this show of weakness.

Taking a glance in either direction, he tucked her under his arm and began walking. It appeared their object was a dirt track that edged the field, alongside a boundary hedge.

"If you need to stop, let me know," he said after they reached the track. "We have some cover, here."

"I feel much better." It was true—if only her head didn't ache so—but at least her stomach seemed to have settled; there was little left in it, after all. She did rather hope they wouldn't be walking for very long.

He seemed disinclined to speak, and she was concentrating on keeping up, so they crunched along the track in silence for a hundred yards. "Are we trying to avoid paying the shot?" she finally asked, panting.

Stopping abruptly, he drew her into his arms to squeeze her, which she didn't think was the best idea, given recent events, but made no protest. "Forgive me, sweetheart—I am distracted."

This was true; she gauged that he was on a low simmer, almost a'boil. If it had been the Colonel, he would have practiced sword-fighting for an hour and then felt much better, but she didn't know Pen as well—not yet, at least—so she simply said, "I don't mind; pray don't feel you must coddle me."

He released her and they continued on at a slightly slower pace. "You will be coddled, and you will like it. I will not be gainsaid on this."

As this seemed an opportune time, she ventured, "I may need to rest—just for a minute."

He glanced down at her with concern. "We are almost there —shall I carry you on my back?"

"No—no, if it's not much longer—" She looked ahead, and

decided that their destination must be a farming shed, up ahead. Perhaps he hoped to steal a horse.

As they approached, the shed door opened slightly on its own. With some alarm, Artemis drew back, but Droughm urged her forward. "No—it's safe; go in."

Slipping inside, Artemis came face-to-face with Lady Tallyer, waiting at the door.

Whilst Artemis blinked in astonishment, Droughm asked, "Anything?"

"No—quiet," the lady replied.

Artemis felt a rush of annoyance—mixed with jealousy—that Lady Tallyer was apparently involved in Droughm's mysterious work, and so she said with a touch of pique, "We are only missing the Investigator to make this reunion complete."

Neither of them acknowledged her remark, and Lady Tallyer informed Droughm, "I made coffee."

"Whiskey may be helpful. Do you have any?"

At her denial, he asked, "Does Tremaine?"

"I've no idea—he's on watch."

Artemis did not appreciate being treated like a child listening to the adults, but she firmly bit back any other sarcastic remarks, because it would only make her appear petty and young, and she half-suspected the lady was hoping for just such a reaction.

Droughm took her arm, and saw her seated on a bale of hay. "Can you attempt some coffee, Artemis? Your cook thinks it will help clear out the opiate."

But the smell of the coffee was not at all appetizing, and Artemis dreaded the idea of being sick in front of Lady Tallyer, who was—naturally—very attractive in a black riding habit. "I am thirsty," she admitted. "But I don't know about the coffee."

"Try a sip," Droughm suggested, crouching before her. "If you can't, you can't." He looked over to his companion, who poured a cup and brought it to Artemis.

Tentatively, Artemis held the warm tin of coffee between her hands for a moment, gathering the courage to take a sip.

Lady Tallyer said quietly, "Please reconsider, Pen. They will be expecting just this."

In a curt tone, Droughm replied, "I'll not leave her again. I was a fool to leave her vulnerable in the first place."

"Not your fault," Artemis offered, turning the cup around in her hands. "I should never have parlayed with Torville; thank God Cook is a suspicious soul." She took a tentative sip, the aroma alone making her stomach heave.

"Shall we step outside for a moment?" the lady asked Droughm with some significance.

"No," he replied.

Despite her misery, Artemis found she was rather enjoying herself—she hadn't known him long, but even Artemis knew you couldn't talk Droughm out of something he'd determined upon. With a furtive gesture, she set the coffee cup aside.

Not so furtive, after all. "Can't do it?" he asked with sympathy, the green eyes worried.

"I just feel as though I've been turned inside-out, Pen." She was careful to use his name, because Lady Tallyer had done so. "Let me give it a few minutes."

"I'll go fetch some whiskey from Tremaine—we need to prepare you for travel." Droughm slipped out the door, and the two women were left alone in the shed.

"My head hurts," said Artemis crossly. "And I am past making conversation."

Lady Tallyer made an impatient sound. "Then don't talk, if you'd prefer, but I should try to pin up your hair. We're to switch clothes, and I've brought your horse."

This was of interest, and Artemis looked up. "Callisto is here?"

"She's in the stall. And you should be kinder to me; I'm to sacrifice my best riding habit for you."

Artemis managed to muster up a smile. "I do thank you, then. Where will I be wearing your best habit?"

"Scotland," the other replied in an even tone, her face expressionless.

An elopement, then. Artemis couldn't help but think how she would feel, if she were in the other's position, and offered, "I am sorry."

The lady arched a brow. "Don't be; I will hold out hope that Pen will come to his senses long before you reach the border."

Artemis found she appreciated the other's honesty and countered, "And I will hold out hope he does no such thing."

With a nod, Lady Tallyer produced a hairbrush. "Then we shall see who has the right of it."

Droughm returned after Artemis' hair had been braided and pinned atop her head, and he produced a flask. "Drink," he commanded, and she took a healthy swallow, waiting whilst she felt the liquor burn; one wasn't a camp follower for seventeen years without having tasted whiskey.

"You'll need to give Katy's dress to Carena," he instructed. "She'll wear a wig, and pose as you in the carriage we came in."

"A feint," Artemis declared in appreciation. "It should work —as long as no one comes too close." As she was feeling more charitable toward the other woman, she refrained from mentioning that close proximity would make the age difference all too apparent.

Droughm brought forth Trajan, and cinched his saddle. "We should leave within the hour. There is a market fair down the road, and we will want to use the distraction of the crowd."

The whiskey had indeed helped Artemis' headache subside, and she retreated into the stall to switch clothes with Lady Tallyer, and to don a riding bonnet that obscured her face. Then Callisto was led out, and the few things they would carry were efficiently tucked into the saddlebags. *It is like being on the Peninsula again,* thought Artemis as she checked the knots, *only with a different sort of enemy, this time.*

"May I speak with you privately for a moment?" asked Lady Tallyer of Droughm.

"No," he said shortly, and helped Artemis mount up.

"You cannot mean to ignore it," she persisted. "Don't be a fool, Pen."

"Have done, Carena." He said the words without rancor as he mounted his horse. "I may be many things, but I am not a fool." Gesturing for her to open the door, the lady did so, and Artemis followed Droughm out into the field.

CHAPTER 23

They paused for a moment, whilst Droughm took a long look around the immediate area, twisting in his saddle to do so. Artemis could see nothing of interest; Tremaine, whoever he was, was nowhere in sight.

With a nod to Artemis, he moved forward, and she moved in beside him, breathing in lungfuls of the cold air—she felt much better, but was not yet fully recovered. An opiate, Droughm has said; that others would willingly take such a thing seemed incomprehensible—she'd hated the feeling of helpless lethargy.

Quietly, he said without preamble, "Carena was alarmed that you twigged the Investigator. She doesn't know—as I do—that you twigged Miss Valdez just as easily."

"I must be sensitive to deception," Artemis replied in an even tone.

He did not pretend to misunderstand. "I cannot reveal very much, I'm afraid. Not as yet."

In a steady voice, she ventured, "When I realized that you and the Investigator were allied, I wondered if perhaps your—your interest in me was mere playacting."

His head snapped around. "What?"

At his professed incredulity, she had to chuckle. "It was a weak moment, and passed quickly."

"Weak indeed. Good God, Artemis, I can hardly keep my hands from you."

"Or from my silver mines."

But he only replied, "I'll remind you that the silver mines are not yours in the first place."

"You ease my mind, then. Where do we flee?"

"Scotland," he said bluntly. "I will have the honor of marrying the Countess of Droughm over the anvil."

"I don't know what that means, Pen," she confessed. "But I don't think your vaunted ancestors would approve."

They were traveling down the dirt track toward the road, and she noted that he kept a sharp eye on their surroundings. "We've little choice. You need only be sixteen to marry in Scotland, and anyone can perform the ceremony; all that is necessary is the requisite number of witnesses. And my ancestors may be damned."

"A good riddance to them," she agreed.

He gave a bark of laughter. "Thank God you are back—don't ever do that to me again."

"Tell it to my poor head, Pen—as if I am at fault in this. What has happened to Torville?"

He flicked his riding crop on the toe of his boot. "I did not remain behind to find out."

"Hooks offered to take a whip to him."

"Hooks is a good man."

She glanced at him sidelong, but then desisted because it made her head ache. "Who put Torville up to it? Lady Stanhope couldn't force him to do such a drastic thing—not after you'd given him a taste of what-for."

He thought about how to answer this, and finally said, "There are some very unpleasant people who are involved in your uncle's mining operations. I imagine they applied some pressure on Torville, and on the heels of Stanhope's murder, very little pressure was needed—indeed, it may have been the entire reason for the man's murder. They are ruthless people, and desperate to keep the mines under their own control."

"And the Portuguese? Why do they take an interest?"

He tilted his head in apology. "I will tell you, but not just yet, I'm afraid. How far do you think you can ride today? I'd like to go cross-country most of the time, and avoid the roads."

She took an inventory of herself. "A good ways, I think— I've done my share of rough riding. What is our goal?"

"That depends on your stamina, and how determined the pursuit is."

This seemed ominous; Artemis had assumed that the changed-clothes feint with Lady Tallyer and Tremaine would solve all problems. "Do you think there will be a pursuit?"

"Almost certainly—much is at stake. Stay close to me, if you please—you have your pistol? Do not hesitate to use it, if circumstances warrant."

She nodded, hiding her concern. Although her knowledge of geography was hazy, she was aware that the Scottish border was not lengthy—it would not be the same as evading pursuit in Spain, where there was a vast expanse available to take cover from the enemy. No wonder Droughm wanted to move quickly —their best chance was to race to the goal before the enemy had a chance to establish a position and block them.

Up ahead, she could see a variety of travelers on the road, all heading in the same direction and drawing wagons, pushing wheelbarrows or even driving dog carts to bring goods to the market fair. Artemis looked about her covertly so as not to show her face, and decided that—except for the appearance of the people—it was very similar to any other market fair she'd seen on the Continent. The destination appeared to be a town, visible in the distance, with the tall spire of a church marking its center. Artemis also noted that the sun seemed to be in the wrong place. "Isn't Scotland to the north?"

"Carena and Tremaine will head north to draw the pursuit;

we will take a less direct route. Stay with me; here we go."

Turning his horse, he casually walked off the road into a copse of trees, and began threading his way through them, glancing to see that Artemis followed, and that no one had taken note of their departure from the crowd. Quickening his pace, he trotted through the stand of trees and after coming out the other side onto a spinney, began to gallop in earnest. Nothing loath, she spurred her own horse and the next few hours were spent covering a great deal of ground, headed in what seemed to Artemis a north-west direction.

Callisto had a smooth stride, and after the horse jumped the first hedge without hesitation, Artemis relaxed and enjoyed herself. It was wonderful to be freed from all burdens—at least for the time being—and to have only one object, keeping up with Droughm.

They stopped only briefly, to water the horses and partake of the cheese and bread that Lady Tallyer had packed in the saddlebags. As they ate, Droughm pulled a map from the saddlebags and muttered to himself as he studied it closely, his compass in hand.

"You forgot your quizzing glass," Artemis concluded.

He brought the map over to her and pointed to an area. "Can you read to me any of the letters, here?"

She followed his fingertip and tried her best, but could not offer any meaningful assistance. "The letters are all looped together—although I think this is an 'M'." Shaking her head, she smiled at him. "We are a sorry pair."

"No matter—I have a good guess. The horses will need to rest, so we will stay in one of the villages that come up along the river. A small, out-of-the-way Inn should be safe enough, and you need a good night's sleep."

And so, after a long day's riding, they cleared a final rise to look down upon a cluster of lights that marked a small village in the lengthening shadows. As the horses picked their way down the hill, Droughm turned in his saddle to face her. "I will reconnoiter to see if there is a place to stay—if nothing is suitable, we'll head on to the next village, or perhaps pay to stay in a farmhouse."

"Lay on," she agreed.

They came to the road, and as they warily approached the village, he said in his abrupt manner, "I have a question for you, but I fear you will take your crop to me again."

Hiding a smile, she responded gravely, "I make no promises."

"Have you already been with a man—in a bed?"

This was plain speaking—even for him—and she could feel her color rise. "No; the Colonel was very strict about such things."

He looked away and nodded. "I will pose as your uncle, then; best take your ring off."

Interpreting these remarks, Artemis eyed him with a smile. "So; we are going to wait until we are married?"

"Yes," he said firmly. "We are. I can be just as strict as the Colonel."

"If you say so," she responded, and kept her own counsel on the subject.

After they'd found a room in a suitably obscure inn, Artemis washed herself in blessedly hot water, and then sponged the dirt from her riding habit as best she could. She was hanging it up to dry before the fire when Droughm gave a perfunctory knock and entered the room, dressed in his shirtsleeves. After observing Artemis in her shift—made transparent by the fire behind her—he paused on the threshold, completely still.

"You may close your mouth." Smiling, she spread the habit's skirts out.

"Good God—you are *beautiful*." Stepping forward, he drew a hand through the dark, thick hair that fell nearly to her waist, and she willingly lifted her face as his mouth descended upon hers. The kiss deepened, and his mouth moved to her throat and neck as she pressed against him, feeling for his buttons.

Impatient, he pulled his shirt over his head and then lifted her in his arms to lay her down on the bed, whilst she ran her hands over the thick patch of dark hair on his chest. In a haze of anticipation, she relished the weight of him along the length of her body, and reached to kiss whatever part of him was nearest, as he impatiently worked off her shift, and flung it aside.

Ten minutes later, matters didn't seem to be going well, and the worse it went, the more tense she became—if Lady Tallyer and Miss Valdez had experienced no such difficulties, the problem must be wholly hers, and Droughm was surely going to regret taking on a young and inexperienced bride.

"Whiskey," he pronounced, and rolled out of bed to fetch the flask.

She sat up, mortified and holding the coverlet against her breasts. "I am so sorry, Pen."

"Not your fault." He took a healthy pull from the flask, and handed it to her to do likewise. "I'm too impatient. You've never done this before, and I've never been with someone who's never done this before, and it's not a good combination." He sat beside her and bent his head to look into her face as he took her hand in his. "We will come about—we have all the time we need."

"I hope we have enough whiskey." In some distress, she took another pull.

He chuckled, resting his head against hers, and she chuckled in response, and soon they were both laughing as he pulled her back to lie within his arms. "I love you," he said easily, without constraint. As he began to idly stoke her body, the liquor began having an effect, and Artemis nuzzled him as his wandering hands created a sensation of pleasure wherever they went.

Slightly breathless, she warned, "You should probably lock the door—else the chambermaid will think you a very odd sort of uncle."

"In a minute," he murmured, and began to kiss her with more urgency.

CHAPTER 24

*T*he coupling was duly accomplished, but the experience had been, truth to tell, more painful than Artemis had anticipated. On the other hand, there was no denying the extreme pleasure he had taken in the act, and any amount of discomfort was well worth it; there'd been such a depth of feeling in the movement of his body against hers, and in the sweet, sweet words he'd whispered to her.

Afterward, Droughm had assured her the marriage bed would become easier for her, and she had assured him in turn that no such assurances were necessary. But she had been a bit taken aback, truth to tell.

The moment that lingered in her memory, however, was as she lay awake in his arms— she was unused to sharing a bed, and it felt so strange—with his chest rising and falling beneath her cheek as he slept. He'd murmured something unintelligible as he ran a light palm across her back, and she'd been overcome with a wave of affection so powerful it brought tears to her eyes. As she lay against him, she thought, *I have more than I could ever ask for—he makes up for every hardship, every desertion; I am fortunate beyond measuring.* Drifting into sleep, she moved her fingertips over his ribs and relished the masculine feel of his coarse chest hair against her face.

The next morning, she awoke to see Droughm dressed and seated on the bed, watching her as he'd done the morning before. He was an early riser, then—this was to the good; she was also an early riser—that was, when she wasn't recovering from her first brush with being drugged, or being bedded.

"Good morning," he said, the warmth in his eyes a remnant of said bedding.

Sitting up, she stretched, rather enjoying the novelty of being naked before another person—this one in particular. "Good morning. What evasive maneuvers are in store for today?"

He dragged his gaze from her body. "More of the same, I'm afraid. Shall I call for tea and toast before we go? You look a bit pulled."

"And pushed," she teased, leaning over to run her fingers down his shirt front.

But he resisted, and stayed her hand by catching and kissing it. "We should be away, and quickly."

She leaned forward to kiss him lingeringly on the mouth and felt him respond, his hand reaching up to cradle her face. "Just yet?" she whispered against his mouth.

Gently, he said, "Let's allow you some time to recover before we try it again, Artemis."

She could hear the thread of remorse behind his words, and thought, *this will not do at all.* With a gesture, she directed his gaze to her naked breasts. "Look, Pen; I believe I am permanently scarred from whisker-burn."

"I know exactly what you are about, you know," he said with a smile, but she could see that he was weakening.

"Please, Pen." She kissed the corner of his mouth, and then slowly planted more soft kisses along his jaw line. "I do need to practice."

They then engaged in a mock-argument about whether they

should or shouldn't, with so many kisses interspersed amongst the words that the outcome was never truly in doubt.

Afterward, she lay with him, watching the early morning light play on the opposite wall as he lightly moved his fingers along her back. *Better*, she thought with satisfaction as she rubbed her face affectionately against him—*or at least, not as bad*. And his own delight was deep and unfeigned; small wonder it is such a weakness for men, if they all took such pleasure in it.

"We truly must go."

"I can decamp in a trice," she assured him, swinging her legs over the side. "Give me five minutes."

Frowning, he pulled on his coat. "I must find some spectacles. The innkeeper had none to spare, but there's a rectory down the way—I will see if the Vicar is awake, and then meet you at the stable."

After washing and dressing, Artemis descended the stairs and made her way out to the stable. As she lifted Callisto's bridle from the hook in her stall, she saw a stable boy, half-hidden behind the wooden partition, and watching her with a wary expression.

He was perhaps ten year old—the same age as the drummers who'd beaten out the march-pace, mile after mile, and Artemis couldn't help but smile at him in a friendly fashion. "Hallo, there."

The boy nodded, but offered no response, and seemed half-inclined to flee.

"Thank you for seeing to Callisto," Artemis continued, patting her mare's neck and buckling the bridle. "Isn't she a beauty?"

The boy swallowed. "Ter were a man, lookin' through yer bags."

"Yes, my—my uncle," Artemis agreed, securing her pistol in the saddlebag.

"Not 'im—summan else. A furriner."

Artemis' hand closed around her pistol. Turning her head, she whispered to the boy, "Fetch mine uncle—quickly."

The boy stared at her, unmoving, and then Artemis heard a heavily accented voice from behind her issue an ominous command. "Come away from the horse—now."

So—Portuguese. Artemis whirled around to face the man who held a pistol on her, and hissed in his language, "Fool! Not me—the man!"

If it were another situation, the man's surprise would have been comical. "*Que?*" he asked, his pistol unwavering.

Artemis cast a furtive glance toward the stable door, and then advanced toward him, furiously emphasizing her point with a slashing finger, and hoping the boy was using the distraction to fetch reinforcements. She continued in Portuguese, "Idiot! You do not take me! I am here on orders from the *senhorita*—who has told you otherwise?"

"Come no closer," the man warned, but he'd stepped back, and it was clear he was confused.

Gesturing for him to stay silent, Artemis moved toward the stable door, as though to look out, but her true intent was to require him to face the morning sun as she hid her pistol in the folds of her riding skirt. She'd learned battle-tactics at the feet of a master, and the Colonel had always taught that a sun-blinded enemy was a helpless enemy.

"Come away from there," the man insisted in Portuguese, and just as Artemis was considering the possibility that she may indeed have to shoot him, he was suddenly struck down from behind by Droughm.

"Well done," she exclaimed in relief. "I didn't want to fire, and draw attention."

"Are there others?" he asked quietly, dragging the man toward the back stall.

"I don't think so—not here, leastways. He must be a scout." She watched him bind the man, and then tear off one of the man's shirt sleeves so as to fashion a gag.

"We must be away, and quickly." Droughm quickly covered the man with a horse blanket.

But Artemis had inspected her saddlebags, and had a more pressing problem. "My doll is missing. Does he have it?"

Droughm checked, briefly. "No."

Frantic, Artemis searched around the stalls. "She must be here, somewhere."

"Artemis," said Droughm as he tightened their horses' girths with deft hands. "We must be away; I promise I will buy you a new one, exactly the same."

"The stable boy," she insisted. "Perhaps he saw what happened—let me find him."

Droughm stopped her with a hand on her arm. "I am sorry for it; but if this fellow's a scout, he will soon be missed and we cannot tarry—I will leave instruction that the doll is to be sent ahead to Sheffield, with a substantial reward. Now, mount up."

Utterly wretched, she faced him, her lips pressed together. "We *must* find her, Pen. The minting plates are hidden inside her."

He stared at her, thunderstruck.

Into the ominous silence, she ventured, "I was working up the courage to tell you—I swear it, Pen."

"Who are you delivering them to?" This asked in a grim tone.

"No one—well, mine uncle, originally, but I thought it all too smoky by half—please, Pen, you must believe me." The look in his eyes made her writhe in an agony of remorse—she'd been a fool to put it off.

Droughm indicated the unconscious man with an abrupt gesture. "Did he know where the plates were?"

"No—no one knows, save me."

He ducked his chin to his chest and swore softly. "I don't know if I can believe you."

"You see—" she paused, and then whispered in anguish, "—you see, the Colonel is the one who gave them to me."

This caused him to raise his gaze to her again, considering. "We will save this discussion for later. Where is the stable boy?"

They discovered him lurking along the exterior of the building, the picture of guilt; unable to face them, and unable to flee. With a friendly gesture, Droughm summoned him over. "I believe you may know what has happened to my wife's—"

"—niece's—" Artemis corrected him.

"—niece's rag doll. If you would return it to me, I will give you a guinea."

But Artemis found this unacceptable, and protested hotly, "You cannot reward him for *stealing*, Pen."

"Artemis," said Droughm in an ominous tone. "Give over."

"You shouldn't have stolen my doll," Artemis accused the boy stubbornly. "It was wrong."

"I sees it when t' furriner was lookin'," the boy admitted, nervously clasping his hands behind his back. "I has a new baby sister."

Droughm crouched down, so that he was on a level with the boy, and spoke in a friendly fashion. "We will have an agreement, then. You will return the doll to my niece, and I will give you a guinea; but I must have your word of honor—as a gentleman—that you will give the guinea to your new sister."

The boy nodded, relieved, and the two solemnly shook hands.

We are going to have children, Artemis realized as she watched them; *he will be the father to my children—that is, if he will still have me, after this latest disaster.*

"Let's go." Droughm strode toward the horses with the doll under his arm, and she leapt to comply, giving him no opportunity to find further fault.

CHAPTER 25

They spent the next several hours riding hard—splashing through rivers and then scrambling along shale outcroppings to obscure their tracks, as the countryside became more mountainous.

Judging from the rigid set of his shoulders, Droughm continued angry with her, and so Artemis did her penance, and kept up as best she could without complaint. Unfortunately, her muscles were stiff from all the unaccustomed riding yesterday, but—since she'd rather fall off the horse than ask for mercy—she bit her lip, and endured.

Finally, Droughm pulled up near a stream to allow the horses to drink, and reviewed his map with his newly-acquired spectacles. He made no comment to her, which she found harder to bear than the physical discomfort. "Forgive me, Pen," she begged, a thread of anxiety in her voice.

Removing his glasses, he contemplated her for a moment. "I will admit my first thought was that it was you who was playacting—pretending an interest to beguile me. But the episode with Torville certainly wasn't playacting. For that matter, neither was that maidenhead of yours."

That he was making light of this miserable disaster was such a relief that she began to cry, holding her hand up to cover her eyes, and finding that she was unable to stop, even when he dismounted to pull her down into his arms. He rested his cheek against the top of her head whilst she sobbed into his chest, feeling young, and foolish, and overwhelmed.

"Why didn't you tell me?" he asked softly, tightening his arms around her. "Did you think I would betray the man who stood as a father to you?"

"I—I didn't want anyone to know," she whispered, trying to catch her breath in ragged gasps. "It was so—so *ghastly*. I was tempted to throw them down a well." Like an anguished child, she began to cry again, so that she could barely get the words out, clutching his coat in both her fists. "He—he must have been a party to it—"

"No—I'll not believe it," he soothed in a steady voice. "He could not have known what was afoot. I imagine he was only looking to make some extra pocket money."

"All his men—" she choked, "—all his men who died for England—"

"That is why it is unimaginable that he knew."

"Treason," she whispered, and made a mighty effort to control herself. Counterfeiting the coin of the realm was a hanging offense, and whilst Droughm was making an admirable attempt to play it down—which she appreciated—they both knew it was very unlikely there was an innocent explanation.

His lips found her temple. "My poor Artemis. What on earth did he tell you?"

Drawing a shuddering breath, she said, "He asked me to deliver them to Uncle Thaddeus, but to let no one know I had them, for fear thieves would try to wrest them. But I seemed a very inappropriate messenger, if they were indeed the official plates. I think I suspected from the start that they were not."

She could feel him take a breath as he thought it over. "Where did he come across them?"

"I don't know—I didn't even know he had them, until the day he gave them to me to hide. I think he said they were made on the Continent, because no one in England could do the work."

"Gerard," guessed Droughm. "One of Napoleon's counterfeiters."

"The Colonel had gambling debts." In misery, she rubbed her face against his coat front. "I couldn't bear to think about it, so I hid them in the doll and pretended they were not there."

"You need to eat something," he said abruptly. "You haven't eaten today. Sit over there, and I'll fetch the food."

Wiping her cheeks with her palms, she walked on stiff legs to sit on a large rock by the side of the rushing stream, wondering what he would do, and feeling relieved, all in all, that he would be the one to decide—that the terrible burden was no longer hers to carry. *The Fourth Terrible Thing,* she thought; *and definitely worse than the other three—although having to murder a madman certainly came in a close second.*

He fetched their cold meal from the saddlebags, and sat beside her in silence as they ate. When he offered her the skin of water, she lifted it high and drank, as she'd done countless times before. The familiar action fortified her, reminding her of all that she had lived through—and of the generous, larger-than-life man who had seen to it. *I must do my best to resolve this—somehow—without bringing disgrace upon him,* she thought; *it is the least I can do.*

Hard on this thought Droughm said, "You will not mention this to anyone, Artemis, and I will make every effort to ensure no one knows of the Colonel's role."

"I think the Investigator already suspects," she admitted. "He asked about any weaknesses the Colonel may have had."

With a grimace, Droughm conceded, "There is little he does not know, I'm afraid."

"Does he know about Wentworth, and Miss Valdez?"

"Almost certainly."

"I am not certain that *I* know about Wentworth and Miss Valdez," she ventured.

"She seduced him, because he holds a position at the Treasury," he replied in his blunt way.

Surprised, Artemis brought to mind the earnest young man at the Museum, and had trouble picturing it. "*Wentworth* is involved in the counterfeiting?"

"Yes—they needed someone on the inside. The Treasury would necessarily make inspections at the refining sites, and someone had to report back that all was well."

"'They' being the French?"

He nodded. "Yes."

But she was having a hard time sorting out the particulars of the scheme, and knit her brow. "So—counterfeit silver coins are being minted? What has this to do with tin, and why would the French take an interest in the first place?"

"It is much worse than mere counterfeiting, I'm afraid." He brushed off his breeches and—after considering a moment—apparently decided to tell her. "The false coins were minted in tin, with only a thin veneer of silver, to disguise this fact. The bulk of the silver was quietly being sent to Napoleon's supporters, to finance the next war."

Artemis stared at him in horror for a few seconds, before disclaiming in a stammering voice, "Pen—oh my God, Pen—there is no *chance* that the Colonel knew of this."

"No," he agreed. "But it does not look well."

This seemed an enormous understatement, and Artemis tried to comprehend the sheer audacity of such a scheme. "The French were arranging for English silver to finance Napoleon's next war—to conquer England."

"There can be no war without the funding for it," he concurred grimly, "And France is out of money."

And it also meant that Droughm's scandal was every bit as hideous as her own—if his heir was involved in this treasonous plot. She asked in amazement, "Wentworth knew all of this, and didn't care? How could this be?"

Droughm ducked his chin and made a sound of impatience. "Miss Valdez fed him some tale at first, and he was so enthralled that such a woman sought his bed that he ignored the obvious, and then he was too ashamed to confess it to me. Instead, he made an attempt to set it to rights—which only made it much worse."

Artemis thought about it, watching the water sluice through the rocks in the stream. "He was coerced to kill someone?"

Droughm nodded. "Yes. It was a trap, of course—he was led like a lamb to the slaughter, thinking that he saved his sweetheart from disgrace, and—as an added measure—saved the Crown from counterfeiters. But in truth, he killed an innocent man."

"How—how *despicable*," exclaimed Artemis with some heat. "Give me honest warfare any day."

He glanced at her, and she belatedly recalled that he was in the same dishonest business, and so perhaps she should temper her comments on the subject. "How did you uncover this plot, if Wentworth was too ashamed to confess to you?"

"His manservant wrote to me."

"Thank God for the servants," she declared fervently. "They have served us well in this particular skirmish."

He nodded in agreement. "I was in Algiers, so there was a delay before I could make an appearance, and by that time the idiotic boy practically fell on my neck with relief. He confessed, and told me—with all sincerity, the fool—that she was pregnant, and so he had no recourse but to marry her."

"They thought to stymie you," Artemis observed with grudging admiration. "It was masterful, truly."

"No one stymies me," Droughm declared.

"I did," teased Artemis.

"Except you," he agreed, his gaze warm upon hers. "You are the exception to my every rule." He took her hand and held it in his lap, as they watched the water for a few moments. "Did Uncle Thaddeus ask for the plates?"

"Almost immediately, upon my arrival. He asked if the Colonel had sent along a packet for him, and so I told him my kit had been stolen whilst I was waiting for the posting coach at the docks."

His brows drawn together, Droughm interrupted in a sharp tone, "You traveled from San Pablo to Sheffield *all alone*?"

Artemis laughed at him. "My kit truly wasn't *truly* stolen, Pen—I made that up." She explained as though to a child, "You can't think I'd allow someone to steal something from me."

But he put his head in his hands. "You have been ill-served, Artemis—what was the Colonel thinking, to allow you to travel such a distance alone?"

She shrugged. "The Colonel was already dead. And Uncle Thaddeus would not pay for a private coach."

He lifted his head from his hands. "Go on."

"After I told Uncle Thaddeus, then I had to explain to the Chief Constable of Sheffield that my kit had been stolen. He was very unhappy about it." Artemis paused, and added with some significance, "It seemed a little strange that he took such an interest."

"The *devil*," said Droughm slowly. "You think he was involved?"

"I would not be surprised—I suppose it is the same situation as with Wentworth; the French needed to make certain the local authorities would not be poking about, noticing anything untoward." She paused again. "Not to mention that the Constable saw himself in the light of a suitor—he brought me flowers, once; it was very unlike him."

Droughm could no longer contain himself, and rose to his feet to stride back and forth in agitation. "The *bloody* bastard. Did he offer you insult?"

She eyed him, gauging his temper. "No—he is what the soldiers would have called a dry stick." She did not betray that she knew very well the "stick" to which the soldiers referred. "He was older and unmarried—spinsterish, I suppose you would say."

"He had an eye on the mines, then?"

"I would guess—although mine uncle quarreled with him; he didn't like to think of anyone else having an eye on his mines."

Frowning, Droughm asked, "What is the Constable's name?"

"Mr. Easterby. He was very unhappy when the Stanhopes came to fetch me, but I couldn't very well stay at my uncle's house alone, and so he was forced to let me go." With an air of resignation, she asked, "Do you wish to hear of mine uncle's untimely death?"

"Save it," he said abruptly. "We must press on, and I fear I will do violence to someone, if I hear any more of this tale of yours."

As she stood and brushed off her skirts, she offered with quiet sincerity, "I am truly sorry I didn't tell you sooner, Pen."

With a soft, strangled sound, he stopped his pacing long enough to face her. "Small wonder—what a cast of characters you've been saddled with, Artemis; it is nothing short of amazing you didn't flee back to the Continent, and take your chances there."

"I would never have met you, then." A powerful wave of emotion rose up within her, and she struggled to put it into words. "I don't think I've told you how very happy—how wonderful it is—" she was perilously close to tears again.

He laid a hand alongside her face and said quietly, "I know—I feel the same."

She leaned into his hand, emotionally spent; she was not one who easily confided in another, and could not be comfortable making herself so vulnerable. As though sensing this, he drew her into his arms, holding her so that she could recover her equilibrium. "We'll head for Kendal, and stay in a farmhouse tonight—I am wary, after having been so easily traced last night. If we stay at a private home, it will make it all the more difficult to track us."

Raising her face to his, she offered, "You know, Pen; we can always sleep in a haystack—it's rather comfortable, actually. And I could snare a rabbit, if you have any string."

"You are the greatest and best thing that has ever happened to me," he pronounced as he replaced her bonnet on her head. "Are there any more revelations to come?"

"No—except for mine uncle's death, that is all of them."

"Then up you go." He kissed her so that she was assured she was forgiven, and helped her mount.

CHAPTER 26

They rode to the north and slightly west, rapidly when there were stretches of open land, and slowing to walk or trot where there was forest. Droughm avoided all roads, and stayed well away from any other persons they happened to see in the distance.

Artemis followed closely, and tried not to think of her weariness, or the fact that there was only more weariness to come. She was unclear on exactly how far they must travel, but tried to remain philosophical, as she'd done on so many advances in the past; hers was to follow without complaint, and provide support where needful.

And hopefully, she'd be providing support to Droughm beneath him in a bed—no question that she needed to improve, since there were plenty of others hoping to supplant her. That he loved her was a certainty, but men were men—as she well knew—and the bed-sport was a priority for them. She hated to admit it, but their less-than-spectacular first night was a cause for concern.

They stopped once to eat, and to rest the lathered horses, then pushed on through the long afternoon. Just as the light was fading, they pulled up to review the valley spreading out before them.

"I believe the lights in the distance are Kendal."

"Excellent," she replied, having no idea where Kendal was. "Are you husband or uncle, this time?"

He considered. "Uncle; I imagine I will have to sleep on the floor."

Artemis nodded; it was just as well—despite her desire to improve on her bed skills, she truly, truly needed some sleep.

They circled around the village as darkness fell, and Droughm decided on an isolated farmstead located on the outskirts. Holding his horse, Artemis watched as he approached, and knocked on the door to be met by an older man, musket in hand. The two conducted a discussion during which she saw Droughm make a gesture in her direction. The terms having been agreed to, he approached and lifted her down.

"You are to go in, and Mrs. Manley will see to you while I help rub the horses down. We are Mr. and Miss Hardy."

She nodded, and mounted the steps to meet Mrs. Manley, a stout, plain woman with cheeks like apples. Her cheerful smile revealed that one of her front teeth was missing.

"Come on in, lass. We'll have ye clean and fed in a lamb's shake—best take yer boots off on the steps, here."

With a relieved sigh, Artemis removed her muddy boots, and then followed the woman into the warm kitchen, stepping carefully on the wooden floor in her stockinged feet. "Thank you so much for your hospitality," she offered in her best niece's voice, and wondered what excuse Droughm had given for their bedraggled appearance at this late hour.

"Wash yer hands and face 'ere at the pump, first; after ye eat, I'll heat-up sum water fer a proper bath."

"That would be wonderful," said Artemis with heartfelt gratitude. "I would so love a bath."

After washing at the pump, she dried her face with the

rough-spun towel proffered by her hostess, who watched her with a speculating eye. "A pretty thing, ye are—sech bonny eyes." The woman's tone indicated that this was not necessarily to the good.

Artemis wasn't certain how to respond. "Thank you."

The woman shook her head. "Pretty is as pretty does, though; mark it well."

"Yes, ma'am." One could not argue with such an observation.

Gingerly, Artemis settled into a wooden chair at the kitchen table, and then watched as her hostess dropped eggs into boiling water and cut a thick slice of ham from the joint in the pantry.

"Ever been this way afore, lass?"

"No, ma'am—I'm afraid I am not very familiar with this area." Artemis refrained from making any mention of Sheffield, thinking she should probably play her cards close to the vest.

"Where's yer family, then?"

The sole representative is currently in the stables, she thought, but instead said vaguely, "Oh—they live to the south."

"Hmmph." Her hostess raised a brow as she served up the food.

Nothing loath, Artemis was wolfing down the meal when Droughm entered with Mr. Manley, deep in a discussion about the quality of the horseflesh now stabled in the Manley barn. Droughm nodded to Artemis, and indicated he would retire upstairs to wash before joining them.

With some amusement, Artemis noted that Mrs. Manley's gaze was openly appreciative as she watched Droughm mounting the stairs. But as soon as he was out of sight, the woman suddenly turned to shake her coddling spoon in Artemis' direction.

"Now missy; my mother didn't raise a fool, and I can ken what's afoot, 'ere."

"I beg your pardon?" Artemis' tone was as mild as milk, but

she was suddenly on high alert. *I hope we don't have to flee again,* she thought, annoyed. *It would be cruel beyond measure to dangle a hot bath before me, only to snatch it away.*

"Yer uncle's fit to be tied, for all he's tryin' to keep it hid."

This was an unanticipated tack, and Artemis could not fathom where it was headed. "He does tend to be fit-and-tied," she agreed tentatively.

The woman pursed her mouth and regarded her with an admonishing eye. "None o' yer sauce, if ye please."

"No, ma'am."

Mollified, the woman relaxed her posture, and tilted her head in a kindly manner. "What be yer name, lass?"

"Carena," Artemis answered promptly.

Mrs. Manley folded her hands over her ample midsection and regarded her with a shrewd eye. "Well, Carena, p'haps ye'll listen to an older woman, who's been about, and has seen what there is t'see."

"Willingly," said Artemis, all attention. "Pray continue."

"Ye'll be wise t'marry who yer family tells ye to. It's the way of it for good reason—yer nowt but a silly flibberbeget, at yer age, and its lucky yer uncle caught ye in time, and is draggin' ye back home."

The light dawned, and Artemis struggled to maintain her countenance as Droughm re-entered the room. Brightening, Mrs. Manley indicated he was to sit whilst she cooked up another batch of eggs. Simpering over her shoulder, the woman said, "I hope ye don't mind, sir, but I bin scoldin' Carena, here. An older woman's advice is needful, betimes—she'll nowt listen to the likes o' ye, right now."

Not surprisingly, Droughm slanted Artemis a covert glance of alarm, and Artemis was forced to cover her face with a hand, lest she burst out laughing.

The woman mistook her hilarity for distress. "Now, now, missy; I'm sure yer uncle won't give ye what fer—no need to be cryin'. But ye canno' be behavin' in such a way—tyin' yer garter in public with a runaway weddin'. Think o' the disgrace to yer pur family."

There was a small silence. "Indeed, Artemis has often been a trial," Droughm offered.

"Carena," Artemis corrected him.

"Carena," he agreed.

The woman shook her head sympathetically at Droughm. "These young lasses—wi' no respect fer their elders."

"Deplorable." Droughm began his meal. "The chit is entirely too hot-at-hand."

"Unfair," Artemis protested. "You are very hard on me." She slid her gaze to him, but he did not dare look up.

"Ye may think yer sweetheart's a good choice, lass, but yer family knows best—ye need to get yer father's consent, and do it all proper-like."

"They want me to marry someone too *old*," Artemis protested with a great deal of heat. "It is *so* unfair—"

"You will do as you are told," Droughm interrupted. "Is there bread and butter?"

Eager to please, the woman fetched a loaf from the pantry, and admonished Artemis as she unwrapped the cheesecloth. "The young lads may turn yer head, missy, but ye'll wind up cryin' by the wayside, wi' no one willin' to take ye in."

"Exactly," Droughm agreed. "Crying by the wayside."

Artemis sulked, in her best imitation of young love thwarted.

Warming to her theme, Mrs. Manley sawed off a thick slice of bread. "And a weddin' in Scotland's the next thing to no weddin' a'tall. The terrible shame—ye'll never live it down."

Artemis had to cover her face again with her hand.

"I was fortunate to put a stop to such a disgrace," Droughm agreed. "I will keep her under lock and key, henceforth."

"Where's t' boy?" asked Mrs. Manley.

"I shot him," said Droughm.

Taken aback, the woman stared at him. "Ye *shot* him?"

"He'll recover," pronounced Droughm in a negligent manner, helping himself to more ham.

But this glimpse into her guest's violent nature only seemed to fascinate the woman, and she gave him a coyly significant look from under her lashes. "I'm afeered if the lass is to sleep upstairs, sir, we'll have to put ye on a pallet, down 'ere by the hearth. I'll see to it that ye're are comfy as can be, though."

He considered this. "Is there a lock on her bedroom window?"

The woman admitted there were no such safeguard, and so Droughm said with regret, "I shall have to guard this vixen, then."

Artemis crossed her arms and sulked.

CHAPTER 27

"You are not to succumb to her wiles," Artemis cautioned, "Or else I will climb out the window in truth."

"I am sorely tempted," Droughm replied. "Give me your hand." They were having a whispered conversation after they'd retired for the night, Artemis on the ancient bed, and Droughm on a trundle pulled alongside, so as to keep a weather eye on her.

Lying on her stomach, she dropped a hand over the side and he held it clasped against his chest. With her cheek against the edge of the lumpy mattress, Artemis looked down on him in the dim moonlight. "I'm a bit shocked, I must say. Where is her husband?"

"Elsewhere. Can you blame him?"

She smiled. "I imagine you are always being propositioned —and by far more appealing women."

"Now, how am I to answer that, without sounding like a coxcomb?" He lifted her hand to kiss her knuckles, his lips soft on her skin. "I will be a married man, by this time tomorrow."

"Tomorrow," she said in wonder. "I'd almost forgotten."

"There's a bit of a disappointment."

"No—no, Pen; I suppose—well, I suppose I feel as though we are already married."

"No; we are merely behaving as though we are already married. For God's sake, don't tell our hostess, or we'll have to hear another 'crying by the wayside' speech."

"I don't think she should be lecturing anyone about morals," Artemis observed in a tart tone.

There was a small pause, as he brushed his thumb across the back of her hand. "You needn't, you know."

"Needn't what?" she asked, a bit sleepy.

"Marry me. It has occurred to me that I haven't given you much choice in the matter."

Leaning her face over the side of the bed, she peered down at him. "What nonsense is this? You will marry me, if I have to force you at gunpoint."

He chuckled, which made his chest vibrate beneath her hand. "I beg your pardon; I thought I should at least pretend to give you a right to renege."

Laying her head down again, she warned, "I've half a mind to renege, just to teach you a lesson."

"Pray do not; I am armed, also."

She smiled. "I've no idea how to be a Countess, Pen."

"You will make an excellent Countess. None better."

"You will help me, when I don't know how to go on?"

He turned her hand and kissed the palm. "There is only one task required of a Countess, and I can already assure you that you excel."

"I need practice," she admitted.

"God willing."

Laughing softly, she squeezed his hand. "We are having such an adventure, Pen—I wish I could enjoy it more."

He pressed her hand against his chest again. "I confess I will be relieved when the deed is done, and this mad flight is over; I lack your experience in covering ground, pell-mell."

"You are doing very well," she told him kindly, which elicited another chuckle.

There was a contented pause, and Artemis closed her eyes, thinking that perhaps the conversation was over, when he asked, "How did you twig Miss Valdez?"

"Are you worried that I truly am a French spy?" she teased, then realized she shouldn't tease—not with the Colonel's ambiguous involvement in these schemes raising that very possibility.

But he said merely, "I am impressed by your instincts."

"Not to mention that Lady Tallyer is alarmed."

"Small blame to her," he noted in a neutral tone.

Artemis wondered if perhaps he did have a doubt, somewhere in the back of his mind, and so she hastened to reassure him. "Miss Valdez lapsed into French, once, without being aware of it. But it is more than that—she just didn't seem Portuguese to me, so I said some things about the peninsular campaign, and she was tricked into betraying her ignorance."

Mulling it over, she tried to explain. "I am constantly on alert, I suppose, from how my life has been lived. And since I've come to England, nothing is what it seems—even you." She waited, to see if he would say anything about his own role in these events.

He did not pretend to misunderstand her meaning. "I'm afraid I am unable to tell you very much—things being how they are."

"Even after we are married?"

"Even then."

She sighed philosophically. "I never really thought much about it—the spies are looked down upon as being rather dishonorable, you know—but I can see that it is important."

He reminded her, "You said the Colonel was warned about an ambush, in the north of Spain."

"Yes—and many lives were saved. And then there is this

business about the money to finance the war, which I'd never considered. It is as though there is an entirely separate war going on behind the actual war, and this one is just as hard-fought."

"That is a very good way of describing it." Idly, he began playing with her fingers.

Artemis thought she may as well ask. "What do you mean to do about my doll?"

He let out a breath which she could feel, warm on her hand. "First things first. We will marry, then head to Sheffield to reconnoiter. It's a delicate situation, because we can't just put a stop to all production; the Treasury needs the new schilling, and we don't want to expose the French counterfeiting scheme to the public—the fewer people who know the truth, the better."

Seeing the wisdom of this, she added, "And I suppose we can't just charge in like the cavalry, because you would like to find out who is involved in the plot, first."

"Yes, although I imagine once it is known that you have married me, those involved will simply melt away—there is little reason to risk capture."

Reminded, she asked, "Why is Portugal interested?"

"It is not Portugal as much as the Ambassador himself. Again, the French needed someone on the inside—this time in diplomatic circles; someone who has the protection of diplomatic immunity."

Puzzled, she could not decipher what was meant. "Immunity for what?"

"Abducting the heiress springs to mind."

Amazed, Artemis leaned over the edge of the bed to look at him. "Nothing would have been done, if they'd seized me at the Ballantine ball?"

"No—the Ambassador and his staff are protected by diplomatic immunity."

She stared in dismay. "Why, it is almost *unbelievable*, Pen—that the enemy would go to such lengths."

"Napoleon's spymaster is a mastermind, and should never be underestimated."

She leaned back, thinking over what he had told her. "What hold do they have over the Portuguese Ambassador, that he would aid the French in such a scheme?"

"He lost his estates to the Spanish, and has been promised that they will be returned in exchange for his cooperation."

Incredulous, Artemis frowned at the low-beamed ceiling. "And that is all it takes? To do such a thing, out of nothing more than greed?" She thought about the Colonel, and her mad uncle, and the Stanhopes and Torville—all motivated by the promise of riches. "There is *nothing* the French could offer me that would convince me to help them."

Droughm pointed out reasonably, "On the other hand— unlike the Ambassador—you have no land that has been in your family for generations before it was stolen."

"Would you do it to save Somerhurst?" she countered.

"Not a chance in hell."

"Well, then," she concluded, justified. "What is *wrong* with everyone, that greed seems to trump integrity?"

"I think good men have been asking that same question since the beginning of time."

"Despicable," she declared with some heat. "And people like me—and Wentworth—are moved about like pawns, to be used as they wish."

"Wentworth, perhaps," he corrected her. "You, on the other hand, are no one's pawn." He kissed her knuckles again, to emphasize the point.

But she had to disagree with this assessment. "I was the Colonel's pawn. I suppose he was my weakness, rather than hereditary estates."

"But you did not deliver the plates. It must be driving them mad, wondering what happened to them; they are not easily replicated."

"Yes; I know Miss Valdez was threatening the Stanhopes

about them—perhaps she thought they were double-crossing her. I can draw some comfort from the falling-out amongst thieves, I suppose."

There was a small pause, and then the tenor of the conversation changed, as he said quietly, "It has been a miserable business. But it brought you to me."

"I love you," she whispered into the darkness. "Truly, Pen."

"And I love you," he replied softly. "I won't keep you awake; tomorrow will come early." He turned over her hand to kiss her wrist at the pulse, sending a *frisson* of pleasure up her arm.

"Oh, Pen—should I practice, do you think?" She wanted to make up for the scare she'd given him today, and she found—rather to her surprise—that she missed having him next to her, his big body taking up the bed.

"Tomorrow," he promised. "Our wedding night."

With a contented smile, she drifted off to sleep, her hand in his.

CHAPTER 28

*I*n what seemed like only a few short hours, Mrs. Manley was leaning over Artemis, shielding a candle. "Wake, missy; yer uncle says yer to begone—he hopes to get ye back quick as a wink, to scotch the scandal."

Artemis struggled to sit up, feeling as though she'd hardly slept at all. "Thank you, Mrs. Manley. Is there to be breakfast?"

"Nay, missy. I'll pack bread and ham fer 'ee."

The fire was not yet lit, and Artemis shivered as she pulled on her riding habit, and buttoned her wool cloak up to the throat. *No matter,* she thought with grim resolution as she re-plaited her hair. *It is my wedding day, and this time—God willing—it will go forward without some disaster striking; they do say that the third time's a charm.*

Feeling her way in the dim light, she descended into the kitchen to see Droughm coming in the back door, stamping his feet on the rush mat and looking up at her. The kitchen fire was only getting started, and Artemis tucked her hands underneath her arms.

"Will you be warm enough?" Droughm asked.

"I has me rabbit-lined cloak," Mrs. Manley offered,

apparently willing to give him anything he desired. "It's precious warm."

Artemis replied, "Thank you, Mrs. Manley, but my cloak has a hood, and I should be warm enough once the sun comes up. Thank you for your kindness."

The woman smiled her gap-toothed smile. "Ye'll mind wot I tole 'ye, missy."

"I will never forget you," Artemis assured her in all honesty, and then they went outside, the light from the sunrise barely illuminating the morning mists.

"No more runaway weddin's." Their hostess gave Droughm an arch look.

"Certainly not," said Droughm, as he cupped his hands for Artemis' boot. "She has learned her lesson."

"Come back, any time," the woman called out as she waved them off, and there was no mistaking that she was not speaking to Artemis.

The horses' hooves sounded over-loud as they struck out along the empty road. "Well, she was a treat," observed Artemis in a tart tone as she tightened her cloak's hood under her chin.

"She does not know that I am spoken for," Droughm pointed out in a reasonable tone.

"I'll have you remember that *she* is spoken for," Artemis replied crossly. "Does loyalty mean *nothing*, anymore?" She was tired, and cold—and the subject was a sensitive one.

He pulled Trajan up so as to walk beside her. "I suppose it depends on the marriage. Many do not marry for love, and never intended to be loyal to begin with."

But Artemis shook her head in disagreement, her stubborn gaze on her horse's ears. "Not always—many of the officers professed to love their wives, but then they took a Spanish mistress. It was accepted, because they were away from home for so long, and men have their weakness."

There was a small pause, and then he asked quietly, "Is this about me?" He glanced at her, as the horses' hooves crunched on the gravel road and the mists rose around them.

Artemis sighed so that her breath formed a cloud in the cold air. "I don't know what this is about, and I sound like an archwife. I'm sorry, Pen."

Droughm looked down the road ahead of them, barely discernable through the fog. "I never intended to marry—never could imagine having to be bound to one woman. And then I saw you in the garden, and ever since that moment—here's a rich irony—I've been in an absolute fever to bind you to me. I am terrified that you will get away, and the rest of my life will be lived without you."

The words were patently sincere, and she decided there was no time like the present to bring up her concerns. She lowered her gaze to her hands as she flexed her fingers in her gloves to keep them warm. "I am worried—" she ventured slowly; "I suppose I am worried that I will always be inadequate, and that you will look elsewhere."

He let out a bark of laughter, and surprised, she looked over at him. "What? You haven't had an easy time of it, Pen—you can't convince me otherwise."

With a smile playing around his lips, he flicked his crop against his boot as the morning birds could be heard calling from the treetops. "I must tell you a cruel and unjust truth."

Reading his tone aright, she smiled slightly. "I am forewarned, then."

"The very difficulty of which you speak is actually physically pleasing, for a man."

Eying him with some surprise, she asked, "Truly?"

"Have you heard me complain?"

Laughing, she accused him, "You are only saying this to make me feel better."

"Upon my word," he assured her. "Ask any man."

"It would make for an interesting topic of conversation, but I will take your word for it." Feeling immeasurably relieved, she teased, "Then I am not such an utter disappointment."

"Definitely not; it is one of the many reasons that I am in a fever to bind you to me."

She laughed at him, and then he led her off the road, so that they walked across a sheep pasture, the scattered sheep not even bothering to look up as they passed. "What is today's plan of action?"

"We'll need to cover forty miles, more or less, and stay to the side roads because the horses are recognizable. We'll try to cross over the border in the countryside, away from the Great North Road where it crosses the border near Carlisle. On the other hand, they may assume I would not be so foolish as to follow the Great North Road through Carlisle, and therefore they won't be watching there—so Carlisle actually might be the best place for us to cross the border."

"Cat-and-mouse," agreed Artemis, who was familiar with the tactics of war. "Should we trade the horses, perhaps? We can always retrieve them on the return."

But apparently, he'd already considered this. "I think not; speed is most important at this point—we've only one day more, and nothing we can readily purchase will be as fast as these. Ready?"

She nodded, and the bulk of the day was spent in hard riding, interspersed all too rarely with a short break to stretch their legs and have a bite to eat. Artemis bore up well; there was nothing for it, after all, but as the afternoon wore on she was aware the events of the past three days were taking their toll. *When this is over*, she promised herself, *I shall sleep for a week— unless Droughm has other plans, which he probably does, judging by his comments about the cruel and unjust truth.*

She was concentrating on the terrain ahead—she was tired, and a fall could mean disaster—when Droughm suddenly pulled up, cursing roundly.

"What is it?" she asked in alarm, automatically scanning the horizon.

"Threw a shoe," he replied tersely, dismounting to examine his horse's rear hoof. "The *devil*."

This was an unlooked-for problem, as any delay only worked against them. "There must be a smithy along here, somewhere," she ventured, gazing out over what appeared to be a vast expanse of uninhabited land.

With his hands on his hips, he let out an aggravated breath. "I believe Carlisle is just over the next set of hills to the east; since it's a large town, there should be a public livery stable. I can get the shoe replaced while you hang back—they'll be looking for the two of us together, and—as I said—they may not be looking for us at Carlisle in the first place, since it would be too obvious."

"And you now sport a beard." It was true; several days without a razor had left him with a decidedly piratical appearance, which was rather appealing, in its own way.

He nodded, and remounted. "We'll take it easy—unless we see anyone, and then I'm afraid Trajan's foot be damned."

"Do we split up, in the event?" Oftentimes, the strategy in retreat was to require the enemy to choose whom to pursue.

"You will not leave my side," he replied, very seriously. "I will have your promise."

"Yes, sir," she teased.

They walked the horses for several miles, and in the late afternoon they finally paused on a hilltop to view Carlisle in the distance, nestled in a sweeping valley.

Droughm gestured with his crop. "The border is perhaps ten miles beyond. Once we are across it, I believe we can conscript nearly anyone to marry us, as long as there is an additional witness."

"Excellent," Artemis replied. "Trajan will have his shoe and I will have my ring, just in time for dinner."

They threaded their way through the outcroppings of rock

and shale, and made their descent toward the town. Despite the fact she was disheveled and bone-weary, Artemis felt a surge of elation; the border was a few miles away, and with any luck, the enemy would not have guessed they would come through Carlisle, as bold as brass. Soon their mad flight would be over.

Approaching circumspectly, they skirted along the perimeter and stayed in the shadows of the hedgerows that bordered the surrounding fields. Droughm was alert and watchful, and Artemis kept her face lowered, respecting his cautious mood. He finally pulled up so that she could come abreast of him, and pulled out a soft leather drayman's hat from his saddlebag.

As he donned the hat, he indicated a livery stable, up ahead. "Stay here in the shadows, and keep your hood up and your head down; I should not be gone above a half-hour, God willing."

Artemis watched him enter the public stable, his shoulders slightly slouched as though he had nothing more urgent to consider than his horse's missing shoe. Callisto shifted her weight and lowered her head to pull at some grass during this welcome opportunity, and Artemis hoped they would not both fall asleep, now that they had stopped moving for a moment.

Lost in her thoughts, she was taken completely by surprise when Callisto startled and reared her head back, pulling away from the man who'd seized her reins. Horrified, Artemis stared in disbelief as Marco from the Ballantine ball raised a pistol to her. "Make no sound," he warned in a low voice.

CHAPTER 29

*T*hey had lost this round of cat-and-mouse; the enemy had out-guessed them. In the course of an instant, Artemis knew one thing; if she allowed Marco to hold her at gunpoint, Droughm would be helpless. Therefore, she sat as though frozen with fear whilst he moved his hand to her bridle, and began to pull the horse toward him, the pistol never wavering.

Choosing the moment when his eyes slid to check on the stable door, she lashed her crop at his face with all her strength, and kicked her mare at the same time, shouting. Marco drew back with a cry, bringing his hand from the bridle to shield his face, as the leaping mare literally ran him down.

Artemis wasted no time, but pelted toward the livery stable to warn Droughm. Behind her, Marco shouted in Portuguese, "Seize her!" and two other riders suddenly burst from the shadows and rushed to block her path. *We are outnumbered*, she thought, assessing—*the Colonel would say that I must try to even the odds*.

"Hah!" she shouted at Callisto, and spurred the startled mare directly toward the livery entrance at full speed. The other horses were no match for the initial burst of speed the Arab mare could produce, and so they were unable to head her off, but instead fell into close pursuit, directly behind her. Artemis didn't hesitate, but galloped straight through the stable doors where the startled patrons stared at her in outraged surprise. She didn't dare look for Droughm, but instead concentrated on taking the easiest route through the building whilst angry men shouted and dove out of her way. Clearing a stack of baled hay with a leap, Artemis exited out the back doors of the livery, and then spurred her mare to race toward the church spire that rose in the distance, gauging it to be the center of town.

Kicking the mare's side and pumping the reins, she frantically tried to maintain her breakneck pace, hearing shouts and the drumbeat of pursuing hooves behind her—not as close; she'd managed to open up a lead—and risked a quick glance beneath her arm to gauge the distance.

Thundering at full speed down the Great North Road, Artemis crouched over the mare's neck and urged her onward, plying the crop from side to side across the horse's withers as pedestrians scattered and fled. Finally, she spotted what she sought; a throng of men, running out onto the road to observe the commotion. Artemis hauled back on the reins and Callisto slid to a skittering stop, her haunches drawn beneath her and the dust rising around them in a cloud.

"Help!" she shouted, her voice hoarse. "I am being pursued —they seek to force me to marry in Scotland."

Surrounding her, the men on the ground stared in surprise and then turned their gazes to her pursuers, who'd become wary, now that they were confronted by a gathering crowd. Artemis deemed it wise to dismount, and one of the men reached out for her bridle and asked, "What's to do, missy?"

"I am an heiress," she proclaimed loudly. "These—these Spanish men have stolen me from my uncle, and seek to wrest my Sheffield silver mines." Hopefully when Droughm appeared he would realize he was an uncle, because a husband would make no sense, given her story.

The crowd began to mutter, their natural antipathy toward the Spanish having been compounded by the idea of good Yorkshire silver falling into hostile hands. More bystanders flocked to join the group as word spread, and the hostile mob blocked any attempt at retreat by the Portuguese men.

"Your pardon," Marco offered stiffly, doffing his hat and speaking in very correct English, despite his disheveled appearance and the livid mark across his face. "We were mistaken, and will take our leave, now."

"Not so fast," proclaimed a man, angrily grasping at his reins. "Jem—send for the Sheriff." Needing no further urging, several men stepped forward to seize the Portuguese horses, as the crowd's mood turned ugly.

"I was forced to hit him with my crop," Artemis embellished in a loud voice. "He tried to have his way with me, so that I would be forced to marry him." This was not exactly an untruth, and so she felt justified in adding this particular fuel to the fire.

As she'd hoped, the revelation of virtue threatened by a foreign menace served to infuriate those assembled, and the foreigners were pulled off their horses and underwent some ill treatment until the local Sheriff waded into the fray, his huge hands pulling the attackers off the accused. "Here, now," he boomed. "What's to do?"

It had occurred to Artemis that Droughm should have arrived on the scene well before this, and she stifled a sudden fear that he'd been injured, or had been attacked, himself. "These good people have stopped an abduction," she explained to the beefy law man, in her best imitation of a helpless maiden. "I am an heiress—from Sheffield."

"She lies! We are not Spanish—we are Portuguese, and with our Ambassador's staff in London." Marco's tone was icy as he scornfully shook off the hands that held him. "We have diplomatic immunity, and your superiors will hear of this outrage."

The Sheriff considered him, apparently unmoved. "Do you have papers?"

As Marco put his hand inside his jacket to present his papers, Artemis cried out, "Do not believe them; they are Spaniards." She pointed to the nearest one. "This man helped murder all the little children at Guarda."

Howling with rage at such an accusation, the Portuguese man lunged toward Artemis and had to be physically restrained from doing violence to her. "Everyone to the station-house," the Sheriff decided. "We'll sort it out there."

"Shall I walk your horse, miss?" the bystander who'd taken hold of Callisto asked. "Give 'er a blow—she's a bit wet."

"Please," said Artemis.

"A fine horse," the Sheriff noted in a mild tone. "You rode her here from Sheffield?"

Hell and damnation, thought Artemis; *where is Droughm?* "Why yes—yes; I am traveling with my Uncle Pen."

"I see. And where is that gentleman?"

Artemis had the uneasy feeling the Sheriff was not buying what she was selling. "He should be along soon," she answered vaguely. "We became separated." She suddenly became alive to the problems that would arise if the local Sheriff discovered that her uncle was not her uncle, that she was underage with no guardian, and that the miscreants indeed had diplomatic immunity. *I could always tell him the truth,* she thought, *but unfortunately, it is more unbelievable than any tale I could come up with.*

Once in the station-house, the Sheriff indicated to his deputies that the men were to be taken to a holding cell whilst he questioned Artemis. "Have them relinquish all weapons," he directed.

"This is an outrage," countered Marco with barely-suppressed menace. "You cannot imprison us; we have immunity."

"It's for your own safety," the Sheriff explained in a mild tone. "We'll wait a bit, and let the crowd cool down."

He then escorted Artemis into his office and offered tea, which she accepted with appreciation, having had little to eat this long and eventful day. She noted that several deputies had filed into the cramped room to observe the proceedings, and concluded that—whilst runaway marriages were probably a commonplace—they usually didn't involve menacing foreigners and international diplomacy.

The Sheriff took up his pen. "Your name, miss?"

After a moment's reflection Artemis decided she could not lie to an officer of the law—or at least not without Droughm's say-so, and so she answered honestly. "Miss Artemis Merryfield."

One of the deputies leaning against the wall straightened up. "Are you related to Colonel Merryfield, miss?"

Artemis looked at him and smiled. "I am his daughter." Or at least, that is what the official papers would say. "Were you in the 3rd Division?"

"No, miss—the Light Cavalry. But I knew of the Colonel." For the benefit of the others, he pronounced, "A true war hero; England's finest."

Stricken, Artemis could only nod, thinking of the disgrace that hovered, like a dark cloud, over his memory. Pulling herself together, she offered, "You may not be aware that he died, earlier this year."

The man's face fell at having ineptly launched such a painful subject. "I'm that sorry, miss—it is England's loss."

Artemis turned to see that the Sheriff was watching her narrowly, and so she added, "Yes—my father's death is why I was shipped off to Sheffield."

At this point, there was a knock on the door, and another deputy poked his head in. "There's a man here says he's an Inspector from the Treasury—he's come after the foreigners, and would like a word with you."

With an air of satisfaction, the Sheriff leaned back in his chair, and crossed his arms. "By all means, let him in."

I hope Droughm knows what he is about, thought Artemis, struggling to present an impassive face; *I have the feeling the wretched Sheriff has already reconnoitered the territory, and is ready to roll us up, foot and guns.*

CHAPTER 30

*D*roughm entered, looking less like a drayman and more like a government official this time—complete to a new black felt hat. *The man needs a costumer*, thought Artemis, and looked for any clues as to how she was to behave.

"Miss Merryfield." He bowed to her as though they were already acquainted.

"Sir." She nodded, having no idea what his name should be.

"Sheriff," continued Droughm, offering his card. "I am Mr. Hardy, an Inspector for the Treasury Minister, and I understand you have seized a contingent of Portuguese men—"

"I believe they are Spaniards, Mr. Hardy," offered Artemis quickly. The crowd would never have turned so ugly, if they were merely Portuguese.

"Ah," said Droughm. "I stand corrected."

"I will see your identification, sir." As the Sheriff's sharp gaze rested on him, Droughm produced a badge, and after leaning forward to scrutinize it, the other man asked, "Tell me—how does Miss Merryfield's situation affect the Treasury?"

"Foreign interests seek to sabotage the production of silver coins originating from Sheffield," Droughm explained in his blunt manner. "It is a complicated scheme."

The Sheriff drew his shaggy brows together, considering. "And yet this affects Miss Merryfield in some way?"

There's a good question, thought Artemis, and waited to see how much Droughm would reveal.

Apparently, he'd decided that the truth—more or less—was called for. "Miss Merryfield's uncle is missing, and presumed dead. She would be the heiress, and whoever marries her has control of the silver mines."

"More correctly, my great-uncle is missing," interrupted Artemis. "Not to be confused with my Uncle Pen, with whom I am traveling."

Turning his attention to Artemis, the Sheriff contemplated her, his expression impassive. "And where is he—your Uncle Pen?"

"We were attacked," Artemis explained without giving specifics. "And I had to flee—as you saw."

It was just as well that Droughm interrupted at this point. "The Minister believes that the men you hold in custody are, in fact, responsible for the death of Miss Merryfield's great-uncle. If given time, I can produce evidence to this effect."

A master-stroke, thought Artemis in appreciation; *I am off the hook for mine uncle's murder, and these blackguards are now firmly on the selfsame hook—or at least for the time being—and at the same time they are removed from the arena of operations.*

"And if they indeed have immunity papers—what am I to do?" The Sheriff spread his hands, and Artemis had the fleeting impression the man was amused, for some reason.

"It would be a mistake to set them free," Droughm cautioned in a grave tone. "Under diplomatic protocols, if they are guilty of murder—or of crimes against the British Crown— they can be detained, and then forcibly deported. Back to Spain."

Oh-ho, thought Artemis, dropping her gaze to hide her satisfaction. *Another master stroke—although surely someone at some point would realize they were not Spaniards at all. There was no love lost between the Spanish and the Portuguese, and if they were indeed sent to Spain, some rough treatment would be meted out.*

She glanced under her lashes at the Sheriff to gauge whether he would cooperate with Droughm's proposal, and was a bit surprised to see his thoughtful gaze resting upon her. Quickly, she lowered her eyes again.

"I don't know about all this—I'm only the local Sheriff; how am I to sort out crimes against the Crown?"

But Droughm had a ready answer. "I suggest you hold them until representatives from London can be summoned to determine the extent of their involvement in the murder plot. It would only be a few days delay, at most."

Thinking it over, the big man nodded. "Certainly a reasonable request, and I have already witnessed their civil disturbance, and their attempt to adduct an English citizen."

Artemis nodded gravely, hoping that no one would actually try to verify that she was indeed an English citizen.

"Just so," said Droughm, and Artemis had the impression that it was now Droughm who was amused.

"Will you remain here, Mr. Hardy, to oversee the process?" the Sheriff asked politely.

"Unfortunately not. I must escort Miss Merryfield back to her uncle, and then continue my investigation; there are others to be apprehended."

"Where did you say her uncle was staying—was it Campine?"

The words hung in the air, and Artemis could feel the sudden shift in the atmosphere as she glanced at Droughm, wondering at it.

"No," Droughm replied easily. "We plan to rendezvous with him to the south of here—the next good-sized town to the south, whatever it is."

"Wreay, then."

Decisively, Droughm nodded his head. "Wreay it is, if anyone is asking."

The other man also nodded, and Artemis felt as though the two had come to some sort of unspoken understanding. The Sheriff then had a deputy fetch letter-writing materials so that Droughm could scratch out a note directed to the Treasury—although Artemis had no doubt it would find its way to the grey-eyed man, instead.

As Droughm wrote, she sat quietly, feeling the Sheriff's thoughtful gaze upon her, but kept her own gaze downcast for fear she would say the wrong thing, and disrupt this unlooked-for deliverance.

As they stepped from the small office and into the hallway, belligerent shouts could be heard from the holding cells located in the recesses of the building. Unable to contain herself, Artemis paused to call out with some heat, *"Bastardo!"*

As the howls of outrage intensified, Droughm took her arm. "Come along, Miss Merryfield."

They exited the station house without further incident, and then waited with the Sheriff on the steps for a few moments, whilst the horses were brought around. "Safe travels," the Sheriff offered.

"Thank you," said Droughm. "You will be hearing from me."

The two men shook hands, and then they mounted up, Artemis following Droughm as they trotted out of Carlisle, turning off the main road and onto a tangent by-way. Evening had fallen, and as she wasn't certain, she asked, "Where do we go now?"

"Scotland. I am taking you across the border, will you or nil you."

"I will." She was glad the moon was full—hopefully Droughm knew their route, as it seemed they were not going to travel up the Great North Road, but take an overland route, instead. She followed him closely, as they struck out toward some distant hills. They progressed at an easy canter for a time, then slowed down to walk through an area thick with brush. As it was growing cold, she tightened the hood around her face. "I am heartily sick of Lady Tallyer's stupid cloak."

He looked at her over his shoulder for a moment. "Your next will be sable."

She smiled at his broad back. "Excellent; I shall wear it when I wear my sapphires."

He made an appreciative sound in his throat, and she laughed. "Well, that turned out well enough—even though we didn't win the cat-and-mouse."

"Oh, yes we did. The enemy engaged with the wrong little mouse."

"It was a close-run thing," she admitted. "Callisto is a wonder." She patted the mare's neck in appreciation. Glancing at Droughm's back in a speculative manner she added, "And we were fortunate that the Sheriff was so cooperative."

As he seemed to be in a good mood, Droughm was willing to enlighten her. "During the war, he must have served in some capacity in Flanders, during the French occupation. He recognized me from when I was there, in another guise. I wondered at his complacence—we did not have the strongest story."

Artemis was fascinated by this glimpse into Droughm's doings during the war. "You do not recall meeting him? He is huge."

"No, I do not. But in my defense, there was a riot at the Clothworkers Guild Hall, and I had my hands full."

"Well, it was a fortunate coincidence that he recognized you. I don't think he is easily fooled."

"No," Droughm agreed. "He should be put to use—his talents are wasted, here."

Artemis suffered a small pang of jealousy that others were allowed into Droughm's mysterious world, whilst she was not. "I could be useful, too, you know."

"No," he said immediately. "My heart would fail."

Laughing, she followed him along the sandy path. "I imagine you were surprised to see me charge full-bore through the livery stable, like a winged Hussar."

"Words cannot convey my extreme surprise."

"Did Trajan manage to get a new shoe?"

"No; he was called away immediately on an emergency."

Smiling, she thought over the events of the past hour with some satisfaction, now that the danger was past. "Why couldn't you be yourself, when you approached the Sheriff? I should think an Earl would hold some sway."

But his answer was sobering. "We are not yet out of the woods—and everyone would remember an Earl. There will now be others to take up the pursuit."

Artemis contemplated her horse's ears, flicking back and forth, as Callisto listened to their voices. "Because the Portuguese are only doing the bidding of the French—I'd forgotten, in the heat of victory."

It was a daunting thought; hopefully they would have a few days rest, before having to take up the task of saving the world, again. She thought about the coming war, and the Sheriff, and how she was slated to be a Countess despite her utter ineligibility, and ventured, "I am not certain that I can stay home tending the gardens if you are out having adventures somewhere, Pen. I would be like a fish out of water, without you there to damn the proprieties."

"Then you will accompany me." Idly, he slashed at the brush with his crop, as they threaded through it.

"I should like that above all things," she confessed, relieved and rather surprised.

"And I would have no need to take a Spanish mistress." Teasing, he glanced back at her.

"None at all," she agreed happily.

He made an appreciative sound in his throat. "I almost feel guilty, Artemis; we need to find you a soft bed somewhere, but

I'll be damned if I allow you to sleep—not after watching you fly through the livery like Artemis, your namesake."

"I'll forgive you," she offered, laughing. "So you will be husband instead of uncle, tonight?"

"Definitely," he pronounced as he leaned back to gauge the stars. "I believe we are across the border."

CHAPTER 31

"We are in Scotland?" She could scarcely believe it—it seemed such an anticlimax, after all they'd been through.

He pulled back to ride beside her, since the sandy track had widened. "There should be a village called Dunby, up ahead six or seven miles—far enough within the border to make a search difficult. We need only to find some soul willing to marry us, and then we can retire someplace quiet."

"Can you stay quiet?" she teased. He was not one to suppress the extreme pleasure he took in the coupling.

He smiled, his teeth flashing in the moonlight. "Fie, Artemis; do you think I have no self-control?"

"No."

He conceded, "Perhaps not. Fortunately, we'll be married, and no longer subject to shame or scandal." They walked a few minutes in silence. " I'm afraid the ceremony will be cursory at best; when we are settled at Somerhurst, we'll throw a wedding breakfast to make up for this hole-in-corner affair."

But she assured him with all sincerity, "I would not change a single moment of this hole-in-corner affair for the finest wedding at St. George's, Pen. Truly."

Apparently, her words inspired a heart-felt accolade. "You are the only woman in the world for me—the silver mines be damned."

"No point in wasting the silver mines," she observed in a practical manner. "Someone's got to have them, and it may as well be us."

"I imagine they will end up belonging to the Crown," he warned.

But she was unsurprised. "That's a relief, actually—I didn't like Sheffield much, and I positively hated the mines." In the grip of elation, she spurred Callisto ahead of him. "Watch this—I think she has been trained to gavotte."

"Careful—the path is uneven."

"Hush, my Dutch Aunt," she laughed, trying to convince the mare to lift her legs in a prancing motion. Suddenly, she felt the horse drop, and saw the ground come up hard to meet her. Artemis had taken many a fall, but her reactions were slower after her long day, and she tumbled in an awkward heap whilst the mare scrambled to regain her feet. In a haze of pain, Artemis slowly pulled herself upright to sit on the path.

"Artemis," Droughm's voice was rough with concern as he crouched down beside her. "You are hurt?"

Indeed she was. Cradling her left arm, she fought nausea and began crying uncontrollably—she'd heard a sickening snap.

"Hush, my darling; you must tell me where it hurts."

"My arm is broken," she gasped, trying to take herself in hand. "I am so sorry."

"Allow me to feel, all right? I'll be careful." His fingers probed gently, and she flinched, then allowed him to continue, trying to stifle her sobs. "Anywhere else?"

Assessing, she answered in a halting voice, "No—no, I think it is only my arm."

He took her carefully into an embrace, his cheek atop her head. "All right then. We will find someone to set your arm."

She drew a shuddering breath. "We must be married, Pen—"

"First things first. Can you stand, do you think?"

With his assistance, she found that she could, but her knees were weak. "Is Callisto all right?"

He turned to observe the mare, who had taken the opportunity to graze on the undergrowth. "She looks to be sound. I'll tie her to Trajan, and you may sit before me—let me find something to serve as a mounting block."

Carefully, she steadied her left arm in her right whilst he gathered up the horses' reins, and they walked along the rough path for a short distance, until they came to an outcropping of shale. Murmuring a command to Trajan, Droughm helped her to climb up the outcropping, and then lifted her onto the gray's saddle. Mounting up behind her, he jarred her arm in the process, so that she bit her lip to contain a gasp of pain, and the tears started afresh. "Sorry, sweetheart; lean back against me, we'll go slowly."

"I am such an *idiot*, Pen; I am so sorry."

"No more, if you please. Are you comfortable?"

"Quite," she lied.

He pulled her gently against his chest as they walked forward, the steady grey stallion picking his way along the track in the moonlight, with Callisto following behind them. Artemis could feel Droughm lift his head to consider the stars, and she dared not think of what would be the result if they became lost here, at the end of beyond.

"We'll go slowly," he said by her ear. "Are you warm enough?"

"I am—truly." She was shivering with reaction, and ashamed of her weakness.

The journey seemed interminable, and although she was cushioned within Droughm's arms, every time Trajan took a hard step on the uneven ground, pain shot through her arm.

Castigating herself for her foolishness, Artemis could not find the wherewithal to be brave, and instead wept silently, hoping Droughm wouldn't notice.

"I love you," he whispered, his mouth near her ear. "We'll come about."

"I know it." She wiped her face with the back of her free hand, and resolved to stop weeping like a paltry civilian.

"Although now that you have a broken arm I may reconsider; shall I take an inventory? Have you ever broken anything else?"

She offered a watery smile. "No—nothing else. How about you?"

"My nose," he admitted. "And a finger or two, when I was a boy."

This piqued her interest. "Your nose? It doesn't look it."

"It is a bit crooked. Fortunately I am not a vain man."

"You won't wear your spectacles," she reminded him.

"If I begin wearing spectacles, everyone will assume I am your father."

"You are not old enough to be my father, Pen, and I am not the type of girl who cares two pins what anyone thinks—recall that I danced with you in front of everyone, when I didn't even know how to dance."

He kissed her temple. "I can still remember how it felt when I held you that night; I was completely undone."

She smiled at the memory, her misery forgotten for a moment. "I told you to hush."

"Indeed you did; it wasn't so long ago."

"No, but it seems so, doesn't it? So much has happened."

He rested his chin on her good shoulder for a moment. "The first of many dances."

She cautioned, "I need practice dancing, too."

"I was already planning to bring you to this, our wedding day. I went home from Ballantine House and told my valet that I'd met his new mistress."

Smiling, she replied, "And I went home to worry about how I was going to confess to the Four Terrible Things."

He chuckled and she chuckled, feeling much better. He was right; they would come about—only see how far they'd come, already. His arms tightened around her, and they continued their journey in silence, the horses' footsteps on the track the only muffled sound.

At long last, Artemis could see a light up ahead, and Droughm said, "That will be Dunby, with any luck. There's an Inn, I believe, but I'd rather stay somewhere less obvious. Let me make an inquiry—perhaps the place boasts a physician."

Droughm carefully slid off Trajan and then led the horse with Artemis atop him toward the nearest structure, a stone residence which displayed a sign indicating it was the Post. "Ho," he called. "Is there anyone about?" It was dark, but not yet late.

A light appeared near the door, and a man's voice could be heard. "Who's out?"

"I require medical assistance."

The door opened and a slight, bespectacled man appeared, holding a lantern aloft and squinting. "Medical assistance, you say?"

Droughm indicated Artemis. "My companion has broken her arm. Is there a physician nearby?"

The man came toward them and lifted the lantern aloft to survey Artemis. "Hallo," she greeted him in a friendly fashion. As they intended to marry, Droughm could pose as neither uncle nor husband, and their arrival together must seem strange at this time of night.

"Poor lass," the man said, shaking his head. "The doctor is from town, attending his niece's wedding." There was a pause, whilst Artemis digested this latest bit of bad news. Brightening, the man added, "It's naught but a bone, though—will the horse doctor do?"

"Let us visit the horse doctor, and solicit his opinion," said Droughm.

"Bones are bones," pronounced the other man. "Hold for a moment, and I'll fetch my coat."

CHAPTER 32

*T*he Postmaster identified himself as Mr. Rayburn, and escorted them down the road to the nearby home of Mr. MacLeod, the area's livestock doctor. As it turned out, MacLeod's quarters were located in a loft above a barn, and it was apparent to Artemis that both men were bachelors. "Roddie," shouted Rayburn from the barn floor, "Rouse yourself; we have visitors."

Once duly roused, the horse doctor proved to be a burly, taciturn man who did not seem at all surprised to find his evening interrupted by Rayburn's arrival with an English girl who required a bone to be set. "Let me have a look, then," he said, washing his hands at the pump.

Rayburn dusted off a joint stool and then went to fetch an additional lantern, as Artemis was invited to sit. "Off wi' yer sleeve," said MacLeod, brandishing a formidable pair of shears.

Droughm placed a cautionary hand on the man's arm. "Be careful; she is in a great deal of pain."

The doctor shot him a look under bushy brows, and nodded. "I will indeed, sir."

A novel experience for him, thought Artemis, hiding a smile. *I imagine his usual patients do not have Dutch Aunts.* As the man applied the shears, she assured him, "You may do your worst; this riding habit belongs actually belongs to another lady, and I am not fond of it."

Rayburn exchanged a glance with MacLeod, and Artemis belatedly realized how it sounded. She hastened to add, "I had to steal away in disguise, you see."

This explanation only inspired another space of surprised silence. "We are to be wed," Droughm revealed, "And were required to leave in haste."

"There were exigent circumstances, you see," Artemis explained.

Since the other men now looked embarrassed, Artemis quickly corrected, "Not *that* exigent circumstance, another one." *I should just stay quiet*, she decided; *before they throw Droughm in gaol.*

"I see," said the Postmaster, doing only a fair job of hiding his confusion. "My sincere best wishes, then."

"Ah," Artemis gasped as the doctor manipulated her arm— she was not paying attention, and had been taken by surprise.

MacLeod leaned back and grunted in sympathy. "Won't be a treat, lassy. I'll fetch the laudanum, t'ease ye summat."

Droughm stayed him with a hand on his shoulder. "No laudanum, I'm afraid. I cannot allow the possibility that she was not in her senses when we conduct the ceremony."

"No drugs," Artemis agreed firmly. "I had a bad experience, once."

Rayburn stared in surprise. "You mean to marry *tonight*?"

Artemis saw an opportunity to regain his good opinion, and offered with maidenly modesty, "I've been alone in the gentleman's company for most of the day, sir. We must wed immediately."

"Of course—of course," agreed the Postmaster hastily. "Quite right. If you will permit, I can conduct the ceremony and draw up the papers; I do, on occasion."

To Artemis, this seemed a godsend, but Droughm cautioned,

"You are certain the ceremony will be valid? It is very important that every legality be observed."

"As long as the lass is sixteen, and we have a witness, all's right and tight," explained Rayburn. "Roddie will bind the lass's arm, and then I will bind the two of you." He smiled his thin smile, pleased with this little joke.

"If I may, I'll be needin' a bit o' help with the arm," interrupted MacLeod, impatient with the talk of weddings. He nodded at Droughm. "Ye're the stronger—I'll show you what to do." He then cocked a brow at Artemis. "Best look away, lass."

Artemis looked away, and tried not to listen to the doctor's instructions as Droughm took a firm grip on her left hand and the Postmaster awkwardly patted her other. "There now, lass. It will all be over in a trice."

On the doctor's command, Droughm pulled hard and the doctor's strong hands manipulated her upper arm. Unable to control her reaction, Artemis cried out in agony as the Postmaster made inarticulate sounds of sympathy, and after a few long moments it was over.

Artemis gasped for breath as the doctor held her arm in a firm grip and gave instruction to Droughm as to how to tie the wooden splint in place. With cautious relief, she realized that her arm almost immediately felt much better.

The doctor nodded in approval after the splint was secured. "A braw lass, y'be. We'll be needin' a sling o' sorts—I'll fetch a length o' rope."

"Now, Roddie; we can't have the girl wearing a rope on her wedding day. Let me find something more suitable when I go to the Post to fetch my papers." Self-importantly, the Postmaster hurried away.

"Could you fetch a brush, also?" called Artemis after him.

Crouching before her stool, Droughm placed a gentle hand alongside her face, his gaze warm upon hers. "Are you ready for this? Tell me honestly."

"I am. I've been ready from the first, Pen."

They shared a moment of mutual awareness that the time was finally here, and then Droughm rose and spoke to MacLeod. "With your permission, I'll bed down the horses here."

The doctor nodded, and Droughm went over to settle them into the stalls. Rather than offer to assist, however, MacLeod turned on his stool to face Artemis, and said in a low voice, "We'll have some plain speaking, lass, if ye don't mind."

Surprised, Artemis nodded. "By all means."

MacLeod glanced toward Droughm, his expression intent. "Is this what ye wish? If ye'd rather nowt marry this man I'll see to it—ye can stay with m' mother and there'll be no questions asked."

Touched, Artemis assured him, "You are diligent to inquire, Mr. MacLeod, but I would ask for nothing more in this world than to marry him—truly."

The doctor studied her, his brows drawn together. "He's a fair bit older; mayhap he's turned yer head."

With a smile, Artemis replied, "I am not one to have my head turned, I assure you. We are very well-suited."

The man persisted, "He's Quality—and no mistakin.' What's t' emergency, if I may be askin'?"

Artemis shook her head slightly. "I'm afraid I am not at liberty to say. But we marry in all honor, I promise."

The man nodded, and they both watched Droughm brush the horses down for a moment, the rhythmic strokes the only sound in the quiet barn.

Artemis hoped the man was not embarrassed by her rebuff. "I do appreciate your concern, Mr. MacLeod. I have no one to stand in as a parent, unfortunately."

But her companion confessed in a gruff voice, "I feel an interest, I s'pose. My grand-dam had eyes t' color of yorn."

"Did she?" asked Artemis with interest. "I've never known of another."

"A Frenchwoman, she was; met my grandfather during the French and Indian War."

With mixed emotions, Artemis looked at the horse doctor for a long moment, wondering if perhaps they were distant kin. Softly she said, "I suppose we are lucky, your grand-dam and I." *It is true*, she realized; *I am lucky because Droughm thinks my eyes are beautiful, and couldn't care less where they came from.* She looked over at her bridegroom, who smiled at her from the other side of Trajan as he methodically applied the brush. *I believe the time has come to let go of all past grievances; it is time to begin the rest of my life.*

CHAPTER 33

*T*he Postmaster re-entered the barn, carrying a length of white lace and a bouquet of hand-picked lilacs. "The bride should have a bouquet," he offered, pleased with himself. "My sister tends my garden."

"Lilacs are my favorite." Artemis glanced at Droughm, thinking that if this was not a sign of Providence, she didn't know what was. "Thank you. And the lace?"

"One of the curtains," he confessed. "But it is the right length for a sling."

Laughing, Artemis asked, "Won't your sister be unhappy with me?"

"No, lass—she'll be that pleased when she hears of it."

The men carefully twisted the sling around her splint, and then tied the ends about her neck so that her arm was immobilized against her chest. With a flourish, Rayburn also produced a hair brush, as well as a bottle of Scotch whiskey. Artemis directed Droughm to unplait her hair so that she could brush it with her good hand, and as no one knew how to re-plait it, Artemis had to be content with having Droughm draw it back, and tie it with a piece of string.

"Are ye ready, lass?" asked the Postmaster, and Artemis

stood in her disheveled riding habit to take her place beside her bridegroom, who'd prepared for the ceremony by splashing his face with water from the pump. She was beginning to experience the ill effects of her tumble, and ached from head to foot, but she smiled at Droughm, and took his offered hand. As she had no hand to spare, the Postmaster tucked the flowers into her sling, and then opened his Book of Common Prayer.

Artemis stood beside Droughm and listened to him answer the timeless questions in a voice that was steady and sincere. *Another memory I will never forget as long as I live*, she thought, as the horses moved about and the subtle scent of leather and dust enveloped them. It was appropriate in a strange way; it felt as if there was no one else in the universe except for the four of them, standing in a remote barn in Scotland.

After she answered her own set of questions, they were duly declared Mr. and Mrs. Penderton Michael Fitzwilliam Vincent St. John, and Droughm presented her with the wedding band she had already worn, when the occasion warranted.

He bent to kiss her as the two bachelors applauded. "Whiskey all around," declared Rayburn, and as there were no glasses, they each took a turn drinking from the bottle, Artemis going first.

The Postmaster was cautious. "Have you had whiskey before, lass? You may not care for it."

"I'll be careful." She was unable to resist a glance at Droughm.

They all toasted the bonny, bonny bride, then Droughm, and then bonny Scotland and then the poor King. Thinking she'd best keep her head, Artemis was careful not to drink too much, although the whiskey was indeed very smooth, and her aches proceeded to fade.

"If you'd like, you may stay at my house tonight, and I can sleep here with Roddie," offered the Postmaster, his cheeks slightly pink.

This arrangement having been agreed to, Droughm thanked

the men and then guided Artemis out of the barn, his arm around her waist.

"It was a great go," Artemis declared to her new husband, as they walked in the cold night air back to the Post. "A wedding like no other."

Smiling, Droughm leaned his head back to contemplate the myriad stars overhead. "I cannot argue. How does your arm?"

"It does not bear thinking about, so I will not."

"My poor Artemis."

"Mrs. St. John, if you please." Despite everything, she was in the grip of a heady euphoria, and laughed up at him.

"The Countess of Droughm." He opened the gate for her with a small bow.

"I'm afraid that does not bear thinking about, either," she admitted.

Chuckling, he swung her up in his arms to carry her into the residence, taking care to avoid jarring her arm. He smelt of whiskey, and it occurred to her that he was rather well-to-go; he had imbibed a goodly portion of the bottle.

As he carried her into the building, she nuzzled her face in his neck, which inspired him to set her down and kiss her roughly, kicking the door shut behind him. Thinking to encourage such behavior, she caressed his head with her good hand, and opened her mouth to his, which in turn inspired him to pin her against the wall with a rather forceful movement, his hips pressed against hers.

"Ouch," she protested. In the heat of the moment, he'd forgotten about her arm.

"Sorry," he breathed, easing the pressure on her. "Let me get you situated, and then I will find some food and light a fire." Despite these good intentions, he did not move, but instead began kissing her neck, his hands caressing the contours of her breasts.

"I'm not very hungry," she confessed, and looked to the stairs. "Where do you suppose the bedroom is?"

"We cannot," he muttered into her throat, his hands busy. "We will re-break your arm."

She gently nipped at his ear and whispered, "You are adorable, when you are trying to be noble."

Cradling her head in his hands, he rested his forehead against hers, breathing heavily. "I don't feel very noble, just now, but I must defer to reality."

"Come upstairs, and we will discuss the matter."

"Artemis," he groaned. "I am too drunk to resist."

"I will be the dragon atop your St. George," she suggested. She'd heard the soldiers use the expression, and was given to understand that it referred to sexual congress where the female was atop the male.

He laughed into her ear. "Good God—I don't even want to know where you heard such a thing."

She reached to untuck his shirt as he leaned his head back and took a deep breath. "Reconcile yourself, my friend; we are going to do this—if we can just figure out how to remove the rest of this wretched riding habit."

This, however, was apparently not a problem; he bent his head to kiss her neck and placed both his hands at her neckline so as to forcefully rip the seam along the shoulder.

"That will do," she teased. "Come to bed, Pen—I feel a draft."

They progressed up the dark, narrow stairs, pausing on occasion to indulge in a heated embrace to such good effect that by the time they tumbled into the bed, Artemis had been divested of the remnants of her shredded habit, and Droughm was shirtless. As her attempt at playing the dragon did not go very well, Artemis ceded to Droughm's urgent need and shifted to lay beneath him, doing her best to shield her splint from his weight because it was clear he was past remembering such niceties. Lying between his arms, she kissed and caressed and accommodated him as best she could—it did seem easier, this time. And there was something so thrilling in the fact he could not seem to resist her—that she could so easily tempt him, despite her inexperience.

Afterward, she carefully sidled away from his weight, and tried to find a comfortable position for her aching body. He'd fallen asleep, and his deep breathing resonated in her ear; he was no doubt exhausted, and the combination of good Scotch whiskey and lovemaking had turned the trick. Idly, she wondered what she was going to wear on the morrow—as the saddlebags were still at the barn—but such practical considerations could not dampen her extreme happiness, as she awkwardly tried to pull the quilt over him so he wouldn't be cold during the night.

He'd spoken of that first night at the Ballantine ball, when they'd each recognized the need to form an alliance, so as to thwart those who schemed against the Crown. But neither one of them could have foreseen the alliance that was formed on a more elemental level—the alliance that had brought them to this night. *We looked upon each other, and were forever mated,* she thought; *it is truly enough to make one believe in Providence.*

He started suddenly, and raised his head.

"All is well, Pen; go to sleep," she whispered, and pulled his head to her breast.

CHAPTER 34

"*H*air of the dog," Artemis suggested. "I heartily recommend it."

"Instead, I think I need something to eat." Droughm lifted a tendril and smoothed it behind her ear as she leaned over him in the bed.

"And I need something to wear."

He ran his hand over her splint. "Did I mangle your arm last night?"

"Only slightly; nothing to signify."

He chuckled, and she chuckled, and soon they were both laughing as he pulled her carefully against him and caressed her back. His hair was disheveled, and his unkempt beard completely covered his chin and throat, but she thought he was the most beautiful thing she'd ever seen.

"My God; I am starving, and you are beautiful. It is a dilemma."

"Eat," she suggested. "You will need to muster your strength for more mangling."

"I'm afraid we cannot stay here more than a day." His voice held real regret as he pulled on a lock of hair so that she was compelled to bring her face to his. "I must go lay claim to your silver mines."

"I see how it is," she murmured into his throat. "Now that you've had your way with me."

He lay back to gaze at her, propping an arm behind his head. "More like you with me, from what I can recall—and that was excellent whisky, by the way; I must lay a case away at Somerhurst."

Tracing a finger on his chest, she asked, "Where exactly is Somerhurst?"

He laughed. "Derbyshire—near Lambton."

"Ah," she replied, having no clue.

But he was on to practical matters, planning the day. "I should reconnoiter a bit, to verify we haven't been followed. Then I'd like to find a doctor, so that you may be examined before we travel to Sheffield—we need to make certain the bone is well-set."

"Are we no longer in hiding?" It had occurred to her that the two men from last night had a very fine story to tell.

"No. Now that we are wed, there is little point in seizing you—or even me, for that matter."

Knitting her brow, she realized, "Wentworth is the heir to the mines, now, until we have children."

He nodded. "Wentworth is the heir, and he is safely stowed away."

The simple wedding ceremony in the barn had changed everything—small wonder that the enemy had tried so hard to prevent it. "So now we march into Sheffield and stake out our position, big as life?"

"A direct foray." Thinking, he pulled his fingers through her hair, and watched it fall back on his chest. "I am of two minds— some very unpleasant people will no doubt descend on Sheffield, but I do not want you out of my sight; I learned my lesson in Carlisle."

"I will stay with you, or know the reason why," she warned

in a tone that brooked no argument. She ran her hand across his chest, feeling the hair spring up beneath her palm.

"Breakfast can wait," he decided, and pulled her atop him.

After another session of lovemaking—this time sober—Artemis lay in the bed and watched Droughm pull on his boots as he prepared to go forth on his errands. "I imagine I'll be away for an hour or more, depending on the nearest doctor. You should be safe; I'll go by the barn to caution the two from last night, and no one else knows you are here—don't answer the door."

"I don't have any clothes," she pointed out. "I couldn't even if I wanted to."

He leaned over her to kiss her, briefly. "I'll bring the saddlebags with me on my return. See if you can sleep, in the meantime—you should rest."

"I will; I need to muster my strength for when you've mustered your strength."

"Artemis," he protested, unable to suppress a smile. "You are mighty demanding—think of your poor arm."

"I am a very hardy Countess, and I am dedicated to my one task."

"Rest," he advised, as he left to search down the stairs for his coat, "and then we shall see."

Artemis did indeed doze for a time—she normally slept on her stomach, and so it was difficult to find a comfortable position, with the splint in the way—and then she lay abed, watching the shadows on the walls until she was heartily bored, and decided to go investigate the pantry. Wrapping the quilt around her, she padded in her bare feet to the kitchen, where she stood on tiptoe to examine the offerings in the cupboards.

"Well, glory be to God."

Startled, Artemis turned to confront a plump, middle-aged woman, standing at the back door and gazing at her in astonishment. The woman untied her straw bonnet, and approached to place it on the kitchen table. "Pray tell me your name, lass, and how you brought about this particular miracle."

Smiling, Artemis shook her head. "I'm afraid you misconstrue the situation, ma'am; your brother is not at home, but he very kindly allowed my husband and me to stay here last night."

The woman threw back her head and laughed heartily. "Ah well—it was too much to be hoped for, a pretty little thing like you. I am Mrs. Tittle, and I'll be hearin' how you came to be here, and how my curtain came to be wrapped 'round your neck."

Taking a seat, Artemis wound her feet around the kitchen stool and described last night's wedding whilst the woman bustled about the kitchen, preparing a meal of stew and bread. "It was such a stroke of luck—Mr. MacLeod set my arm, and then your brother married us, all in a trice."

"And what brought you to such straits, if I may be askin'?" Mrs. Tittle chopped the carrots, and allowed her thoughtful gaze to rest upon Artemis for a moment.

"I am not of age in England." This much was apparent, and so Artemis thought it did no harm to disclose.

Slicing her turnips with quick precision, the woman cocked an eyebrow at her. "And your parents did not approve, I s'pose?"

"My parents are no longer alive, and my guardianship is unclear—the Court of Chancery is sorting it out, and it is all very complicated."

The woman shook her head philosophically, gathering up the vegetables and dumping them into the cast-iron pot. "And he couldn't wait, I suppose. Ah, youth."

Artemis hid a smile. "He was indeed eager to be wed."

With both hands, Mrs. Tittle lifted the heavy pot by the handle, and then hung it on the hook in the hearth. "What's done is done. Where is this husband of yorn?"

"He is searching for a physician, your own being out of

town. He wants to be certain my arm is well-set—no offense to Mr. MacLeod—"

The other made a derisive sound. "Of course he wants to be certain; by the looks of ye, he managed to do his duty last night despite that contraption on your arm."

Artemis' eyes twinkled. "Yes, ma'am. It was our wedding night, and so it seemed important to make the effort."

"For the men folk, it always is." The woman cast a shrewd look at her guest. "If ye don't mind plain speakin', now's the time to ask any questions ye may have, being as yer mam is no longer with us. I been married over twenty years to Tittle, and there's little enough that I don't know about men and their doings." Taking a handful of flour from the bin, she spread it on the table. "Best that ye know what to expect."

Not one to shrink, Artemis found she did indeed have several questions, and so passed a very interesting hour discussing her difficulties with Mrs. Tittle whilst the bread baked and the stew simmered.

"'Twill ease, over time," the woman assured her. "And a bit o' warm oil will help—that, and havin' the boy slow down, and pay some attention to what is best pleasin' to you."

"He does try to please me," Artemis defended, embarrassed. "But then I worry that I am not pleasing him, and it builds from there."

Wiping her hands on her apron, Mrs. Tittle addressed her with a twinkle. "Here's the secret, lass, and hark it; it takes remarkably little to please a man—only good food, and a willingness in the bedroom."

Artemis had to laugh. "You sound remarkably like a cook I know."

"'Tis the simple truth," the other insisted, giving the pot a stir. "And it's all you'll need to know—he'll be happy as long as you lay yerself down, and there is no need to fret over it."

Satisfied with the stew, the woman glanced up at her. "I'll brew up a pot of tea while you dress yerself; my brother will show up soon for his supper, and he'll swallow his tongue if yer here with nary a stitch on."

"I'm afraid I have no clothes at hand," Artemis confessed. At the other's astonishment, she added, "It's rather a long story."

"It is apparent to me," the other pronounced with a great deal of emphasis, "that neither one of you young 'uns is possessed of a lick of sense."

"You may have the right of it," Artemis agreed in a meek tone.

CHAPTER 35

*I*n short order, Artemis bathed with Mrs. Tittle's assistance, and then was bundled in Mr. Rayburn's robe to sit on a chair before the kitchen fire so that her hair could dry.

"I'm not one to be criticizin' others," Mrs. Tittle noted as she brushed out Artemis' hair, "but I think that new husband of yorn could do a sight better than to leave ye alone in a strange house and with no clothes."

"Yes, ma'am." Having her hair brushed reminded her of Katy, and Artemis wondered where she was, and how she did, and whether Lady Stanhope had ever returned or had simply fled, once the plot to ruin Artemis had run aground. *A good riddance,* she thought sleepily, her head pulled back with the force of the brushstrokes. *A thoroughly detestable woman.*

The door opened, and Rayburn poked his head in, tentatively. "I smell stew; may I come in?"

"You may, Gerry," said his sister. "The bride had need of your robe, is all."

"Mrs. St. John." He nodded in greeting, his cheeks pink. "How does your arm?"

"Very well," said Artemis, who privately wished everyone

would quit asking. "Thank you again for offering us your home; you are very kind."

"Ach—it was only fitting, after all. Your husband should be along soon—me and Robbie sent him to fetch Dr. McIntosh." He sat at the stool, and his sister began serving his supper.

"A fine doctor." Mrs. Tittle brought a steaming bowl to Artemis by the fire, and carefully balanced it in her lap for her, so that she could eat with the one hand. "He's from over the way, in Annan."

"I'm afraid I know little of the local geography," Artemis confessed, her bare feet propped up on the hearth as she tasted the stew. "Or any geography, for that matter. I've followed the drum all my life."

"Is that so?" Mrs. Tittle straightened up, very much surprised. "And you so well-mannered."

"Oh, I can be as rowdy as any half-pay officer," Artemis assured her.

"Did you see any action?" asked Rayburn, and Artemis had the impression he was a bit wistful—too old to fight, he had probably followed the war avidly, and from a distance.

"I was with the Third Division, and we saw a great deal of action." In the event they were unaware, she concluded with spirit, "We were the best."

"The 'Fightin' Third,' under Picton," Rayburn agreed with a show of keen interest. "You were in the thick of it, then. Did you travel with the artillery?"

"Infantry," she declared, her mouth full. "The First and Foremost, for King and Country."

He was all admiration, as he crumbled the bread into his bowl of stew. "Then you have some tales to tell; you should write your memoirs—or at least the dates and the battles, so that you do not forget."

Artemis was amused by the very idea. "I can't imagine I will ever forget anything—and I never learned how to write, anyway."

"Didn't ye?" exclaimed Mrs. Tittle in surprise. "Fancy that."

But her brother found this particular fact only one more piece to the puzzle that was Mr. and Mrs. St. John, and he regarded Artemis covertly from under his brows whilst he continued with his meal. "If I may ask, how did you meet your husband, lass?"

Hiding a smile, Artemis said only, "We met at a dance, in London."

"Isn't that nice?" Mrs. Tittle folded her hands under her apron. "It just goes to show—you never know."

"Never," agreed Artemis.

"Have you known him long?" Rayburn ventured, still probing.

"Gerry," his sister admonished with a small frown. "You mustn't pry."

"We danced, and then he came to call the next morning," Artemis reminisced, gauging the dryness of her hair with her fingertips. "It is rather a simple story." She thought it would be best to omit large and horrifying parts of it.

"Where will you settle?" asked Mrs. Tittle as she rose to gather up Artemis' bowl. "Is he training in a trade?" Apparently, she'd resisted her own impulse to pry as long as she was able.

"His family is from—" She frowned, trying to remember the name Droughm had given her. "Lamb—something."

"He's not one to have a trade," commented Rayburn dryly.

Misconstruing the remark, Mrs. Tittle turned to admonish him. "Now, Gerry; he has a wife, now, and responsibilities, and I am sure he'll do right by her." With a significant look, she sent him a clear message not to dishearten the new bride.

Suppressing a smile, Rayburn mopped up the remains of his bowl with a crust of bread, and made no further comment.

"Ye're welcome to stay as long as you like, until you find your feet," Mrs. Tittle assured Artemis. "It's no easy thing, just startin' out."

Any response was interrupted when, with a preemptory knock at the door, Droughm entered, carrying the saddlebags over his shoulder and bringing another gentleman with him. Scrambling to her feet in surprise, Mrs. Tittle rendered a respectful curtsey to the newcomers. "Dr. McIntosh; Sir."

With a twinkle, Artemis called out from her perch by the fire, "Allow me to introduce my husband, Mrs. Tittle; Mr. St. John."

After an astonished moment, the woman pulled herself together and bobbed another curtsey, slanting Artemis a sidelong look. "I am that pleased to make your acquaintance, sir."

"Indeed," said Droughm abruptly. "What is that I smell?"

Whilst Droughm sat at the kitchen table and put away two bowls of the stew in short order, the doctor sat next to Artemis to remove her splint, and examine her arm. "Sound," he pronounced. "Roddie knows his work." He regarded her with his brows drawn together as he immobilized the arm in the splint once again. "It must hurt—I'll give ye a vial of laudanum for the pain. Take a few drops at a time; it should ease in a few days."

"No thank you," said Artemis firmly. "I'll manage without."

The doctor shook his head. "Take it at least to sleep, then. You can't be sleepin' well."

"That is true, I am not getting much sleep."

She heard Mrs. Tittle chuckle, as Droughm walked over to accept the vial and secure it in the saddlebags without comment. "Is there more bread?" he asked.

"I'll make scones," offered Mrs. Tittle, and happily rose to commence this task.

Addressing Rayburn, the doctor remarked, "I told Mr. St. John that the nearest place to secure a carriage is Gretna, or even Carlisle—he'll not want what old McElroy has to offer."

"There's the right of it," agreed Rayburn. "Break-downs, mostly."

"Do we need a carriage?" asked Artemis in some dismay. She could hardly imagine a worse fate—carriages were for paltry civilians.

Droughm met her eyes to convey a message that she would not prevail on this particular subject. "I'm afraid we've little choice; I'll not risk further injury."

At Artemis' unhappy silence, the doctor added his own caution. "Come now, lass; ye can't risk another fall."

"Oh—did ye fall from a horse?" Mrs. Tittle clucked her tongue from her station at the counter. "Big, nasty things, horses."

Nonplussed, Artemis could make no reply.

"Gretna, then," said Droughm, pulling his map from an inside coat pocket. "We'd like to avoid Carlisle." The men gathered to pore over Droughm's map, and then discussed the most expedient route from Gretna to Sheffield in the common language of men everywhere.

Whilst they were thus occupied, Artemis signaled to Mrs. Tittle to bring over the saddlebags. "I have a dress packed away, and my hair is nearly dry. Could you help me, ma'am? I suppose we'll have to cut off the sleeve."

"A wee dolly," declared Mrs. Tittle, removing Artemis' rag doll from the bag, and holding it fondly in her hands. "Brings me back, it does—my Janey had one similar." She tucked the doll in Artemis' sling, and then pulled the day dress from the depths of the leather bag to shake it out. "Sech fine quality; I'd hate to ruin it—we can pin the sleeve on the inside, mayhap."

"It is not one of my favorites," Artemis assured her. "Feel free to slice it up." Lady Tallyer had indeed been generous in her choice—the dress was a very pretty green. On the other hand, the neckline was modestly high.

"'Twill need a pressin'," noted Mrs. Tittle. "Let me heat up the iron."

Artemis turned to watch the fire, as the aroma of scones filled the kitchen and the men debated the merits of various posting houses. Out of habit, she pressed her doll's midsection to feel the edges of the minting plates within, and then stilled her hands, suddenly wide awake. Glancing quickly under the doll's threadbare dress, she verified what she'd suspected—the abdomen had been re-stitched. Over the course of the war, she'd learned to sew a fine seam, and she could feel that the repair in the doll's midsection was not her handiwork.

Careful to give no indication of her discovery, she thought about it for a moment and then came to the only logical conclusion—Droughm. She'd wondered why he'd not brought the saddlebags in with them last night, and this must have been the reason; he had planned to use some of his time away from her today to open the doll and then re-stitch it—although his stitching was not as fine. The plates were still within, though; she could feel them. Perhaps he wished to see them for himself, but it seemed strange that he hadn't simply asked her—unless he didn't quite trust her, at least not yet. The thought was a bit disturbing, and she tucked the doll back into her sling, wishing she hadn't made the discovery.

CHAPTER 36

"I am *begging* you, Pen. If you have the slightest shred of compassion—"

Twisting his mouth, Droughm lifted his gaze to the horizon. "What am I to do with you?"

Artemis had engaged in a war of wills with him ever since he'd hired the carriage in Gretna to make the three-day journey to Sheffield. To add insult to injury, he did not join her within, but rode Trajan alongside, speaking to her from time to time in an attempt to alleviate her misery. Artemis found it hideously stultifying, and implored him to allow her to ride beside him instead. "Callisto is very biddable—I can easily manage her with one hand." Gauging his expression, she could see that he was weakening, and redoubled her efforts. "*Please*, Pen."

"Perhaps for a time—but I'll have your promise that you'll stay on the road, and maintain an easy pace."

"I will, I *promise*."

As they stopped to saddle Callisto, Artemis hoped that he wouldn't notice that she wasn't wearing suitable riding dress and use this excuse to change his mind, but he made no comment as he helped her mount up. Once they were underway, she lifted her face to the breeze and sighed. "Much better—thank you, thank you."

"You do not make a good invalid," he noted dryly.

"I've never been an invalid before, and I do not recommend it. If anyone else inquires after my arm, I am tempted to smack them with my splint." Holding the reins in her teeth for a moment, she tugged on her skirt in an attempt to arrange it over the sidesaddle, but then gave up, aware her ankles must be showing. "I suppose I'm lucky it's only my left hand, and not my right that is out of commission."

"Speak for yourself—I am very fond of that hand."

Laughing, she cast him a playful glance. Last night at the posting inn, she'd introduced Mrs. Tittle's suggestion about warm oil, and the result was so satisfactory that the experience had been eagerly repeated, with Artemis having to caution him to stay quiet on more than one occasion.

They rode in companionable silence for a time, Artemis carefully keeping a sedate pace so that he wouldn't change his mind. It was so enjoyable—the weather was mild, and the open countryside pleasing to look upon. However, there was a subject that had to be broached, and Artemis decided there was no point in shrinking from it. With a small smile, she glanced over to him. "I must ask you a question, and I am not certain how to go about it."

He raised his brows. "This sounds ominous."

"It's about my doll, you see."

He did not pretend to misunderstand, and immediately sobered. "Forgive me, Artemis; I did not think you'd notice."

"I noticed," she replied, and waited.

"I wanted to see the plates—to examine them. I think I was half-hoping that you were mistaken."

"And was I?"

"No."

Nodding, she looked ahead again and decided this made sense—she'd not been able to imagine any other reason to do what he'd done. If he wished to take them away from her, after all, he would have simply done so—and she would have willingly relinquished them.

He shifted in his saddle to face her. "I am sorry; I should have asked your permission."

To show she was not offended, she asked, "Do you wish to leave them in the doll, then?"

He ducked his head for a moment, considering. "It seems as good a hiding place as any."

Having to address the subject brought back all her misery over the Colonel's involvement, and her buoyant mood evaporated. "I wonder—I wonder if perhaps they should be destroyed." She lowered her gaze to contemplate her hand on the reins. "I was so tempted, and more than once."

"I'm afraid we must deliver them to the Treasury Inspectors." Reaching over, he touched her knee. "I will see to it that any necessary revelations are discreetly handled—you have my promise on it."

She teetered on the edge of asking if he could use his rank and standing to sweep the matter away, but then drew back. He might do it for her, but she shouldn't ask it of him—shouldn't put it between them. Things were going so well, they were so happy together—and the lovemaking last night had ascended to a higher, more blissful level. She must not allow him an opening to think her a spoilt child, unable to face the consequences of her actions.

Watching her, he said gently, "When this matter is resolved, we will take a wedding trip. Where should you like to go?"

All too willing to change the subject, she thought about it. "I don't know—I've never had a choice, before."

"Anywhere you'd like," he reiterated, flicking his crop on his boot.

"I suppose we cannot go to the Continent, if Napoleon is planning a re-conquest," she reminded him.

"An excellent point. Anywhere else, then."

"If there is a re-conquest, though, I imagine you will be busy." She eyed him.

"Artemis," he said. "Choose."

But she had literally no ideas, having only a hazy knowledge of world geography outside the theatre of the last war. "What was Algiers like?"

"Abductions, pirates and slavers," he replied succinctly. "A miserable cess-pit."

Then he must have been there in connection with his work, as she'd already guessed. She decided that she didn't have any preferences—as long as she was with him, and didn't have to ride in a carriage. "What would *you* choose, Pen? Have you a favorite?"

He thought about it, gazing out over the countryside. "Can you swim?"

"No," she admitted with regret. "Where would we swim?"

"The West Indies—Tortola, perhaps. I have a friend who has a plantation there, and I could teach you to swim."

"That sounds wonderful; you are a very useful sort of husband," she noted with approval.

"Save for those times when I am defiling your doll." His worried gaze skewed over to hers, contrite. "I feel terribly, Artemis—I must remember that it is now the two of us, and that I should consult with you—and perhaps even defer—on occasion. I'm afraid I am not used to thinking in such terms."

"And no blame to you; you've done as you wish for a long time, and with good reason. Truly Pen—I've not an ounce of insubordination in me, and I will gladly follow orders." She felt badly for him—he was remorseful about the doll, and she had the feeling this was unfamiliar territory for him.

"If you do not mind, this may be a good opportunity to tell me of your uncle."

For a brief instant, she harbored the uncharitable thought that he'd deliberately manipulated her to open her budget on the subject, but then decided it didn't matter—she would willingly tell him the whole without prompting. "Where should I start?"

"You were to bring him the plates—start at the beginning, if you do not mind. We've plenty of time."

It occurred to her that she would be allowed to ride for as long as the story continued, and so she was determined to spin it out. "Uncle Thaddeus was a miser—and that was the least of his sins, I assure you. He begrudged even a peat fire, and would rather lose a finger than light a candle."

"Good God; the man was as rich as Croesus," Droughm declared. "Unfathomable."

"Tight as a drum," she confirmed, and considered for the first time how much better it all would have gone, if the Colonel had inherited just a modicum of this trait. "And he was much struck when he met me at the posting inn—where he haggled about the fare, and caused a *horrific* scene. He said I was his *'pretty chicken'*."

"Did he? You did say he was fond of *Macbeth*."

She marshaled her thoughts for a moment, in an attempt to explain the inexplicable. "Yes; he recited lines from it constantly, and there was a good reason—at least in his mind. He told me that Macbeth was based on a real-life thane—one who'd been awarded his estates after conquering a Viking."

Droughm frowned, skeptical. "Is this true? I'd never heard such a thing."

Artemis shrugged, then winced as her shoulder reminded her she should not. "I have no idea, but I would put no faith in anything he said—he had determined that the real Macbeth was his ancestor, you see, and for reasons that are unclear, he was also very fond of the conquered Vikings—there was that famous battle near Sheffield, with the Vikings involved."

Droughm considered this. "The Battle of Constantine, I believe—perhaps a thousand years ago."

"That is the one," Artemis exclaimed, happy that he knew of it. "It was all melded together in his mind—he was Viking and Macbeth, all at the same time. He was quite mad."

Frowning, Droughm wondered aloud, "And yet the Treasury contracted with a madman to mine silver for the Crown?"

"Oh, he was very shrewd in his own way, and he did not invite others into his strange world. He explained it all to me, however, because I was his shield-maiden."

Her companion stared at her. "And what is a shield-maiden?"

"I had no idea—not at first, but it seemed apparent he was very pleased that I'd arrived, and treated me with some kindness. He even allowed a coal fire in my chamber when I complained of the cold, because a shield-maiden should have a fire, if she liked." Artemis made a wry mouth. "I was to find out why this was, later."

"One cannot help but pity him," Droughm observed. "But at least he did not mistreat you."

She lifted a brow at him. "Oh-ho, you have yet to hear my tale, Pen. He was very eager to show me the mines—very proud of them, and I'll admit that it was interesting to see how it was all done. Such hard work, and the men deep in the tunnels for hours and hours at a time. He took me aside and explained— very seriously—that the god—Thor, I think it was—required a sacrifice to make up for the taking of the silver from the mountain."

Droughm made a sound of incredulity. "It is nothing short of bizarre—did you tell no one?"

With a grimace, she confessed, "I thought he was mad, of course—but I felt a bit sorry for him, and remember, I had literally nowhere else to go; I didn't even know the Stanhopes existed—not that they turned out to be much help. And mine uncle did treat me well, as though I was his pet; it was a balm to my soul—I was still so sad. I wasn't yet ready to strike out on my own."

"My poor Artemis."

The warmth of sympathy in his voice triggered a need to speak of that which she had heretofore simply endured, and she said quietly, "Everything I had ever known died the day the Colonel died. I remember standing at his funeral; watching the splendid ceremony and hearing the guns salute, but it was no comfort to me. We had only each other, you see." She paused, dangerously close to tears.

With a hand on her reins, Droughm pulled the horses up, then placed a gentle hand on her knee, whilst she recovered her equilibrium. "Surely, *someone* should have taken you in; a man of his standing—"

She mustered a wan smile. "Oh, I had several offers of marriage; from his officers, of course, and from a very kind Chaplain from Shropshire. But I thought I should do as he'd asked me, and travel to Sheffield to deliver the plates. At the time, I would not have made a very joyful bride."

"It was Providence," he insisted. "You came here to make me a joyful bridegroom, instead."

"Yes." Her gaze searched his face. "It *was* Providence—that's what I think, too."

But he had waxed romantic as long as he was able, and now sought to return to her story. "So; you did not deliver the plates."

"No, I did not. Once I took my uncle's measure, I thought it foolhardy—and I'd begun to suspect—" here, she paused. "I'd begun to suspect it was all not on the up-and-up, and I worried that the Colonel's part would be exposed. So I told mine uncle that the packet had been stolen—I feigned ignorance as to what was inside. Mine uncle and the Constable were very unhappy with this turn of events, and it motivated mine uncle's next move; he decided that Thor must be angry, and therefore the god must be placated."

With growing incredulity, Droughm exclaimed, "You don't mean—"

"Definitely; it was time to *screw his courage to the sticking point*, and present a sacrifice, with no further ado."

CHAPTER 37

"*T*ell me," Droughm insisted, and she could see that he was controlling his temper only with an effort.

"To appease Thor, the shield-maiden would have to be sacrificed."

"Good *God*," exclaimed Droughm angrily, and Trajan started at the vehemence in his tone.

"Not exactly," Artemis teased. "I can't imagine such a thing would be considered proper Church doctrine."

"He tried to kill you?"

"Well, yes—but it was a paltry attempt, Pen. He'd no experience in taking prisoners, or with conducting executions; that much was evident." Artemis found she was rather enjoying herself.

"Artemis," he prompted ominously. "Tell me."

"It was on a Sunday, and he professed a desire to show me the mines when there was no one working. I was willing—there was precious little to do there, I must say—and he showed me where the silver ore was most plentiful, and explained at length the importance of appeasing the gods—I believe he very much regretted having to sacrifice me, and was trying to talk himself into it, now that I look back upon it."

"The *damnable* bastard. Go on."

"He told me that he had something important to show me, and led me into the recesses of the oldest tunnel—he held a lantern, as it was quite dark." She reflected for a moment. "There is something very unnatural about being underground with no light, with the sounds echoing off the hewn rock; it makes one long to turn and scramble for the sunlight."

"I can well imagine. Continue, if you please."

"We traveled through the tunnel; it was very narrow because it was an ancient one—he told me even the Romans had mined in the hills, there—and led me into a chamber where he'd constructed an altar of some sort—a lot of kindling, and some artifacts scattered about."

"An *altar*?"

"Well, remember that he was mad, Pen. He kept a robe hanging on a hat rack and put it on—along with a crown—with a great deal of ceremony. I suggested we return to where it was warmer—it felt as though there was snow on the ground, Pen, it was that cold—but he explained that he would start a fire on the altar and that I—as the shield-maiden—I was to throw myself on the fire, once he'd got it started."

There was a stunned silence. "He honestly thought you'd volunteer?"

"Well, yes—he saw it as an honor, of sorts. I refused, but then he hoisted his Brown Bess and held me at musket-point—the sacrifice was slated to occur, will I or nil I."

"So you shot him?"

Artemis shook her head. "Not immediately—I made an attempt to dissuade him, but I'm afraid the die was cast when he lit a lucifer from the lantern and then threw it on the kindling. There was nothing for it; I drew my pistol and fired. He was that surprised, Pen, and went down like a straw-target."

Droughm considered this recital for a moment in the silence it deserved. "Good God," he said again.

"The place was filling with smoke, so I had to scramble out. There was some blasting equipment in a crate near the entry, so I scattered some blasting caps and black powder—I learned about explosives from the men in artillery."

Droughm made a strangled sound.

"What?" she defended herself, warming to the subject and rather proud of herself, despite everything. "It worked wonderfully—I waited outside, and once the fire reached the blasting caps you could feel the ground tremble with the explosion. Fortunately, it had started raining—it was always raining in that miserable place—and so the smoke did not attract attention."

"What was your purpose when you engineered the cave-in —did you seek to conceal what had happened?"

The question was posited in a mild tone, but she could sense his sharp interest, and looked at him in surprise. "Well, yes. I suppose I thought to conceal everything; I truly, truly did not want to have to explain the circumstances—can you imagine?" She thought about it, and then admitted, "I can see now—with the benefit of hindsight—that it may not have been the best thing to do, but during the war, no one ever worried about a potential murder investigation. And I did not know that I was the heiress, then, or how it might look."

He nodded. "I see. And so now—once the rubble is cleared away—they will discover a burnt corpse. Will it be clear that he was shot, do you suppose?"

"There'll be a hole between his eyes," she confessed.

"Remind me not to vex you," he remarked absently. "So, once they clear it out, a murder investigation will open, and—as his heiress and companion—you will be the prime suspect."

"Yes—but that is my last dreaded confession; I swear it, Pen."

He flicked his crop against his boot. "Who knows you went there with him that day?"

"No one," she assured him. "It was Sunday; the servants

had the day off and—since he planned to murder me—he didn't want anyone to know of the excursion."

"Good; we will place the blame on someone already dead. Your Uncle Stanhope, perhaps, would make a likely candidate."

"A falling-out among thieves," she agreed with relief. "An excellent strategy."

"You have no idea what happened, and did not see him that morning."

"Yes, sir," she teased.

"And you didn't have a pistol."

"Oh," she said doubtfully. "The servants know I had a pistol. We would set up target practice by hanging pie tins from the trees."

Droughm was mightily amused. "Did you indeed?"

"There was precious little to do there, Pen; you would have gone mad."

"Not as mad as Uncle Thaddeus, I hope."

She quirked her mouth. "Wait until you get there, Pen; you can easily see how such a thing could happen—all that rain, and grim mining. I hope Somerhurst is not like that."

He gave a bark of laughter. "Not even remotely."

"Well, that's a relief." Recalled to her situation, she added belatedly, "Not that I would not gladly live wherever you were, Pen—truly."

"At present, my main concern is that you do not end up living in Newgate."

Surmising that Newgate was a prison, she agreed with some fervor, "I would appreciate it."

They rode through the rolling countryside for another quarter hour until Droughm decided that her reprieve was over. "It is time you returned to the carriage, if you please."

"Perhaps you should join me." She slanted him a look.

"I'll ride alongside; I'm afraid I can't abide riding in a carriage any more that you can."

As he hadn't understood her innuendo, she made it plainer.

"I could see to it that the ride was abidable." In a meaningful manner, she arched a brow.

Grinning, he regarded her. "Artemis; you shock me."

"I am desperate for company," she confessed. "And willing to make any sacrifice."

Regretfully, he advised, "As much as I think it a fine idea, it is too difficult to do the deed in a carriage on a rough road—trust me on this."

Laughing, she nonetheless remembered the soldier's euphemism for a different kind of sexual service. "I could play the piper, instead."

At this reference, her husband professed his profound shock that she knew about such things and chided, "You were allowed too much fraternization with common soldiers, Artemis."

"I imagine that is true," she agreed with mock-contrition, watching him from the corner of her eye.

"You must be careful to watch your words—not with me, of course, but when you are amongst others."

"Yes, Pen," she agreed meekly.

Eying her, he continued, "Because soldier's cant is very vulgar, and you may not even be aware of the meaning of what you say."

"Oh, I am well-aware of the meaning," she said mildly.

He whistled for the coach to pull up, and considered for a moment. "I suppose I can tie up Trajan and join you—just this once."

Having entertained no doubt that he would do so, she hid a smile as he lifted her from her horse. "I may require some instruction," she confessed, and his only response was to make a strangled sound.

CHAPTER 38

$\mathcal{T}$he local posting house at Sheffield was the Green Goose Inn, and as the carriage clattered to a halt in the yard, Artemis couldn't help but think of the last time she'd been here, in this very yard. After her uncle disappeared, Lord and Lady Stanhope had come to fetch her, striking quickly to take custody of the presumed heiress, and returning to London with all speed so as to apply to the Court of Chancery for her guardianship.

At the time, Artemis made no demur to this unlooked-for godsend, due to the plates hidden in her doll, and her uncle's corpse hidden in the mines. Vaguely, she held an idea of striking out on her own—if matters did not work out—but at the time, she was grateful for any form of escape, particularly since she'd no money, and she shrank from the idea of having to steal some—although needs must, when the devil drives.

And now—through an extraordinary turn of events—she'd returned in triumph with a very useful husband who would—hopefully—resolve all problems. *If anyone had told me what was to happen within the next month's time,* she thought with some bemusement, *I would have thought them stark, raving mad.*

Droughm dismounted from Trajan to give instruction to the

post-boys, and then came around to help her step down from the carriage. With a great deal of relief, Artemis discreetly stretched her back, grateful that the miserable journey had finally come to an end. "I hope they've water on the boil, Pen; I'm longing for a bath."

She turned to accompany him to the Inn's entry doors, but her husband took her elbow to retain her for a moment. Meeting her eyes, he said, "I'm afraid I must give you unwelcome news. Artemis."

Surprised, she asked, "What is it?" Hopefully, it was not going to involve any more time in the wretched carriage.

"I have arranged for Lady Tallyer to stay here with us, for those times when I must necessarily leave you alone."

Artemis stared at him in astonished dismay, and, reading her aright, he continued in a low tone, "She works with me—as you know—and understands the enemy, and what is at stake. There is no better candidate to attend to you—to keep you safe."

"I am well-able to keep myself safe," she retorted.

"Do you think you can you be civil?"

He asked it in an even tone, and she was immediately contrite; she shouldn't allow him to think her a sulker—she detested sulkers.

"I can. I am sorry, Pen."

He tucked her good hand into his arm and escorted her across the yard. "Try to avoid shooting her between the eyes."

No, I cannot engage in a battle with her, thought Artemis as they entered the common room. *There is no point, and it would only make me appear petty. Besides, I've carried off the palm, and therefore I can afford to be gracious.*

This time, Droughm used his title, and the Innkeeper could not scramble fast enough to appoint servants to attend to them, and to prepare the best suite of rooms.

They were asked to wait in the private parlor, and as she

accepted the man's bowing offer of tea and cakes, it was suddenly brought home to Artemis that there was nothing for it; she'd now stepped into Droughm's world and the old Artemis—the one who was a simple soldier—would have to be let go. Instead of speaking her mind and living by her wits, she was now slated to become a completely different person—one with whom she was not yet familiar. *I must become accustomed,* she thought, struggling to maintain her poise as she sipped her tea. *He is who he is, and as I intend to be with him, I must learn how to go on; we are not bivouacking across the countryside anymore, and I must give him no opportunity to harbor regrets—I've brought enough problems as it is.*

Her husband's voice interrupted her thoughts, as he set down his own tea cup. "I may have to leave you to do a bit of reconnoitering, I'm afraid. Will you be comfortable, here?"

"Of course, Pen," she replied, and hoped that it was true.

Fortunately, a welcome surprise was in store; upon entering their suite of rooms, Artemis was treated to the unexpected sight of Katy, who rose to bob a curtsey—hiding a grin with only limited success—and saying "My lady," in a self-conscious voice.

Artemis did not hesitate to fold the former 'tweenie in a one-armed embrace. "Katy; thank you for saving me from the odious Torville."

"It was Cook who twigged it," said Katy modestly. "I only helped."

Artemis released the girl. "Whatever became of everyone? Did Lady Stanhope ever return to the house?"

"I don't know, miss—I mean, my lady." With a self-conscious glance at Droughm, she added, "Me and grand-dad went straightaway to Somerhurst."

Artemis turned to smile warmly at Droughm. "I'm so glad, Katy. And Cook?"

Droughm responded, "She is our new pastry cook."

Paying no mind to Katy, Artemis walked to him and clasped

her good arm around her husband's neck. "Thank you," she said quietly into his neck cloth.

"It was I who owed the thanks." He returned her embrace and kissed her brow. "Now, if you would like to rest for a bit, I will make my presence known to the local authorities. We will reconvene for dinner."

Rather surprised by this abrupt announcement, Artemis nodded, remembering her new role and fighting the urge to ask to go with him; they hadn't parted in a over a week, and it seemed very strange to watch the door close behind him.

On the other hand, the sooner he could lay claim to the mines and thwart the enemy, the sooner they could put all this behind them and settle-in at Somerhurst, wherever it was. Hopefully, it wouldn't be as daunting as it sounded.

"Oh, miss," exclaimed Katy. "Your poor arm."

Artemis shook herself out of her abstraction. "I'd rather have a hundred broken arms than marry Torville, Katy. What's happened to him, do you know?" Artemis was curious, herself —she was vaguely aware that he would not be thrown in prison like a common criminal, but *surely* he'd be punished for his actions.

Katy began to unpack the saddlebags, shaking out the much-creased nightdress with a dubious eye. "I don't know, miss; we were escorted back to the house to fetch our things the next day, and Torville was not there. No one was."

"A good riddance; if fate is kind, I'll never see him again." Not to mention that she couldn't vouch for her temper, if such an event were to occur.

Katy shook out the remaining contents of the saddlebags onto the chair. "You've no other dress, my lady?"

"I'm afraid not—and I am heartily sick of this one." Artemis sighed with resignation. "I suppose we'll have to do some shopping."

But Katy was enthusiastic. "May we, miss? His lordship must give you a lot of pin money."

Artemis blinked, as this was another topic she hadn't seen fit to even think about. "We haven't discussed it—not as yet."

But Katy was happily calculating the purchases that would be needed. "Day dresses—and under-things, and stockings. Another nightdress—something pretty, this time. Another cloak —a bit heavier. Will ye—*you* be attending parties, d'you think?"

"I doubt it." With a small sigh, Artemis sank into the other chair and tucked-up one leg beneath her. "Mine uncle is missing, after all, and I am burdened with this wretched splint."

The maid made a sympathetic sound. "Does it hurt very much?"

"Not so much, anymore—only when I accidentally jar it. The doctor gave me a dose of laudanum, but I haven't used it—I hated being drugged." She made a face, and Katy nodded in remembered sympathy.

At this juncture, a knock sounded at the door, and Katy opened it to reveal Lady Tallyer, who approached Artemis to sink into a deep curtesy. "Lady Droughm."

With a smile, Artemis held out her hand to lift the other woman up. "I am Artemis, and never do that again, if you please."

The lady rose and removed her gloves, smiling as Katy took them. "Then I am Carena. I was sorry to hear of your injury— beyond vexing."

Artemis paused, and managed to keep her countenance only with an effort. *I've been an idiot*, she realized grimly. Whilst Droughm could have arranged for Lady Tallyer—and Katy—to meet up with them in Sheffield before they'd left on the elopement, he wouldn't have been able to inform Lady Tallyer of Artemis's injury unless he'd told her since Dunby. So; the lady and Droughm had been in very recent communication, and this fact had been kept from Artemis. *Something is afoot,* she realized, suddenly on high alert; *and I had best discover whatever-it-is.*

With this in mind, she indicated the poor heap of belongings that Katy was now clearing off the other chair so that Lady Tallyer could sit. "Would you mind helping me shop for clothing tomorrow, Carena? Your pretty green dress is the only one I have, and I'm afraid your riding habit was ruined." Charitably, she did not mention that Droughm had been so eager to take her to bed that he'd ripped it to pieces.

Lady Tallyer sank gracefully into the other chair and asked Katy to ring for tea. "With pleasure; although it will be nothing like London, I'm afraid."

"I cannot hope to match your taste," Artemis admitted generously. "And so I imagine that whatever Sheffield has to offer will be more than adequate."

But the lady would not allow Artemis to defer in such a way, and leaned forward to say with all sincerity, "Nevertheless, we must make try to make appropriate choices; you must dress in accordance with your new station, after all."

Artemis nodded, thinking with reluctant admiration that there were all variety of subtle insults contained in that last remark.

Oblivious to all undercurrents, Katy offered brightly, "Grand-dad and Cook are to be married, miss."

Artemis turned to her with genuine pleasure. "Are they? How wonderful—did he succumb to her brisket?" To include her in the conversation, Artemis explained to Lady Tallyer, "The cook and the butler, at Stanhope House."

With a smile, Katy shook her head, "I don't know anything about briskets, but Grand-dad thought it best, if they were going to be spending their evenings at cribbage together. He didn't want the Somerhurst folk to think the worst."

Artemis offered, "I am so happy for Cook—she's carried a torch for him, I think."

"Truly?" asked Katy, who paused in her sorting-out with a dubious expression. "She was always so unkind to him."

"Sometimes, that is the first clue," Lady Tallyer observed with a smile. "It showed she was not indifferent."

"But love shouldn't be unkind, my lady," Katy insisted. "It should be kind, and giving."

"I suppose it should, but sometimes it does take a very strange turn." Artemis couldn't help but think of Lady Macbeth, from her mad uncle's favorite play. "Lady Stanhope is a good example."

But Katy disagreed with a little shake of her head. "I think that one's never loved anyone, miss—I mean, my lady." With a fond smile, she carried Artemis's rag doll across the room, and propped her up on the window bench.

"Sometimes, love is very hard to fathom," agreed Lady Tallyer absently, her sharp gaze following Katy's actions.

Ah; another subtle insult, thought Artemis; *and I believe it was not Droughm who re-stitched my doll, after all—something is indeed afoot.* Whilst Katy poured out the tea, she smiled brightly, and resolved to stay sharp.

CHAPTER 39

o Artemis' relief, Lady Tallyer did not remain with them once Droughm returned in the evening, but instead took her leave, citing a desire to rest after the day's long journey. Rather than make an appearance downstairs, Artemis and Droughm decided to have their dinner served in their rooms, and sat before the fire to partake. Now that she was on the alert, Artemis covertly scrutinized her husband for signs of distraction, but could find none. Instead, he seemed well-content.

"Do you note I haven't asked after your arm?" He looked over at her with a gleam. "I have no desire to be knocked about with your splint."

"I appreciate it," she replied gravely. "Truly, I do."

"I met your Constable—"

"Not 'my' Constable Pen; for heaven's sake."

"No, and a good thing. He's a rum touch—and insolent, which is not a good sign."

She teased, "Insolent? That is unthinkable, my lord. Will you throw him in the stocks?"

But he tilted his head, unwilling to joke about it. "Not a laughing matter, I'm afraid. The High Constable of Sheffield should not be insolent to an Earl, and I can only surmise it is because he believes he holds the whip hand over me."

Sobering, she guessed, "Because he's part of the counterfeiting scheme, and knows about Wentworth's murder."

"No doubt. I will visit the mines tomorrow morning—I have some questions for the Overseer that I'd like to have answered without the Constable listening in—and I'd like you to be there with me, concerned, and very much not guilty."

Artemis readily agreed, relieved that the shopping expedition would be postponed—she'd a million times rather be with Droughm—and resigned herself to yet another day spent in Lady Tallyer's borrowed dress. "Do you think I can manage it? I am not very good at pretending things."

"You'll have to, I'm afraid—even if they find your uncle's corpse, and parade it before you."

Nodding, she decided there was no time like the present to discuss her latest concerns—she could not imagine stewing in silence, afraid to broach the subject; it was not in her nature.

Lifting her face, she met his eyes. "When I first met you, Pen, I thought you were not one for roundaboutation, but now I wonder if perhaps that is not so."

She noted that the expression in the green eyes was suddenly wary—not a good sign. As he made no reply, she explained, "I would not make a very good spy—I am much better suited for direct action. Can you not tell me what is planned?"

Considering, he regarded her for a long moment, his dark brows drawn together. "What has made you doubt me? You should not believe everything Carena tells you."

"I won't, then," said Artemis, watching him. "What, in particular, am I to disbelieve?"

He ducked his chin to his chest, debating.

Artemis decided to help him out. "I think it was she who re-stitched my doll, and I suppose that means your people have been shadowing us the whole time."

Holding her gaze with his own, he admitted slowly, "I told them you had the plates. I had to, Artemis; it is too important to take any chances. They are concerned—understandably— that you are working against our interests, and that I am too besotted to take a clear view of the situation."

Surprised, she thought this over. "You *are* besotted," she acknowledged fairly.

With an abrupt movement, he stood and pulled her upright against him in a tight embrace, his cheek against her temple. Alarmed, she felt the tension in his arms and waited for whatever was to come, as she shifted her splint out of harm's way.

In an intense tone, he spoke from over her head, "They do not know you as I do, and it does not look well. Your uncle—"

"Great-uncle," she corrected him.

"Your great-uncle—"

"Who is truly not my great-uncle at all," she reminded him anxiously, speaking into his neck cloth.

"Artemis, have done. You killed him shortly after you arrived with the plates; you will inherit the mines; your father was French, and Colonel Merryfield has some complicity in the scheme. They cannot look upon all these factors without grave unease."

Acknowledging the truth of this, she leaned back to look up at him. "But they *cannot* believe you married a murderess, and a traitor. They cannot think you such a fool, Pen, besotted or not."

His arms tightened fiercely around her. "I shouldn't even be telling you this."

She said slowly, "So it is cat-and-mouse, but between us?"

Making a sound of frustration, he took a long breath. "I suppose that is one way of looking at it."

Pressing her lips together, she asked in a level tone, "Are we truly married?"

With an impatient gesture he ran his hand down her back.

"Good God, Artemis—of course we are truly married; how can you doubt it?"

This was a relief; it had occurred to her that perhaps everything that had happened since the Ballantine House ball had been a sham. She thought over their situation, and asked, "Can you simply tell me the truth—what is planned? I could do whatever is necessary to clear my name—without letting on I am aware you told me."

"I cannot," he said quietly. There was a thread of grim emotion underlying the words.

"Because some things are more important than the truth." She quoted what he had told her, back in London. He couldn't take the chance—even if it was a very small chance—that she was indeed a murderess and a traitor. "I understand, Pen—truly I do."

"It is a damnable situation."

"We'll come about." She laid her cheek on his shirt-front. "But I am glad you told me."

She felt his chest rise and fall, and then he suddenly said, "I may decide it is best to take you away from here—away from England. Be aware that this is a contingency, and do not mention it to anyone, even to Katy."

"My poor Pen," she sympathized with some bemusement. "You must be worried indeed, if you think we may have to cut and run."

"I'll not take any chances. Circumstances—circumstances may conspire against you."

"I'm not involved in any of this—except for killing my wretched uncle, of course. I swear it, Pen."

"I know. But I must at least give the appearance that I am cognizant of the possibility." He rubbed his cheek against her hair. "Forgive me."

"I can hold no grudge—no one is to blame in this, except the Colonel." She could not keep the edge of bitterness from her voice.

"He loved you, Artemis."

"Not as much as you do; you who are willing to live abroad as an outlaw." She reached to kiss his chin. "Go ahead with your shadowy plans—I will trust you, come what may."

He said nothing for a moment, bringing his cheek down to rest against hers, and she had the impression he was debating whether to tell her something.

"What is it?" she whispered. Whatever it was, it was not good.

He drew back from whatever he was on the verge of saying, and said instead, "I love you. You know that—even when I tease you."

"I do," she assured him. "I think it is most evident when we do tease each other."

He spoke with quiet intensity into her ear. "Damn Merryfield, and damn your uncle."

"No argument here. Shall we go to bed?"

Amused, he drew back and looked at her. "Now?"

"Yes, now. I think I am longing for reassurance."

"Then by all means." He steered her toward the bedchamber, where there was no further discussion of treason, or flight.

Afterward, she lay in his arms, relieved by his attentions, even though she wasn't certain why she felt relieved. That he was in contact with his people shouldn't surprise her; it was only the fact that she'd been kept unaware that bothered her. But there was nothing for it—he couldn't take the chance that she was conspiring to bring about the ruination of England. It was understandable, even as it was vexing. And she mustn't sulk about it, or provoke a quarrel—Lady Tallyer was hovering in the wings, no doubt hoping for a misstep on her part. Despite the woman's determined civility that day, Artemis had seen her gaze rest on the bed for a long, ambivalent moment.

CHAPTER 40

$\mathcal{T}$he next day looked to rain, and so Droughm asked to use the Inn's chaise carriage for their trip to the mines. He overrode Artemis's protests: "Since you cannot use both hands, I would not be easy having you ride horseback over the terrain. You've been in that area, and you know how rough it is."

As though I've not seen more rough terrain than smooth, Artemis thought with an inward scowl. But she was trying to find her role as his wife, now that their lives had swung so drastically, and so she did not challenge his stricture. There would be plenty of time for riding—there was precious little to do here, after all.

With a servant accompanying them on horseback, they made their way in the one-horse chaise to the outskirts of the city proper, and then climbed the wooded hill that led to the famous Merryfield mines. A gatekeeper guarded the entrance to the mining area, and at Droughm's signal, the gate was levered up, and the man tugged his cap respectfully as they passed through. They tied their horse at the tie-rail, and then approached the small wooden building that served as the office for the mining operations. Upon being informed that the

Overseer was in the Old Mine, a worker went ahead to fetch him, and they climbed the tiered path, the servant hoisting an umbrella over them against the rain.

On the hill, there were two parallel shafts, the Old Mine—which was not in use, as it had been mined out centuries ago—and the main mine shaft, which continued to produce a rich vein of silver. Droughm greeted the Overseer, and introduced Artemis as they stood in the tunnel's entrance, out of the rain. Artemis had forgotten the distinctive, musty smell of the place, and resisted an urge to stand out in the rain, rather than within the hewn-rock walls.

"My lady," the man said, removing his cap with a grave expression. "As I told your husband yesterday, we believe that there was a fire somewhere in the Old Mine—there are new smoke stains on the rock entry—and a fire doesn't just start in the tunnels without a lantern or such. I'm afraid you may need to brace yourself for bad news, as it seems likely it was old Mr. Merryfield—he did like to come to the mines, when there was no one about."

"It is indeed grave news, but not unexpected, as we have not heard from him in so long," Droughm agreed. "We can only presume he met with an unfortunate accident."

"When will you know for certain?" asked Artemis, doing her best to appear concerned.

"We're taking the rock-fill out now, and depending on how large a blockage we're dealing with, it may take a few more days." The Overseer bowed his head in commiseration. "I'm sorry, my lady—I fear we'll have bad news."

"It is fitting, in a way," Artemis offered. "He did love the mines."

"That he did," agreed the man, and gave her a glance that made her think that perhaps he was not unaware of her uncle's strange obsession.

"What is the status of the Treasury's contract for the new schilling?" asked Droughm.

The Overseer made a gesture toward the men who were pushing the wheeled hand-carts, piled high with rock. "As far as I know, there has been no change in the plans, and as soon as we remove the rock-fill, we'll be back at it. The Constable—Mr. Easterby—said we were to keep going, despite Mr. Merryfield's disappearance, and that the men would be paid, same as before."

Droughm continued to speak to the Overseer, asking questions about the mining process and the refinery, whilst Artemis listened with only half an ear, having already heard much of it from her late, unlamented uncle. The rain had dissipated, and as she gazed out over the wooded valley, she noted that there was a horseman coming in through the gate, seated upon a very fine chestnut horse. As he came closer, she recognized the Constable himself—this was of interest, as Droughm had been hoping to avoid the man, but it appeared he was well-informed as to their activities.

The Constable dismounted to tether his horse, and climbed the path toward them, greeting Droughm with a nod and taking Artemis' hand with a dry smile. "We meet again." He was an in his forties, compact and lean with a perpetually somber expression. "You've been informed that we believe your uncle was buried when the Old Mine collapsed?"

Artemis gently extricated her hand from his. "Yes; I suppose the news is not unexpected—his disappearance does not bode well."

"And you hardly knew him, of course."

The observation was rather abrupt, and Artemis had the brief impression that the man was hoping to disconcert her. "I'd never met him before my visit here; that is true."

Almost before she'd finished the sentence, Droughm interjected, "Hardly a surprise, after all; Lady Droughm has followed the drum all her life." He placed a slight emphasis on her title, and Artemis belatedly realized the other had not used it—although she was not one to notice.

But the other man needed no further prodding, and said to her, "It is a shame your first visit to England has been marred by this tragedy, my lady." There was the barest undercurrent of irony to the statement.

She nodded, not certain what the appropriate response should be in light of the very evident fact that she'd not hesitated to marry in the midst of the aforementioned tragedy.

Droughm clasped his hands behind his back. "We should discuss the transfer of the mines to my control." The comment seemed deliberately provocative, and Artemis awaited the other man's reaction, hiding her trepidation.

But she needn't have worried, because the Constable offered no protest. "I can't imagine the transition need be delayed for any reason; it seems a forgone conclusion that Mr. Merryfield is no longer with us."

"I will need to examine the accounts, of course."

"Certainly," the man agreed without hesitation, and indicated the Overseer with a nod of his head. "As soon as we make the recovery of Mr. Merryfield's remains."

He excused himself, and walked away to confer with the Overseer, and it occurred to Artemis that she'd rather not be present in the event her uncle's burnt corpse was indeed recovered. She glanced at Droughm. "Do you know as much as you need to know, Pen?"

"Nowhere near." He watched the Constable walk away, a frown between his brows.

"Not very friendly," she observed, watching her husband. "He doesn't seem to like us aristocrats much."

Drawn from his abstraction, he smiled—as she'd intended—and tucked her good arm into his so as to support her down the tiered path. "Come along; this particular aristocrat is sharp-set."

She teased, "Are you hungry again already? If you were in the army, you'd be the bane of the Brigade Cook, and have to be put on the rationing list."

"I don't know as I would make a very good soldier."

"No." Fondly, she squeezed his arm. "I imagine you are better suited for whatever it is that you do; you're not one who would follow orders without question."

"But you are?" He allowed his skepticism to show.

"I am," she affirmed, a bit stung. "I am a good soldier, Pen."

"And now you're a good Countess." With a gleam, he glanced down at her, and she could see that he was referring to her one task.

She laughed, and he paused for a moment on the dirt step, his thoughtful gaze on the tie-rail. "Have a look at the Constable's horse."

Following his gaze, she noted, "I already have; he's a fine animal."

"Very fine, indeed." He helped her down the step, and continued on toward the chaise.

Hearing his tone, Artemis made a wry mouth. "I think the Constable is one of those men who hides a self-indulgent streak —you know the sort." She'd known a few herself; many of them were the Colonel's gambling cronies.

"I can only agree; the pearl in his tiepin is also very high quality. And if what we believe is correct, he is indulging himself with purloined silver, courtesy of the British Treasury."

Artemis admitted, "I wouldn't know a fine pearl from a paste one."

"Pearls are paltry," Droughm pronounced, as he helped her into the chaise. He then came around to climb up beside her, and to gather up the reins. "You are never to wear pearls, and that's an order." He nodded to the servant to release the horse.

"What pearls?" she teased. "I've yet to see my sapphires. Perhaps it was all a hum, to lure me into marrying you."

"Too late," he said bluntly. "You are well and thoroughly ruined."

"Then I certainly deserve my sapphires," she insisted.

But instead of replying with a ribald comment, he stilled for a moment, his gaze on his hands. "You deserve far better from me, Artemis."

The light mood had vanished without explanation, and the atmosphere between them was suddenly thick with undercurrents she did not understand. Nonplussed, she tucked her good hand into his arm, and tried to tease him out of his sudden seriousness. "I do? Your best seemed more than adequate, last night."

With an abrupt gesture, he slapped the horse with the reins. "*Damn* your uncle—he did you no favors."

"No argument here, Pen; and we can only hope he's been thoroughly damned—although he's just the sort of person who would haunt me, like Banquo's ghost."

"*They say blood will have blood*," quoted Droughm.

"I certainly hope not," Artemis replied.

CHAPTER 41

*A*fter luncheon, Artemis felt she could no longer postpone the shopping expedition if she wished to remain clad, and so she sent Katy to inquire as to Lady Tallyer's availability. "Unless you'd like to accompany me," she asked Droughm with little hope—she gauged that he was not the sort of man to endure such an activity.

He was reading the newspaper, and held it aside for a moment. "I will regretfully decline; surprise me."

Self-consciously, she ventured, "How does one go about paying for things?"

The level look he gave her from over the top of his spectacles held a trace of amusement. "You explain that you are the Countess of Droughm, and that you are staying here at the Green Goose Inn. You will encounter no difficulties."

"I see." It was quite the turnabout; oftentimes the Colonel's credit was disdained.

"Carena will help you go on."

This was the wrong thing to say to Artemis, but she was not going to make a childish retort, and so she nodded without comment. Unexpectedly, however, her husband rose and crossed the room to take her into his arms. "Now, that was clumsy of me. You will do whatever you think right; you have better instincts than anyone I know."

Mollified, she admitted, "Lady Tallyer does have excellent taste."

Placing a finger under her chin, he lifted her face to kiss her gently. "I intend to take an inventory at the refinery, and I will look forward to seeing your new finery this evening."

She mustered a smile, ashamed that she'd allowed him to see her pique. "Yes, sir."

Although Artemis didn't look forward to spending the afternoon with Lady Tallyer, she was nevertheless determined to be civil, and so with Katy and another servant in tow, the two women strolled into the first dress shop that presented itself. To alleviate the awkwardness, Artemis cast about for a topic of conversation. "Is Tremaine here in Sheffield, also?" Tremaine was the unknown donor of the whiskey flask the morning this mad adventure began—when he and Lady Tallyer had posed as Artemis and Droughm, to confuse the enemy.

"I shouldn't be surprised," Lady Tallyer said, as she paused to finger a length of light weight wool. "Let me ask if the proprietress has anything ready-made."

So, thought Artemis, *we are not going to refer to the mysterious business she shares with Droughm; fair enough—I won't refer to what he shares with me on a nightly basis.*

The shopkeeper was only too willing to take them into the back room so as to display her collection of dresses already made up, which would need only limited tailoring. "There's a blue," said Lady Tallyer, indicating a deep blue frock. "Best seize it."

Artemis concurred, and then added a black, thinking that no one could fault her, after the grim news at the mine today. As she stood before the cheval mirror, waiting to be pinned, she asked, "How long do you suppose we'll stay in Sheffield?"

"I've no clue," the woman responded, watching with an unreadable expression as the modiste clucked her tongue, trying to decide the most expedient way to accommodate the splint. "I suppose it depends upon how long it takes to resolve the situation with the mines."

Artemis raised her good arm as directed, and then stood still as the seam was pinned. "I hope it's not very long; there is so little to do, here."

"Droughm controls the mines," the other woman reminded her. "I imagine he will have to travel here often, even after the current problem is resolved."

As Droughm was the last person to tolerate such a task—not to mention he'd already indicated that they were to leave this place as soon as possible—Artemis could only surmise that her companion was trying to paint a grim picture of an oft-absent husband. Hoping to avoid any further petty sniping, she changed the subject. "Where do you hail from, Carena?"

With a small smile, the other answered, "Shanghai."

Surprised, Artemis returned her smile. "That is quite a distance."

"My parents were missionaries," the other explained briefly. "Perhaps we should go to the glover's before we head back; your poor gloves are threadbare."

So; any discussion about the lady's life history was apparently to be turned aside, also, and Artemis resigned herself to long silences; making polite conversation would be heavy going, and in truth, she was not interested enough to make the effort.

They consigned their packages to the servant for delivery to the Inn, and then resumed their shopping journey along the boardwalk, looking in the windows and stopping to enter an occasional shop, if the wares were of interest. They passed a small hotel that fronted the boardwalk, and the gilt lettering on the windows advertised a tea room. Lady Tallyer paused, and began pulling off her gloves in anticipation. "Perfect; we should take tea."

There seemed little point in demurring to this plan, and they were soon seated at a small table, with Artemis reconciled to another tedious half-hour of Lady Tallyer's company. Since Droughm was scouting-out the refinery, she needed to fill her time anyway, and the other woman had been kind enough to take her out on this expedition—certainly Artemis could be civil, if she put her mind to it.

After they'd placed an order, Artemis looked around the hotel's interior in a desultory fashion, thinking that it was perhaps not Sheffield's finest establishment. She'd been seated facing the narrow hallway that led into the kitchens, and so she saw a maid emerge from the servant's stairwell, just a few feet away. That the girl was unhappy seemed evident, and she whirled to speak intently to the companion who'd also emerged from the stairwell, and who followed her out toward the kitchen door. In an instant, Artemis recognized Droughm. Even before she'd processed the implications of this, she realized—with a jolt of abject shock—that the maid who'd briefly appeared was Miss Valdez, the enemy spy.

The two paused with the kitchen door ajar, engaged in a low-voiced, intense conversation; Droughm's hands on the girl's elbows. She made a gesture that cautioned him to be quiet, and then they both exited out the door, his hand on her back.

If someone had asked Artemis what her reaction would be, were she to witness such a hypothetical scene, she would have assured them that Miss Valdez would immediately be on the receiving end of yet another take-down. The reality, however, was completely different; Artemis could hardly breathe through the frozen feeling in her breast, and she had to stifle an intense desire to flee—to hide away somewhere, and curl up in utter misery.

Turning to Lady Tallyer, she said though stiff lips, "I am afraid I feel ill. I must return to the Inn."

"What?" The lady lifted her brows in surprise. "Now?"

"Katy can take me—I am so sorry; please continue on without me."

But the lady insisted on escorting her outside, making excuses to the proprietor as she did so, and signaling for Katy. Supported by her maid, Artemis stood on the wooden boardwalk as the carriage came around, and began to regain her equilibrium. *Steady*—she thought, *steady. The reason you are shocked to the core is because it makes no sense at all.*

"Do you need to sit, miss? You're that pale."

"No, Katy—I'll lie down once we're back at the Inn." But her mind—functioning once again—could not stay silent. *He is consorting with the enemy—what to do? Had they shared a room?* She made an involuntarily sound in her throat that prompted Katy to put an arm under hers for support. *It cannot be true. They were arguing—or not exactly arguing.* She furrowed her brow, trying to remember. *He was trying to persuade her of something— and she was unhappy. But they were definitely not angry with each other—he kept touching her, and she did not recoil. Why was Miss Valdez not in prison? Because she had some hold over Droughm?*

Grasping at this faint hope with eagerness, she thought it over. *Miss Valdez was in disguise, and they were meeting secretly— perhaps without the knowledge of his people; thank heaven she'd said nothing of it to Lady Tallyer. Was he still protecting Wentworth? Perhaps*—here she paused, struck—*perhaps Miss Valdez truly was pregnant with Wentworth's child.*

Analyzing this possible explanation, she had to reluctantly discard it. Droughm was not behaving as though the woman was pregnant with his great-nephew's child; there was an intimacy between them—an intenseness.

Taking a deep breath, she climbed into the carriage, and sat quietly during the journey back to the Inn. *There is nothing for it,* she thought, staring out the window with unseeing eyes. *I must speak to him about it, and hear whatever answers he will give me.*

CHAPTER 42

*O*nce back at the Green Goose, the Innkeeper informed Artemis that Lord Droughm had sent a message saying he'd been detained, and would instead return home after dinner. Unsurprised, she immediately decided she needed to evade Lady Tallyer, and so announced, "I am going to lie down for a bit."

"Allow me to keep you company."

"I'd rather be alone," Artemis replied with a touch of annoyance. She was well-sick of Lady Tallyer, and wondered what on earth Droughm had ever seen in her in the first place—aside from the obvious fact that she was sophisticated, and beautiful, and closer to his own age. In her current frame of mind, she could not trust herself not to push the woman down the stairs.

"I'm afraid we have little choice," the lady said in a low voice. "I am entrusted with your safety; I will read in a corner, if that is agreeable."

I imagine it was not my safety they are worried about, thought Artemis as she mounted the stairs; *more like they are afraid I'll take the stupid minting plates and abscond. Hell and damnation, but I am in a foul mood.*

Although she would have much rather gone riding—or even taken a brisk walk to sort out her unhappy thoughts—Artemis dutifully entered the bedchamber to rest, whilst Lady Tallyer sat quietly in a corner of the sitting room, reading.

Katy brought Artemis a flannel soaked in lavender water, and laid it on her brow. "May I bring you anything, miss—I mean, my lady?"

"I feel much better, Katy—I think I just had a weak spell for a moment."

Katy eyed her with a speculative gleam. "Do you suppose—"

"No," said Artemis shortly, and then was ashamed she'd snapped at faithful Katy. "I don't enjoy shopping, is all."

"Oh." Katy looked a bit taken aback by the revelation that shopping could bring on such a reaction. "But you did buy some lovely things—his lordship will be that pleased with your new nightdress."

Artemis could not bring herself to answer, and wondered if perhaps she should actually start wearing a nightdress, just to punish her husband for this little episode. "Katy—when Droughm returns, I'd like to speak with him in private, if you don't mind."

"Yes, miss." The girl leaned in to whisper, "And Lady Tallyer won't be staying long, I think. She keeps checking the time, so she must have an appointment with someone."

If she is also going off to rendezvous with Droughm, I will not be answerable for the consequences, thought Artemis, and then calmed herself; the lady was no doubt going to meet with her compatriots—perhaps this Tremaine-person, who was clearly lurking in the background—and as long as she was away from Artemis it hardly mattered.

When Droughm did return, he apologized for his late arrival and took Artemis' good hand in his as he kissed her cheek. Not an ounce of shame or guilt could be discerned as he said easily, "Matters took more time than I'd anticipated."

"No matter," Artemis disclaimed. "I have been well-entertained by Carena."

Reading her aright, he shot her a cautionary look, and thanked Lady Tallyer, who gave him a rather sad smile and then glided out the door, her hips gently swaying.

"I hate her," said Artemis crossly. "And I am perilously close to hating you."

"What is this?" he asked in surprise, shooting her a glance as he poured himself a whiskey.

Charitably, she allowed him to take a healthy swallow before she asked, "What was your business with Miss Valdez today?"

His head snapped up, and he regarded her, his expression unreadable. "What have you heard?"

In a quiet tone, she replied, "That is not much of an answer, Pen."

They stood for a silent moment, then he gestured for her to sit, as he pulled up a chair so that they were nearly knee to knee. The pale green eyes searched hers, and she wondered if he was hoping she would speak first, so as to give him some insight as to how much she knew. The thought was annoying in the extreme, and she remained silent, waiting.

He leaned forward, his forearms resting on his thighs and his hands clasped between his knees. "She is here," he admitted in an even tone. "I must meet with her, because I have no choice."

"Why?"

He ducked his head. "It is a delicate situation."

For some reason—perhaps it was his choice of words—Artemis leapt to a horrifying conclusion, and stared at him as she felt the blood drain from her face. "She carries your child."

"Good God, Artemis—no—no, of course not." There was no doubt that he was genuinely stricken as he reached to cradle her face, running his thumb over her cheeks. "Oh, my darling; is that what you thought? I am so sorry—" Speechless with remorse, he pulled her rather roughly into his lap, and brought his forehead to rest against hers.

Nearly overcome with relief, she nevertheless persisted, "If it's not that, Pen—then what? Is it Wentworth again? What can be worth this?" Hearing the thread of anxiety in her voice, she pressed her lips together and took a breath, to steady herself.

His arms still restless on her, he said slowly, "I'm afraid I cannot say."

She drew back to allow her gaze to search his. "Even to me?"

"Even to you. I am so sorry, Artemis."

"Did you take her to bed?" Despite her best efforts, Artemis could feel her lower lip tremble.

"No." He lifted her hand to kiss it, his eyes still anxious on hers. "No—my word of honor, Artemis."

Ashamed of her loss of composure, she dropped her gaze. "I was worried you may have. For Wentworth, or England, or some such thing."

"Not even for England," he said softly, and stroked her hair back at the temple. "My poor Artemis."

"Will you meet with her again?"

"I can speak no more on the subject," he said gently. "Have you eaten?"

"Have you?" she asked sharply, shooting him a look.

Sidestepping an answer, he offered, "Allow me to have something sent up—anything you'd like."

"An ice," she decided. "No opium."

He rose, and she sank back into the chair as he summoned a servant and issued the order. Watching him, she contemplated the unbidden thought that had suddenly crept into her mind; Droughm had been guarded and a bit withdrawn toward the beginning of their conversation—wary—but then he'd broken into genuine and heartfelt remorse, when she'd expressed her fear of Miss Valdez's pregnancy.

I think, she realized in dawning puzzlement, *that he was going to lead me to believe he'd bedded the wretched woman—or at least, leave the possibility on the table—but then couldn't bring himself to do it. But why on earth would he willingly cause me such misery— what would be the point?* Following this train of thought, she realized something she'd been too upset to think about previously—how strange it was that a supposedly clandestine meeting between Droughm and Miss Valdez took place at a public hotel, and directly in her line of sight from the table in the tea room.

With some wonderment, she thought, *Why, I believe this was all done on purpose—and I am being goaded into taking some action. But what? They have the wretched plates, for heaven's sake—do they want me to leave Droughm? Why?*

Her husband returned to take his seat across from her, watching her with a hint of concern. Remembering when he'd advised her to be ready to flee the country, Artemis debated whether she should simply ask him outright what was afoot. *Best not,* she decided—*or at least not yet. He does have to worry that I am committing treason, after all, and perhaps whatever is going forward will alleviate his fears, once and for all.*

"Are you angry?"

"I don't know what I am," she answered honestly.

He made a gesture toward the settee. "Should I sleep out here tonight?"

"Of course not," she replied with some surprise. "I love you, and I always will."

He ducked his head, and swore.

Watching his reaction with some alarm, she ventured, "Is it time to pack my bags, Pen?"

"Not as yet; but stand ready." He was completely serious.

"Yes, sir," she replied in a small voice.

CHAPTER 43

"*Menina.*"

The word was spoken quietly, but Artemis' reaction was immediate. Closing her hand around the pistol hidden beneath the pillow, she whirled to draw upon the woman who sat upon the foot of her bed. Miss Valdez did not outwardly react, but Artemis saw the flash of alarm in her dark eyes. *Ah*, thought Artemis. *The penny drops; apparently I am to discover what this is all about.*

"*Bonjour.*" Artemis held the pistol steady, aimed at the woman's head. As had been the case at the hotel yesterday, Miss Valdez was dressed in maid's clothes, her thick, dark hair pulled back tightly under a cap. Droughm was not in evidence, but Artemis knew better than to take her gaze off her visitor, and continued in French, "Start talking."

The other girl responded in Portuguese, "There is no need for your weapon—"

"English," interrupted Artemis in that language. "My Portuguese is not very good."

"Very well," the other agreed. "Perhaps you will put the pistol down."

"I think not." Artemis drew herself to a sitting position, and pulled the sheet across her breasts. She was aware the other woman sought to place her at a disadvantage— confronting her in bed with no warning—but Artemis knew better than to give the enemy an advantage, and so she showed no embarrassment or discomfiture. "I need little excuse to shoot you—best start talking."

"You are very pretty," the other opined thoughtfully. "Except for the eyes, we could be mistaken for sisters. Perhaps he married you because you look like me."

But Artemis was having none of it. "Or he married me because he found you lacking."

Ah, this hit a sore point; Artemis could see the woman press her full lips into a thin line and felt an unexpected twinge of pity. *She is not one who tolerates weakness, even in herself,* she thought; *and I believe Droughm is a weakness for her.* Artemis drew back the hammer with a click. "You must leave, now; I shall count backwards from three. Three. . . ."

"I am here to make a bargain," the other interrupted. "I did not mean to startle you, but I did not have any other opportunity."

It occurred to Artemis that this must be the reason Droughm wanted to sleep on the settee last night—but the poor man couldn't bring himself to make her angry enough to throw him out.

With a pout, Miss Valdez continued, "My throat is still sore from when you hit me at the Museum."

But Artemis had no sympathy to offer. "You must learn to better defend yourself."

"*Tiens*; how was I to know you were such a violent one? Droughm must be very sorry he married you."

Artemis narrowed her eyes. "You will stay away from my husband."

Contemplating her with a trace of amusement, her visitor shrugged her pretty shoulders. But will your husband stay away from me?"

"Remind me why I haven't shot you already."

"Because I have—information—that Droughm would like to me to forget; but first I must have something in exchange."

With a trace of scorn, Artemis replied, "So you are trying to blackmail Droughm into your bed? Can't you find anyone else?"

The other's lips thinned again. "No; I have no need for such a trick, believe me. But Droughm tells me that you know where your uncle kept the items I seek."

This was of interest, and Artemis asked warily, "What sort of items?"

The dark eyes sharp upon her, the other girl held her hands in a circle shape so as to demonstrate. "Plates for coins. This big —made of metal."

Artemis could not imagine that Droughm's people would want her to turn over the plates, and so she said with all honesty, "Mine uncle told me no such thing—Droughm is misinformed."

The other regarded her for a moment in silence, whilst Artemis held her gaze with her own steady one. "I can ruin him," the other woman finally threatened.

"Have at it," suggested Artemis. "Although I cannot imagine such a course would make you more attractive to him."

Her visitor leaned forward, her gaze intent. "You must think where they could be—think of a hiding place; I have searched your uncle's house—and his safe—"

"Had he a safe?" asked Artemis in surprise. "It's probably where he kept the candles."

"The candles?" the other girl asked, bewildered.

"He was a miser—*muito barato*," Artemis explained.

"Ah," the other nodded. "It is often the way, with the rich men."

"But not Droughm," Artemis noted.

Miss Valdez smiled fondly. "No; Droughm is *très genereux.*"

"You are lapsing into French," Artemis warned her.

"I accidentally broke his nose, once," the other girl reminisced. "He is like a tiger, in the bed."

"Out," said Artemis, gesturing with her pistol. "Now."

Reminded, the other was contrite. "I am sorry—I forgot I should not say this to you; but we need to make our bargain."

"I cannot help you, I'm afraid." Artemis balanced the hilt of her pistol on her bent knee and casually sighted down the barrel at her visitor.

Her gaze on the weapon, the woman tilted her head as though studying an interesting specimen. "Droughm seemed to think you would know."

"Then he should ask me, and not you."

"You must see that he cannot—not with honor," the other pointed out reasonably. "He will be happiest if you give them to me without his knowledge. You tell me, and I will be gone from you, and leave him alone—my promise."

Artemis decided the best course at the moment was to stall for time. "I am going to think this over. Why should I trust you?"

"You will tell me," the girl warned with a hint of menace, "Or I will make things much the worse for you."

"I am not certain how things can get worse," Artemis observed.

Miss Valdez narrowed her eyes. "Yes, they can."

For whatever reason, Artemis was convinced this was a bluff. "Well, if you have to kill me, promise you won't let Lady Tallyer have him."

"Never," the other retorted, her color high. "*Elle est une chienne.*"

"Good—we are agreed, then. Now go, and I will consider what you have asked."

"Tomorrow morning, or I will not be so generous," the other warned as she rose with a swish of her skirts. "*Au revoir.*"

Lowering her pistol, Artemis sat in bed, and stared at the door as it closed behind Miss Valdez. It was hard to believe that

Droughm had arranged matters so as to allow for this alarming confrontation, but on the other hand, where was he? And it was all so difficult to sort out—it had occurred to Artemis that perhaps the woman was actually aligned with Droughm's people, in which case she may be setting up a trap for Artemis to reveal her supposed treason. On the other hand, there was the chance—remote, but nonetheless a possibility, that what the woman said was true—Droughm was willing to look the other way whilst Artemis relinquished the plates, if it meant avoiding the stain of a treasonous scandal. Frowning, she discarded the idea immediately—he'd said he'd even sacrifice Somerhurst, rather than betray his country, and she believed him.

As a welcome distraction to her tangled thoughts, Katy knocked, then backed through the door, carrying the breakfast tray. "His lordship said to see to it you were awake and made ready by eight, miss, so I took the liberty."

Artemis drew a blank. "Am I slated to go somewhere?"

Her manner reflecting the gravity of the news she had to import, Katy informed her, "They've found your poor uncle, miss—it's as they thought; he was killed in the mines."

"Oh—I see," said Artemis, thinking with some annoyance that she truly didn't need any more complications, just now.

"His lordship has gone to speak with the Constable, but he asked that you be informed—he said you'd best be up and about."

Because, of course, it would be apparent in short order that her uncle's death was no accident. "Thank you, Katy—I suppose my black dress can make an appearance. Is Lady Tallyer about?" Artemis thought it interesting that she'd been left unguarded—although it seemed clear she was meant to be unguarded, so as to allow for the meeting with her uninvited guest.

"Shall I fetch her?"

"Not just yet; give me a few more moments of peace." This last was said in a tart tone, and Katy giggled.

Contrite, Artemis begged, "Pretend I didn't say it, Katy—she's been very kind."

But Katy had an opening to make an observation, and took it. "At first I thought that she was a bit too kind to his lordship," said the maid with a meaningful look. "But the kitchen maid tells me that she has other interests."

"Lady Tallyer does?" asked Artemis in surprise. "Truly?"

The girl lowered her voice. "She says a man creeps into the lady's room for a cuddle every night."

"*No,*" breathed Artemis, completely agog.

"She says it is the gatekeeper from the mines." Katy's eyes gleamed. "And she so fancy!"

Artemis absorbed this astonishing information, and almost immediately perceived the truth of the matter; information—rather than affection—was being passed between the two during these clandestine meetings. Casting back into her memory, she tried to remember the gatekeeper, and came up empty; he was a nondescript individual, but one who certainly was positioned to know who came and went from the mines. Again, Artemis felt a faint sense of distaste when presented with further evidence of the spies' activities; battles should be fought honorably—head to head, not by skulking about, so that persons like herself were unable to ascertain who was friend and who was foe and what was what and whether one's husband was knee-deep in the skulking.

"No better than she should be," pronounced Katy with a sniff.

"One of many," observed Artemis darkly.

CHAPTER 44

*T*he Sheffield Constable was questioning Artemis at the station-house, Droughm having reluctantly agreed to it as long as he could be present. To no one's surprise, the questioning centered upon the obvious motive the orphaned and penniless Artemis would have had in putting a period to her previously-unknown rich uncle's existence.

With a narrow gaze, the Constable pressed, "And you kept a pistol with you, when you were visiting here, I believe."

"I did," Artemis agreed. "I still do." *Put it to good use this morning*, she thought with no small satisfaction; *certainly surprised that French hussy.*

What was unsettling, or at least it was to Artemis, was the fact that her illustrious husband's extreme displeasure in the proceedings seemed to have little effect on the officer of the law. *There's little point in marrying an Earl*, thought Artemis, *if he hasn't enough influence to intimidate a Yorkshire Constable*. For it seemed apparent that the man was not intimidated, but was instead enjoying the power he held over them—it did not bode well, as Droughm had already pointed out.

"And his death meant you inherited the mines," the Constable continued, leaning his hands on the table.

"Not exactly," interrupted Droughm. "My wife is underage —legally, she could not have inherited without a guardian."

But the Constable only lifted his sharp gaze to Droughm. "The mines certainly made for a fine dowry, and she attracted a titled husband in short order."

Amazingly short order, Artemis had to agree in all fairness; *and the Constable himself was attracted by the self-same dowry. But if it hadn't been Droughm, it would probably have been Torville, which would have been nowhere near as enjoyable, because I'd have been forced to punish him for his misdeeds, and then we'd have two corpses to explain away, instead of just the one.*

"Next you will accuse Lady Droughm of arranging for the cave-in," Droughm exclaimed in outrage. "This is intolerable."

"A man has been murdered," the Constable countered. "I must make my investigation, my lord."

"The matter is more properly one for the Coroner, certainly."

The other man raised a brow in surprise. "Come now; there can be little question the death was by homicide."

"An inquest must be conducted," Droughm insisted. "The wound may have been self-inflicted."

This suggestion invoked a mildly derisive reaction. "Unlikely, my lord; there was no pistol at the scene. If he shot himself, the weapon would be present."

"Has a thorough search been made through the rubble?" demanded Droughm with narrowed eyes. "Or are you a bit too eager to charge the late Colonel Merryfield's daughter?"

For the first time, Artemis could perceive a slight wariness in the lawman's demeanor. "A search was made; however, another canvass could certainly be taken as a precaution."

"Then do so," commanded Droughm, at his most autocratic.

With a nod, the Constable conceded. "Nevertheless, I must ask that Lady Droughm step into the next room and write out a statement under oath—setting forth a chronology of her actions on the day her uncle disappeared."

Hell and damnation, thought Artemis, flushing with

embarrassment. But before she could confess that she was unable to write, Droughm interjected smoothly, "My wife writes with her injured left hand—perhaps I could write out her statement as she recites it."

But the Constable was not to back down again. "I must insist that you not be present while she completes this task, my lord—surely you understand. Instead, I will send for a clerk."

"I cannot be comfortable with such an arrangement—to have my young wife closeted with a strange man," Droughm countered immediately. "Such a course is unacceptable."

Amused by this out-and-out mischaracterization of her maidenly sensibilities, Artemis awaited the other's response with interest. After a small pause, the Constable offered, "I will fetch my mother to sit with her, then; she lives here with me."

Unable to think of any further objection, Droughm nevertheless made his displeasure very clear as he escorted Artemis into the holding room next door, pausing at the doorway to assure her that he would await without until she had completed her statement. As he leaned in to kiss her cheek he murmured, "Caliber?"

She murmured in return, "Forty-four." He then left, presumably to arrange to have a pistol planted at the scene of the crime. *A very useful sort of husband*, she thought, as she watched him leave; *when he wasn't being tiger-like with annoying Frenchwomen*. Although to be fair, she couldn't fault him for anything he'd done before he'd met her. Of course, he was currently involved in some sort of plot to trip her up, but she couldn't really hold it against him—there was little doubt that he was unhappy about it; a haunted look dwelt in his eyes, and he'd not slept well.

"I will fetch my mother to you, and send for a clerk." The Constable indicated she should be seated at the small table. "I'm afraid I can allow no visitors, but if you have need of anything, you have only to knock."

With an inward sigh, Artemis settled in to wait in the

sparsely-appointed holding room—Droughm had instructed her to tell a fish tale, and she would follow orders, even though she didn't much like all the dishonesty. Although in this case, the truth would probably sound more like a fish tale than a fish tale.

Within a few minutes, the Constable returned, escorting an elderly woman with greying hair who leaned on a cane to assist her progress. As he saw her settled into a chair, the Constable said in clear tones, "This is Lady Droughm, mother. You must stay with her while she gives her statement to the clerk."

The man then left, closing the door and leaving Artemis in the small room with the older woman, who was regarding her with over-bright eyes as she sucked on her teeth.

Artemis ventured, "Good afternoon," raising her voice so as to be heard.

"Her house is the way to hell, going down to the chambers of death," the woman announced in a malevolent tone.

"I see," replied Artemis with a twinge of pity—the woman was clearly a bit addled. "That is alarming."

"A just death—and then my Danny will have riches and honor." The claw-like hand gripped the head of the cane with such strength that it trembled.

"Yes—mine uncle has died," Artemis explained. "Great-uncle, actually."

But the older woman continued as though Artemis hadn't spoken, narrowing her red-rimmed, rheumy eyes. "The Rebecca, she will steal the birthright by her evil deeds. But it matters not; the other is a foul Delilah, and will descend into the pit. In the end, my Danny will be glorified."

Thinking this a rather disjointed outlook, Artemis ventured a smile. "My name is Artemis; have you any grandchildren?" She had little experience with the elderly, but had heard they could not resist discussing their grandchildren.

There was a small pause, and then the woman continued with some heat, stamping her cane on the wooden floor. "Back!

You'll not inveigle me—not with your pretty eyes, and your sweet way. No; not since Mary Queen of Scots will Sheffield hold such a prisoner—my Danny will be the talk of the kingdom."

"The Queen of Scotland?" Artemis wasn't at all clear on this reference. "Are you from Scotland, then? I have only just now returned from there."

But the woman paid no attention, and seemed to be lost in her own reverie. "It will be the talk of the kingdom. My Danny —my Danny will be glorified. *Wealth and riches shall be in his house.*"

Artemis hadn't the heart to argue with the poor woman, who seemed to be rejoicing in Artemis's anticipated imprisonment. "I think it is all a misunderstanding—my uncle may have shot himself." May as well start laying the groundwork for Droughm's falsified evidence.

"No; no. They'll have him dead to rights." Malevolently, she eyed Artemis and cackled, as though amused.

A small alarm sounded in Artemis' mind. *This is important,* she thought. *Pay attention, Artemis.* "Him? But isn't the murderer a woman? A Queen, I think you said."

"A death in Sheffield," the other repeated, allowing the syllables to roll off her tongue like a portent. "And a good riddance to the foul Delilah, with wealth and riches to my Danny."

Nonplussed, Artemis decided that further conversation was futile. "Well, I hope no one will be injured."

The woman covered her mouth and cackled, as a young man entered only to pause on the threshold, taking in the strange scene.

"The Constable's mother," Artemis explained. "Come to chaperone."

"I see," he said, although it didn't seem as though he did, and for the next half hour he took down Artemis' false recitation of events the day her uncle died. The Constable's mother made no further remarks, which was a relief, as Artemis needed to keep her story straight without the distraction of dire warnings.

The clerk looked over what he'd written down. "So; you stayed in the empty house during the day without going out-of-doors, and you did not wonder what had happened to your uncle until dusk began to fall, and he had not returned."

Artemis nodded unhappily. "Yes—I suppose that's the brunt of it." *I cannot be honest because too much is at stake,* she thought. *If it weren't for the French, and the treason, and my having the stupid plates, I could simply explain that the man was insane and tried to murder me. But I cannot be honest because—to quote Droughm— some things are more important than the truth.*

Suddenly struck, she raised her gaze to consider the opposite wall for a long moment. Droughm was miserable for the same reason; too much was at stake for him to trust his new bride, even though he was inclined to do so. *I believe I can alleviate this dilemma for him,* she thought, her mind turning over a new-hatched plan; *I cannot like all this deception, and I believe— at least in this instance—that honesty may well be the best policy.*

"Thank you, my lady," said the clerk in a respectful tone.

"Repent, in dust and ashes," pronounced the old woman in a malicious tone.

"Hush," said Artemis absently. "You are annoying."

CHAPTER 45

"*What* do you know about laudanum, Katy?" Artemis held the brown vial in her fingers and turned it this way and that, in the fading afternoon light.

Katy paused in sponging off the hem of Artemis' black dress, which would be seeing a great deal of use for the foreseeable future. "I've taken it for a toothache, my lady. Are you needing a dose?"

"How much would it take to put Lady Tallyer to sleep, do you suppose?"

After a surprised pause, Katy offered, "Well, three drops for a toothache, and it makes me sleepy—I suppose ten drops would do it."

"I'll need your help, Katy—my wretched arm has cashiered me."

"We're putting Lady Tallyer to sleep, then?" Katy's eyes shone and she abandoned her project without a qualm. "What's to do?"

Artemis debated, then said with regret, "I'm afraid I'd rather not say, Katy—best you not know the particulars."

With a smile, the girl assured her, "I'll stand bluff, my lady."

"Good. I will invite Lady Tallyer to play cards in the private parlor downstairs, and at my signal you're to bring us tea, and see to it she has her drops."

Katy considered the obvious drawback to this plan. "She'll fall asleep at the table, miss."

"Leave it to me, Katy; I'll have the servants help me get her back into her room, and then I will attend to her—it is important that we are not disturbed, once we are in her room, so you're to return to your own room straightaway."

"Very good miss—I mean, my lady."

I'm sure she thinks I'm going to search the wretched woman's room, thought Artemis, *which is as fine an explanation as any.* "Thank you, Katy—you are a trump."

That evening, Artemis watched Droughm as he pulled the brim of his drayman's hat low over his face, in preparation for a clandestine night journey. "What time do you think you'll return, Pen?"

"My best information is that the Coroner is conducting official business two towns over. I'll leave quietly, and track him down for a little discussion—preparing the ground, so to speak. Say nothing—no one should notice, but if anyone asks, you don't know where I am."

"I'll be as subtle as a serpent," Artemis assured him. "How much does it cost to bribe a Coroner, nowadays?"

Shrugging into his greatcoat, he tilted his head in demurral. "Not so much a bribe as a friendly conversation; a bribe might give the impression you are indeed guilty."

"I *am* indeed guilty," she reminded him, reaching on tiptoe to kiss him goodbye. "You'd best give him the sapphires, so as to outbid the Constable when he offers up his paltry pearls."

He tugged on the braid that fell down her back, a hint of remorse in his eyes. "I don't deserve you, Artemis. You are one in a million."

"Oh, I don't know about that, Pen—the Constable's mother didn't like me much."

He began to button up his coat. "Didn't she? I thought you were slated to be her daughter-in-law."

Artemis made a face. "It was ridiculously awkward, actually. She's a bit addled, I think, and kept making dire predictions, rather like the witches in *Macbeth*."

As he pulled on his leather gloves, he gave her a look. "Eye of newt?"

Knitting her brow, Artemis tried to remember. "She kept referring to a death in Sheffield, but it didn't seem that she meant mine uncle, but instead someone else. There was a famous prisoner, too; a Queen."

He walked over to pause at the door, listening. "Mary, Queen of Scots?"

Artemis brightened. "Yes—that was it. Do you know of her?"

Droughm opened the door a crack, and scouted the hallway. "She was held prisoner in Sheffield centuries ago—it does sound as though the woman was addled, if she was speaking of her."

"I don't know." Uneasy, Artemis frowned. "I can't shake the feeling that what she said was important, for some reason."

Droughm lifted a shoulder in dismissal. "I think it is her son who is addled, to be antagonizing me without fear of reprisal. If he was involved in the counterfeiting scheme, he should be putting some distance between himself and the others, and trying to curry favor; he could easily be hanged for treason."

"It makes no sense," she agreed. "Unless he is annoyed with you because you stole a march on him, and carried off my wealthy self."

Pausing before he left, he threw an arm around her, and drew her to him, holding her a bit too tightly for the comfort of her splint. "I am sorry to put you through this, Artemis."

"I could say the same to you, Pen."

His hands on either side of her neck, he drew her apart from

293

him, so that he could look into her eyes, very seriously. "Know that I love you, Artemis; this—episode—with Lisbetta—"

His voice trailed off as he struggled to decide how much he could say. Artemis resolved to help him along, being as she wanted him out the door so as to put her counter-plan into action. "I know there's a cat-and-mouse in play, Pen. Please don't worry; I understand."

"I can't antagonize Lisabetta; not just now." His thumb reached up to brush her cheek. "I'm afraid I'm not at liberty to explain."

This seemed a veiled reference to the French girl's insistence that Artemis turn over the doll, to save Droughm from having to do it. "So many crossings and double-crossings to keep track of," Artemis observed in a mild tone. "I can't help but think that an honest dose of pound-dealing would not come amiss."

"I can't antagonize her," he repeated more firmly. "It is damnable, but there it is."

"I understand," she repeated, and didn't mention that she was never one to hesitate in antagonizing the enemy, and had even excelled at it, on occasion. But first, she needed to find out what was what—no need overset poor Pen's careful plans, after all. With a final kiss, she bid him goodbye.

Lady Tallyer appeared promptly upon Droughm's departure, and Artemis recited an abbreviated version of the day's gruesome discovery to her, concluding, "But they need to call in the Coroner to determine the exact cause of death."

"Oh? I thought the cause of death was clear." The woman slid her gaze to Artemis.

Matter-of-factly, Artemis informed her, "Apparently, the possibility of suicide has been raised."

After considering this, Lady Tallyer nodded. "Suicide would certainly be the best conclusion for everyone concerned."

"Definitely best for me."

"For *everyone*—not just you," the other woman emphasized. "If it was determined that you murdered your uncle, you would not be eligible to inherit the mines—under the law, a murderer cannot inherit from the victim."

"Oh." Artemis had not considered this aspect of the tangled plots and counter-plots that were currently in play. "Then who *would* inherit, if I were determined to be the murderess?"

"I think it is not certain, the lady said. "Let us hope it doesn't come to that."

Soberly, Artemis remembered there was more at stake than keeping the new-minted Countess out of prison; the mines could not be allowed to fall back under the control of Napoleon's evildoers. Small wonder Droughm was moving heaven and earth to clear her name.

Artlessly straightening her sling, Artemis suggested, "Shall we go downstairs and play cards to pass the time? I am weary of these four walls, and that way we could have tea and cakes brought in from the kitchen."

"Very well," agreed the lady with little enthusiasm, as she turned toward the door. "What would you care to play?"

"Piquet? We could play penny-a-point." Artemis had played cards all her life with the savvy Colonel, and was certain she could thoroughly trounce her companion.

This was agreed to, and as they descended the stairs, Artemis remembered to ask something that had been niggling at the back of her mind, ever since her visit to the station-house. "You must be familiar with the Bible, if your parents were missionaries."

"Very true," the other responded, and offered nothing more.

Artemis persisted, "Wasn't Delilah a Bible character?"

"Yes," the other answered absently as they settled in the private parlor, the proprietor fussing to make them comfortable. "She was infamous for betraying her husband to the enemy."

As they called for cards and candles, Artemis considered this information. "And there was another woman—I think her name started with an "R."

With an amused smile, Lady Tallyer suggested, "Ruth? Rachael?"

Frowning, Artemis tried to remember, as she dealt the first hand. "It had to do with stealing a birthright."

"Rebecca, then."

Artemis looked up. "Yes—that's it. Who was Rebecca?"

The other woman absently spread her cards. "Rebecca schemed to steal one son's inheritance, so as to give it to another."

Thinking it over, Artemis made a discard. "I'm asking because the Constable's mother was spouting off dire warnings, and seemed to be very pleased that I was about to meet my comeuppance. I had the impression that I was the foul Delilah —going down into the pit—but there was someone else who was the Rebecca, and the Rebecca was going to steal the birthright and bring riches and honor to the Constable."

Lady Tallyer paused, and lifted her gaze with an unreadable expression. "Who was saying this to you?"

"The Constable's mother—she's a horror. Do you know what she meant?"

"No," said her companion thoughtfully as she made a discard. "But I should find out. I've been meaning to ask you if I could borrow your mare, while we are here."

Hiding her dismay only with a mighty effort, Artemis felt she had no choice but to politely agree. "Of course; Callisto does need the exercise, and I've been unable to ride her."

"Thank you," the other replied, and returned her attention to the game.

Katy poked her head in the door. "Would you care for tea, my lady?"

"Definitely," said Artemis with relief.

CHAPTER 46

*S*oft-footed, Artemis approached the Innkeeper at his desk, and asked in a low voice, "Excuse me—may I speak with you privately, for a moment?"

Eager to grant any request for his exalted guest, the man stepped out and bowed low. "Certainly, my lady."

"I'm afraid my friend, Lady Tallyer, is quite drunk."

Aghast, the man stared at her, as Artemis nodded sadly. "It is true; she is passed out in the private parlor."

"Goodness—this is most unfortunate—" the man stammered.

"Yes. I wondered if I could enlist a servant or two to carry her to her room with as little fuss as possible, and then I will sit with her until she recovers. The least said the better, of course." Privately, Artemis hoped the servants here gossiped as much as they did at Stanhope House.

"Of course—of course; allow me to call for assistance."

Artemis supervised the transport of the unconscious woman to her room upstairs, where she instructed the servants to lay her down on the bed. "Thank you," she told them gravely. "I will sit with her, whilst she sleeps it off."

Eying the woman's prone form askance, the two men bowed

and exited, followed by Katy, who closed the door behind them after giving Artemis a conspiratorial wink.

Artemis pulled a chair up beside the bed, checked her pistol, and laid it on her lap. She then settled in to wait, hoping it wouldn't be too long.

After an hour, a soft tapping pattern could be heard on the door, and Artemis lifted her pistol and held it on the doorway. Without waiting for a response, an unknown man entered and then froze in the doorway as he took in the tableau before him. Artemis recognized the grey eyes of the Bow Street Investigator —now dressed as the gatekeeper, complete with a beard and cap. "Sir," she said in an even tone, as the man stared down the barrel of her pistol. "I must beg a word with you."

"You have my undivided attention." He sketched a little bow as he turned to close the door, and she saw his hand slide toward his waistband.

"Hold." She pulled back the hammer of her pistol with a click, and wondered how many more times this fine day she'd be required to hold someone at gunpoint. "There'd be none to gainsay me, were I to shoot a gatekeeper bent on ravishment. Show me your hands, and you will suffer no harm from me— which is more than I can say of you."

Slowly, he turned back to face her, holding his hands where she could see them. "On the contrary; I dare not harm you— your husband is vehement in your defense."

"As well he should be; I am true. And I do not appreciate your making him miserable, so let us put an end to it."

The gentleman stood at his ease, but Artemis had the impression he was on high alert, and carefully assessing enemy terrain. "How so?"

"I am tired of trying to determine what is afoot here, and so I would appreciate it if you would tell me straight-out what it is you are trying to vex me into doing."

He answered without hesitation, "I would like you to give your doll to Miss Valdez."

Artemis stared at him. "Truly?"

"Truly," he assured her.

Her brows snapped together. "Oh; oh—I am *such* an idiot. You have switched the plates; *that's* why the doll was opened."

Bowing his head in acknowledgement, he continued, "I would appreciate it if you would make a show of reluctance, nonetheless."

"I will," she agreed. "How are the new ones different?"

"I am afraid I do not care to discuss the matter further. Perhaps you will be kind enough to set down your weapon."

But Artemis did not move, and said slowly, "This one—" she indicated Lady Tallyer with her head. "Are you certain *she* is true?"

He cocked his head, and regarded her narrowly. "Explain yourself."

With reluctance, Artemis admitted, "Nothing specific; only a feeling I have."

The other made an impatient gesture. "Your husband has been a bachelor for some time; if you are going to enact a Cheltenham tragedy every time you meet one of his former lovers, you will have a very rocky road of it."

But Artemis would not be taunted. "You are trying to vex me again," she replied in an even tone, "But I assure you, Miss Valdez is the more trustworthy of the two."

He made a derisive sound. "We must disagree, then."

"Who is the Rebecca, who seeks to steal the birthright?"

The grey eyes regarded her without expression. "I have no idea."

"No," she replied with a frown. "Neither do I."

There was a pause, and then he asked, "Where is my lord Droughm, this fine evening?"

Artemis matched his impassive tone. "I have no idea."

With narrowed eyes, he made it clear he did not appreciate her impertinence. "Do not trifle with me."

"No, sir," she said steadily.

He watched her without speaking for a moment, and then asked, "Are we quite finished?"

"We are; although I will warn you that if you cause any harm to Droughm—any injury whatsoever—I promise I will hunt you down, and put a period to your miserable existence."

"You terrify me," he said with a full dose of derision, and then turned to open the door, and slip out.

He doesn't like me much—not that I care, Artemis decided as she stood to remove Lady Tallyer's shoes and cover her with a blanket. She had a lot to think about, as she performed these services—the plates had been switched, and presumably the new plates could be traced. Did this mean the counterfeiting would be allowed to continue? There seemed little benefit to switching the plates, if the process was to be shut down as soon as Droughm seized control. Or perhaps—here she paused, thinking—or perhaps they wished to be certain the scheme would not simply pick up and make a new start elsewhere—the new plates were presumably not as good a counterfeit, and could be easily spotted, unlike the old ones. Whatever the reason, it seemed evident they did not mean to arrest Miss Valdez on her receipt of them, but instead they wished to see what she would do with them next.

Artemis gave up trying to puzzle it out—perhaps she would never discover the reason behind the subterfuge. With one last look at her unconscious companion, she locked the door behind her, and returned to her rooms.

It was late when Droughm carefully rested his weight on the bed, but despite his efforts, the movement woke her, and she sleepily moved over to him, receptive. He needed no further urging and wordlessly took her in his arms as he rolled his warm body atop hers, his mouth searching in the dark.

There was something to be said for lovemaking born of remorse; the man went out of his way to please, and as a result, she lay in an aftermath of drowsy contentment, feeling as though her bones were made of jelly.

"Who was the noisy one, tonight?" he murmured, very pleased with himself.

"You are a master," she murmured in response. "I will ask how it went with the Coroner, when I can muster up some energy."

"I am cautiously optimistic." He nuzzled her neck.

"That is to the good; I had my own conversation with the gatekeeper, this evening." Earlier, she'd debated whether to tell Droughm of it, but then decided that she would always be honest with him—she was more soldier than spy, and didn't know how to be otherwise.

His mouth paused on her neck, and she could feel his wariness. "Did you?"

"Yes; I will need you to go on some sort of errand tomorrow morning so that I can give my doll to Miss Valdez. Although I'm supposed to feign reluctance, so I hope I can be half-way convincing."

There was a pause, and then Droughm began to laugh—such a glorious sound, she hadn't heard it in a few days. "Good *God*, Artemis; what have you done?"

"I took matters into my own hands," she replied complacently. "I happen to think there is nothing *more* important than the truth."

"How did this come about?"

"I held him at gunpoint, I'm afraid. He is not very happy with me."

"Good *God*, I should have liked to see his face—he doesn't like to be outwitted." He laughed again.

It was so wonderful to hear his laughter, to feel his relief. She rubbed her cheek against his chest, feeling the coarse hair on her skin and thinking it was all—finally—coming to an end, so they could settle into some semblance of a normal life.

"How tired are you?" he whispered, his hands drifting down the sides of her hips.

"I suppose we will find out," she murmured in reply.

CHAPTER 47

*A*rtemis and Katy took a leisurely stroll around the grounds of the Inn the next morning, putting themselves on display so as to draw-in Miss Valdez. Katy reported that she'd seen Lady Tallyer depart on Callisto earlier that morning, but Artemis had missed it, having overslept as a result of the conjugal demands made upon her the night before. "How did she seem, Katy, did she look the worse for wear?"

"She did look a bit cross," Katy disclosed with a gleam.

"A shame Droughm didn't see her at her worst; she's always so well turned-out." Artemis's husband had gone into the town so as to remove himself from the scene, and also, Artemis surmised, to be close at hand when the Coroner made his arrival today.

"It is a lovely day," Artemis commented as their footsteps crunched on the gravel in the yard. "And by lovely, I mean it's not raining."

Katy smiled. "How long do we stay in Sheffield, my lady?"

Artemis grimaced. "Not much longer, I hope; I hate this place."

"Oh, but miss; you were married, here."

"Not here—Scotland, instead," Artemis corrected her. "And

it was a close-run thing, I will say. I wish I'd taken your grand-dam's tuppence when we left London—we could have used some luck."

Wide-eyed, Katy had to disagree. "Oh, but miss—what with your new husband, and him being Quality, and everything coming out like a fairy tale, I think you had all the luck you needed."

With a smile, Artemis conceded, "I don't sound very grateful, do I? But I am; it has all turned out much better than I could have hoped."

"Grand-dad always said you could take care of yourself."

"I've never known anything else," Artemis replied honestly. "Katy, may I ask you to go purchase another black dress at the dressmaker's shop? I'll be in blacks for a while, I think, and it would be nice to have another."

"Of course, my lady—when shall I go?"

Artemis teased, "Quickly, before Lady Tallyer comes back and wants to choose it herself."

Katy was dispatched on the errand, and Artemis wandered back to her rooms, hoping she needn't wait very long for her anticipated visitor. Her wish was to be granted, because upon entering her rooms, she discovered Miss Valdez—again, dressed as a maid—and thumbing through Artemis's armoire.

"You have so little," the Frenchwoman complained, looking at her over her shoulder. "I think he does not mean to keep you."

"I think he does. I would post a wager on it, but I don't like gambling."

With narrowed eyes, Miss Valdez threatened, "He will be ruined, unless you do as I tell you."

Artemis advanced to firmly close the armoire door. "I think you are bluffing, but I've decided to give you the plates, anyway, so that there will be one less annoyance in my life."

Astonished, the other girl arched her dark brows. "What is this? Are you not afraid of me?"

"No. You rather remind me of me."

Her visitor paused, seemingly much struck, and then nodded thoughtfully. "That is what I thought, also. But you are *très ingénue,* and me, I am not so; I am *plus sage.*"

"It doesn't seem very wise to be chasing a married man."

With a show of superiority, the Frenchwoman tossed her head. "You see? *Très ingénue.*"

With her best attempt at a sigh, Artemis indicated they should walk into the sitting room. "Come along, then; I'll give you the plates, but you must promise to relinquish all claims to my mines and to my husband."

"I have no claim to the mines," the other pointed out. "You are the heiress."

"And you have no claim to the husband," Artemis prompted, over her shoulder. "I am the wife."

But as the other girl followed, she stubbornly insisted, "What if he grows tired of you? Then it would not be my fault."

Artemis came to a stop before the window seat. "You cannot hedge your bets; either we have a deal, or we do not."

With a calculating expression, her companion countered, "We have a deal, but with the understanding that I will not try to take him away. If he wishes to leave—well, that is something different altogether."

Exasperated, Artemis couldn't help but laugh. "I was right— you are the more honest of the two."

"*Que?*"

Artemis decided it would do no harm to tell her. "I think you are more honest than Lady Tallyer."

Miss Valdez curled her lip in scorn. "Bah—that one; she has —how do you say it? *Normes peu élevées*—the low standards. She cannot have Droughm, and so she runs over to console herself with the Constable. *C'est incroyable.*"

Artemis stared at the other woman in surprise. "Whatever do you mean?"

The other woman shrugged. "*Rien*; I shouldn't have said."

But it wasn't 'nothing'; Artemis could think of no good reason for Lady Tallyer to have gone over to see the Constable—although —although she'd said she was going to investigate the story about the Rebecca, which seemed to have piqued her interest. Maybe the lady was visiting the lawman on orders from the grey-eyed man, and if that were the case, Artemis should probably not be discussing this particular subject with an enemy spy.

Thus reminded of her orders, she lifted her doll from the window seat. "Here." She handed it to the other. "The plates are hidden inside—you can feel the edges."

"*Oui.*" The Frenchwoman felt the doll's midsection, and then lifted her head. "Do you wish to keep your doll? We can remove them now, if you'd like."

"No," Artemis replied, having already thought about it. "She's from another life—one that is over, now."

"*La guerre,*" acknowledged the other, her gaze resting on the doll, and Artemis had the impression that Miss Valdez had her own war stories to tell.

Resisting the urge to empathize, Artemis drew herself up. "You should go, now."

But before Miss Valdez could make her exit, there was a knock at the door, which caused both women to freeze, and then glare accusingly at each other. Wary, Artemis answered the door to behold a servant, who handed her a folded note. "From Lord Droughm, my lady."

Artemis stared at the man, and then stared at the note, a leaden feeling in her breast. "Thank you." After she closed the door, the two women stood in silence, assessing each other. "What ploy is this?" Artemis asked through stiff lips, indicating the note. "What have you done with Pen?"

"I do not know what you are talking about," said the other, alarmed. "*Qu'est-ce c'est?*"

"If you have hurt him—"

Impatient, the Frenchwoman gestured with her hands. "I am

not going to hurt him, I am going to steal him away from you. What does it say?"

Artemis looked at the note, with its bold, black scrawl, and fingered it in alarm. "I do not know—I cannot read, and Pen knows that I cannot read; therefore, he did not write this."

Snatching it, the other woman walked over to the window to peruse the writing, but gave up in exasperation. "I do not read the English."

Snatching it back, Artemis strode over to take her pistol from under the pillow. "I am going to find out what is afoot." For whatever reason, she believed that Miss Valdez was not involved in—in whatever was happening, which actually made it all the more alarming. Who was behind this subterfuge, if not the enemy? It was beyond frustrating, not to know what the note supposedly said.

She was not to be kept in suspense long, however, because when she descended the stairs to the front desk, it was to face the Constable and a deputy, waiting alongside the unhappy Innkeeper.

Reading their faces, Artemis mentally braced herself and asked in a steady voice, "What is the meaning of this?"

"You're to come with me, my lady," said the Constable in a clipped tone. "Lord Droughm was very unhappy to discover the disturbing news about you. He feels that he's been made a fool."

Flushing, Artemis retorted, "He said no such thing—what are you about?"

"Perhaps you would like to step into the private parlor," suggested the unhappy Innkeeper, glancing at the other guests who were not hiding their acute interest in the confrontation. "Discretion is advised."

"Lord Droughm is in a thundering rage, I assure you," the Constable said with a thread of satisfaction. "I am to escort you to the station-house immediately."

Stalling for time, Artemis replied, "I will go nowhere until I have spoken to my husband."

Turning on her heel, she made to retreat up the stairs, but instead nearly ran into Miss Valdez, who had crept down to stand behind her, obviously eavesdropping.

"My lady will need her maid; may I accompany her?" The Frenchwoman addressed the Constable with a soft English accent.

"Come along, then," the lawman nodded, and Artemis immediately leapt to the conclusion that the two were colluding —he must have needed a signal that the plates were now secured, before he hauled Artemis away; it was too much a coincidence that these two had descended upon her within the same hour.

Furious, Artemis whirled around. "No; you will stay right here." Cocking her arm, she struck Miss Valdez square under the jaw with a closed fist, and as the bystanders gasped, the Frenchwoman sank down into her skirts on the stairs.

Artemis' arm was immediately grasped by the Constable, who announced grimly, "In the name of the King, you are under arrest for treason, murder—and assault."

CHAPTER 48

J am not in the infantry anymore, Artemis thought with deep regret; *I truly cannot go about knocking people down.* Sitting ramrod straight, she gazed out the window of the transport coach, and refused to look at the two men who accompanied her. *On the other hand, I was completely justified in clocking her—I'd forgotten, for a moment, that she is an enemy combatant, and it was a good thing that I was reminded before I started thinking that we were friends, of sorts.*

That Artemis' arrest was part of an ulterior scheme seemed evident, and in particular, she couldn't like the public nature of the event—it was as though the Constable wanted an audience and was certain there would be no retribution, which seemed a foolish conviction in light of her husband's uncertain temper.

Also, they'd used a questionable subterfuge; the note from Droughm—which apparently accused his wife of murder, and treason—would easily be shown to be a fake. As Droughm had already noted, there was an insolent tone to all of this which made no sense—no one was afraid of Droughm, even though they should be. And—come to think of it—they didn't seem very concerned about Miss Valdez, either, who'd been left unconscious at the Inn.

She stilled for a moment. If everyone was working for the French, and Miss Valdez was the French agent tasked with securing the new plates, then how come the Constable didn't know who she was? Could it be possible that the Constable was *not* colluding with Miss Valdez, after all? Perhaps—perhaps Miss Valdez was *not* involved in the little drama that had been conducted at the Inn. But then, what was its aim?

The enemy's object is to wrest the mines, she reminded herself, furrowing her brow; *but how? What can they possibly hope to do? The Crown's agents are already working hard to ensure that I'm the heiress, so that Droughm can control the mines as my husband. The English aren't going to stand idly by whilst I am accused of murder — it would overset their fake-adoption story, since a murderer cannot inherit from the victim. Therefore, if it is proved that I killed Uncle Thaddeus, the mines are not mine in the first place — and wouldn't be Droughm's, either.*

And—now that she thought about it—if this were indeed the plot, it seemed mighty far-fetched. The enemy was well-aware that the Coroner was on his way, and as a representative of the Crown, his jurisdiction would prevail over the Constable's with respect to her uncle's death. And—aside from the matter of Droughm's planted evidence of suicide—it seemed very unlikely that the Coroner would find a Countess guilty of murder unless there was irrefutable evidence, which there wasn't.

Not to mention there was no reason to set up this false-note pretense that Droughm was enraged with his new bride—either Artemis was a murderess and she couldn't inherit, or she wasn't a murderess and her claim was iron-clad; whether Droughm wanted to set her aside was neither here nor there. It all made little sense.

Pen will sort it out, she thought, trying to reassure herself. *I need only be patient, and try to control my temper so as not to commit any more felonies.*

Once at the station-house, she was ushered into the holding-room, and hoped with some trepidation that she would not be required to converse with the Constable's mother again. The alternative was hardly better, however, because—to her extreme astonishment—Artemis came face-to-face with Lady Stanhope, who sat regally in a straight-backed chair, and watched Artemis' entrance from hooded eyes.

"My—my lady," stammered Artemis, when she'd recovered her voice.

"I have tracked you down," the other said in awful tones. "You'll not get away with it."

Immediately angry, Artemis retorted, "I could say the same to you."

"Insolence," hissed the other woman. "When I think of how I took you in—"

"For your infamous purposes—" countered Artemis hotly.

"Enough." The Constable gestured Artemis back with an out-flung arm. "Lady Stanhope has made a very serious accusation under oath, and her testimony is enough to support a warrant for your arrest."

"You should instead arrest *her*," Artemis replied with a full measure of contempt. "She conspired to ruin me, so that I would have no choice but to marry her loathsome nephew."

As though she hadn't spoken, the Constable continued, "You are accused of murdering Lord Stanhope. How do you plead?"

Nearly speechless, Artemis stared at him. "*Lord Stanhope* —why, what madness is this?"

"I have a witness," insisted Lady Stanhope in her cold voice. "My cook will attest to it."

For a moment, Artemis was tempted to tell the lady where her former cook now held sway, but decided the least said, the best. "That is utter nonsense, as you well know—your husband was killed in a brothel."

But the Constable only regarded her narrowly. "Coupled

with your other uncle's death, this leads to a very ominous conclusion."

"Why would I murder mine Uncle Stanhope?" asked Artemis in exasperation.

Apparently, the lawman did not take kindly to being chided by a seventeen-year-old girl, and leaned his hands on the table to reply with heavy menace, "It is believed he'd discovered your treason, and so you resolved to silence him."

"Utter nonsense," declared Artemis again, clutching the edge of the table with her good hand so as to bring herself under control. "I demand to speak to my husband."

"In due time," the Constable replied.

There was a knock at the door, which then opened to reveal Lady Tallyer, who slipped into the already crowded room. Unable to control her tongue, Artemis demanded, "And you! Are you involved in this—this farce?"

"Hush, Artemis," the lady cautioned in a tone that made Artemis feel all of ten years old. She then said to the Constable, "May I speak with you privately for a moment?"

Outraged, Artemis retorted, "No; I am entitled to hear what is being said and besides, I refuse to stay here with this—this harridan."

"Insolence," Lady Stanhope hissed, her cheeks reddening.

The Constable intervened, "Please, Lady Droughm—no brawling; I should not like to be forced to hold you in a cell." This said in a tone that made it clear the he would like it above all things.

Artemis ignored him, and confronted Lady Tallyer. "Where did you go, this morning? Did you know Lady Stanhope was here? Are you the one behind these *ridiculous* accusations?"

But the lady addressed the Constable instead of Artemis. "Please; allow me to take Lady Droughm to the back, and explain the situation plainly to her—she doesn't realize how matters stand, and how precarious her position."

During this speech, Lady Tallyer met Artemis' eye for the

merest second, and she was given to understand that the lady was attempting a subterfuge, and that Artemis should cooperate with this plan.

I am so tired of everyone, and of their layers-on-layers of play-acting, thought Artemis. "As you say," she said stiffly, and then allowed Lady Tallyer to steer her toward the back of the station house, where the holding cells were located.

"Say nothing," Lady Tallyer murmured, as they moved through the hallway.

"You will tell me what is afoot immediately," warned Artemis in an ominous tone, "Or I will conclude you are hip-deep in this nonsense."

Glancing over her shoulder, Lady Tallyer closed the door behind them, and then turned to Artemis. "Listen carefully," she said in a low voice. "You are in danger, and you must go warn Droughm—I've tied your horse out back. I'll stall them, but hurry."

This was a surprise, and Artemis could not help but be suspicious. "I don't know that I can trust you—I am worried that you are allied with the Constable."

With a quick glance at the door, the lady continued in a low whisper. "I am only pretending to conspire with him, so as to monitor the situation, but things have taken an unexpected turn. Best go warn Droughm, and quickly."

This seemed plausible, and Artemis nodded; after all, the lady wouldn't be aiding Artemis' escape if she were allied with the Constable. "Where is he?"

"He is at the mines, waiting for the Coroner to meet him. Tell him what has gone forward, here, and I'll make it appear as though you've escaped—can you mount your horse without assistance?"

"Yes. Will you be in danger?" Artemis felt a qualm, albeit only a very small one.

The other shook her head. "Not if they believe me—good luck."

"Thank you," Artemis said sincerely, and then slipped out the back door.

Callisto was tied outside, and by sheer determination, Artemis managed to pull herself up with one arm, before she urged the mare down the mews in the back—not moving too quickly so as to incite notice. Once clear of the buildings, however, she let Callisto stretch out into a gallop toward the wooded hills, and used the opportunity to berate herself for poor judgment. *I am indeed unseasoned*, she admitted with a twinge of shame—*or at least not at all savvy with respect to this spying business. Lady Tallyer is not the villainess in this tale, instead it is Miss Valdez—I had it all backwards.*

That her suspicions of the lady derived from petty jealousy made her all the more ashamed. *I must never leap to conclusions again,* she chastised herself—*I am beyond lucky to have escaped. I was so certain, the way Lady Tallyer behaved when she heard the Bible names last night at cards*—here, Artemis paused in her thoughts, her brow knit as the horse kept up her steady pace. There was no question the names had meant something to the lady—and indeed, it seemed that the revelation had inspired today's sequence of events.

Perhaps Lady Tallyer had been afraid that Artemis would say something she oughtn't, and spoil whatever double-crossing trap had been set-up for the Constable. That must be it —the Constable's mother, in her strange Bible ramblings, had let it slip that the Constable was aware of the Crown's plans against him.

Which begged the original question—what did the conspirators hope to accomplish, if they knew that the Crown had unearthed their plot? It seemed ridiculous to pin all their plans on the hope that a sitting Countess would be found guilty of her uncle's murder, and thus unable to inherit the mines— surely they knew the Treasury would never allow them to continue the counterfeiting operation, regardless.

Glancing behind her, she could see no pursuit—not even in

the distance, and so she let out a breath she hadn't realized she'd been holding. With a sense of relief, she made for the gate at the entrance to the mines—the grey-eyed man would be an ally, although it would probably annoy him no end to have to come to her aid.

"Hallo," she called out, as she didn't know the man's name. "Are you there?" She walked Callisto up to the small gate house, and saw that it was empty—and the path to the mines was quiet, also. *It is Sunday*, she realized; *no one is working*. Lady Tallyer had said Droughm was here, waiting to meet with the Coroner, but she saw no indication that either man was here— there were no horses tied in front.

Riding back a small distance, she urged Callisto forward, and the mare leapt easily over the gate. As she approached the tie-rail, Artemis waited for a moment, listening, but heard only silence. Assessing the situation, she decided she should remain mounted, and watch for any pursuit. Perhaps Droughm had ridden out to meet the Coroner as he approached on the road—soften him up, a bit, before they inspected the crime scene—or perhaps Droughm had already received warning of the latest disaster that was unfolding at the station-house, and he'd gone into town. She'd wait a bit, and if the Constable tried to come fetch her before Droughm did, it would be best to flee toward the hills—west, perhaps? —until she ran into another town; she dared not allow him to seize her again.

While she contemplated this unhappy plan, she heard a noise, echoing from within the mines, and turned in surprise, shading her eyes and peering toward the dark entrance. Could it be Droughm? Or the Coroner, perhaps? Strange that there were no horses. "Hallo?" she called out, but was met with only silence.

She was certain she'd heard something, though, and it seemed likely it was the two men, inspecting the area deep in the Old Mine, where her uncle's corpse had been found.

Perhaps they'd led the horses into the mine's entry—it did look to rain again.

After taking another long look down the valley to be certain there was no pursuit, she dismounted, and led Callisto up the tiered pathway to the mine's entrance.

The eerie silence reminded her of the day she'd come with her mad uncle, and she tried to shake off her uneasiness. *I wish I had my pistol; there is nothing like being arrested to catch one unprepared.*

"Pen?" she called out, as she stood just within the entry. Lady Tallyer had seemed certain that he would be here, but Artemis was not so sure—and in a strange way, she felt as though the Colonel was standing beside her, and giving the usual warning against entering any contained space without a pre-planned escape route. *I won't go in; instead, I'll remount, and hide along the tree line, watching,* she decided. *Then I can make a quick exit if need be; I cannot like this set-up.*

Turning to retreat back down the path, she heard a soft footfall behind her and whirled too late; standing before her, his pistol leveled at her breast, was her cousin Torville. "Into the mine," he said, gesturing with the gun. "Now."

CHAPTER 49

*I*n an instant, Artemis calculated her chances of escape and what she knew of Torville, and decided to feign ignorance. "*You*?" she asked in astonishment as they marched to the entry. "Why, what are you doing here, Torville? Where is Droughm?"

"He'll be along." Taking her arm, he pushed her against the rock wall and patted her down, looking for weapons as he held the pistol on her. His hand lingered on her breast as he smiled unpleasantly into her eyes.

"You mustn't, you know," she said matter-of-factly. "I am a married woman." Hopefully, he would be reminded that her lawful spouse was not someone who would take kindly to such insults.

"I can't believe he actually married you—our mutual aunt thought there wasn't a chance in hell." Relinquishing her, he stepped back, and glanced down the hill, toward the gate.

Droughm must be coming, she thought in acute alarm. *Is Torville going to shoot Droughm? Or me?* She didn't understand his purpose, and so was at a loss as to how to proceed. The only thing she knew for certain was that she could not allow Torville to be holding her at gunpoint when Droughm made his

317

appearance; therefore, the best strategy would be to ease her cousin into complacence, and then break away at the right moment so that Droughm could shoot him with no further ado.

In furtherance of this plan, she stood docilely. "I don't understand what you hope to gain—am I to be ransomed, or something?"

"You don't need to understand," he said shortly, and glanced at the gate again. He seemed reluctant to engage in conversation with her.

Thinking of the way he'd caressed her, she struck upon a new strategy. "I'm not certain he would pay very much—he doesn't seem very happy with me."

With full scorn, Torville replied, "Of course not—he's used to the best, and you're barely out of the cradle."

Artemis confessed, "I probably should have stuck with you, all in all. You are closer to my age."

Ah, this caught his interest, and his gaze sharpened as he took a step toward her, his gaze deliberately dropping to her breasts.

Good, she thought—*just move a bit closer, now*—but they were interrupted by the sound of a horse approaching.

Thinking it was Droughm, Artemis made ready to gauge the timing so as to break away from Torville, but was brought up short when she saw that the approaching horseman was not her husband, but the Constable.

She watched in dismay as the man dismounted and strode up the pathway, his gaze on Torville. "Take her in the shaft— and wait for my signal. He should be along any time; Carena will have sent him."

But Torville considered these instructions for a moment with a sullen expression, his head bent down. "*You* take her back."

His manner very cold and deliberate, the Constable replied, "No—it has to be you, so that you dare not grass. Without this leverage against you, the whole deal falls apart, and you don't get the mines."

With a curt nod of agreement, Torville prodded Artemis to walk before him. "Into the mine, cousin—we'll wait for your lord and master back there."

But Artemis was having trouble moving her wooden legs, because her mind was reeling from the implications she'd gleaned from their conversation. *I believe I am slated to die,* she thought in horror. *I believe they were discussing whether Torville had to be the one to kill me. But—but if they kill me, then Droughm inherits the mines; the mines wouldn't go to Torville. Unless —unless—*

"Let's go," Torville urged. "Quickly."

Artemis began to walk, firmly tamping down the panic that threatened to overwhelm her. *It must be Torville,* she realized; *Torville must be the next heir, after me. It's a weak claim—through our mutual aunt—but it's the only one left. So; Lady Stanhope is the Rebecca, she wants to steal the birthright for Torville. First, however, she has to get rid of me, and she has to get rid of my husband, since we both stand in the way.*

"Stop here," said Torville. They had come to a wider portion of the mine shaft, normally used as a staging area for supplies. "Just be quiet, and we'll wait for your illustrious husband to arrive."

And the reason they were waiting for Droughm had already dawned on a horrified Artemis. A murderer could not inherit from his victim, so they were going to stage the scene to make it look as though Droughm had murdered his treasonous wife in a fit of rage. It only made sense; it was the reason for the dramatic scene at the Inn—none would be surprised at the news, and no one would believe his protestations of innocence. The Sheffield gaol would hold another famous prisoner, and Torville would inherit the mines—with a healthy share going to Lady Stanhope and the Constable, for cooking up the scheme to begin with.

It was so obvious, that if she weren't so terrified she'd be ashamed. *I've been so distracted by the spies and the counterfeiting and the treason that I'd forgot the mines are valuable all on their own, and therefore worth a murder or two.*

Fighting a sense of panic as she waited in the cold, dark tunnel she thought, *Think, Artemis; you have to stop it, somehow. The Colonel would say you must even the odds, and exploit your strengths.*

But I have no strengths, she thought in despair, her mouth dry; *I have no weapons, and my arm is in a splint—not to mention I am only a woman, fighting against two men.*

Suddenly, she could hear the Colonel's voice in her head. *"Marshall your strengths,"* he commanded. *"Tactics!"*

Why, why yes—I do have strengths, she realized. *In fact, I have two; my weaknesses are actually my strengths—I only need to exploit them.*

Hiding her grim determination, she eyed her cousin with a benign eye. "Surely, you cannot think that you'll continue on with the counterfeiting operation, Torville—the Home Office obviously has discovered it. You would do much better to flee the country."

At this suggestion, Torville scoffed. "No; the counterfeiting operation is finished—and a good riddance, it was more trouble than it was worth. But we'll pin the blame on you, and your dead uncle. And in the end, I'll inherit the mines."

"I should have married you," Artemis declared with all admiration. "You are so very clever."

"You should have," Torville agreed, grimly glancing toward the dim light that filtered in through the dust motes. "But no—you were too particular."

"If it meant I'd save my life, I would gladly marry you." She met his eyes with all the sincerity she could muster. "Droughm will set me aside in an instant after all this, and then you may have the mines with my blessing—I'll not say *anything*; not a word, I promise."

"Too late." His thin mouth was drawn into an unpleasant line. "You have to be the scapegoat—the traitor; we have to pin the blame on you. We have to say it was you, your father and Uncle Thaddeus who were working with the French, and that we knew nothing about it."

Artemis stared at him, hiding her abject horror. There could be nothing worse—nothing whatsoever—than to die a disgrace to the army she'd served her whole life, and the very idea only strengthened her resolve. Looking up at him from under her lashes, she smiled coyly. "*Please*, Torville; here, let me show you what you would be missing." To emphasize the point, she reached out a hand and gently touched the front of his trousers.

Good—she could see the calculation in his eyes. He would still kill her, but there was no harm in taking his pleasure, when it was offered. "All right then; have a go, and I'll see whether you can change my mind."

Crouching down before him, she pretended to fumble with his breeches buttons whilst gathering her feet solidly beneath her, and then carefully lifting her splint from its sling. With a burst of strength, she suddenly thrust upward, driving the end of her wooden splint squarely into his chin. With a grunt, he collapsed backward, but not before his pistol discharged, and the ricochet could be heard pinging off the walls whilst Artemis stayed low, hoping she wouldn't be hit.

Once the sound subsided, she groped in the darkness for his pistol, and pulled it from his hand only to make a sound of frustration because it was a single-load. She felt in his pockets, but couldn't find any ammunition on his person—trust Torville not to be adequately prepared.

There was no point in hiding—there was nowhere to go, and at any moment the Constable could come to check on Torville, and he wouldn't hesitate to kill her himself. She somehow needed to subdue the Constable, but she had no weapon other than the splint, and at the moment her arm hurt like fire. She could try to seduce him also, but she had the uneasy conviction he was not so easily distracted—the man lived with his mother, after all.

Struck with an idea, she stumbled across the shaft, and rummaged in a burlap sack for blasting caps and a flint, and then ran light-footed back toward the entry, cradling her splint in her good arm and trying not to think about how much it hurt.

She held a vague plan of lighting one of the fuses and then threatening to blow up the mine, but was to be deprived of even this questionable threat when the Constable appeared, silhouetted against the sunlight at the entrance to the mine shaft and peering into the darkness. "What was that? You were supposed to wait for my signal."

"I'm coming to fetch you, sir; Torville is hurt—he—he accidentally shot himself." Artemis stood docilely in the shaft, and hoped the lawman would not decide it was best to shoot her, then and there. More likely he would be more concerned about Torville; if Torville did not survive, their evil plan would be for naught because there would be no one left to inherit. *If he raises his pistol*, she thought, pressing her lips together, *I must charge him, and try to use my splint as a shield.*

But—as she'd anticipated—the man was more interested in Torville's status, and made a sound of frustration as he holstered his pistol. "Where?"

Artemis gestured down the shaft, and the Constable jerked his chin, and commanded, "Follow me."

A tactical mistake, thought Artemis. *A prisoner should always precede you—otherwise, something like this may happen.* Gritting her teeth in anticipation of the pain, she shoved the end of her splint up at the back of his head; unfortunately she couldn't buttress the splint with her other hand this time, and the blow was not a mighty one—he stumbled forward, cursing, but was not cashiered.

Hell and damnation, she thought, and turned to flee up the shaft toward the entry. She heard the discharge of his pistol, unnaturally loud in the small space, and gritted her teeth as she pelted up the tunnel, waiting to feel the ball hit her back. He missed—and she could hear him cursing and presumably re-loading. *The Colonel would say I am too easy a target, silhouetted against the sunlight,* she thought and whirled to slam shut the wooden door that marked the entrance to the mine shaft. With frantic fingers, she lowered the horizontal wooden brace-bar into place just as she heard him crash into the other side, furious and pounding on the barrier. It was not a stout door, and he would break through it in short order, but at least she had a moment to plan a strategy.

Gasping for breath, she paused to assess as the Constable cursed and hammered on the wooden door. She could try to flee on Callisto—she honestly didn't know if she could pull herself up into the saddle again—or she could try to find a weapon; perhaps her uncle's musket was still in the Old Mine—the one that ran parallel to this one.

Torn, she hesitated, reluctant to go back into the bowels of the mine where she could be so easily cornered. Looking to Callisto again, she then saw a horseman in the distance, entering the road that led up to the mines. In an instant, she recognized Droughm.

Behind her, the Constable had stopped cursing, and was now methodically pounding on the door with the butt of his pistol—soon he would break through. She could run to warn Droughm, but if Constable freed himself first, she would make an easy target. She could try to shout a warning for him to stay back, out of range, but Droughm wouldn't stay back—not if she shouted a warning—he would only come toward her faster.

Behind her, Artemis could hear the repeated blows, and she struggled to suppress her panic. There was no time; the important thing—the important thing was that even if she was killed, she needed to make it clear that Droughm could not have possibly killed her—she needed to thwart their plot, and warn her husband that it was a trap. *Think, Artemis, think.*

Coming to a decision, she whirled to race down the abandoned Old Mine.

CHAPTER 50

I *hate this place, and if I survive this, I am never, ever*
coming here again, Artemis promised herself, as she
ran over the uneven stone floor toward her uncle's altar
chamber. The acrid smell of smoke still lingered in the stale air
as she burst into the stone chamber where she'd been forced to
kill Uncle Thaddeus, and she could make out the shapes of
supply sacks, still lining the walls. Frantically feeling with her
hands in the near-darkness, she grasped what she had hoped to
find; her uncle's old musket, left where he'd dropped it.

Running at top speed back toward the entrance, she held a
sack of black powder in her teeth as she primed the musket
with her good hand, her actions sure and familiar. As she
emerged at the entrance, it took a moment to adjust to the
sunlight and assess Droughm's position—he was almost close
enough. The Constable continued pounding on the wooden
doorway to the newer shaft, and she could hear that the door
was beginning to splinter—not long now; time was short.

Kneeling down in the gravel, she braced the musket across
the edge of a rubble cart—no easy task, with a useless arm—
and cocked the hammer, watching Droughm ride into range as

the Constable hammered away behind her, methodically breaking down the door.

I can do this, she thought grimly, bracing the musket-butt against her good shoulder. *I can do this, because I am not first a Countess, or a daughter, or even a wife. First, I am a soldier. God save the Fightin' Third.*

Her cheek against the stock, she closed one eye and sighted carefully. "The First and Foremost," she whispered against the smooth wood. "For King and Country."

Carefully, she squeezed the trigger, and—as the musket recoiled with a thunderous roar—Trajan dropped in his tracks. Artemis had no time to watch as she dropped the musket and fled back into the shaft, pulling open the powder bag, and hoping the fuse for the blasting cap had not gotten damp from its storage in the tunnel. She'd done this once before—the day she killed her uncle—but she hadn't been frantic, then, nor one-handed.

Her good hand trembled as she poured the powder on the ground in the narrow opening to the Old Mine, and then she struck the flint on the stone wall, sparking a flame to light the fuse on the blasting cap. Turning, she ran back toward the altar chamber, holding her hands over her ears as she had seen the artillery soldiers do when they waited for the cannons to fire—there was no doubt this was going to be loud.

It was—the blast knocked her off her feet, deafening in the close confines of the tunnel. Momentarily stunned, she lay on the stone floor, then gingerly propped herself up on her elbow to view her handiwork.

With acute disappointment, she could see sunlight slanting though a drifting cloud of dust—the blast had not blocked the tunnel; perhaps the miners had shored it up, after the last cave-in. *Wonderful*, she thought wearily, and was gathering up her strength to climb to her feet and flee once again, when she heard an ominous groaning sound overhead. Eyes wide, she paused and listened as the groaning grew louder. *Hell and damnation*, she thought in a panic—*the whole place is coming down.*

Choking on the cloud of dust, she scrambled to her feet as the floor beneath her began to move, and the groaning sound turned into a thunderous rumbling. Between the movement of the ground and the ringing in her ears, she stumbled several times in her frantic flight deeper and deeper down the ancient shaft. Rocks and debris were beginning to rain down around her when suddenly she was grasped around the waist.

The Constable, she thought with dismay, and swung her splint at him, knowing she had little strength left.

"Artemis," shouted Droughm over the horrific noise. "Let's go!" With his arm around her, they lunged and scrambled down the tunnel, he supporting her when she lost her footing, until they burst into the altar chamber. Pinning her against one of the walls, her husband covered her head with his arms whilst the earth rumbled and the roof of the tunnel crashed down behind them.

After a few perilous minutes, the terrible noise finally subsided, and Artemis coughed and sputtered, as dust clogged her nose and mouth.

"Are you all right?" Droughm's anxious voice was near her ear.

Artemis lifted her head and gasped out, "You—you weren't supposed to come in after me, Pen; and now I've killed poor Trajan for *nothing*."

She could sense his surprise, and his voice said near her ear, "*You* killed Trajan? I thought it was that bastard, aiming for me."

"I had to; I had to stop your approach—" Turning within his arms, she faced him and saw that he was covered with dust— his hair was grey with it, and his face was marked where the dripping sweat had left a trail. "Oh," she stammered, her mouth trembling. "I—I am so happy to see you, and I shouldn't be."

He rewarded this sentiment by leaning in to kiss her, but she twisted away.

"Listen to me, Pen; you are in terrible danger—the Constable—"

"He's dead," Droughm informed her in his abrupt way. "The bastard tried to shoot me, but the trestles in the shaft collapsed on him as he took aim. He's buried under a ton of rubble."

She stared at him, much struck. "Perhaps mine uncle was right; perhaps the gods *are* angry."

"No one's angrier than me," he assured her. "Tell me the truth; are you hurt?"

"My arm hurts," she admitted. "Nothing to signify."

"Let me see." As he examined her splint, she realized that the area was illuminated by sunlight when it shouldn't have been, and she looked toward the ceiling to see that the dust was drifting upward through a small, perfectly circular opening. "Look," she exclaimed in wonder.

He turned and regarded the opening for a moment. "This must have been an old smelting room, and the blast knocked the plug loose—it was probably packed with mud."

In silence, they stepped over the debris to stand beneath the opening and peer up at the sky, visible through the dust. "It must have been very old," said Artemis. "Was it built by the Vikings?"

"More likely the Romans; they were the engineers, and this chamber didn't collapse."

She tried to wipe her stinging eyes with her sleeve, but as it was covered in dust, this action only compounded the problem. "They were plotting to kill me, and frame you for my murder."

Droughm stared at her, thunderstruck. *"What?"*

"Yes—you couldn't inherit, if you killed me, so the mines would go to Lady Stanhope and Torville. May I wipe my eyes on your shirt sleeve?"

"Torville is here?" asked Droughm as he removed his coat, and presented a clean sleeve to her. "Where?"

"He's over in the next tunnel—I knocked him out." As she rubbed her eyes, she added, "He has a pistol, but no ammunition."

"Then he's probably dead—or will soon be. The other entrance came down on the Constable, remember? They won't be able to get to either one of them any time soon."

Blinking, she straightened up. "That proves it, I guess—the gods are indeed angry. All that's left is to have them smite Lady Stanhope and Lady Tallyer."

There was a small silence, as he drew his brows together. "You think Carena was a part of this?"

"Yes, she was," Artemis informed him. "Although I don't think she was involved with the counterfeiting ring. She only got involved when it became a murder-Artemis-to-steal-the-mines plot—in fact, she's the one who lured me here, where they were waiting to kill me."

He stared at her. "Good *God*."

She tried to keep a childish note of vindication from the words with only limited success. "I imagine she was to be paid handsomely, and would be close-at-hand to comfort the new widower, as an added incentive. Don't you *dare* let her get away."

With some satisfaction, she listened to him recite an impressive litany of swear words in the general direction of the stone floor. When he concluded, he promised, "She will pay for her sins, believe me. I knew a few bad moments, when I saw your horse outside as the mines were exploding."

"And poor Trajan—" she added in a stricken tone.

"Perfectly justified," he said immediately, and gently drew her into his arms. "You were trying to protect me."

Artemis bit her trembling lip, and fingered one of his buttons. "We lost so many horses at the Battle of Vitoria, Pen—the soldiers were so grieved. The Colonel made a speech, and spoke of their amazing courage. He said there was a place in heaven—like Valhalla—especially reserved for the horses, because they gave their lives even though it wasn't their war." Unable to control it, she held her hand over her eyes, and began to sob. "I—I am *so* sorry, Pen."

He held her gently as she sobbed on his shoulder. "Trajan was nearly sixteen, Artemis, and he was a good soldier, himself. Don't mourn him; he wouldn't want you to."

"I-I didn't know what was best to do," she wept. "I couldn't let you come any nearer." As her eyes had begun stinging again, she rubbed her face on his shirt, leaving black steaks behind. "I wished that I could see you—just one more time," she whispered, "and then—like a miracle—there you were."

He said nothing in reply, but rested his cheek on the top of her head, and much was left unsaid. After she took a steadying breath, she offered, "When the Coroner arrives, he won't know what to make of all this."

"On the contrary, all is easily resolved; the late Constable is now the villain of the piece."

She smiled into his chest. "I thought we'd decided it would be Lord Stanhope."

"Certainly; the Constable was working hand-in-glove with Lord Stanhope, which puts paid to any chance of Lady Stanhope inheriting the mines."

"Excellent," said Artemis. "And the unjustly accused Countess of Droughm is out of the dock."

"Now it's only left to get her out of this place." He set her from him, and then stood back to assess the opening overhead, his hands on his hips. "If you stood on my shoulders, do you think you could climb out?"

"Perhaps," she replied doubtfully. "If you could launch me over the lip, by putting your hands under my feet."

"Your arm," he acknowledged with a regretful tilt of his head. "Sorry; I'd forgotten."

"We could signal, and hope someone sees it," she suggested. "Do you have your spectacles? We could try to reflect the sunlight."

"Unfortunately, no." He thought about it for a moment. "How about a signal flag?"

"My sling would make an excellent signal flag."

After her sling was untied from her neck, they hunted around in the chamber, and came up with a marker stake, on which Droughm threaded the lace sling.

"Try to drive it into the sod so that it is upright, but even if you just toss it over the edge it will attract notice—I imagine there will be searchers in short order." He crouched down, so that she could climb onto his shoulders, and once seated with her legs wrapped around his neck, she found she had an uncontrollable impulse to giggle.

"Not the time nor the place, Artemis."

She caressed the top of his head. "I love you, Pen."

"Hold that thought for later. Now, take my hand, and try to stand—slow and careful; I'll catch you if you fall."

Her good hand in his, she maneuvered onto his shoulders in her stockinged feet—no easy task without another arm to balance—which elevated her head and shoulders into the circular opening in the ceiling. "Hold still," she instructed, "I'll brace myself on the edge." She took a fortifying breath, and then quickly transferred her hand to the edge of the stone opening.

"All right?" he asked, his voice muffled beneath her skirts.

"Hand me the stake." He carefully fed it into her hand, but she made a sound of frustration. "I don't see how I can do this one-handed; I'll try, but I may be only able to toss it over the top —although perhaps if I can lean my shoulders on the rim, I can brace myself."

As she was contemplating the best course to take, a voice spoke out from immediately over her head. "*Alors*, you live."

Startled, Artemis dropped the flag, and gazed up into the face of Miss Valdez, who peered down at her, accompanied by an unknown man.

CHAPTER 51

"*Y*ou!" accused Artemis, forgetting for a moment her precarious position. "You handed me over to the Constable, and it almost got me killed."

But the Frenchwoman shook her curls and angrily disclaimed, "Me, I did no such thing. I try to help you, because you say Droughm is in danger, and then you hit me—again!"

"I don't trust you," Artemis retorted.

"Tell her!" Miss Valdez demanded of her companion.

"She did come to fetch me," the gentleman verified. "And I don't believe we've yet met, Lady Droughm—"

But Miss Valdez interrupted, "Enough. Where is Droughm?"

Droughm's voice floated up. "Lisabetta, fetch a rope; Artemis should see a doctor."

On her hands and knees, the woman shifted to peer beneath Artemis to Droughm. "First, she must promise never to hit me again—*jamais*."

"Promise her, Artemis."

"I'll do no such thing," retorted Artemis. "I'm sorry if I was mistaken the one time, but I will hit you as many times as is needful. And you have no right to demand any promises of me; I didn't make you promise about Droughm, remember?"

"Promise what?" asked Droughm.

The Frenchwoman considered, her hair dangling down around her face. "*Bien*—that is fair." The two faces overhead withdrew, presumably to find a rope.

"On the count of three," said Droughm to Artemis as he stretched up his hand. "Put your hand back in mine, then fall forward, and I will catch you. Easy, now."

Once this was accomplished and Artemis had been carefully lowered to the ground, she turned to him. "I don't know if we should trust her, Pen—and there is a man with her."

"It's Tremaine."

Artemis stared at him. "Tremaine is with Miss Valdez? Is she working for you, then? But that makes no sense, if I was to feed her the false plates—"

Droughm tilted his head. "We've been trying to convince her that she can be useful to us—she has a sister who's been very useful in Egypt. But it seems we can never be quite certain of her."

"She did come to the rescue—there's that," Artemis pointed out fairly. "Athough she probably wanted to rescue you more than me."

He shrugged. "I am out of play."

Artemis decided this remark deserved a reward, and so she wrapped her good arm around his neck to bring his mouth down to hers. There was nothing like a near-death experience to make one wish for a soft bed and a hard husband, even though she was aching from head to foot and the kiss was slightly grimy. "Perhaps Tremaine has another whiskey flask, Pen. We can try to recreate our wedding night."

"I don't remember our wedding night," he confessed. "But I'm willing."

"I am a *shambles*, Pen."

"A beautiful shambles," he corrected, and kissed her again.

They were interrupted when a rope dropped through the

opening, and a man's voice echoed down. "Ho, there; I've fashioned a foot loop—we'll have my horse pull you out."

Artemis stepped into the loop, and was pulled aloft as Droughm carefully guided her, his hands on her hips as he called a warning to Tremaine to mind her broken arm. Once she was pulled over the lip of the opening, Artemis laid her cheek against the green sod and breathed in its scent, reveling in the blessed sunlight whilst the rope was lowered for Droughm.

"You are filthy," observed Miss Valdez from where she manned the horse at Tremaine's direction. "What happened?"

"I blew up the mine." Propping up with her splint, Artemis wriggled upright, brushing herself off matter-of-factly. "Then the tunnel caved in."

"Ah. You will not live long." The other nodded sagely as she maneuvered the horse forward. "I have only to be patient."

"I will live a long time, just to spite you," Artemis countered.

The Frenchwoman cocked her head, considering this. "Perhaps we can all live together, á la ménage—we can share him, you and I."

"No," said Artemis, a bit shocked. "No sharing."

"Come, now; it is what is done in Algiers," the other argued.

"Well, it's not what is done here."

Droughm was pulled out of the mine, and he and Tremaine immediately began a low-voiced conversation. Whilst the two men quietly conferred, Miss Valdez walked over to Artemis and sank down beside her, cross-legged on the grass. "Will you help them?" Artemis asked bluntly. "It must be exhausting to always be double-crossing everyone—perhaps you should take a break."

The other girl idly plucked at a blade of grass, and then lifted her head to meet Artemis' gaze. "*La guerre,*" she said. "You saw much of it, yes?"

Slowly, Artemis nodded. "Yes."

"After what you have seen, would you ever help the enemy?"

"There is not the smallest chance," Artemis admitted. "I see."

"*Oui*," the other replied, and the two sat in silence.

Another soldier, thought Artemis. *I can respect it, even if I cannot appreciate it.*

"I will write you letters," the Frenchwoman offered after a moment. "Droughm can read them to you."

Artemis smiled. "I would like that very much. I hope you will be careful."

"I will—remember that I must outlive you."

Droughm approached, whilst Tremaine mounted up on his horse. "He'll ride into town to report—we'll need to make some arrests before the enemy realizes matters have not gone as planned. I'll commandeer the Constable's horse, since I've lost mine—"

"Good one, Pen," said Artemis with all admiration.

"—but first we'll wait here a bit; we don't want to arrive before the arrests are made."

The Frenchwoman rose to brush off her skirts. "Then I am *de trop*; I will leave, before you arrest me, too."

"Lisbetta—" Droughm began.

"Ah! Do not fear, you will hear from me." The girl walked over to kiss him formally on both cheeks, after flashing an impudent glance at Artemis. "*Au revoir.*" After mounting up, she turned her horse toward the hills, and took off at a trot.

"Are you just going to let her go?" Artemis asked Droughm in surprise.

"Yes," he replied in his abrupt way. "Recall that she has the plates."

"Oh—oh, yes, I see." *I would not make a good spy*, she thought for the hundredth time. *It is all far too tangled, for my taste.*

Tremaine departed, leaving Artemis and Droughm seated on

the knoll with a fine view of the peaceful, wooded valley, spreading out below them.

"I hate this place," Artemis announced, as Droughm lay down on his back to contemplate the sky. "Let's hand the mines over to the first person we meet."

"My fault." He reached to run a hand down her back. "I thought once the plates were delivered, the French would clear out with all speed, and there would no longer be any threat."

Artemis turned her head to him. "How could you have known that Lady Stanhope was scheming to steal the birthright, or that Lady Tallyer was scheming to get me killed? My only consolation was that Miss Valdez promised she'd not let her have you."

Amused, Droughm ran his fingers through the ends of her tangled hair. "I am not such a puppet, you know; I am well-able to choose for myself."

"You did not choose very wisely before you met me, Pen."

"Point taken. Is your arm still hurting?"

"A bit—it is getting better."

He reached to gather up a lock and tug. "Don't ever do that to me again."

Laughing, she replied, "I can make no promises. If an explosion is called for, then an explosion shall be had."

Absently, he played with her hair, winding it around his wrist. "What do you think about the South of France, for a wedding trip?"

Surprised, she turned to meet his gaze. "I thought we'd ruled out the Continent, being as your people seem to think Napoleon is on the verge of escape."

Rather than reply directly, he said, "I'd rather not leave you back at Somerhurst."

With a sigh, she turned her gaze back to the valley. "No— I'm staying with you, and that's that. Do they think it's imminent, then?"

"They do. But the next war can't last long; France has run out of money."

"Thanks to the war behind the war." She plucked a dandelion, and began to pull it apart. "I suppose I should appreciate it more than I do, but since no one ever sees it, no one knows how successful it's been."

He offered, "We could probably purchase some fine Spanish bloodstock while we're on the Continent. Napoleon is not the only one who's run out of money."

With a delighted smile, she turned to him. "What a wonderful idea, Pen; if you are trying to sweeten me up, it's working."

He closed his eyes, a smile playing around his lips. "But no more racing down the road, hell-for-leather—I'll have your promise, Lady Droughm."

Laughing, she lifted her face to the sun. "You are so very droll, Pen."

Made in the USA
Monee, IL
22 September 2021

77824797R00204